TURNING TIDES

MIA MARSHALL

An Elements Novel

Match
Books

ISBN 978-0-9889761-60
ISBN 978-0-9889761-22 (ebook)

Book design by Cynthia Fliege

This one's for the readers.

Yeah, I mean you.

CHAPTER 1

I expected it to rain the day my life changed forever.

It wasn't an unreasonable request. Sure, it was early June, but the Pacific Northwest was notorious for its wet weather. I saw no reason it shouldn't storm during my trial. I wasn't asking for much, just a few fat, angry clouds hovering over my head, prepared to split open once my sentence was read.

Instead, I stood beneath a cloudless blue sky while the ocean lapped against the shore of my family's island. I supposed I could make it rain, if it came to that, but that felt like cheating. Everyone knows omens and dramatic symbolism don't count if you create them yourself.

It would have been more practical to hold the trial inside, but elementals never did anything important inside. Our lives took place in nature, with the open sky above us, earth beneath our feet, and, in our case, water as far as the eye could reach.

Behind me, practically all my relatives had gathered to witness my trial. This island was the home of the extended Brook clan, fifty or so elementals who were once the only family I knew. I also spotted several unfamiliar faces, a couple of waters from the other old families and even a few who lived in the human world, as I did. They'd flown in just to witness my trial. A council visit was rare enough. A council visit to banish the daughter of a powerful old one was a once-in-a-lifetime event, and no one wanted to miss it.

No one except Great-grandma, of course. She'd muttered something about how unseemly it was for a Brook to be involved in such a scandal and decided it was a good time to visit her cousins in Martha's Vineyard. Great-grandma did have an impressive history of ignoring any events that upset her world view.

The rest of my family were all present, and though I hadn't been granted even five minutes to speak to them, I appreciated their support.

When the seaplane landed, I was led directly before the council and the makeshift court they'd constructed on the beach, just above high tide. There wasn't much occasion for the council to make an appearance, so the island had no permanent court. Instead, my family dragged an eight-person dining table to the shore and covered it with plastic white tablecloths, the kind you could buy at the Fred Meyer on the mainland. They were pinned in place with a variety of small shells and rocks, and only the wind's lack of interest in the proceedings kept them from flying away.

Really, the court looked a lot like a low-budget wedding except, instead of cake, I was about to receive a lifetime banishment. A few weeks ago, I'd been okay with my punishment. Though I'd prefer not to be exiled from the elemental community, this wasn't really my life. My life took place a thousand miles south of my family's island in the San Juans, in a cabin in Lake Tahoe, where elementals and shifters alike stopped by on a regular basis. It was where a man who regularly made my toes curl lived in an Airstream trailer just behind the house.

That was the home I'd chosen, but this was where I'd been born. Though I hadn't visited in well over a decade, now that I'd set foot on its familiar shore, I couldn't help feeling melancholy at the thought of losing it, and most of my extended family, forever.

However, unless I was able to concoct some mighty convincing lies in the next five minutes, lose it I would.

"Aidan Brook," said the woman in the middle. She had short, wispy blond hair the wind enjoyed playing with, and she looked to be in her early thirties, if we were counting in human years. As council members were always full-blooded elementals with lifespans of thousands of years, I could count her age in centuries, rather than decades. Like most waters, her clothes were built for comfort—a cream jersey dress and belted cardigan with an oversized collar—but I sensed little softness in the woman herself.

"Yes," I answered. I was tempted to keep speaking, but I was doing my best to follow the one bit of advice everyone had given me over the last week: keep your answers short, volunteer nothing, and for the love of all that was holy, tell no jokes.

In other words, pretend I was someone else for the next hour or two.

Edith Lake stared at me, as if expecting a longer answer. Normally, the council consisted of six waters, one representative from each of the old families, and leadership revolved between the families. I didn't know much about the Lake clan, other than their family lived on an island off the coast of one of the Carolinas, and it was their turn to take the reins.

Also, based on the sour look Edith fixed on me, they might not like me very much.

Normally, my family held the sixth seat at the table, but for some reason they thought my grandmother might be biased in my favor. This might have something to do with the way she whispered, "Don't let the bastards get you down," when I walked past her.

Therefore, this incarnation of the council contained only five members, four women and one man. I'd like to believe that coming from a matriarchal society meant they'd be more inclined toward mercy and forgiveness, but their stern expressions suggested I was being overly optimistic.

Edith consulted her notes. "Fiona's daughter. Half-blooded water elemental."

"Yes," I said again. It only took me two questions before I started lying. That might be a record, but sadly not one I could brag about. I was most definitely Fiona's daughter, but I was a full-blooded elemental. Unfortunately, the other half came from Josiah Blais, my fire father, and that made me an elemental freak. I was a dual magic, which meant I was capable of controlling two elements. It also meant I was prone to no small amount of madness if I accessed both sides of my magic too often.

Madness in a human was tragic. In an elemental, it could lead to murder or natural disasters that destroyed entire cities. That sort of thing tended to be frowned upon by the old ones. For now, I was sane, but the council wouldn't care. The punishment for being a dual magic was death. If they learned what I was, they wouldn't hesitate to order my execution.

All things considered, I had few qualms about lying in this particular case.

"Do you admit or deny you told two FBI agents about the existence of elementals?" And it appeared the easy part of our Q&A was at an end. Edith pinned me with hard gray eyes.

"Well, see, they already knew. Not those two in particular, no, but the FBI in general knew we existed and already had a secret branch to deal with magical creatures, so it's really not the problem you seem to think it is."

Two people cleared their throats about twenty feet apart

from each other. One came from the direction of my family's section, and I'd heard that sound too many times growing up not to recognize my mother. The other was directly behind me and sounded almost amused. Sera Blais, reminding me that, as usual, I was my own worst enemy.

"That is to say, I admit. With reservations." I muttered the last sentence, but Edith continued to stare at me, catching every word.

"And do you admit or deny that you raised Lake Tahoe over twenty feet in front of hundreds of human witnesses?" Her words were precise, her voice clipped. She kept one hand braced on the table, the other tightly gripped around a small black case. In general, she looked tense and painfully self-contained, making it hard to believe she was truly a full-blooded water. There were exceptions, but for the most part we were a relaxed group and easily distracted. I began to regret that it wasn't the Ponds' or Rivers' turn to take the lead.

"Really, it was more a tilting than a raising. Just to be clear. And I had no choice. We were in a vehicle that was crashing down the side of a mountain. We would have died if I hadn't called the water. It slowed our fall." I raised my chin. No, tilting one of the most popular tourist lakes in the country on end hadn't been the stealthiest move, but it had been necessary.

"We?" Edith raised a perfectly shaped eyebrow.

"Myself and three friends," I elaborated as little as possible. The eyebrow didn't dip, and she continued to watch me. I had to literally bite my tongue to keep from speaking, but I managed to stay quiet.

"Tell me about these friends," she pressed.

She knew. Somehow, she already knew. That was the thing about living for hundreds of years. You developed an impressive network of resources.

"It was Sera, a fire." I turned to the side, acknowledging her. She nodded, her face impassive, but I saw the steady tattoo of her fingers against her black jeans. She knew exactly where this was going. "Our friend Vivian, a low-level earth who also lives in Tahoe, and Mac." I paused for a breath, then met the woman's eyes. "A shifter."

I might as well have said I'd befriended the Loch Ness monster. The spectators erupted, hissing and booing and generally naming me a liar in an impressive range of ways, some of which required profanity even I wouldn't say.

Again, I looked toward Sera, whose fingertips had begun to spark. She was the only one allowed to insult me, after all.

I felt my own fire uncoil and raise its head in interest. It did so more and more often these days, ever since I accessed both sides of my magic simultaneously in order to heal Mac from a bad case of dead. Prior to that night, it only stirred when I felt angry, and for years before that I hadn't known it was there at all. I'd only felt that something inside me wasn't quite right.

Things were different now. I'd called on my fire side too many times of late, and it was no longer complacent. I was aware of it all the time. It was part of me, a constant burn in my core.

I might know the fire was there, but that didn't mean I chose to access that side of my power. When I allowed it free rein, it insisted on total control, and I was rarely happy with the results.

Over the last several weeks, my fire side and I had reached some sort of compromise. I no longer attempted to thrust it into a tiny compartment and deny its existence, and it no longer attempted to burn things without my permission. It was a tenuous control, but I'd take whatever I could get.

I sensed its curiosity, its desire for release, and I ignored it, focusing on my water heritage. Grumbling, it quieted, no longer challenging me as it used to.

I was grateful for the increased stability. As I was currently awaiting a lifetime banishment from the entire elemental community and being denounced by my extended family for the company I kept, I'd take whatever good news I could get.

I studied the faces I'd grown up with. While many looked calm and supportive, there were an equal number that were enraged or accusatory. Just your typical family.

There were lots of problems with elementals. We were slow to change and didn't always integrate with humans as well as we ought. We lived a long time, and it wasn't uncommon to turn a little odd as the millennia passed. We tended to believe that, as descendants of the earth's original magic, we were just a little superior to every other creature in existence.

We also liked to pretend an entire race of magical creatures didn't exist, all because we didn't want to share our origin story with creatures born from the union of magic and beasts.

I faced the leader of the council. Her gaze never wavered from me. When she spoke, she did so in a soft voice, forcing the others to quiet if they wished to hear her—and they all did. "You are saying that shifters exist."

"Yes." She did not blink. The existence of shifters was a poorly kept secret among the old ones. I'd wager at least half the people at my back knew about them. They simply chose to deny this fact as often as possible. Denial, it seems, runs in the Brook DNA.

"You are also saying you have befriended one."

"Yes." Behind me, the murmurs started again. It was shocking enough that one of their own might have revealed our existence to humans. To have done so in the company of a despised shifter might be unforgivable.

Listening to some of the people I'd grown up with denounce me, I decided banishment couldn't come soon enough.

"And you are saying you chose to save one of their lives at the cost of our secrecy."

"It was necessary to keep all of us alive. The elementals, as well. Sera and Vivian might not have survived the crash."

"Hmm," she said. Such a non-committal word, capable of conveying so much doubt.

"Shall we discuss this?" The question came from the woman on her right, the Pond's council representative. Her expression was softer, and I suspected if she was handling the questions the day would bear less resemblance to a witch trial.

"Is there much to discuss, Lydia? There is no question that Aidan Brook recklessly and repeatedly revealed our presence to humans. By her own admission, she did so while consorting with tainted creatures, as if her own elemental blood meant nothing. We are the pure creatures of magic. We might integrate with humans out of necessity, but there is no excuse for fraternizing with those vile beasts. Even worse, she chose to save one, regardless of the cost to our secrecy. Through her own actions, she is no longer one of us. It is time to vote. Michael, would you begin?"

The man at the far end stood. He was a Bay, the only water family with a habit of popping out more boys than girls. Given the circumstances, I figured it wasn't the best time to make a joke about his unfortunate name.

He walked into the ocean until it reached his knees. A heavy table was stationed in the water, the metal legs dug into the sand for stability. Our traditions stated that we needed to connect with our element during all significant life events. This allowed waters to be at full strength as they married, attended funerals, gave birth, or decided the fate of a woman they'd never met before.

The table held writing supplies and something that looked rather like a small urn. He scribbled his vote on a scrap of paper, placed it in the container, and returned to his seat.

Lydia Pond repeated his actions, her mouth set in a grim line. On her way back to her seat, she nodded at me, just once.

Deborah Rivers followed, and the crowd perked up as she moved toward the voting table. She hadn't said a word during my trial, but it wasn't due to her lack of prestige. If the waters ever decided to elect a queen, she would cruise to an easy victory. As far as anyone could track these things, she was the oldest and most powerful of us all. I'd only met one elemental who could rival her rumored strength, and he'd fathered me.

She didn't even glance at the crowd as she wrote my fate on a slip of paper and returned to her seat.

Rachel Strait went next, her movements hurried. She wanted this trial finished.

At last, Edith Lake moved to the box. Each step was graceful and precise. When she reached the table, she cast her own vote but didn't replace the lid. Instead, she shook the urn slightly so the votes wouldn't be pulled out in the reverse order they were cast. The council's votes were supposed to be anonymous.

She withdrew the first piece of paper. "Guilty." Her voice rang across the beach. Though the gulls called and the waves continued their gentle lapping, the elementals were eerily silent as the votes were read.

She pulled the second slip of paper. "Guilty."

Chairs creaked as everyone leaned forward to hear her

read the third vote. "Innocent."

Unwanted, hope rose in my chest, only to be instantly squashed with the fourth vote.

"Guilty. There is no need to read the final vote. Aidan Brook, this council, in its role as protector of the water elementals, has found you guilty of revealing our existence to humans and recklessly endangering the elemental race through your actions. Do you have anything to say before your sentence is decided?"

She paused as a matter of form, though she didn't seem to expect me to speak. Since I doubted "Fuck you and the broom you rode in on" would make me any friends, I held my tongue.

I braced for the words, trying to ignore the sting of regret. Not regret for the actions that had placed me in this position—they were choices I'd make again and again. The regret was for my absence, for the years I could have visited my family, floated down the canals in summer, swum in the sea.

Once the sentence was read, that would all be in the past. I'd be escorted back to the seaplane, never again welcome at any elemental enclave. I'd be a pariah, and those who refused to cut me out would be tarnished. My mother and Sera—their lives would change, too.

As I waited to be banished forever, I held the image of my friends in my mind, a reminder of what I could return to. Mac, quiet and mysterious and yet, somehow, everything I'd never known I wanted. Sera, my sister in every possible way, who would remain at my side no matter what a bunch of uptight elementals said. Simon and Vivian, who were exploring their own paths but were never far from my thoughts. The shifters who'd grown to trust me, Miriam and Will and Carmen. There were so many people waiting for me in Tahoe. I just had to receive my sentence, then get on the plane and return to my real life. By evening, I'd be curled up on one of the cushions in the A-frame cabin's living room, surrounded by ugly orange curtains and upside down teddy bear wallpaper, and everything would be okay. I'd be home. It was where I belonged.

Edith lifted her chin, letting the sun fall on her face, and offered the gathered crowd a gentle smile. Perhaps it was only my imagination that saw malice in the gaze she turned to me.

"Please stand. Normally, in such cases, we choose the mercy of banishment. However, given the severity of your actions and the company you have chosen to keep—"

I stood straighter, my spine growing rigid. There should be no "however." There was only one punishment for my crime. Only murder of another elemental earned the harsh sentence of death. For everything else, it was banishment. There was no other option.

The current leader of the water council disagreed with me.

"We believe an example must be made. Aidan Brook, you will submit to…"

She never finished the sentence. As the entire island watched, the councilwoman exploded.

The noise shook the island, then everything was muffled, like cotton had been stuffed into my ears. At a distance, I heard screams, the creak of metal as dozens stood as one, chairs flying backwards as half the island ran away and the other half ran toward the water.

One second the councilwoman stood in the ocean, prepared to read my sentence. The next, pieces of Edith Lake floated alongside the voting table, flames still clinging to her clothes.

Even as I stared in horror, my fire roared in joy.

The island's old ones, the healers, rushed toward her,

but it was futile. There was nothing to heal. Though the lower half of her body was still mostly intact, her torso had been obliterated. One arm clung to the body, the tendons and bones exposed for all to see, but the other was in the water. Maybe the old ones could have repaired that, but they could do nothing about the fact she was missing half her head. Even Dr. Frankenstein couldn't put Edith back together at this point.

My mother and grandmother stood in the water, and though they remained at least ten feet from where Edith had blown up, body parts bobbed around them in a grotesque tableau. They turned in circles, fear stamped across their features, as they looked for any explanation. Any way they could help.

When my mother raised her eyes to mine, I only saw panic in their depths.

All around me, I heard shocked and horrified whispers. The words made no sense. I couldn't concentrate on anything but the carnage in the water and my mother's terrified face.

"What is it? What happened?" Michael Bay stood at the water's edge, lines on his face that hadn't been there five minutes ago. He sounded like a child, begging the adults to tell him he was only imagining the awful scene before him.

"She's dead," my mother whispered. "I've never seen anything like that." Once again, my mother looked at me, her eyes fierce and desperate.

She wasn't the only one. The remaining council members, hell, everyone on the island, stared at me.

No, not at me. They stared over my shoulder, at Sera.

Rachel Strait was pale, and her eyes were wide and scared, but when she spoke, her voice did not waver. "Only one person on this island is capable of creating an explosion from thin air," she announced, in a clear voice that carried to everyone on the beach. "We all witnessed it. That was the work of a fire elemental."

Too late, I understood what my mother was trying to tell me.

She'd been telling me to run.

CHAPTER 2

Chaos would be one description of what happened next. Utter, complete insanity would be closer to the mark. At Rachel Strait's words, the crowd panicked, pushing against each other and, in some cases, pushing each other over, desperate to flee the homicidal fire in their midst. They knocked over chairs and ran in every possible direction. A few brave souls struggled against the crowd in an effort to get closer to Sera and personally observe the murderous fiend. However, far more ran away, arms wrapped tight around their torsos as if they could prevent her deadly magic from entering their fragile bodies.

Deborah and Michael stared between me, Sera, and the remains of Edith Lake. Sera's wild black hair and defiant eyes left little doubt about her heritage. She looked like what she was—an intense, powerful fire used to getting her way in all things.

At that particular moment, she wouldn't have wanted my mysterious sentence to be read. We might not have known what it was, but the details weren't important. When someone talks about making an example out of another person, it's pretty clear things aren't going to end well.

Anyone who knew the first thing about our friendship would know Sera wouldn't allow me to suffer, not if she could stop it. It wasn't much of a motive, but considering the lack of any other fires on the island, my best friend looked damn guilty.

One council member didn't share the others' helpless confusion. "Could whatever passes for law enforcement on this island isolate that woman?" Rachel Strait waved in Sera's direction. Despite the horror she'd just witnessed, she sounded almost bored. She didn't raise her voice, but her words were enough to catch my relatives' attention. She was the only one on the island in a suit, a flawlessly tailored white linen outfit that likely originated in Europe. Her hair was cut in a severe bob, her lips outlined in red. I'd seen porcupines who looked softer and more cuddly.

Having accepted that there was nothing she could do for the dead woman, Grams returned to the beach and stepped toward Rachel, her face deceptively polite. "Why would we have enforcement? We're a peaceful enclave. There's no crime here."

The internal organs currently drifting out to sea notwithstanding.

Normally, she was right. The island was pretty damn close to utopia, if your idea of utopia was having all your material needs met and never worrying about violence among a bunch of easy-going waters. If your idea of utopia involved seeing the world and understanding people outside your small circle, you were shit out of luck.

We didn't have crime. Like all the old families, we'd been saving money since humans first began minting coins, and we were embarrassingly wealthy. No one lacked for funds, no one could be bothered to hurt others, and if someone wanted a different life, they simply stepped onto a boat or plane with their enormous trust fund and disappeared for a while.

Rachel curled her lip. "No crime?" She slid her gaze toward a dismembered hand washing up on the shore. "How reassuring. Here I was worried my colleague had been murdered, but now that you've told me it's not possible, I feel quite relieved."

More people were drawing closer, wanting to hear the discussion. They might fear Sera and her potentially lethal magic, but this was the most dramatic thing to happen on the island in centuries. No one wanted to miss a moment and be forced to hear about it secondhand.

"Just to clarify, am I being accused?" Sera's voice cut through the murmurs. "I'm assuming that's the case, based on the way everyone's staring at me, but I'd like to confirmed."

Grams sighed heavily and looked upward, as though a skywriter might appear with an answer. She'd met Sera once before, when my fire friend visited the island during sophomore year. My relatives had all liked her well enough, and at the time none seemed to think she was capable of immolating others.

"Sera, normally I'd say you were under no more suspicion than anyone else present. However, you are the only fire on the island. Unless you have a possible explanation for how this could have happened, I fear you are very much our best suspect." It was about as fair as one could be, considering the circumstances.

Unfortunately, Grams wasn't wrong. I scanned all the remaining faces. Most were familiar, and almost all were water, with the telltale tall, skinny bodies, golden hair, and eyes in varying shades of gray. I thought I picked out a stone in the crowd, but he'd be no more capable of burning someone to a crisp than my relatives.

Based on the people in attendance, Sera was the only one who could have committed the murder.

Someday, our lives were going to be peaceful again. We would find ourselves on a beach with umbrella drinks and cabana boys, and there would be no dead bodies in sight. I would surround myself with friends and wake up every day to a calm, stress-free life in which I could enjoy however many sane days I had left.

Unfortunately, it didn't look like today was that day.

"I didn't do it," Sera's voice remained strong, and she met each of her accuser's eyes in turn.

Rachel sniffed. "I'm glad to hear it. In that case, we'll just stick you back on the plane and forget all about this brutal attack on the water elementals' governing body and the destruction of a woman who, by rights, should have lived for another thousand years. Thank you for saving us the paperwork."

I narrowed my eyes at the councilwoman. "No one is saying that. We understand how this looks. But Sera is claiming she is innocent, and she deserves a fair trial. We require time to determine what happened." Rachel Strait looked unimpressed, and she opened her mouth to deliver what was sure to be a snide denial. I rushed to finish. "We're not barbarians, after all. Or animals." I smiled pointedly. If they were going to insist on being prejudiced assholes, I was not above using that against them.

The tone of the crowd's murmur shifted from fear and excitement to understanding, even agreement. There was only one sentence for murdering another elemental, and I was glad to see no one was in a hurry to order Sera's death.

Apparently, if you were going to be accused of murder, the best place to get caught was on an island full of easily-distracted pacifist waters.

That description didn't apply to all waters—the councilwoman seemed a notable exception—but she was overpowered by numbers. Rachel gave a curt nod, though I suspected her agreement would only last until she could think of a better option.

We tried to beat her to it. "Shouldn't I be tried by my

own council?" Sera asked.

Rachel appeared surprised by the question. "Surely not. You have murdered a water, and we shall decide your fate. I will inform Allison Ash, my equivalent on the fire council, and she can decide if you will have a second trial with your own people. If it proves necessary, that is."

"Your equivalent?" I choked out, overlooking the suggestion that, if Sera was dead by the order of the water council, there'd be no need for a second trial.

"With Edith gone, it becomes the Straits' turn to lead the council."

That's what I'd been afraid she was going to say. I grasped at my last straw. "But how can we have any trials? With Edith dead, there are only four of you."

This time, it was Grams who spoke, her voice resigned. "Four members are considered a quorum, Aidan. If there is a tie, the verdict defaults to innocent. They have enough people to try Sera and decide your sentence."

"In the name of efficiency, we will do both at the same time. The fire's trial will be held three days hence, at which time your sentence will be read before witnesses. You have been granted a seventy-two hour reprieve. Do you have any other questions, Ms. Brook?"

I wanted to ask how the hell she expected me to find a killer in three days, but somehow I doubted she would share my concern.

"Good. The fire will need to be kept isolated, and at least one hundred feet from all other elementals."

My mother pointed to the west. "We have several guest cottages on the other side of the island. One is unoccupied, and the remaining visitors can be moved while we resolve this issue. Will this suffice?"

"Guards?"

Blank stares greeted the question. This wasn't an island

full of people who understand the value of a work ethic, and no one was going to volunteer to stand around all day to make sure a murderous fire didn't escape her prison.

"I'll stay with her," I said.

"That is hardly appropriate security, a best friend and convicted traitor to elementals."

The woman sure as hell didn't mince words. I could practically see the collective feathers of the gathered Brook clan ruffle at her words.

"Regardless, I'm also determined to prove her innocence, which means I won't want her wandering about the island. If someone else blows up, distance is her best alibi."

"If someone dies, are we supposed to take your word that she was in the cottage?" Rachel forced a smile, doing her best to appear the calm water despite her contemptuous words.

"Sera didn't do it. This means someone else caused Edith's death, and they're still wandering around the island, free to burn any unsuspecting water who pisses them off. My friend will not be responsible for anyone else's crimes. Sera will stay in the cottage because she wants to prove her innocence even more than I do. We all know that if she wants to escape, she would just burn down a wall, grab a boat, and get the hell out of here. She doesn't want to spend her life on the run, so she will accept this temporary jail. We can mount a surveillance camera on the porch to prove she doesn't leave the cottage, if it makes you feel better. If anyone dies, we'll have proof she wasn't involved."

Rachel's smile didn't waver, and when she agreed, it almost sounded like she meant it. "Fine." She turned to stare at the ocean, no longer interested in discussing Sera's fate.

"Another thing. Once the camera's mounted, I can come and go as I please from the guest cottage. Whatever else

I've been convicted of, it didn't involve physically harming other elementals, and I need to be able to move freely about the island. It's the only way I can prove Sera is innocent."

This time, Rachel hesitated, but she knew she was trapped. No one else was volunteering to defend Sera. If the councilwoman didn't acquiesce to my request, she could be accused of conducting an unfair investigation. "That is acceptable. Now get that woman locked up before she finds another target."

"Don't tempt me," muttered Sera, too low for anyone but me to hear.

"Let's go." I urged her toward the west side of the island, where the unoccupied cottage waited for its prisoner.

Umbrella drinks and cabana boys would need to wait a bit longer.

CHAPTER 3

In college, I'd done one or two walks of shame, returning to my dorm room in the previous night's clothes after a night with a guy I'd been seeing. I'd keep my head low, hoping no one I knew recognized me, and I'd swipe my finger under my eyes over and over, trying to remove the residual mascara. On those mornings, I felt tired and stretched and embarrassed, but I also felt glee, the sort of buoyant happiness that came from pushing the boundaries on my formerly narrow life.

Those days were long behind me, but the memory of the contradictory feelings had nothing on the torrent of emotions that crashed through me as I walked across the island that had once been my home.

It was, still and always, one of the most beautiful places I'd ever seen, as striking in its own way as Lake Tahoe.

It rested on the outer ring of the San Juan Islands, far from the more popular tourist spots, and elementals went to great lengths to ensure our small piece of land appeared on no map. Our only pier was well hidden, so any boaters who happened past would find landing difficult. There was enough room for small seaplanes to land, which remained our primary way on and off the island. Boat and plane travel were monitored, and all incoming and outgoing visitors were painstakingly logged.

Our caution was necessary. From above, the wealth of

firs and maples helped disguise the network of canals cut into the entire island, but they'd be visible the moment someone stepped foot on our shores. While one or two waterfalls or fountains might be expected, we had them in every garden. There were even a few houses with moats.

In short, it was an island custom made for water elementals, and it called to that part of my soul like few other places could. Everywhere I looked, water flowed and bubbled, looking for someone to play with it. I tentatively reached out my magic and greeted it as it coursed through the canal on my left side. It responded instantly, the water exploding in an ecstatic spray. I was a daughter of the island, and it recognized me.

I'd been raised here. As the island's only child, I'd been adored and pampered by my family for the first twenty years of my life. Things changed when I came of age. I'd wanted to see the world. My mother wanted to hide me from it. Before long, the island I loved felt as much like a prison as a home, one I longed to escape.

It appeared I'd come full circle.

"How long has it been?" Sera asked.

I was doing my best to pretend half the island wasn't following us to confirm that the dangerous fire was truly locking herself away. Sera remained focused on me, as she had been since we learned I was a half fire who would likely go crazy some day. I hated it, but I hadn't figured out a way to change our dynamic yet.

"Senior year of college. I came home on Christmas vacation. Then…" I stopped. We both knew what happened after that. We'd gotten involved in a series of murders, and the fire magic I'd not known I possessed helped cause the deaths of several innocent people. I'd gone into hiding for ten years and hadn't seen anyone. Not my mother, not Sera, not the island. It hadn't been my finest decade.

With a head tilt, Sera indicated those who followed us at a careful distance, always remaining outside the reach of Sera's magic. "I'm thinking there's something to that whole 'you can't go home again' thing."

The words were irreverent, but tension marked her body. Her spine was straight, her shoulders set, her eyes fixed on the path before us. "I didn't blow her up, either," I whispered, too low for anyone else to hear. It seemed a point worth clarifying. "I didn't even know fires could do that."

Her gaze flicked to me. "I never thought you did."

Half a mile later, we arrived at the western edge of the island. It was less sheltered and prone to higher winds than the rest of the island. It was therefore less populated, with only a handful of stilt houses at the high tide mark. No permanent residents lived in these cottages, and the few visitors were already evacuating the nearby homes, bound for guest quarters where they didn't need to worry about their neighbor incinerating them in a fit of pique. They cast nervous glances in our direction. I waved cheerfully.

The gathered crowd stopped behind an invisible line, always keeping their distance. It didn't matter how close they were, or whether I could still hear their quiet murmurs. In the end, it was just me and Sera. We'd fought plenty of battles already and come out on top, and I had no doubt we'd do it again. I wouldn't consider any other option.

I marched up the stairs to the cottage and opened the front door. It wasn't locked. None of our homes ever were. It was a guest cottage, and so held little in the way of personality, but it was clean and comfortable. For a jail cell, we'd both seen worse.

I threw my bag on the sofa and performed a quick study of the house, calling back to Sera.

"You can take the room on the right. Accused murderers get the pastel bedspread. I'm sure I read that somewhere." I turned to discover I was talking to myself. Sera stood on the threshold, frozen. Her eyes held the closest thing to fear I'd ever seen on her face. "What is it?"

"Once I go in…" She didn't finish. Elementals weren't meant to be trapped inside. She needed constant access to nature, and more specifically to her element. This small cottage perched on the edge of the ocean would soon feel as much a prison as any county facility ever could.

"I know. It won't be long, I promise. And there's a fire-place."

She nodded, but the tension I'd noticed earlier ratcheted up several notches. She looked like she wanted to sprint back to the seaplane and learn to fly the damn thing her-self, if that's what it took to get off this island. This wasn't her natural habitat. She'd only come with me to offer moral support. It's what she always did.

Now, it was my turn to do it for her.

"Come on. I'm better company than those behind you." I reached out a hand, and she only hesitated a moment before taking it. With a gentle tug, I pulled her into the house and closed the door on the gathered crowd.

Sera turned in a slow circle, studying her prison. The cottage looked like an issue of *Coastal Living* had exploded all over the room. The color scheme was primarily blue and white, and far too many of the decorations had a starfish theme. It was as comfortable and bland as any luxury hotel, with any hint of personality deliberately removed.

"It's only temporary."

Sera's face was drawn and tight, and she ignored me in favor of loading up the fireplace with wood, despite the fact that it was seventy-two degrees outside. A flash of her magic, and a fire blazed. She sat before it, absorbing its power, and I sat next to her.

Though I didn't consciously stretch my forbidden magic toward the flames, the proximity was enough to feel renewed, and for the despair of the day to ebb slightly. Sera's shoulders relaxed, as well.

"Hungry?" I asked. Neither of us had eaten anything since a plastic-tasting breakfast in the Reno airport.

She shook her head.

"Thirsty?"

"Anything stronger than water around here?"

"Please." I jumped up and headed toward the small kitchen. "It's an island full of near immortals who never have to work or worry about their livers. What are they going to do but drink? Plus, I think my aunts technically own this cottage, and they always kept booze stashed around the island."

I rummaged through the cupboards, calling to Sera across the breakfast bar. "Lots of dried soup mixes, some pasta, pancake mix, of course." I bent and opened the last cabinet. It was a temperature controlled wine cellar, fully stocked. We wouldn't need to be sober for the next month, if that was our wish.

"Good news is I found the booze. The bad news is it's all wine."

"And so my punishment begins. Is there a cab, at least?"

I pulled out several bottles until I found a big Australian cabernet sauvignon. I uncorked it, grabbed two glasses, and returned to my spot by the fire. Sera grabbed the bottle from me and took a hefty swig. She grimaced, finding the high-end wine vastly inferior to cheap tequila, but she still filled her glass.

"So, you want to talk about what happened or do you want to get drunk?"

"I can multitask." She took another long gulp. "What

the hell happened out there?"

I shook my head, helpless to offer any plausible explanation.

"Could this place be bugged?"

I had no idea. I knew nothing about how the island was run these days. I supposed anything was possible. "Doubtful, but I can't say for sure."

She nodded, and our eyes met in silent understanding. We could talk about the murder, about Sera's involvement, about possible explanations, but we couldn't say a word about my fire side. It wouldn't take much for someone to put the pieces together—a single throwaway comment, a flash of rage darkening my eyes—and I wouldn't even be given the time to defend myself. I'd be too busy being dead.

Sera took another hefty swig of wine and topped up her glass. The bottle was already half empty, but that meant nothing. Fires can burn off any excess booze, meaning Sera could maintain the perfect level of intoxication as long as she wanted to. "So, I narrowed it down to three possibilities, each less likely than the last."

I took a sip of my own glass, much smaller than Sera's. "You're ahead of me. I'm leaning toward the island housing an invisible dragon at the moment."

"One, I lost control for the first time in my life and somehow failed to notice it happening."

I wrinkled my nose. An invisible dragon was more plausible than Sera losing control.

"Two, there's another fire hidden somewhere on the island. There were several buildings within magic range of the council. Someone could have hidden there."

"Someone who snuck on the island without anyone noticing them, who will need to continue to hide now that all transport off the island is shut down?"

"I didn't say these were good theories," she reminded me.

"And the last?"

She lowered her voice. "There's another fire somewhere on the island, hiding in plain sight."

Our eyes met in silent understanding. In the sea of blonds on the island, there was no chance one of them was a fire—unless they were, like me, a dual magic. Neither of us wanted to even speak the words, lest anyone overhear, but we were both aware of the possibility.

It was unlikely. Dual magics were extremely rare. They only resulted from the pairing of two different full-blooded elementals. Full-bloods were uncommon enough, and they weren't especially fertile. Plus, any full was well aware of the risk of bearing a dual magic. Immediate death to the child, and a century of imprisonment to any parent who concealed the abomination.

Once, there'd been many more dual magics. However, when elementals are capable of producing floods, tsunamis, ice storms, earthquakes, avalanches, rock slides, and forest fires, it really helps if they're in their right mind. The previous dual magics weren't, and one after another they were slaughtered. Now, there was just me, and a sad man locked in a mental hospital on the California coast, and the two others Josiah found after a long search.

And yet, another dual magic was the most plausible explanation for Lake's death.

It also meant, if someone else was using fire on the island, I had a way to find them. It wasn't a method Sera would approve of, I knew, and I tried to school my thoughts into a neutral expression before I gave anything away. Her eyes narrowed, letting me know I hadn't been that successful.

Before she could say anything, the doorbell rang. I barely

had time to stand before it rang again several times in short succession.

I opened the door to see several familiar faces crammed in the doorway. My three aunts rushed in, followed by my much calmer mother. Before I could even speak, I found myself in the middle of a group hug, my aunts wrapped around me while they alternately cried about how unfair it all was and scolded me for staying away so long.

"I missed you, too," I said. They were nuts, every last one of them, but they were family. "Sera has a bottle open."

Their faces instantly brightened. Marie, the middle aunt, shook her head. "Just one? That will never do." She bustled into the kitchen and pulled out a bottle of white from the wine cellar. Georgina, the oldest, followed and grabbed a light red.

It was strangely comforting to see that there was no occasion, even a gruesome murder and their niece's best friend standing accused of the crime, that didn't call for copious amounts of wine. These days, I felt like my life was constantly changing, the ground shifting beneath my very feet, and I was glad to see a few things remained constant.

Tina was the youngest of my aunts, only a century old. She joined the others and began filling glasses.

I offered my mother a tentative smile. Her brows drew together, revealing a crease on her forehead that hadn't been there when I left for college. I raised my index finger to her face, smoothing out the line. "We've been through worse," I reminded her. "We'll figure this out."

She blinked, just once, but with that simple move her face transformed. She was the oldest of her sisters, the first born of my unusually fecund grandmother, and she carried the air of responsibility seen on older siblings the world over. But she was still a water, and she rarely stayed in a bad mood for long—particularly when there was wine nearby.

I turned from her to the last people who'd stepped through my door. "Lana?" My voice rose sharply on the single word. If Santa Claus had ridden through the door on a reindeer with a technicolor nose, I wouldn't have been much more surprised.

Lana Pond was a half-water who lived less than an hour from our cabin in Truckee. I'd only met her once, when I'd still believed I was, like her, half-human. She'd pointed me toward her brother, Trent Pond, the institution-bound dual magic who helped show me what I was. As far as I knew, she had no idea dual magics even existed.

Lana was loopy and odd but mostly harmless. Unfortunately, she was also one of the few who'd seen me lose control of my water magic. If she started telling stories to those who understood what that loss of control could mean, she'd quickly go from mostly harmless to a woman capable of ruining my life, if not ending it entirely.

"Aidan!" Lana exclaimed. "I haven't seen you since you visited me and…"

Marie returned with a glass in either hand. I grabbed one and thrust it toward Lana, hoping to distract her. Fortunately, a pretty piece of dust could distract Lana, and soon she was exclaiming over the oaky notes in her chardonnay.

I swallowed, fighting panic, and grabbed a second glass just for me. Lana couldn't be here. Not with the council, not with her knowledge. Either she needed to get off this island immediately, or I did.

I caught Sera's eye. She'd never met Lana, but she'd heard about our encounter. "Lana Pond," I mouthed, tilting my head in the other woman's direction.

A mask dropped over Sera's features, as it often did when her thoughts were in turmoil. She whispered to my mother, whose eyebrows leapt in alarm.

I'd never met the man at Lana's side, but I was certain

he was the stone I'd spotted in the crowd earlier. A strong one, too, based on his traditional coloring. He was average height, and there didn't appear to be a single part of his body that wasn't covered in a muscle of some kind. His short hair was a medium brown undiluted by highlights, and his eyes were a dark slate gray. He was handsome enough, if your taste ran to body builders who looked like they smiled twice a year.

Me, I preferred a man who could destroy this one in an arm wrestling match, one who smiled damn near every time I walked in the door. I felt a sharp pang for Mac, still in Tahoe and expecting me home in a couple of days. We weren't together, exactly. We'd agreed to wait to take the next step until I'd resolved my issues with the council and knew what my future held. At the time, it seemed the mature thing to do. With this new delay, I was beginning to regret that decision. Maturity is seriously overrated.

Forcing my thoughts back to the man in front of me, I stuck out my hand. "Welcome."

He shook my hand somberly. I suspected he did most things somberly. "It's nice to meet you, Aidan. I'm David Flint."

One of the old names, too. I couldn't remember the last time I'd been surrounded by so many strong elementals.

These were supposed to be my people, but my thoughts and my heart kept returning to an A-frame cabin by the Truckee River, where shifters and elementals were equally welcome, regardless of how much magical blood they could claim.

Lana's heart, however, was clearly right in front of me. "Isn't he lovely?" She wrapped her arms around his waist and leaned her head on his shoulder, her face soft and dreamy.

David gave her an indulgent smile and pressed his lips

to her forehead in a warm kiss. In a way, I guess it made sense. Someone as batty as Lana would likely do best with a man who had patience of a saint, someone stable and reliable and predictable. In other words, a stone. I guess there really was someone for everyone.

That pang hit again, sharper than before, insisting I was too far from Mac. Whatever was happening on the island, I needed to figure it out quickly and get back to Tahoe. Every cell in my body yearned toward him. Being with him made everything else just a bit more bearable.

"What brings you by?" The question was more abrupt than I'd intended, but Sera and I needed a night of drinking and plotting, and only one of those looked to be happening now. "I mean, aren't you all scared Sera's going to burn you to ash?"

David cast a speculative eye toward Sera. Somehow, his face grew even more rigid. He was seriously considering my question. "Until she is convicted, I'd rather not behave as if she were guilty. Also, I can't imagine any reason she would want to incinerate me or Lana."

Stones always were a serious and pragmatic lot.

David nodded at my mother. "Fiona assured me that Sera was innocent and asked me to study your porch to see what kind of camera you need. A branch of my family owns a home security company, so I guess that made me the best option."

I nodded, grateful. Without Vivian and Simon to help, I hadn't thought how we'd manage the surveillance camera on an island full of luddites.

"I've been granted permission to fly into Bellingham tomorrow for the camera. Until it's set up, Lana offered to stay with you. A witness, to confirm that Sera doesn't leave."

"That's very... kind. But aren't you worried Sera will

hurt you, Lana? If you're sleeping, you won't be able to defend yourself at all. Perhaps you should stay far away."

While we spoke, my mother and Sera inched closer to us. Hearing Lana's offer, my mother didn't even attempt to pretend she wasn't eavesdropping. "She's right, Lana. No reason to take an unnecessary risk. Please, come stay at my house. I have a lovely guest room already made up." The offer was graciousness itself. No one would ever guess she was trying to keep us apart—or keep Lana under tight surveillance and away from the council.

Lana laughed, light and airy. "Don't be silly. Look at that face." She gestured toward Sera. "It's such an honest face. I don't know why we're going through this charade of gathering evidence when it's so obvious she didn't do it."

Sera looked between me and Lana, as if unable to believe this woman even existed. Her face, it should be noted for the record, looked very much like she could kill someone at that moment.

"Even so," I continued, "I think my mother will stay. We haven't seen each other much lately and…"

Lana shook her head, already dismissing my words. "And she's your mother. Her testimony will never be believed. I, however, have no reason to lie for you."

That's what I was afraid of. Still, as much as I dreaded having to watch my every word and action while Lana was around, it beat letting her run around the island unsupervised.

Lana was already heading toward the back of the cottage. "Now, which bed is mine?"

"The pink one," Sera and I announced in unison. Then, with a long look at me, Sera drained her glass before refilling it to the top. I suspected she had no plans to burn off the alcohol that night.

CHAPTER 4

To our unending joy, Lana proved to be an incompetent witness. It took two glasses of wine before she was leaning against David's shoulder, a decidedly slack look on her face, and she made no protest when he guided her toward the second bedroom. He left soon after with a promise to return the next morning and trade Lana for a security camera. I thought we were getting the better end of that deal.

My aunts wandered off a few minutes later, their last bottle clutched in Georgie's hands. Before leaving, they covered my cheeks with enthusiastic kisses and insisted they didn't believe I was guilty of murder, not for a second. My aunts never had been good with details.

My mother left with them, though she first murmured quiet promises to help exonerate Sera. They were vague words, though, and I knew she didn't have any real idea where to begin.

The moment we were alone, Sera turned to me. "No."

I raised both eyebrows. I was pretty good at filling in the blanks with Sera, but even I needed a little more to go on.

"I know how you're planning to find the other fire. No."

"I have no idea what you're talking about." It was a lie, and about as successful as all the other ones I tried to tell her.

She listened for Lana's quiet snores, then pulled me into

the kitchen and turned on the water, disguising our voices. "You are not going to wander the island while accessing your fire side, looking for someone else doing the same."

"No one would expect it, which means any hidden fires on the island wouldn't try to hide their magic from me. It's the best way."

"To be discovered? To learn how far you can push it before something in you snaps? It's not worth the risk." She shook her head, the issue already decided in her mind.

"Shut up. *You* are worth the risk. You'd do the same for me. Don't deny it."

"I'm not a freaking dual magic, either, which means I'm a hell of a lot more stable than you are. It's not even apples and oranges. It's apples and tractors. We can't begin to compare our magic."

I opened my mouth to protest. I was perfectly stable. Sure, I might occasionally want to scream and throw things in a way a proper water would never do. It was possible I'd done two entire pushups the other day before I came to my senses. And yes, maybe I was aware of my fire side as I never was before, the individual threads of magic becoming dangerously familiar.

Oh, and there was the part where I might have given Mac a small measure of my elemental magic when saving his life after an FBI agent shot him, a freak occurrence I couldn't even begin to explain.

Really, stable is such a subjective term.

"Well, we need to do something. You have a better idea?"

"What do we always do when things go wrong?"

I grinned. My burst of happiness was inappropriate, considering the current situation, but if nothing else we now had a valid reason to contact Simon and Vivian. Yes, they'd moved out of the cabin, but they'd never leave Sera in a lurch if they could help it.

"Didn't Simon call earlier? Right before the trial?"

She groaned. "I forgot about that. He asked for Fiona, said he had a question about healing, but he wouldn't go into details. I was supposed to deliver the message to her, but got distracted by the whole accused of murder thing. I'll let her know tomorrow."

"No, let me handle it. I may hate healing, but I can still answer some basic questions."

Sera took a seat at the small laptop computer set up for guests and booted it up. "In the meantime, let's see if Vivian will help. You do have internet here, right?" She didn't wait for me to answer, already opening her favorite music program. If she was going to be trapped for several days, she would damn sure have Social Distortion for company.

I was relieved to see the cottage was connected, as elementals were historically quite anti-technology. Rumor had it we refused to ride in a passenger train until 1932. However, even we recognized the benefits of internet shopping. We might resist big scary metal things that rumbled along iron rails, but it was a lot harder to resist the lure of books and clothes being sent to the island with the click of a button. Even if it did force me to listen to Sera's music, having access to the internet would make our investigation much easier.

Sera found the site she needed and opened a video chat window. "Wait. This isn't right."

I peered over her shoulder, trying to see the problem. Unfortunately, after my decade as a technology-free hermit, video chat was still relegated to the "freaky science fiction" category.

"Vivian's not online," she explained, pointing at the gray dot. "Vivian is always online. What has that woman done to her?"

The woman to whom Sera referred was Olivia, Vivian's

live-in girlfriend and the subject of my and Sera's irrational dislike. Sure, Vivian chose to move out of the cabin
because she needed a break from the non-stop chaos and
murder attempts, but we preferred to blame Olivia.

We hadn't heard from Vivian since she left, and we were
trying to respect her need for distance. Still, she was a
friend, and I had to believe she'd be willing to help Sera
avoid a murder conviction and the subsequent death pen-
alty.

I pulled out my phone to call our earth friend. It went to
voicemail, and I left a short message, asking her to call us.

"What about Simon?"

"In what world would Simon sit around, waiting for people to contact him?" She had a point. "Mac's never online,
either. When did you last talk to him?"

"When the plane landed, just to check in. He sounded
tired, but he brushed it off when I asked him about it.
Think they're having wild parties without us? Maybe
they're all sleeping it off."

I was joking, but my words triggered a thought for Sera.
A few keystrokes later, a familiar and utterly adorable face
filled the monitor. "Ladies," said Miriam, her voice booming. Sera adjusted the volume down. "How the hell you
doing? Homesick already?"

Miriam was an otter shifter, and she looked it. Physically, she was as cute as a basket of, well, otters, with big
melting brown eyes, a button nose, and cheeks that begged
to be pinched. Of course, if you followed through on that
urge, you were likely to lose your hand. The woman was
brash, outspoken, and often seemed to speak entirely in
curse words. I kind of wanted to be her when I grew up.

Like Vivian, Simon, and a handful of other shifters, she
knew my secret and hadn't told anyone. I trusted these
people, far more than I trusted elementals these days.

"You have no idea how homesick we already are," I answered.

"Brook, I'm looking at your tits, and let's be honest, there ain't that much to see. Get in the damn frame."

I knelt until only my disembodied head appeared in the bottom of the frame. "Better?"

Miriam nodded. "So what's up?"

"Sera's been accused of murder," I announced, like any older sister tattling on a younger one.

"Again? Did you at least do it this time?"

Sera shook her head, disgusted. "I was thinking unflattering thoughts about the victim, but nothing incendiary."

"It was awful," I said. "I'm going to have nightmares about what we saw today. The problem is we have no idea who did it. All we know is the councilwoman was about to deliver my sentence, then she freaking exploded. So far as we know, there aren't any other fires on the island. We're pretty much as a loss here."

Miriam nodded, then a smile lit up her face. "I could come up and help."

Sera dumped the last of the cabernet into her glass. "No offense, Miriam, but what could you do?"

The otter's grin remained firmly in place. "I could smack some elemental heads together. That would definitely help me feel better."

"Maybe later," I said. "Have Vivian or Simon been around? We could use their help with some surveillance and research stuff." The otters liked to hang out in the river behind the cabin and seemed to know more about what went on in our house than we did.

"I was last there yesterday morning. Simon's been by to visit Mac, and those agents have stopped by a couple of times, but that's it."

That was news. We hadn't heard from the FBI agents

for weeks now, ever since the night Carmichael acciden-
tally killed Mac while trying to protect me. I'd managed
to revive Mac, but that didn't mean I was ready to forget
how he'd ended up dead in the first place. I imagined I'd
forgive Carmichael eventually, but I wasn't sure it would
be in this century.

I pulled my notebook from my handbag and began
rifling through the pages until I found Olivia's address. I
handed it to Sera, who typed it into the chat window while
speaking. "Miriam, could you wander over to this apart-
ment building and let Viv know what's going on? I think
she might be ignoring us, so maybe find a way to convince
her that's a bad idea?"

There was a beep on the other end as the address went
through. "Will do. You want me to tell Will and Carmen?"

I considered it. We'd recently helped find several missing shifter children, and I was sure their parents would be
happy to help, if only to even the score. No shifter wanted
to be indebted to an elemental. Unfortunately, I couldn't
think of anything they could do, and I feared their involvement would only worsen matters with the council.

"Just Simon, if you see him." We said our good-byes and
closed the chat program.

I'd waited all night to make the next call. Mac might
not be able to do any more than Will and Carmen, but just
hearing his voice would provide more comfort than every
bottle of wine in the kitchen.

The call went to voicemail. It was one of those auto-
mated responses, too, so I couldn't even be pathetic and
enjoy the sound of his voice telling me to leave a message.

I tried to hide it, but Sera saw the disappointment
cross my face. "Get some sleep, H2O. You've got a busy
day tomorrow, what with exonerating me and figuring out
where the hell all our friends have gone." She grabbed a

blanket out of the closet and chucked it to me, indicating the sofa with a jerk of her head. "And accused murderers always get the bed. See you in the morning."

She walked into the second bedroom and closed the door, leaving me alone in a silent room.

To MY SURPRISE, I managed several good hours of sleep, only waking when the risen sun peered at me through the blinds. Sera and Lana were still asleep, so I started a pot of coffee for them and put on the kettle for my morning tea. I eyed my journal, craving the clarity I always found in writing, but I didn't feel safe jotting down my thoughts while surrounded by a bunch of old ones. I always described my life in broad strokes, not wanting to give away the existence of elementals should the journal fall into human hands, but these days that was the least of my concerns. If an elemental read it and guessed that my two halves didn't refer to one side that liked peanut butter and another that liked chocolate, there'd be no laughing. Blood and death, perhaps, but no laughing.

Instead, I pulled off my sweats and, in just my underwear and a cotton camisole, I stepped outside, ran around the porch, and dove into the ocean.

It swallowed me instantly, and I sank to the rocky bottom. I stayed there for a long time, letting the water recharge me and fuel my magic in a way sleep never could. So long as I accessed my element, I could go weeks without eating or sleeping. I had a sense I'd need to be at full power today, and I definitely wanted my water side to be in charge. Even in June, the water was cold, but I didn't feel it. It just felt like home.

At last I rose, ready to face whatever new insanity this day felt like throwing at me. I pulled myself up the ladder and drew the water from my body, drying off a bit before heading inside.

I returned to the quiet living room, pulled my sweats back on, and grabbed my phone. I stepped onto the front porch for a bit of privacy, in case the others awoke. I didn't care how early it was. I hadn't spoken to Mac since noon the day before, and that was too damn long. Hell, sometimes an hour felt like too long.

It rang four, five times, and just as the heavy weight of disappointment settled in my stomach, someone picked up. Unfortunately, that someone wasn't Mac.

"We are on our way."

"Wait, what? Simon?"

"Of course."

"But this is Mac's phone." I wasn't sure if I was the one being simple-minded or if it was him, but one of us was definitely confused.

"Mac is sleeping. I answered. Are you going to continue to offer inane commentary, or are you going to tell us where to meet you?"

I was at least three minutes behind on this conversation, and I wasn't sure I could blame it entirely on my lack of caffeine. "How did you know we needed help?"

"I'm psychic. Or I have no idea what you are talking about. Choose one."

"Wait, then why are you coming up here?"

"He did not tell you?"

It was with a great force of will that I didn't bang my head against the porch railing in frustration. Unconsciousness might be more productive than this conversation.

"Simon. You know I love you, but if you were speaking in Swahili, you couldn't make less sense. What is going on?"

A brief wave of static interrupted whatever response

Simon was preparing. "We're cutting out. I'll tell you when we get there. Meet us in Seattle tonight?"

My gut clenched. As much as I wanted to think they were rushing to visit because they so missed me and Sera, experience suggested they were bringing some fresh hell my way.

We set a time and place. "Can you tell me anything? Cause you're kind of freaking me out here, Simon."

"Mac's…" His voice cut out, leaving me with only fragments of words. "In… mountains." The line cleared for a moment. "Why do you need help?"

"Sera's accused of murder."

"Again?" Simon asked, just before being disconnected.

I hung up and stared at the phone, hoping it would provide an explanation for what had just occurred. It remained frustratingly silent. I knew I should be worried, and I was, but a larger part celebrated the news that, in a few more hours, I'd be seeing Mac.

My mind still struggling to make sense of the conversation with Simon, I stumbled into the kitchen where a cup of tea waited, along with a bright-eyed water elemental.

"What's the plan for today, Aidan?" Lana asked, hands clutched around my cup. Without a word, I refilled the kettle and dropped a teabag into a second mug.

Lana was kind, gentle, and more than a little annoying. Some elementals reached centuries of age roughly the same person they'd always been. Others, particularly those who lived alone, tended to go just a little bit weird. Lana fit squarely in the second category.

One more reason to be grateful Sera saved me from my hermit ways.

"What brings you to the island, Lana?" *And more to the point, when do you plan to leave?* I added silently.

"Oh, David and I are traveling the country this summer.

This island isn't far from David's home, so we decided to pay your family a visit."

"You two are that serious?"

"Mmmm," she said, a wordless reply that nonetheless managed to be quite eloquent. Lana was a goner for her stone boyfriend, that much was clear.

"David's coming over soon, isn't he? With the camera?"

Lana smiled and poured the now boiling kettle into the second mug, which she proceeded to claim as her own. I did not attempt to set her on fire, which I thought said loads about how my emotional control was developing.

"He's already texted me five times this morning. He's so romantic that way. He said he couldn't sleep without me, so he was on the plane first thing this morning."

I did some quick math in my head. The flight back and forth would take just over an hour. Add in the time needed to purchase the camera in Bellingham and the travel time to get back across the island, and I was looking at another hour alone with Lana. I had the distinct feeling that, so long as the other woman remained in our living room, Sera wouldn't make an appearance.

"Once he arrives, I'm going to head over to my mother's, to learn as much as I can about what happened to that councilwoman."

"The poor thing," she murmured.

"Indeed. You should come." I was sure my mother wouldn't mind getting stuck with Lana babysitting duty.

I didn't give her a chance to come up with some daft reason why she needed to stay at the cottage. Instead, I disappeared into the bathroom and showered for the next forty-five minutes. The islanders piped in their water from the canals and never bother to heat it, so I didn't even need to feel guilty about the waste. Instead, I reveled in the privacy.

When enough time had passed, I dressed for the day in a clean pair of jeans and a blue tank top. I combed my hair into a neat ponytail. I was almost desperate enough to start applying makeup when I heard the stone's low voice in the other room.

I rushed out, barely remembering to offer David a civil greeting in my hurry to get out of the cottage. I taped a note to the coffee maker, where Sera would be sure to see it, then dragged Lana away from her boyfriend.

"I'll be back soonish. Let me know if you have any problems with the camera."

He nodded, unperturbed, as he removed each item from the box and lined them up on the kitchen counter. David was a stone. He'd read the instructions from beginning to end, then reread them to make sure he understood. He would be there for a while.

At last, with Lana at my side, I stepped out into the bright light of morning, bound and determined to prove my best friend innocent and get the hell off this island.

CHAPTER 5

The island hadn't been so much planned as built around hundreds of years of various Brooks planting a stake and declaring the land theirs. There weren't property lines, just canals that ran between houses, and not a single home was built along a straight line with another. The gravel walkways zagged in every direction, often doubling back on themselves when they encountered a large fountain or random building. Even so, it never took more than thirty minutes to walk from one end of the island to the other.

The unprotected west shore belonged to the guest cottages. The east held the pier, where the seaplane and all the island's boats rested when not in use, tucked into a small cove and hidden by the tall fir trees that lined the shore. The south shore was the calmest of the lot, and the only part of the island that had a true sandy beach we would lounge on during the warm summer months. Our version of a town center was plopped in the middle of the island.

There were houses scattered all over, in every possible style. The younger elementals favored the Craftsman and Art Deco styles, while the older ones built Colonials and faux Tudors. Nothing matched, not in color or style or size. The first time I'd seen a planned development in the human world, I'd stood on the sidewalk for a full five minutes, unable to imagine the mind that could produce such order.

The northeast shore belonged to my nearest relatives. The house I'd grown up in was furthest west, a simple white Cape Cod home with green shutters. Grams lived to the east in a large brick two-story Georgian that was completely dwarfed by its proximity to my great-grandma's house. Hers sat between the other two homes, a neoclassical monstrosity complete with columns and a curving driveway, despite the island having no cars.

Great-grandmother was the oldest resident of the island and its proud matriarch, and her home was more than a house. It was where the island gathered for companionship, entertainment, and news. Despite her absence, the house maintained its role as community center, and the porch and living room were crammed full of people looking to relive the scandalous trial and murder. My aunts, who lived in matching bungalows close to town, had appointed themselves hostesses, keeping the gathered masses content with food, gossip, and mimosas.

My mother was already there, working on damage control. When I entered, she was patiently suggesting to two distant cousins that it was perhaps overkill to require all members of the Blais family to register themselves as deadly weapons.

There were too many people around for an open conversation, so I stayed just long enough to suggest she entertain Lana for the day, then rushed out the door before she could protest.

Alone for the first time since landing on the island, I headed for the transportation center on the eastern side of the island, hoping to convince Robin to lift the travel ban just long enough for me to pop into Seattle and meet up with Simon and Mac.

On a whim, I detoured through town. It wasn't much of a town, at least according to most definitions of the word.

There was a general store that stocked basic necessities and a private post office that delivered mail whenever someone bothered to take a trip to Friday Harbor and collect from the island's P.O. box. There was one coffee shop and a restaurant with three tables, both run by people who liked to cook and thought it seemed like a fun way to pass the time. The stores were only staffed for an hour or two a day, as more often than not the proprietors didn't feel like coming in. People would take what they needed and leave an IOU behind, which the owners never bothered to collect.

Today, most of the island was at Great-grandmother's, leaving the town center nearly silent. I stopped at the empty coffee shop to make myself a cup of tea. While it steeped, I dialed Simon, hoping for news that would lessen the ball of anxiety taking root in my stomach. The call went straight to voicemail.

I muttered a few uncomplimentary things about black cats who weren't nearly as forthcoming as they ought to be, then stretched my magic toward the canals, seeking balance in the water. When I felt ready to face the day, I headed east.

After the silence of town, the transportation center was surprisingly busy. At least ten people struggled with large suitcases while arguing with the pilot, who was trying to explain that he had as much money as they did, thank you very much, and would not be bribed into taking them off the island so long as a travel embargo was in place.

I sidled over to Robin, a third cousin who'd been tracking everyone coming on and off the island for as long as I could remember. It was a volunteer position, one I thought she chose because it allowed her to spend all day with her feet on the desk, a romance novel in one hand and a never empty mug of coffee in the other. As she was one of the few waters capable of keeping detailed records, everyone was grateful for her dedication.

"What's going on?" I asked.

She grinned at the sight of me, the smile cutting across slightly weathered skin. She was a quarter elemental—strong enough to live on an enclave, but still prone to a few human weaknesses, like aging. She was blond like the rest of us, but a slightly darker shade, and I thought she might be the only water on the island with hips worth noticing. There was a medium-sized shed behind her that doubled as an office, but I'd never seen Robin sitting anywhere but her outside desk.

As I approached, she bookmarked her place in her latest novel and set it aside. "Aidan! Glad you stopped by. I was hoping to see you before you left for good."

"It looks like I'm here for three more days. Still no flights out?"

She made a face. "Unfortunately. These fools here seem to think they're in danger, and they're acting like such idiots I'd be plenty happy to get them off the island. I know we're supposed to assume everyone's a suspect until your friend is convicted, but that seems like a lot of bother to me. No offense."

I offered a noncommittal noise. I wasn't offended, but I didn't welcome the reminder that most weren't viewing this as an "innocent until proven guilty" situation.

I studied the panicked waters and saw no familiar faces. At least it wasn't my relatives trying to flee for their lives. Visitors, then, come to witness the trial. "They know how elemental magic works, right? Sera can't stretch her murderous claws across the island."

"I'm not sure there's a lot of thinking going on at the moment. Still, you how how waters are. As unpredictable as they are fickle. They'll find something new to panic about in an hour or two."

I wasn't so sure. This wasn't a typical situation, and I didn't think we could count on normal behavior.

As if to prove my point, three people decided arguing was getting them nowhere and dropped their suitcases, rushing up the stairs and into the plane. It was the possession is nine-tenths of the law approach to winning an argument.

The pilot rolled his eyes and left the pier, the plane's keys presumably safely on his person.

Robin shook her head and sipped her coffee. "If they want to sit and try to will the plane to take off, I'm just going to leave them be. Now Aidan, what can I do for you?"

As I watched, five more people pushed their way onto the six-seater plane. "I was hoping to get on that plane this afternoon. That's not going to happen, is it?"

An emphatic snort was my only answer. "What's your hurry? You'll be gone soon enough." She actually sounded sad about it.

"Oh, people to meet, more unbreakable elemental laws to flout. You know how it is."

"You shouldn't joke," she admonished, though she didn't seem offended.

"I shouldn't have done a lot of things. That's why I'm in my current situation." I glanced at the neat pile of paperwork on her desk, kept from flying loose by a heavy black rock. "Hey, could I get a copy of the flight list? Everyone who's on the island right now. Boats, too."

"Sure thing." She rifled through the papers, pulling out the records from the last week. She disappeared into the shed, and I heard the groan of an ancient copy machine being summoned to life. A minute later, Robin returned with a thin folder in hand. "This should do it. You really think someone else killed Edith? Not your friend?" She sounded more curious than disbelieving.

"I think it's worth looking into all options." I tucked the folder into my bag. "Thanks for the help, Robin." She smiled, eyes already darting back to her book. I left her to her tale of rugged and misunderstood Highlanders.

I had eight hours before I was supposed to be in Seattle, no idea how to get there and even less idea how to begin clearing Sera's name. During my brief time working with Carmichael and Johnson, they'd taught me a thing or two about how to approach an investigation. List the suspects. Gather facts. See the big picture. I hadn't done any of that yet.

The folder in my bag was a place to start, at least. I could return to the cottage, share it with Sera, and attempt to form an actual plan.

Five hundred feet from our cottage, I passed one of the guest houses that had been emptied the night before. Though travel was limited to the other side of the island, where Robin could track it, this house reached far enough into the ocean to double as a dock. A decrepit rowboat and a modest houseboat were tied to its stilts. The houseboat looked new, and I wondered if it was intended as an additional guest accommodation.

I stared at the dock, a truly terrible idea forming.

"Planning your prison break?"

I turned to see David at my side, the empty camera box in one hand.

"What gave it away?"

"Something about the longing look and evil grin. Gives it away every time." He glanced to his left and right, then lowered his voice to a conspiratorial whisper. "Also, I know how you feel."

"What, an island full of drunken waters isn't your idea of a good time?"

He shook his head in disbelief. It was the standard reaction when someone met my aunts for the first time. "I noticed you weren't partaking much last night. Are you sure you're related?"

"When I drink, I tend to miss things, and that's not an option right now. When this whole thing is over, I'll down a glass or ten, I promise."

David handed me the empty box. "Speaking of not missing things, the camera is up. Sera won't be able to step outside without it being captured. I set it to wide angle, too, so the windows are in the frame. If anything else happens, she'll have an unbreakable alibi."

I took the box and studied the image on the front. It was your bog-standard motion sensing camera, the kind I'd become all too familiar with recently. "Thanks. Where does the footage go?"

"There's an SD card in there, and if something happens to that, there's a wireless backup drive. Who should have access to that?"

"My mother. Fiona."

"I'll take care of it."

"You're being so helpful. Like you think Sera might be innocent."

"Is that a problem?" His brows knit, and it wasn't a rhetorical question. I hadn't known many stones in my life, but they rarely wasted words.

"No. It's just unusual in the current climate."

David stared at the ocean, and I waited. Okay, I bit my lip, counted to ten, and forced myself not to speak before he replied, but I also waited.

"I've known fires," he said at last. "They're hot-headed, but they also have tremendous control. I can't see one of them losing it and causing an explosion in front of dozens of witnesses. It just doesn't feel right."

Something inside me unknotted at his words. It wasn't much support, but it was more than I'd had five minutes ago. "I appreciate you doing this," I said, holding up the box.

He shook his head, waving off my thanks. "It's good to be useful."

"Are you and Lana planning on staying long?" I worked hard to keep the hope from my voice, and when he shook his head I worked even harder to keep the smile from my face. Lana—or what she knew about me—was simply too dangerous to be around the old ones. The sooner she and David were off the island, the sooner I could relax and just worry about little things like my best friend's murder charge.

"A few more days. We'll leave once the embargo is lifted. I'm eager to get some rocks under my feet, but Lana's enjoying herself too much. I can't blame her, I guess. There aren't many places in the world like this."

"Someday, you're going to have to explain how a calm, staid stone ended up with a flighty water."

He gave me a small, close-mouthed smile, but it was genuine. This crazy man truly liked Lana. "I'll tell you as soon as I figure it out. Maybe over one of those ten glasses of wine."

"Deal."

He kept staring at the water. With no warning, his placid stone expression distorted into shock and confusion. "What the...?" He took long strides to the water, face darkening with every step.

I walked after him, my gaze following his own.

Then, I started running.

A black speedboat pulled away from the rear of the house. There were two figures in the boat. One was Sera, struggling to free herself from the driver. He steered with his left hand while keeping his right arm locked tightly around her waist. It was a familiar figure, a man with an average height and build that belied the power he wielded. A man with the same bronze skin and dark hair and eyes as the woman in his arms.

Josiah Blais. Sera's father—and mine.

I didn't think. I didn't give the anger time to build and interfere with my water magic. I gave into the fear instead, the panicked certainty that I would lose my best friend if I didn't act. Our father loved us, in his way, but his pathological need to protect both his daughters meant Sera would be locked in a chamber somewhere on her family's Hawaiian compound and not released until Josiah had eliminated everyone who dared threaten his daughter's life.

It wasn't the first time he'd tried that maneuver.

They were moving fast. In a matter of seconds, they'd be out of range.

I flung the magic from my body. It flew toward the boat, grabbing molecules of water as it rushed toward the target. I didn't bother with finesse. I just needed enough power to force an enormous wave into the escaping boat, and I had more than enough control to do that.

The water crashed over the speedboat, filling the hull and seeping into the electronic controls. The boat sputtered and paused, but it didn't stop. The engine had too much horsepower to give up so easily.

I dove into the ocean, calling my magic back and demanding it push me through the water at unnatural speeds. The water fed off my desperation until I was nearly as fast as the speedboat. I only needed to delay them for a few seconds, just long enough to reach Sera.

I begged the magic to fly toward the boat. I felt the water molecules attach, felt the control in my fingers. I pictured the magic spinning, turning in faster and faster circles until a whirlpool began to form, one capable of swallowing the boat whole.

I didn't know if Josiah could swim. I didn't much care, either.

The engine roared, trying to escape the ravenous water, but whichever direction it turned, the whirlpool followed, relentlessly pulling it down. From my position under the water, I saw the moment the boat gave up the fight. It was sucked under the waves, along with its passengers.

I released the whirlpool and raced for Sera. She was still in Josiah's arms. He stared at me through the water, unmoved. He wouldn't let her drown, I knew. He was counting on the fact that I wouldn't either, and was waiting for me to save them both.

Most people move slowly under water, their muscles unable to work at full speed with the ocean's weight pressing against their bodies.

I wasn't most people. I pulled back my right arm and punched Josiah hard in the nose.

His head jerked back, and his grip lessened. I hit him again, enjoying it probably more than I should. I wasn't strong, but I had my element on my side. Plus, I hated this man, and it's staggering how much fuel hatred provides.

The second time, he flew a foot backwards through the water, releasing Sera. I grabbed her arms and wrapped them around my neck, giving her an underwater piggyback ride, then burst upwards. It wasn't far to the surface, but I only stayed above the water long enough to ask her a question.

"Can you make it a hundred feet?" She tapped my shoulder in silent assent. I dove with her, then raced toward the shore.

We emerged from the water. Sera crawled onto the shore on her hands and knees, gasping for air. I only felt recharged. With the crisis over, anger blossomed in my gut, a sure sign that my fire wasn't far behind. I kept my magic in the water, drawing on its power until I felt something akin to calm. Well, in the general neighborhood of calm. Maybe the same zip code.

Once I confirmed that Sera was safe, I turned back to the water. A dark head moved in our direction. It seemed he could swim, after all. Without the magical boost, it would take Josiah longer to reach the island, but he'd make it.

David still stood on the shore, watching Josiah swim toward us. I don't think his position or expression had changed since we'd first spotted the boat. I spoke his name twice before he seemed to notice I was there.

"You saw that, right? Sera had the chance to escape and turned it down. Maybe this will buy us some good will, if you tell the council." He nodded, but his expression was so distant I wondered if he'd heard a thing I said. "Can you get them? The council and my family? They should be here for this. The council's staying with my Grams, in the red brick house."

He gave one terse nod, then took off for the other side of the island at a run.

While we spoke, Sera pulled herself upright. She still looked worn, but the steel behind her eyes told me she hadn't even begun to fight yet.

"If we return to the cottage, what are the odds he'll burn down the house?" I asked.

"If he does, I'll stop him." Sera might have only been three-quarters fire to Josiah's full-blooded status, and a fraction of his age, but the set of her chin told me she'd find a way.

I nodded, seeing no better option. "Let's get inside and wait for the cavalry. I have a feeling things are about to get ugly, and I'd rather you not be accused of whatever havoc that man is about to unleash."

Together, we stepped inside our temporary home and bolted every door, and I pretended those small metal locks would keep the world at bay for a bit longer.

More than that, I pretended Josiah's presence didn't mean things had just gotten far worse.

"SHOULD WE OPEN the door? Tell them our side of the story?"

Sera pulled back the curtain just enough to observe the confrontation happening outside our front door. Josiah stood nose to nose with four council members, my grandmother, and my very pissed off mother. While we couldn't make out individual words, their raised voices and emphatic gestures told me this was not a calm discussion.

"Why would we do that? It would just invite that whole mess inside."

She had a point.

"Should we make popcorn?"

One side of her mouth lifted. "No, look. They've reached a decision."

She was right. Though Josiah still pointed toward us, he was moving away. I wasn't so naive as to think he was giving in. There was a spring to his step that suggested he was exactly where he wanted to be, and this had been his plan all along. For once, I took some comfort in Deborah Rivers's presence, along with the rest of the council. On her own, Deborah might be a match for Josiah. In combination with so many other fulls, Josiah could actually be contained.

Of course, even a contained Josiah was more dangerous than a human with an AK-47, a belt full of grenades, and laser beam eyes. I wasn't going to relax anytime soon, particularly as no one was giving him a one-way ticket off the island. In fact, they appeared to be inviting him to stay in one of the other guest cottages, or perhaps the houseboat just behind it.

I swore. "Oh, hell no."

"What?"

"I'll be right back." I stepped outside and slammed the door before she could ask any more questions. It was poor form to take advantage of her inability to leave the cottage. I planned to feel quite bad about it later, but first I had to get Josiah far away from the dock.

I ran up to my parents. They turned at my approach. My mother looked concerned, my father pleased. I disliked that.

"He's not staying? Tell me he's not staying."

"Aidan," he scolded, "I do wish you hadn't interrupted me earlier. I'd have thought you would want Serafina rescued."

In Josiah's world, there was little distinction between being rescued and being stolen away to Hawaii and locked in his compound for a decade or two. "I'd rather prove her innocence so she can have her freedom again. And since she's not leaving with you, there's no reason for you to stay on the island. So, you know. Bye."

The look he gave me suggested I was being disappointingly slow. "Aidan, you know I would never leave a daughter of mine to fend for herself." I didn't miss his double meaning.

"You can't stay. I don't want you here."

The council's eyebrows raised as one, curious why I'd have such a strong reaction to my friend's father.

"He'll try to take her again," I explained. "We can't prove she's innocent if she's not here."

"I'm afraid I can't leave. My ride off the island has been incapacitated. Perhaps you'd know something about that."

His tone was mild, his eyes amused. That was the problem with this man. The world was a joke to him, until he found something he felt like setting on fire.

"You can stay on the other side of the island. Away from Sera. Near witnesses. Lots and lots of witnesses."

My mother's eyes darkened, and I knew her maternal instincts were kicking in. Like my father, she'd do anything to protect me. She was even mostly sane in the strategies she employed to do so. If I said my father needed to be far from me, she believed me.

The council tired of being left out of the discussion. Deborah's brows drew together as she considered her options. "We were trying to keep the fires to this side of the island, away from other people," she said. "So, if something else happens, we at least know whether they were physically capable of the crime. It was your idea, if you recall."

I shrugged. "That was for Sera. You can accuse Josiah as much as you want. I'm fine with that."

"Aidan," my mother admonished, more for my overt rudeness than the words themselves. Josiah just laughed.

"I don't mind," he said. "If something happens, my daughter will be exonerated, and I can defend myself." He meant it, I knew. He'd willingly sacrifice his own freedom to keep her safe. He might even sacrifice his own life. If his love didn't come with so many strings, it might almost be a comfort.

Almost.

"Can he stay with you?" I knew I was asking too much of my mother. Yes, they'd had a fling over sixty years ago, but so far as I could tell, my mother had taken a "what happens in Hawaii stays in Hawaii" approach to their time together. I'd never seen a single romantic spark between them, and I was glad of it.

Plus, I'd already foisted Lana on her. She was becoming

the halfway house for people who knew too damn much about my magic.

My mother only hesitated for a second before agreeing.

Josiah, of course, was not so easily convinced. "On one condition. You visit every day and update me."

I knew my face was pulling into a grimace, but I felt powerless to stop it. The small quirk of Josiah's mouth, too much like Sera's for my comfort, told me he saw it and found it downright adorable. He really was a bastard.

I nodded once, then turned toward the cottage. I made it five steps before a worrying thought hit me. "Josiah," I called. "No setting someone on fire just to clear Sera's name, okay?" For most people, this would be a ridiculous precaution. In his case, the precedent had been set.

He only laughed and walked away, the remaining waters following.

As I watched him leave, I was certain of one thing. I needed to exonerate Sera fast, before someone else died.

Because, based on my recent experience with Josiah Blais, it was only a matter of time before another body appeared.

There was only one thing important enough to distract me from that goal. One reason I'd give up some of the precious hours I needed to clear Sera's name.

Despite the morning's unpleasant turn of events, a smile pulled at my lips. My eyes drifted to the still vacant houseboat.

Right now, I had an appointment with a bear and a cat.

CHAPTER 6

I hadn't learned to drive a car until college, but I'd practically been raised on boats and knew how to work all
of them, from the smallest rowboat to the largest, P. Did-
dy-worthy yacht. All I needed was access to some type of
watercraft, and I'd find my way to the mainland.

Luckily for my plans, I was on a crime-free island where
everyone left their keys in the ignition.

Current unsolved murder aside, I was about to increase
the island's crime rate by about one hundred percent. I
hadn't wanted to get my father away only because he made
me nervous. I also didn't want any witnesses when I committed a felony.

The houseboat was nothing fancy, but it had two small
bedrooms with double beds, a decent-sized sitting area and
a kitchen about the size of a Post-it note. It was a little
larger than Mac's Airstream trailer, but I wasn't concerned
about its comforts. All that mattered was it could get me to
Seattle, which it would.

Eventually.

This particular vehicle wasn't intended for transportation so much as gentle floating. I had several hours before
I was supposed to meet them, but the houseboat would
never make it on time, not without help.

No one was on the shore. With my stomach in knots,
I started the motor and was grateful to see the previous

owners had been kind enough to leave it with a full tank of gas. I waited just long enough to confirm that no one was rushing from the trees to demand I stop, then put the boat in gear. With sluggish, reluctant movements, the houseboat reversed, pulling away from the dock.

I couldn't simply point the bow toward Seattle. I needed to head at least half a mile in the opposite direction, putting distance between the boat and the island before looping back around. It wasted precious minutes, but it was better than being spotted and finding a speedboat chasing after me, demanding to know what trouble I was getting up to this time.

As the miles grew between the boat and the island, tension slid from my shoulders, and I took a moment to play with the water. It responded gleefully, recognizing the ancient power that resided within every elemental. I let the water soothe me, recharge me, strip away the fear and panic of the last two days. There'd be time for that again, I was sure, but for now all I cared about was reaching the city in time to meet Mac and Simon.

The water sensed my impatience and wrapped itself around the boat's hull, pushing it along at a pace no speedboat could match.

The closer I drew to the city, the more my nerves rose to the surface, straining toward what lay ahead. I was eager to see them, certainly, but I also felt a slow-building dread.

Something inspired Simon and Mac to drop everything and drive north. In the last day, something had changed enough to convince them to make the twelve-hour drive to see me—a decision made before they knew I would remain on the island for several more days.

The closer I drew to Seattle, the more my vague unease threatened to turn into blind panic. The water could only do so much to soothe me.

This time of year, full dark didn't descend until nearly ten o'clock. Even so, the sun worked its way steadily across the sky, growing weaker with each passing hour, and the air was changing. It was no longer a warm caress. Instead, chilled fingers plucked at my skin, calling goosebumps to the surface.

I still didn't close the boat's windows. The open sea and sky were too precious to keep a plate of glass between us. Only two days on the island, and already cabin fever was setting in. This illicit freedom was temporary, so I was going to enjoy every second of it.

At last, the city rose before me. Though I still looked no older than your average grad student, I'd been born not long after the Second World War, and over the decades I'd watched Seattle grow, one building after another joining the skyline. The sun glinted on metal and glass, gold and silver against a pale blue sky. The city had a beauty all its own, but it wasn't a beauty that pulled at my soul. The sooner I could escape the concrete and crowds, the better.

The docks in the downtown were reserved for the ferries, tour companies, and a few enormous cruise ships. I eased the houseboat toward West Seattle, a neighborhood that straddled the line between suburban and urban. My family kept several slips reserved for just this sort of trip.

I called a cab, and while I waited, I tried reaching Vivian yet again. When she failed to answer, I texted. *You've had enough alone time. Sera needs your help.* I wouldn't win any points for subtlety, but we'd passed tactful about three phone calls ago. Right now, the one thing we needed was information, and few people on the planet were better at convincing a computer to give up its secrets. Sometimes I thought the NSA might fear Vivian, rather than the other way around.

She didn't reply, and the taxi arrived before I could send

a second, more pointed message.

Six hours after leaving the island, I pulled up to the designated meeting spot in front of the Pike Place Market.

I wouldn't have expected Simon to choose this location. The Olympic Forest would have made more sense, or maybe the Cascade Mountains. Simon and Mac weren't city people any more than I was, and I assumed they felt as ill at ease among the skyscrapers and neon.

Of course, I forgot what the place was famous for.

I found Simon on the ground floor, eyes riveted to the fish being chucked between vendors, a noisy show for the benefit of the tourists who still thronged the market.

"I always wanted to see this," he said in greeting. He didn't need to look at me. He knew my scent and my walk well enough to sense the moment I appeared at his side. "It is not as appealing as I expected it to be. I thought they threw fish to the tourists, not to each other. What is the point in just tossing fish back and forth? It is a waste of perfectly good salmon." His eyes never left the fish sailing through the air, and I wondered if I should get him out of there before he tried to pluck one out of mid-air.

"It's good to see you, too."

He turned to me. "Did I forget pleasantries again?"

"A bit. It's okay. I know you love me."

His mouth lifted, just a tiny close-mouthed smile, but on Simon that said as much as most people's grins. I studied him for a moment, trying to figure out what was different. There were a few freckles on his pale skin, suggesting he'd spent some time in the sun. His black hair was a bit shorter, perhaps cut for summer, but there was something else.

"Your eyes." I stared. His eyes were a remarkable shade of green, but I was used to that. I wasn't used to seeing a perfectly round pupil.

He tilted his head, a silent acknowledgement. "Carmen

taught me how to control them. I did not want to, but she suggested it was nice to have the option to appear more human."

I couldn't argue with that logic, but I still missed the slightly slit pupil, that hint of his feline nature he never hid before. Simon was living with a family of big cats in Tahoe, learning more about what it meant to be a cat shifter. Granted, when he shifted, he became a ten-pound black housecat, rather than a hundred and fifty pound mountain lion, but apparently the basic principles were the same.

While I wanted Simon to better understand his shifter nature, that didn't mean I wanted the mountain lions to change him. I pretty much loved Simon exactly as he was.

As if guessing my thoughts, he blinked, and when he looked at me again, his pupils were elongated and considerably more Simon-esque.

"Not that I'm not thrilled to see you, but where's Mac?" He was a difficult man to miss, as he took up at least twice the space of an average man and towered above most people. Even without his impressive size, I knew my eyes would have gone directly to him if he'd been there. They always did.

"We need to go to him. Did you bring cash?"

I nodded slowly. I'd hoped I'd get answers as soon as I found Simon, but he was only raising more questions. "Why?"

"We need a cab. We weren't able to find a parking spot, so we're in an industrial area a couple of miles to the south. I'd rather not walk." He cast one last, longing look at the soaring salmon, then headed toward First Avenue, leaving me to wonder just how bad traffic had become in downtown Seattle that a single vehicle couldn't find parking.

It was a short ride, no more than ten minutes. I spent most of that time trying to pry information out of Simon, but he only offered responses that ranged from non-committal to downright evasive.

"You will understand in a minute," he said, peering out the window. "Turn right up here."

We were in a new neighborhood south of downtown. I'd visited the area long ago, during summer break. Then, it had been a rundown neighborhood, as so often happens near the shipping centers of major cities, but artists were already discovering the cheap rent and huge loft spaces unavailable in the rest of the city. A decade was more than enough time for gentrification to run its course. Now, it was a mix of posh coffee shops and galleries, once derelict buildings rebuilt as condominiums.

Still, even real estate-hungry computer money needs more than a decade to completely claim a neighborhood. Simon guided the cab driver to a graffiti-covered brick building with boarded up windows. There was an empty lot attached to it, the pavement pockmarked and worn. The parking lot was surrounded by a chain link fence with a broken padlock hanging from the gate. Considering there were only two vehicles in the lot, I suspected the lock was only recently broken.

I also saw why they'd had difficulty parking. It was one thing to find an underground parking lot for an SUV. Even Seattle, a notoriously difficult city for parking, would offer some options.

The Airstream trailer it pulled was another story.

No one was visible through the car windows. It was a Bronco, much like the one recently demolished, though this one was newer and dark blue. If Mac was here, he was in the trailer. Part of me itched to run toward him. The other part was growing more certain by the minute that something was terribly wrong, and I wasn't sure I was ready to face that reality.

"Simon, what haven't you told me?" I kept my eyes on the trailer, willing the Airstream door to open and for Mac to come bounding out, healthy and smiling and claiming he simply couldn't wait another day to see me.

"Pay the man." He opened his door and stepped out, waiting.

I shoved a twenty at the driver without looking at the meter, then joined Simon. The driver pulled away, leaving us alone in the abandoned parking lot.

Simon turned to me, and the sadness in his eyes made my stomach turn to lead. "Mac is sick. It is as bad as anything I have ever seen, and it is getting worse. The shifter doctor in Tahoe could not help. You can. You have done it before."

"No. God, no. For fuck's sake, Simon. That was an extreme situation. He was *dead*, if you recall." My voice rose with each sentence.

I hated healing. I hated moving my magic around in another person's body, controlling the blood and organs by controlling the water that makes up a large portion of the physical body. It felt too intimate, and it was more control than I ever wanted.

Most elementals can kill with their magic. I'd seen too much proof of that recently. We could burn someone's insides or turn their hearts to ice. We could calcify bones or drown them in water we pulled from the air.

I also knew it wasn't a power we should have. We shouldn't get to decide who lived or died. When I sent my magic into another person, for that moment I held their life in my hands. It wasn't a role that fit me.

I'd made one exception, for Mac. Just once, I'd used my water and fire magic together. It brought him back to me, but it also changed us in ways we still didn't understand. And, despite what I'd said to Simon, for Mac I'd do it again.

I'd do whatever I needed to do to keep him with me. If that meant healing him now, I would do it, and I'd just find a way to live with any consequences.

I was halfway across the parking lot when the trailer's aluminum door slammed open and Mac himself filled the doorway. If I'd been dying of thirst in the desert and someone gave me a bottle of water, I don't think I'd have greeted it with more joy than I did the sight of that man.

He didn't look ill. Hell, he didn't even look mildly uncomfortable. He looked like a freaking god.

Mac wasn't just tall, or strong. He was immense. Near him, all other men looked a bit puny and underdeveloped, like they were just a step below him on the evolutionary ladder. He was a bear shifter, and sometimes I was embarrassed I'd needed to be told that. I should have known, just to look at him. He had the strength and size, the broad, tanned face, the dark brown eyes and hair, but it was more than that. He was gentle, until he wasn't, and he was calm, until provoked. He was as protective as any mother bear, and anyone who threatened those he cared about might find themselves missing a spine. Somehow, I'd become one of the people he cared about.

Not just one of them. We were becoming more than one of many to each other, and though neither of us were in a hurry to put it into words, we both recognized there might be something real between us, something rare and unchanging. Something that could destroy us both and maybe, if we were lucky, put us back together again, better than we'd ever been before.

I stared at him, a smile spreading across my face, washing away the fear and tension that had gathered under Simon's dreadful words. I launched myself across the parking lot, crossing the ten feet that separated us in the time between one heartbeat and the next. I didn't stop when I reached

him, either, but I didn't need to. He already had his arms
out, ready to catch me as I landed against him. I wrapped
my arms around his neck and buried my face in the warm
curve of bare skin where his shoulder met his collar bone.

"You're here," I murmured, lips pressed against his skin.

A rumble coursed through his chest, a silent laugh. "So,
we're not doing the take-it-slow thing anymore?"

With one hand, I lightly smacked the back of his head,
then simply held on tighter, squeezing for all I was worth.
Granted, between my absolute lack of muscle mass and his
excess of same, he probably didn't feel much, but I didn't
care. I wasn't letting go, and he should know that.

"If you need a room, I'm sure Simon and I can vanish for
a bit," said a familiar voice.

It was enough to pull me back to reality and remind me
that, abandoned building or not, we were still in public. I
should probably hold off trying to climb inside Mac's skin
until we were alone.

I drew back, looking for the source of the voice. "Miriam?"

The otter shifter lowered herself out of the trailer somewhat cautiously. In water, few were more graceful than she
was, but on land, she was a bit awkward, at least by shifter
standards.

"Hey, Brook. So, I checked on them like you asked."

I looked between her, Simon, and Mac. "Bit of an over-
achiever, aren't you?"

She laughed, a big booming sound that made me think
everything was going to be okay. "Well, I hadn't planned
on catching a ride north, but when I stopped by the cabin,
they were hooking up the trailer and fixing to leave, and
I decided a road trip sounded like way more fun than
babysitting my sister's brats again. Good fucking thing, too.
It turns out the cat isn't much of a driver. He's been nap-

ping most of the way up."

I nodded as if any of this made sense. I still hadn't let go of Mac, and though it was almost physically painful, I disengaged and met his eyes, remembering the reason they were here at all. "Simon said you were ill."

He shook his head, a small smile appearing. "I was, but I'm finally on the mend. Must have been a two-day bug or something. Or maybe I just really missed you." The smile took on a decidedly wicked slant.

"Good thing I've got the cure for that." I grinned, not even caring that the line could win me the cheeseball of the year award.

"Are you done?" Simon's voice had more edge than I'd ever heard. "Because I can assure you, we did not travel several hundred miles to watch the two of you and your amateur flirtations."

Mac leaned toward me until his mouth was right next to my ear, and I shivered from the warm brush of his breath. "Wanna go pro?"

I giggled. Heaven help me, I giggled.

That was apparently the last straw for Simon, who stepped between us, forcing an end to our teasing.

Simon was shorter than both of us, with a mere fraction of the muscles Mac possessed. Even so, the glare he split between us was more than enough to cow me. Simon was not a frivolous man, and he wouldn't drive Mac to Seattle for an interstate booty call.

"Okay, okay." I took a closer look at Mac. While he looked perfectly healthy, there were small signs this was a recent development. Lank hair fell across his forehead, as if it hadn't been washed in days, and he was wearing worn sweats and an old t-shirt. He looked like he'd spent most of the day in bed, and not in the fun way. "Tell me what was wrong with you, and don't even think of doing that macho dude thing where you insist it was a bad case of indigestion."

Mac looked at his feet, and I knew he was debating how much of the truth to actually share.

"I mean it. If something's wrong, I need to know, particularly since we have no idea how my magic is affecting you." He still didn't look up, so I played my trump card. A dirty trump card. "How mad would you be if I was feeling off and didn't tell you?"

His head jerked up, the reminder of my tenuous mental health doing what I hoped it would. Neither of us wanted to see me go off the deep end, but if I started heading that way, he'd insist on knowing.

He grimaced, but at least he started talking. "It didn't start off too bad. It was two or three hours after you left, I guess. I wanted to sleep a lot, and I usually only do that in winter. It felt like a flu, or what I would guess a flu feels like, and it kept getting worse. I didn't want to eat or move. That's how Simon found me."

I glanced at our friend, who didn't look impressed with Mac's accounting of his symptoms. "I stopped by yesterday morning. He was in bed, the sheets kicked off, sweating so much he could have filled a bucket. It was quite disgusting, really. He could barely stand, he had not eaten in a full day, and it took him several tries before he remembered my name. By evening, he did not know his own name, which is when I made the decision to drive to you. Miriam stopped by to check on us, and she helped hook the Airstream up to the Bronco. Mac has been in a state of constant delirium across three states, until about five minutes ago. Until you appeared, that is, and he was magically cured."

Mac shook his head. He didn't argue with Simon's list of his symptoms, but he wasn't ready to agree with his conclusions. "It was just a thirty-six hour flu, maybe food poisoning."

Simon leveled his green eyes at Mac. "Bears often get the flu, do they?"

Mac muttered something about having human DNA. Neither Miriam nor Simon looked particularly impressed. I hadn't known shifters very long, but in that time I'd never seen one have so much as the sniffles.

"What do you want me to say?" His voice rose, the anger I'd witnessed on more than one occasion rising to the surface. Mac would never hurt anyone he cared about, but he had a tendency to destroy inanimate objects when pushed to his limits. I stepped closer to him, offering silent comfort, and I felt rather than saw the tension ease. "I was sick, and now I feel fine."

Simon looked between us. "I know you are both all loved up, which likely makes you stupid, but are you truly telling me neither of you sees it?"

Miriam shook her head. "You can't just blame the love endorphins, dude. I don't know what you're getting at, either. It sounds like you're saying Aidan has some magical healing aura, except that would be fucking insane."

Simon looked at her in surprise, though I thought it had less to do with her confusion and more to do with calling him dude. If he was in cat form, he'd be bathing while steadfastly ignoring us in an attempt to regain his dignity.

He spoke slowly, picking each word with care. "Aidan healed Mac with her magic. She quite literally returned him to life." We waited for the part we didn't already know. "Aidan leaves, and Mac grows ill. Aidan returns, and Mac instantly recovers."

I understood where he was going with this, but I didn't want to hear it. Based on the vehemence with which Mac was shaking his head, he felt the same.

Simon watched us, saw the fear creep into our eyes, and

finished anyway. "Mac's health, maybe his very life, is tied to Aidan. If she leaves him, I think he will die again."

CHAPTER 7

Since the day Sera had landed on my porch and insisted I rejoin the world, I'd been working to curb my denial reflex. Ten years in hiding had trained me a little too well to ignore painful truths, and I feared that, during my lost decade, it had become less of a coping mechanism and more of an attempt to construct my own false reality.

It was a work in progress, but most days I at least made a token effort to acknowledge what was directly in front of my face.

Obviously, that was the wrong choice. Denial was awesome. Denial kept me from facing awful, life-changing things. I should do it more often, not less.

"No." I looked between Mac and Simon, the movement so sharp my neck muscles would complain later. "That's crazy talk, Simon. That's not how it works."

Miriam watched us, though she looked considerably more relaxed than we did. To be fair, a jet pilot on stimulants might feel more relaxed than I did at that moment.

"You used your magic to heal him," she noted. "We all saw you do it."

Mac appeared frozen. He wasn't looking at Miriam or Simon. He didn't even acknowledge their words. He looked only at me, but with none of his earlier warmth. Uncertainty clouded his eyes, as if he wasn't sure he'd seen me before. Panic clawed at my chest.

"Yes, but waters have been healing for years. My great-grandmother once cured a man who'd been electrocuted, and he showed no ill effects when she traveled. It just doesn't work that way."

"But you are more than a water." Simon was determined to make me consider his ludicrous theory. "You are a dual magic. We cannot assume your healing method is the same as a pure water."

He didn't even know the half of it.

After I healed Mac, my mother had examined him, and she was the only one who knew I'd left traces of my magic behind and that Mac could now manipulate small amounts of water. We'd told no one else. It was a secret we'd held close, something that belonged only to us.

Also, we hadn't wanted to run around shouting that I'd created the first elemental/shifter hybrid. That seemed like the sort of thing that could bite us in the ass down the road.

"Can we be alone for a bit?" Mac spoke the words I'd longed to hear only a few minutes before. Not like this, though. Not spoken in a low growl, his brown eyes locked on my face. Normally, they looked like melted chocolate, full of warmth and humor, but now they were as hard and flat as packed dirt. I couldn't even guess what Mac was thinking, but I doubted he wanted privacy so he could indulge his more amorous intentions.

Miriam hesitated. She didn't know Mac very well, but even she could feel the anger building across his skin, the rage he kept tamped finding its way to the surface.

"It'll be okay," I told her. There wasn't much in this world I knew for sure. I knew that Johnny Cash was the coolest man who'd ever lived and pancakes were the best argument for waking up each day, and I knew that Mac would never deliberately hurt me. That last one, in particular, I had to believe. I couldn't accept a world in which that was no longer true.

Simon tugged on her arm, and she reluctantly let him pull her away. Even so, she didn't leave the parking lot, climbing instead into the back seat of the Bronco and turning to look through the rear window, keeping the trailer in her sight. Simon followed.

Mac opened the trailer door and waited. There was nothing to do but step inside.

This really wasn't how I'd imagined our reunion.

Normally, the trailer was pristine, the bed neatly made and Mac's few possessions tucked away in the drawers and cabinets. For the first time, it looked like someone lived in it.

The acrid smell of sick hit me as soon as I stepped into the trailer, and half-full mugs filled the sink. The door to the bedroom was open, and I could see the bedsheets were twisted and damp, covered in his sweat.

"Simon would make tea when we stopped for gas. I drank what I could."

I nodded, mute. The hale man who'd greeted me wasn't the same one who'd ridden up from Tahoe. Simon hadn't been exaggerating.

There was a small table, surrounded by two benches bolted onto the sides of the trailer. It was the only seating available, and I sank into one of the chairs. My mind churned through options, desperate to find any explanation that made more sense than Simon's.

Mac eased into the other seat. It was a tight fit, but he made it. The table sat between us. It might as well have been a city block for all the distance I now felt from Mac.

"Is he right?"

I held my hands out, palms up. "I have no idea. There's not any precedent for what happens when a water and fire dual magic brings a shifter back to life, you know." A bite crept into my words. I didn't want to fight with him, but neither would I sit here and beg forgiveness. I'd done what I had to do, and I would change nothing.

He was silent. He watched me, and waited. Damn Sera for teaching him that nothing made me speak faster than silence.

"I still don't even know what I did. It was like the magic possessed me. It told me what I needed to do to save you, and it worked. It fucking worked, Mac, so whatever's going on now, we'll deal with it, because at least you're alive, and you sure as hell wouldn't be if I hadn't done whatever I did. So I'm not apologizing, and you can stop giving me that evil look any time now, okay?"

He closed his eyes and released a heavy breath, and when he opened them again, he looked like Mac. Maybe not with as much warmth in his face as earlier, but the stranger who'd taken over his face since Simon's damning words was retreating.

He ran his hands over his face and tugged on his hair. It was still dirty and damp from his sweat. Now that I knew what to look for, his face showed signs of two days without food, the cheekbones jutting angrily against the skin.

"Are you hungry?"

He looked at me in surprise. "I am." He laughed, a quiet, rueful sound, but at least one that was identifiably Mac. "That might partially explain the bad mood. Sorry about that." He stood and rifled through the cabinets, returning with a box of plain crackers, several pieces of sliced watermelon, and a large glass of water. He put them between us, indicating I should help myself, but my stomach was too tied in knots for food to sound tempting.

I waited while he polished off at least half a watermelon and a bag of crackers. If I was going to face an angry bear, it seemed a good idea to at least face one with balanced blood sugar.

At last, he leaned back in his seat. "Let's try this again."

The water in the glass bubbled, then rose a fraction of an inch above the rim before sliding back down. "The water magic is weaker. A week ago, I raised it several inches above the glass."

"You were desperately ill less than an hour ago. Maybe it takes more time to recharge."

He let out a heavy sigh and pushed the water across the table, as if he couldn't stand to have it so close.

"We know you weren't able to retrieve all your magic when you healed me."

I waited. He didn't need me to confirm what we'd known for weeks.

"Which we thought made me just a tiny bit of an elemental, something we agreed to keep to ourselves until we understood what we were dealing with."

He recited the facts as though, by speaking them aloud, they'd begin to make sense. Unfortunately, we had very few facts to work with. I'd never heard of anything like this happening before, and we couldn't ask other elementals without revealing my own heritage.

"Have you noticed anything else?" I asked. "Other than getting ill and being able to manipulate water a bit."

He shook his head. "Nothing. Which is why I wasn't too worried about having some extra magic. It was weird, yeah, but I supposed it beat the alternative. But this, I'm not okay with this, Aidan."

"We don't even know what 'this' is yet. We're jumping to conclusions, based on a half-assed theory Simon came up with on the fly. This could all just be a massive coincidence. It could have been the flu. Hell, it could be your body adjusting to the new magic, but that doesn't mean your life is tied to me."

As I babbled, Mac's expression softened into something dangerously close to pity.

"This isn't denial," I insisted, pointing a finger at him. "This is considering the situation from more than one angle. Is it still just the water? No rogue fire magic showing up?"

He stood and withdrew a plain white candle from a kitchen drawer and set it on the table. Still standing, he focused on the wick, his face contorting, as if he was straining to lift a large boulder. After a minute, he shook his head, and the tension left my body, as well. "Looks like I'm not that much of a disaster just yet. One dual magic's enough for now."

"That's good. So, let's keep going. Process of elimination and all that. We've been apart before. I ran errands, checked on my mother when she was recovering from the anti-magic drug. It's not like we were attached at the hip."

"And you were never very far away or gone more than a few hours. You were too worried to leave me alone for long, remember?"

"Okay, but that doesn't mean distance or time is the problem. When was the last time you were ill before this week?" He looked blank. All right, then. "Never? Seriously?"

"I had the sniffles once when I was fourteen."

I tried to picture that. I didn't get ill often, but colds still snuck up on me if I didn't access my element as often as my body needed.

I sat up straighter. "That's it. You weren't actually feeding on water, were you?"

Mac glanced across the room. A large bucket sat next to his bed. I'd assumed Simon placed it there in case of emergencies, but once I focused on it, I could feel the gallons of water it held.

"I've had my hand in that for the last twelve hours, Aidan. I may be new at this whole elemental thing, but I've been watching you for months. I know you need water to stay balanced."

At that moment, I felt many things, but I wasn't sure balanced would even make the list.

"Oh." I tried to come up with something, anything else, but apparently intelligent wasn't on the list right then, either.

He moved to the other room, which was dominated by a large bed. He sat on the edge with his feet planted on the ground and his elbows resting on his knees. His wide shoulders hunched, just a little, but he kept his head up and his eyes fixed on me.

Neither of us said anything, and after a minute I moved to his left side, mirroring his pose. We both stared straight ahead, but our thighs touched. After a long stretch of silence, I took his left hand, threading my fingers through his.

"It's you. We can come up with a hundred different explanations, but that doesn't change what's happening." His voice was pitched so low I strained to hear it. "Though it's in my body, it's still your magic. It doesn't belong to me. It barely even responds to me anymore. It only answers to you. And if you're not around, it becomes sick."

Shifters needed to change, and elementals needed to connect with their element. Bad things happened when magic didn't get what it needed.

Things like Mac falling gravely ill.

"Maybe this was a one-time thing. Maybe you were already getting ill, and you just needed an extra boost of magic to kick it. It's okay. I can be around when you get sick. Just consider me a walking, talking bowl of chicken noodle soup."

He was kind enough not to scoff. "Maybe."

"Look, I have an idea. We need to keep you close until we figure out what's going on. We'll separate for a couple of hours. If you don't feel any different in that time, maybe we'll be okay. We could just be overreacting."

He faced me then, and his eyes were once again the warm chocolate brown I knew, the eyes that looked at me and somehow saw only the good. His right hand rose to stroke my cheek, an almost tentative touch.

"It is good to see you, you know. Even when I was horribly ill, I missed you."

It was exactly what I needed to hear. "Me too," I managed.

He leaned into me then, almost cautiously, as if he was unsure what would happen when our lips met. The kiss was slow and gentle, his mouth fitting against mine. It was pure warmth, a touch that could light a fire in a frozen room, and I savored it.

And then, it changed from a simple kiss to something more. My magic rose, calling to him, and I felt his own respond. It wasn't only his magic, though. It was mine, the threads of magic that had found a home in Mac when I healed him, but also different. Weeks in close proximity to his shifter magic had altered it, turning it savage and hungry.

It took over, needy, demanding, feeding on and fueling our emotions. I felt it expand through my body, from my lips to my neck, my collarbone, dancing along my arms and fingers and legs. My core grew warm, a heat that spread everywhere until I wanted to push him backwards onto the twisted sheets and forget everything in the wild heat of his body.

He pulled back, gasping, and I saw the same desperate craving in his eyes. Then, with no warning, he stood, putting several feet between us.

"I need to clean up. Go see Simon and Miriam, let them know your plan, whatever it is."

I stared, uncertain what I'd missed. He didn't look angry. He looked lost.

"Aidan, I've been slowly getting used to the idea that I don't want to live without you, and I think I'm okay with that. I just wasn't prepared to literally be unable to live without you. I need some time, okay?"

I agreed. There was nothing else to say.

He entered the small bathroom and turned on the shower, closing the door behind him. I stepped out into a Seattle twilight that didn't look like the same world I'd known when I entered the trailer half an hour earlier.

CHAPTER 8

I met them two hours later outside Bremerton, an old Navy town an hour's ferry ride from the city. Like most towns within commuting distance of Seattle, recent years had brought steady renewal to the once forgotten town, but it was still far enough out from the city to have plenty of underdeveloped and working class neighborhoods, and therefore more trailer parks than we'd find in the city itself.

The parking situation was only one reason I'd chosen to meet here. While I could easily sail to Bremerton, they needed to drive an hour south to Tacoma and then back north along the peninsula, putting both distance and time between me and Mac.

It's possible I spent the entire trip back steering with crossed fingers, hoping Mac felt fine and dandy during our separation.

I dug through my memories, looking for any time we were apart with no ill effects. We hadn't been inseparable since the night I healed him. In fact, we'd spent more time apart than either of us would have liked while he healed and I tied up loose ends from our last FBI case.

But we'd never been apart for long, not until I boarded the plane the day before. Before that, I'd provided lots of opportunities to feed his water magic through me, and whenever I was at the cabin, I constantly tapped into the river, creating a rich source of elemental fuel.

Part of me wanted to speed toward Mac, hungry for reassurance that everything was fine and, somehow, we'd get through this new problem. A louder part wanted to take a lengthy detour, possibly through Canada, to give him the time to prove he was perfectly healthy, regardless of my proximity—or lack thereof.

In the end, I neither rushed nor tarried, but it didn't matter. I reached the dock first and waited while they arranged parking for the trailer and Bronco. By the time the three shifters joined me, over three hours had passed, and Mac looked as healthy as he had in Seattle.

Simon's and Miriam's worried expressions told me this was a recent development.

I cast off, asking the water to remain calm while the three shifters boarded. "Welcome aboard." I gestured behind me, showing off my stolen wares. "Or maybe I should say welcome home, at least for now."

Miriam made no attempt to hide her pleasure. As much a creature of water as I was, she acted like a child with a new toy. Simon, on the other hand, appeared decidedly green at the thought of spending any time aboard the houseboat.

Mac just looked resigned.

"How are you?" I whispered as he stepped past me onto the boat. I only received an unimpressed glance in reply. All right, then. If he wanted to do the stoic and stubborn bullshit masculine thing, he could, and I would silently mock him for it.

It didn't take them long to unpack. They hadn't brought much from Tahoe. I'd need to make a supply run to make sure they had food and clothes for at least a few days.

"You know how to drive this thing, Miriam?" I asked, calling her over to the wheel.

"Brook, if I managed to fly a fighter jet, I'm pretty sure I can handle the three buttons on this boat. Hand me the keys."

I couldn't. I was too busy staring at her.

"What? I was in the Air Force. Is that so shocking?"

I nodded, vehemently. "Yes. Don't they require you to follow orders in the military?"

She laughed. "Yeah, well. That's why we parted ways after a year. I'm used to being considered disreputable, but the military are the only ones who've ever called me dishonorable and gotten away with it. So, which direction am I heading?"

After that, it was just a matter of choosing rooms and settling in for the long ride back.

Simon agreed to take the pull-out couch. I thought that had less to do with his inherent selflessness and more to do with the sitting room being further from the water than the two bedrooms.

I filled them in on the recent disasters on the island. "I'm not bringing you along to help. Let's be clear about that. There are two problems here, Mac's health and the murder investigation, and the two will not meet." I put on my serious face, so they'd know I wasn't messing around.

Miriam snorted. "If you say so, Brook." My serious face still needed some work.

My friends knew little about elemental enclaves beyond what Sera and I had told them, and it was difficult for them to fully grasp the insular mentality that had developed among people who'd lived isolated for centuries. They knew the island was filled with elementals who either detested shifters or believed they didn't exist, but knowing something and experiencing it are two very different things.

I refused to give in to Miriam's teasing. "You'll need to drop anchor at least half a mile off shore, on the western side. It's less crowded, since everyone is staying far away from the accused murderer. Though if you have a cloak of invisibility, now would be a good time to mention it."

Miriam shook her head. "Aw, c'mon, Brook. It can't be that bad. You're saying we need to be prisoners on this boat until you figure out the next step?"

Simon looked longingly at the land receding in the distance.

"Pretty much."

She harrumphed. "Please. How bad can it be? They wanna start something, I can take a bunch of skinny water fuckers. No offense."

"Miriam, you don't really understand. You've only met elementals outside the enclaves, and they weren't old ones. As far as you know, a quarter-blooded elemental is strong as hell, but for us, it's a baby. Right now, the council is in residence, too. You're going to an island full of some of the most powerful magical beings in the world, and they *hate* you. Not dislike or are annoyed by or have grumpy thoughts about. Hate. They pretend you don't exist. You show up and provide living proof of their lies? I have no idea what they'll do, but I'm gonna go out on a limb and say it will be unpleasant. Sera and I are struggling with enough right now. If they think we're palling around with shifters, we'll be fighting even more of an uphill battle."

They all looked disgusted, as they ought to. I felt dirty even making the request, as if they were a secret I was determined to hide.

"And these are your people?" Miriam squinted at me, and I worried she was viewing me in a new light.

"You know. Family." It sounded like such a weak excuse, and yet I knew we'd all offered it at one point or another in our lives. A single word that explained so much.

"Fine," she said, in a voice that sounded like she meant the exact opposite. "I must actually like you and Sera to agree to this."

"Right back at you, Miriam."

"Are we done being sappy now?"

"Yeah, we're good."

Simon waited until we were done. "The magic does not stretch half a mile. If Mac needs regular access to your magic, you'll need to be closer to prevent him growing ill again."

"No." It was a flat denial, and not open to discussion.

I still tried, of course. "He's right, Mac. You get, what, three hours if you're not within my magic's range? I can't swim out every couple of hours to recharge you, not right now. Maybe you could park the houseboat by the cottage where I found it, and just keep the blinds drawn."

Mac was shaking his head before I finished speaking. "It's too risky. Anyone could board the boat. I won't be the reason more suspicion falls on you and Sera. We were separated a day and a half before you met us in Seattle, and I can do it again. Besides, when you appear, I'll instantly feel better. Just visit me once a day, and I'll be okay. I can handle a bit of sickness."

"But…" He stared at me, jaw set in an expression I already knew too well. "Fine. But if he gets worse than before, you call me right away. Got it?" I glared at both Simon and Miriam, who kindly did not laugh at my poor attempt at authority.

They both nodded, and there seemed nothing else to say. Miriam moved back to the steering wheel, and Simon shifted into his cat form. He curled up in a tight ball on the built-in couch, black tail wrapped around his face, covering his eyes and allowing him to pretend the rest of us no longer existed.

I sat by Mac. We didn't speak or touch, but I was aware of him the entire way back to the island. Aware of his warmth and his scent, of the thin coat of hair on his forearms, of the muscles clenching and unclenching as he circled through one frustrating thought after another.

More than anything, I was aware of distance, even as mere inches separated us.

I'd just taken the strongest, most capable man I knew and made him physically dependent on me. I suspected there would be an adjustment period.

I mentally revised my to-do list. Prove that Sera didn't murder the council member. Get Josiah off the island and permanently out of my life. Find out what my mysterious sentence from the council was supposed to be.

Those all mattered. They were all necessary. And yet, all I could think during the long ride to the island was that I needed to break the magical link between us.

Years ago, Mac's father had forced him to live as a bear, never allowing him full control over his own body. I knew what his independence meant to him, and I would not be the one to take it away.

Even if I had absolutely no idea how to give it back.

"So, GUESS WHO I found roaming around Seattle?" I asked, opening the door to the cottage.

There was no response, likely because I'd need a bullhorn to be heard over Blondie, currently blasting from the computer's speakers. Sera was nowhere in sight.

Rather than shout again, I crossed to the desk and turned the music down to a volume that wouldn't cause my ears to ring.

The minute the music dropped, Sera's door opened and she rushed into the living room, reaching me in several quick strides.

"Where have you been? It's been fucking hours.

Couldn't you at least answer your phone?"

"What do you mean? No one's called." I pulled it out of my pocket to show her. "Oh. I guess I should charge that. Anyway, I was just in Seattle. I didn't have a chance to tell you, what with Josiah's unexpected visit. What's up?" My fire fought against its chains, wanting to tangle with Sera's manic energy. "Oh, god. Did someone else die?"

She glared at me, and I took a good look at my best friend. Her hair had crossed "untamed" and was heading for "mad scientist," the curls sticking up in every possible direction. Her eyes were almost as wild as her hair. "I've been *trapped*."

I waited for more, but nothing seemed to be forthcoming. "And?"

"What do you mean? Trust me, that's enough."

"Nothing's different since this morning, then? You did know you wouldn't be able to leave the house, right?"

"Yeah, but no one told me how *boring* it would be. I've walked through the entire house six times. I've counted the light fixtures. I did laundry, just to have something to fold. I did one hundred sit ups and watched so many hours of Netflix I think my butt fused to the couch. I opened the front door every hour on the hour, just to flip off the camera. You have to get me out of here, Ade."

She finished, her eyes imploring, even desperate.

"What's going on, Sera? You weren't like this when you were arrested. You acted like a career criminal in the Tahoe jail."

"That was different. I knew I could escape any time. It would be ugly and public, but I could get out and I knew Josiah would clean up any messes. This time, I might be able to get away, but then I'd have to spend my life in hiding. Or worse, on the Hawaiian compound. Neither of those are options." As she spoke, she began pacing through the room, her right hand flicking against her thigh with every step.

I sat on the sofa, forcing my body to calm. "Can you be still for a bit? Your fire energy is a little pronounced right now."

She froze, reading between the lines. Her slightly unhinged expression vanished, and while she looked more than a little exhausted, she also looked like Sera. Instead of joining me on the couch, she folded her legs beneath her and sat on the floor. "Sorry. I actually forgot. You've been acting balanced these last couple of weeks, shocking as that is."

I waved off her apology. She had no way of knowing I felt the fire all the time now.

I hadn't told anyone, not yet. I wanted to be known and loved for myself, not feared and pitied for the crazy woman I might someday become.

"So, Mac, Simon, and Miriam are floating about half a mile away." I told her, enjoying the surprise and pure glee that flashed across her face.

I told the entire story as quickly as I could. Since Mac and I had been close-mouthed about the side effects of my healing, that part took longer than it should have, mainly because I had to stop several times so she could swear at me for keeping the secret.

However, when I finished, I received only silence. It was a silence I knew well, the one where Sera studies me as if wondering how she became best friends with an alien life form. She shook her head, bemused. "Only you. You couldn't just leave your earring at his place so you had an excuse to see him again. No, you had to leave some of your magic behind."

"Well, you know. I'd hate for him to think I was like other girls."

"Little risk of that. Mutant freak."

"Like anyone normal could be friends with you."

She grinned, and for a moment, all was exactly as it should be.

It was late, well past bedtime, but neither of us wanted to move. We'd found a moment of peace within the chaos, and we clung to it. Only when the little hand on the clock pointed toward the two did we reluctantly stand and head for bed.

"Sera." She turned in the doorway to her room, waiting. Though she was calmer than she'd been when I arrived, tension still coursed through her body. "This isn't different from the jail, not really. If we need to, we'll bust out of here. We'll take the houseboat, or I'll carry you on my back the whole way, or we'll train a freaking dolphin army. I don't care. You're not trapped. I'd never let that happen to you. And if we have to go on the run, well, I always wanted to do a road trip across the country. You know you're not in this alone, right?"

She met my eyes a long time, this friend and sister I'd lost and found again, and she let her guard drop. I saw fear and frustration and anger, but more than any of that, I saw love, and I saw trust. "I know," she said, and closed the door gently behind her.

I claimed the now vacant pink bed. I'd worn myself out with the trip to the mainland and back, and I fell asleep within minutes.

I woke with the sun, my thoughts already turning to the houseboat full of shifters. They'd need supplies, and I needed to check on Mac's progress through the night.

I packed up what little we had in the cottage, at least enough for breakfast. Like most elementals, Sera and I ate no meat, so I'd need to figure out a way to sneak some tuna to Simon and Miriam. For now, at least, they wouldn't starve. I went heavy on the fruit in a blatant attempt to win Mac over by appealing to his stomach.

Sera was still sleeping, but that changed when I opened the front door and screamed like a banshee watching a particularly scary horror movie.

It's the natural reaction when one finds a dead body spread across the front steps.

CHAPTER 9

It said something about how accustomed I'd become to fear and chaos that my shock was short-lived. Rather than stand and gape, I ran down the steps to the prone form at the bottom. It was a woman, lying facedown, and at least this time the body was in one piece. However, it was deeply burnt, covered in angry red welts. The skin was misshapen and melted, with a few patches of hair clinging to the scalp. The body had the height and slight build of a water.

Except this one had hips.

"Robin. Oh, hell. Please don't be dead."

I pressed two fingers to her neck, feeling for a pulse and sending a silent prayer to anything that might be listening that a spark of life still flared inside the ruined husk, something I could heal.

It was a desperate hope. I knew it, even before her silent heart confirmed it. There's something about a dead body, an intangible absence of life and spirit, that told me Robin was gone.

"Oh, hell." Sera stood at the top of the stairs and echoed my own words. "Who is it?" Energy pulsed from her every pore, but it was no longer manic like the night before. The Sera who stared down at Robin's body looked focused, intense, and as horrified as I felt.

I sat back on my heels and released a humorless laugh.

"Other than a blatant attempt to make you look more guilty? I can't say for sure, because of the burns, but I think it's Robin. She monitors the traffic on and off the island. Monitored," I corrected.

"Can you flip her? If she isn't burned all over, we can confirm her identity."

"I know." I made no effort to do so. "Let's call my mother. We need a witness before we start disturbing evidence."

Sera looked dubious. "You planning on getting a CSI team out here?"

She had a point. We had no law enforcement on the island, and we damn sure didn't have our own forensics team.

I scanned the porch, looking for the camera David installed the day before. It was tucked under one of the beams and pointed at the cottage door. Unless the killer chose to run up to the porch and wave after depositing the body on the bottom step, it wouldn't have caught a thing.

That would have been too easy.

I pulled out my phone and arranged for my mother to meet us.

While we waited, I sat on the top step, as far as I could get from the dead body.

Sera sat beside me, though she was practically vibrating me with suppressed energy. "You knew her?"

"My whole life. Robin Brook was a third cousin. Older than me, but weaker. She used to slip me her favorite romance novels after she'd read them. I'd hide them from my mother and read the dirty parts over and over again. She was kind, Sera." A sob threatened, and I closed my eyes and took slow breaths until it passed. This wasn't the time for grief. Sometimes, it felt like it was never going to be the time.

"Does she have anything in common with Edith Lake?"

"I don't think they even knew each other."

Sera was asking questions to distract me, and I welcomed it. Facts, evidence, logic. Such coldness kept pain and anger at bay and gave no fuel to my fire.

"Could she know something? Someone might have been trying to keep her from talking." She pointed to the undisturbed ground. "I don't see any sign the body was dragged. It looks like she was on her way to our front door and never made it."

I struggled not to feel responsible. It was hard when Sera's words made me think, if we weren't here, Robin would still be alive.

Focus. One breath in, one breath out. "Maybe. I already have a list of everyone who's landed on the island the last few weeks. I got it from her yesterday."

"Would the killer know that?"

I let the possibilities run through my head. "I don't think so. The only people there yesterday were a bunch of visitors, desperate to flee the crazed fire." She waggled her eyebrows, and I breathed easier after that single moment of silliness, proof that there was still room for teasing in our lives. "We should probably study that list, huh?"

"It would be a start."

My mother was silent in her approach, face drawn in taut lines. "Oh, Robin." The words escaped on a sigh.

With her confirmation, the shard of hope I'd clung to since finding the body shriveled.

"Help me turn her?" I asked.

It wasn't easy. My mother and I tried to be gentle and respectful, but in the end I gripped the hips while my mother took the shoulders, and we rolled her until gray eyes stared, unseeing, at the cloudless summer sky. I didn't want to touch the body, but I couldn't leave her like that. With hesitant fingers, I drew her lids closed.

We stood for a long time, lost in our own thoughts as we looked at the body of a woman we'd known for decades.

My mother broke the silence first. "In all the time our family has lived here, we've had one murder. It was over three hundred years ago, and it was a crime of passion. Jealousy. That scared some people so much they left the island permanently. This… I can't even imagine what this will do to our community."

She was right. The enclave was our haven, the one place where the pain and trauma of the outside world was never supposed to find us. Those who chose to live here did so partly to avoid the crime and stress found in the human world. This death, only days after the murder of Edith Lake at my trial, would challenge the residents' understanding of their own world.

"We could hide her death," I suggested, though I hated the idea. Robin deserved better, and the true killer didn't deserve to get away with it.

"And say she left despite the embargo? That wouldn't be inconceivable, particularly given her job. We'd need to fake a plane or boat leaving the island, but that shouldn't be too difficult with Josiah's help."

I'd offered the possibility because I thought it needed to be said—and then rejected. I was appalled my mother was actually considering it.

"No." Sera's voice wasn't just firm. It was immoveable, her certainty in that single word as inflexible as steel. "I will not lie, and I will not deny this woman an honest burial in an attempt to save myself. I'm innocent. That's going to have to be good enough."

I agreed. "Plus, we need to keep Josiah out of this, as much as possible. We know he'll do whatever is necessary to save Sera, but his methods are questionable."

"Batshit crazy," Sera corrected.

My mother sighed, the heavy and world-weary sigh that belongs only to a mother whose offspring refuses to fall into line.

"Your choice complicates matters and further implicates Sera, but I agree it is the moral path."

My mother might acknowledge that honesty was the moral choice, but she didn't sound convinced it was the best one. It wasn't that she was unmoved by Robin's death. It was more that the old ones had lived for centuries and seen the world's beliefs shift and change too many times to believe there was one true set of values that should guide our actions. It gave them a moral flexibility Sera and I had yet to acquire.

My mother pulled out her phone. "Then I will inform the council, and they will arrive shortly. Perhaps you should brush your hair, Aidan. Appearance does matter, you know."

"Yeah, yeah," I grumbled, heading up the stairs. As I left, I called over my shoulder. "Oh, also? There might be a houseboat full of shifters about half a mile to the west, so if you can make sure no one studies the horizon too closely or notices there's a boat missing, that would be awesome."

If possible, her second sigh was even heavier than the first one.

An hour later, I was barely holding panic at bay. I hadn't been able to slip out to the houseboat, and the texts I'd sent went unanswered. Images of Mac writhing in pain played over and over in my mind. It didn't matter how many times I assured myself they'd call if he grew worse. I wouldn't truly believe it until I saw him again.

However, as the cottage was now crammed with my mother, my aunts, and the remaining members of the council, a quick escape seemed unlikely.

"Aidan, darling, where'd you put the wine opener?"

I gaped at Georgina. "It's eight in the morning."

"Yes, but I understand drinking is expected at a wake, and we want to honor Robin properly." She held up a bottle of Malbec. "This will do, right?"

I opened my mouth several times, trying to explain that this death should be handled no differently than one of the island's natural passings, then gave up and pointed to the dish drainer.

In truth, the deaths were completely different, and no one knew how to cope with Robin's unexpected and violent end. I supposed we needed to create new rituals, and I couldn't imagine any ritual on this island that didn't involve vast amounts of wine.

While my aunts sat on the steps with their glasses, fighting back tears as they steadfastly avoided looking at Robin's body, Sera and I perched on the living room sofa, surrounded by four council members.

I decided my aunts might have the right of it after all. Facing down a councilwoman convinced Sera was guilty might be easier with a big glass of wine. I'd thought Edith had been overly focused on the whole justice and punishment thing, but Rachel Strait made her look like an amateur. While Michael, Deborah, and Lydia seemed more concerned with Robin's horrific death than with convicting Sera, they weren't in charge. Rachel was.

"It proves nothing," my mother insisted.

"Fiona, I understand you wish to protect your daughter's friend, but the evidence is undeniable."

I stood so I was at Rachel's eye level. "Oh, I can deny it. There were no witnesses. The camera didn't capture anything from that angle. All we know is the body of a woman Sera doesn't even freaking know and has no reason to want dead was found on our steps."

Rachel raised one perfectly plucked eyebrows. She had the same regal bearing as my mother, lacking the ease most waters displayed. Unfortunately, she had none of my mother's maternal warmth to go with it. "She was found dead, covered in burns, well within the radius of Ms. Blais's magic. It is not difficult to connect the dots. She came to visit Aidan, perhaps to offer her support, and she was killed by a fire elemental. The facts are all that matter."

The councilwoman turned to me with the same superior expression she'd worn the day of my trial. I was unused to seeing a permanent sneer on the face of a water, but she managed it.

I wouldn't give up. "And the fact is, Josiah Blais is on the island. He could have done it." Josiah would never do anything that would cast further suspicion on Sera, and if he did kill, he'd leave no evidence he didn't want found.

Though I was certain he hadn't committed this particular murder, I felt no compunction whatsoever about throwing him under the bus.

Rachel smiled. I doubted that was a good sign. "Indeed. I spent much of last night with Mr. Blais. He hoped to sway me to his way of thinking, to convince me his daughter is innocent. It was a valiant effort. It seems unlikely that, a day later, he'd choose to frame her for Robin's murder."

Damn.

Sera stared at the woman, her face unreadable. "Why, exactly, did I kill this woman? I know my motive for the first one was to spare Aidan her sentence, but for the life of me, I can't remember why I chose to kill Robin."

The councilwoman refused to be drawn in. "I have little interest in guessing your inner thoughts. What does matter is that since you arrived, two people have died in ways only a fire could manage."

Lydia Pond opened her mouth to speak, but whatever

she'd planned to say died on her tongue. Rachel's glare likely had something to do with that. Michael stared at me, as if hoping answers would appear if he just waited long enough, and Deborah stared out the window, eyes fixed on the burnt corpse.

Lydia's brief interruption quelled, Rachel continued. "We have run string around the cabin, a line no one else should cross. That includes your relatives, Ms. Brook. We will move the camera to capture more of the house. Sera Blais's trial is scheduled for tomorrow evening. I suggest you prepare yourself."

One more day. I had less than thirty-six hours to figure out why people were dying and find the actual murderer, and I still had no idea where to begin.

I'd solved cases before, but I'd always done so with Sera at my side, with Mac and Simon and Vivian offering support. This time, Sera was trapped, Mac and Simon would never be welcome on the island, and Vivian was refusing to answer her phone.

I was on my own, and while I was clueless, confused, and borderline incompetent, I was also Sera's best hope. If I didn't start figuring things out, her life would change forever—and mine along with it.

"Get out." Perhaps I could have phrased that more politely, but I doubted Rachel would have appreciated the effort. I looked her in the eye. "Sera and I would like some privacy to discuss why, exactly, she is being framed for these murders."

To my surprise, the other woman didn't fight me. If anything, she seemed in a hurry to leave, and she insisted everyone on the steps move outside the border she'd created. It was just string, hung in a one hundred foot radius around the cottage, but it sent the message clearly enough. Those who crossed the line forfeited their safety.

Though the council remained outside, making arrange-
ments to remove the body, at least Sera and I were alone in
the cottage. I studied my friend, wondering why the actual
killer had chosen her. She might just be a convenient person to pin these murders on, but I was beginning to fear it
was personal. "I think it's safe to say someone doesn't like
you."

Free from Strait's scrutiny, Sera dropped the impassive
face and began to pace. The living room was small, and
she could only take three steps before she needed to spin
and trace the path in the other direction. The carpet would
likely need to be replaced once we left.

"Can I light a fire?"

I swallowed. She was asking if I could be around her
while she accessed her magic. I was so agitated, I wasn't
certain I could handle it, but neither could I deny her the
comfort of her element. I nodded once, then sat on the
other side of the room, as far from the flames as I could
manage.

The distance didn't matter. I still felt my magic stir,
wanting to answer the call of the flames. No, that was a
lie. *I* wanted to answer the call, to feel the hungry energy
of the flames. For a moment, I imagined letting my gentle
water magic be consumed by the fire's strength.

I didn't give in. I packed it away, as I had time and time
again over the last few months, ignoring the loud voice of
protest.

It was getting closer, I knew. Someday, I wouldn't be
able to fight it anymore. Accessing both sides of my magic
would create a schism in my own mind, and I'd become a
permanent resident of Crazyville. It's what happened to all
dual magics eventually.

If I couldn't stop it, I'd damn sure make the most of
whatever time I had left.

I would start by proving Sera was innocent. She'd saved me, the day she appeared on my porch and forced me to rejoin the world. It was time to return the favor.

"Any theories about what the hell is going on?"

She shook her head and pointed at the walls, a questioning expression. We still didn't know if there were bugs. It seemed unlikely, but so did most recent events. At some point, unlikely had just become another word for our normal lives.

This, at least, was something I could manage, and this time the damn woman was going to pick up her phone.

CHAPTER 10

It took nearly forty-five minutes for Robin's body to be removed and for our side of the island to be evacuated, leaving me and Sera once again alone in our makeshift prison.

I was surprised the council allowed us to stay, now that Sera was suspected of a second gruesome murder. Perhaps they counted on the fact that, while we could escape and eventually swim to land with the help of my magic, we'd do so in waters well known for their orca population. Though I'd meant it when I told Sera I'd escape with her if it came to that, I was in no rush to discover whether I could control an animal colloquially known as a killer whale.

More than anything, though, we stayed because we didn't want to spend our lives on the run, hiding from elementals for, literally, thousands of years.

So long as there was any chance I could prove Sera's innocence in the next day, we'd stay put.

The moment everyone else was out of sight, I decided the makeshift boundary didn't apply to me. No one told me I had to stay behind them, and without a specific order, I saw no reason not to duck under the string and head toward a small copse of maples several hundred feet from the water and far from any possible listening devices in the cottage.

I waited, listening for any sounds other than the rustle

of leaves or the chirps of the local birds, and then I waited even longer, turning in a slow circle. This wasn't a phone call that needed witnesses.

I tried Vivian's phone first, and again I was sent to voice-mail. I left yet another message, begging her to call us back.

I checked her Facebook page next, and while she was tagged in several recent photos of her and Olivia hiking the Lake Tahoe loop, she hadn't updated her status in weeks.

I pulled up four different chat programs, but she wasn't logged into any of them. I pinged her anyway, hoping she was hiding behind an invisible status, but received no response.

I phoned her three more times in quick succession, hitting redial the moment her message clicked on. Nothing. Frustrated, I settled for an irate text written while abusing the caps lock key.

My phone remained silent. While I was glad neither Simon nor Miriam were calling, insisting I get my ass to the houseboat and cure Mac, the phone seemed to be mocking me, its flat black screen a constant reminder that we were no longer one of Vivian's top priorities.

I didn't want to return to the cottage without informa-tion, and I couldn't travel out to the houseboat without first dropping off my phone at the cottage, so I sat on a rock and hoped inspiration would smack me upside the head if I waited long enough.

Inspiration wasn't feeling so violent that day. It chose to buzz instead, the chat program notifying me of an incom-ing message.

Relief poured through me at the sight of Vivian's famil-iar face. "Let me guess," I answered. "You were kidnapped by aliens. The FBI finally figured out what you were up to and confiscated all your equipment. Your girlfriend spilled soda on all your keyboards so you'd spend time with her."

She winced, and even I knew enough to shut up at that point. "She's at the store. I have no more than thirty minutes. What's going on?"

"Seriously? Olivia knows she's not your keeper, right?"

Vivian shook her head. Her dreads were shorter than they'd been a month ago, cut to just above shoulder-length, and she was wearing a yellow button-down shirt rather than one of her nerdy tees. They were small changes, but they reminded me she'd moved on.

She'd always had a beautiful complexion, her smooth dark skin a perfect complement to her hazel eyes. Now, it was marred by an inch-long pale scar on her forehead, earned during the car crash that nearly killed her. It reminded me how close she'd come to never moving again. It had to remind her of the same thing whenever she looked in a mirror.

"It's fine," she said. "She just wants some time for the two of us to reconnect. Considering what I put her through when we broke up, I can't blame her."

"Uh-huh." My skepticism was evident.

"Also, she pretty much hates you and Sera."

Call someone a selfish bitch behind their back just once, and they never let you forget it. "She hasn't gotten to know us yet. We'll have you over to dinner when we get back." I'd even serve humble pie, if that's what it took.

It was Vivian's turn to look skeptical. "Maybe. You two are an acquired taste."

"Like fine wine?"

"Or Marmite. What's so urgent?"

"Haven't you listened to the messages?"

She said nothing, but in her silence I heard both embarrassment and defiance.

"Wow. You weren't kidding about needing space, were you? Well, get over it. We need you. Sera's been accused of murder."

"Again?"

"Why does everyone keep saying that? It's only the second time. It's not like she qualifies for a punch card."

Vivian said nothing. Her lids lowered, hiding her thoughts. I tried to wait her out, but she was quiet for so long I feared Olivia would return before I got to the point of my call. "Vivian?"

When she at last raised her eyes to me, I had no idea what she was thinking. It wasn't that her expression was shuttered and enigmatic, as Sera's often was. Rather, I saw so many conflicting emotions I had no idea how to interpret them. Sadness and regret and curiosity intertwined, and I couldn't even guess what fueled them all.

"Remember why I left?" Vivian asked.

"Something about how we lived in a constant state of chaos and danger?" I kept my voice light, refusing to let her see how bad things truly were.

She released a heavy breath. I had the feeling she wasn't fooled. "I can't get dragged in again. I need to try to make it work with Olivia."

"And she hates us."

"She doesn't really. Okay, she kind of does. But it's more than that. I didn't leave just for Olivia."

"I know, but…"

"I left for me, Aidan. The two of you see danger and run toward it, waving your arms to catch its attention. I'm not like that. I have a fraction of your power and a fraction of your lifespan. I don't plan to spend it dodging people who want to kill me. I wish I could help, but you're asking too much."

I heard the pleading note, and I ignored it. "I know things have been bad recently."

She refused to let me finish. "You really think things are

going to settle down? Fine. When they do, come and find me. I'll even drag Olivia over for dinner. Until then, you have to leave me out of it."

I turned her words over, looking for any loophole, any room for misinterpretation. There was none, and yet I couldn't let her go. "Vivian, Sera's being framed for murder. There are already two bodies, and no evidence pointing to a single other person. Her trial is tomorrow evening, and if she's convicted, the sentence is death. If that happens, the best she can hope for is to escape and spend her life running and hiding. Any help you can give, we need it, and we need it now." I kept my voice level, the words straightforward. This wasn't an emotional plea. It was a statement of fact, one I insisted she hear.

She closed her eyes and took a long, slow breath. "What can I do?"

I wanted to sob with gratitude, but decided that could wait until after our thirty minutes expired. "We're trying to figure out if our house if bugged. Aren't there, like, radio frequencies you can track or something?"

She nodded, mind already five steps ahead. "If it's being sent wirelessly, I should be able to detect the signal. Address?"

"We don't have them on the island. It's about two hundred feet west of me. If you find any transmissions, we can assume they're coming from our house. There will be a video feed, from Sera's surveillance camera, but there shouldn't be anything else."

I'd already lost her. While I could still see her face, she was no longer looking at me, intent on whatever window she'd pulled up. I heard the clack of keyboard keys as Vivian did the thing she was born to do. She was a weak earth, as close to human as an elemental could be and still call themselves a member of our race, but that wasn't her true magic. Her magic was her ability to make any electronic do her bidding.

It only took a minute. "It's clear. Nothing except the camera. You and Sera are just being paranoid."

"We've had good reason to be. As you pointed out, people are trying to kill us all the time."

"Yes, but you're also surrounded by a bunch of old ones who don't know how to program a VCR. Covert surveillance is rather beyond their skills. Is that all?" The words were abrupt. Perhaps I shouldn't have reminded her why she was avoiding us.

"One more thing. If I email you a list of names, can you do your magic research thing?"

She was clearly torn. On the one hand, this favor would only keep her tied to me and Sera. On the other hand, it might give her an excuse to hack into a high-level government database. "Fine," she agreed, resigned. "What am I looking for?"

"We think we might be dealing with another dual magic here, so our first priority is any connection to fires, burnt people or objects, that sort of thing. Other than that, you know. Suspicious stuff." I nodded solemnly, the very image of a serious investigator.

She didn't even crack a smile. "If I find anything, I'll email you. And Aidan, I meant what I said about needing distance from all this. You get my help until Sera's safe. After that, I'm done." She hung up before I could respond.

Her dismissal stung. I understood why she wanted out. Based on just the last few months, any reasonable person would run far from us, and Vivian was an earth, grounded and eminently sane. Her reasons were valid. It didn't matter. I still missed her. I still felt abandoned.

I sent my magic rushing toward the water, needing its comforting touch before the fire decided to stir. Only when

I felt calm enough to fake a smile Sera might believe did I stand and head back toward the cottage.

After all, Vivian might think she didn't need us anymore, but I still had several people who did. I was long overdue to check up on one of them.

THE OLD ROWBOAT looked like it might sink if someone so much as looked at it funny, but somehow it held long enough to get me to the houseboat.

No one came out to greet me. I secured the rowboat, chucked the bag of supplies on the deck, and ducked inside. The reason for the silence was quickly apparent: the boat was empty. Neatly folded blankets lay on the sofa and two empty mugs were still in the sink, but there was no sign of Simon or Miriam.

Only the rear bedroom held any sign of life. I found Mac buried deep under a small blanket fort.

I sat on the edge of the mattress and rested my hand on his shoulder. I felt the heat of his skin through his gray t-shirt, several degrees warmer than he should be. As I waited, his body temperature settled, returning to normal as his magic fed off mine.

There was no slow return to wakefulness. One moment he was sound asleep, his breathing long and steady. The next, his eyes were open and his left hand covered mine, holding it against his shoulder.

We looked at each other, saying nothing, searching for answers the other couldn't provide. I couldn't apologize, not when this magical dependence was the side effect of being alive. He couldn't assure me it was okay when he didn't believe it.

Instead, I offered him the only hope I could. "I'll try to sneak my mother out here today. Now that we have some idea what's going on, she might be able to fix it. You know I'm not giving up until you're back to normal, right?"

He nodded, but he didn't say anything. Instead, he threw off the weight of the blankets and pulled himself up, leaning against the padded headboard.

The movement made my hand fall off his shoulder, but it gave me the chance to examine him. I meant to look for signs he'd been ill, but I was distracted by the sad discovery that Mac wore modest pajama bottoms rather than boxers. When it came to Mac, my libido never had a particularly good sense of timing. I dragged my eyes upward, but the gleam in his eyes told me my perusal hadn't gone unnoticed.

"Where are Simon and Miriam?" When in doubt, change the subject.

He stretched, long arms reaching forward with the fingers interlaced. My eyes followed the movement, the slow expansion of his biceps. When I at last remembered to look at his face, he was fighting a smile, the bastard.

"They shifted. Miriam is off looking for the local otter population, and Simon said he wanted to do recon. There are housecats on the island, right?"

There were, as well as plenty of otters. They sometimes even drifted along our canals, as much a part of our natural world as the water that surrounded us. So long as my friends remained in their animal forms, no one would guess what they were.

A bear, on the other hand, would stand out a fair bit. It was a good thing Mac stayed behind.

"Wait, they left you?"

"I insisted. I was feeling okay, and they were going stir crazy on the boat."

"No, you weren't, you liar." I pulled back the sheets, still damp with his sweat. "The fever came back."

"And now it's gone. It's barely been twelve hours. I knew I'd be fine."

"You don't know anything about this. None of us do."

He didn't even have the grace to look chastened. "I don't need a nurse, Aidan. They couldn't do anything."

"They could have called me if you got worse."

He gestured at the phone on his bedside table. "So could I. You're on speed dial, so I only needed to push one button. Even I could manage that. If it got bad enough, I would have called."

I grumbled several unflattering things under my breath, then decided he deserved to hear at least one of them clearly. "You are a big, stubborn, annoying oaf of a man. You know that, right?"

He shrugged, unconcerned.

"So, I'm really on your speed dial?"

That smile spread across his face, the slow and wicked one that made breathing difficult. "Number one."

I swallowed. I was pretty sure that was the modern version of going steady.

"How are you feeling?" I refused to let him distract me.

His smile vanished. "Are you going to ask me that every time you see me?"

"Well, it's either that or stare at you creepily in an attempt to read your vitals from afar."

My attempt at a joke fell flat. "Aidan, it's hard enough being an invalid. It really doesn't help when you look at me like I'm going to drop dead any minute."

I fixed my sternest glare on him. "You're not an invalid. Stop whining and get up."

My sternest glare remained a source of amusement. "Yes ma'am," he said, swinging his legs off the bed.

A red duffel bag rested on the floor. He unzipped the top and grabbed a clean t-shirt, a white one this time, then pulled the one he was wearing over his head.

I forgot how to close my mouth.

I'd seen him without a shirt before, but that was a long time ago, before I'd been ready to admit what we could be to each other. Before I'd allowed myself to think too much about how it would feel when that chest pressed against mine, and my arms wrapped around him, pulling him to me until our skin felt like it was becoming one.

It was one hell of a chest. I might be falling for the man underneath the muscles, but that didn't mean I couldn't appreciate the view.

"Hand me my jeans?"

"Hmm?"

"The jeans. The pants made of denim."

I chucked them toward him, making a face. "You're enjoying this way too much."

"If you want to even things up, you could take off your top." The words were teasing. The heated gaze that accompanied them was anything but.

There were few things in the world I wanted more than to take him up on his offer. Unfortunately, one of those things was clearing Sera's name. With only one day to prove her innocence, that had to take priority over naked fun time.

Even so, I was really starting to regret our earlier plan to take things slow.

He saw the decision in my eyes. "I know. Still not the right time." I listened for frustration or resentment, but the words were a simple statement of fact.

He stepped into the bathroom, closing the door behind him for privacy while he changed into the jeans.

"What, I don't get to see if you're a briefs or boxers man?" I asked through the thin door.

A low rumble reached me, the sound of his laughter.

"Today, I'm neither."

The door opened again, presenting me with the disappointing view of a fully dressed Mac. "Commando?" I did my best not to think about what was underneath the jeans. My best wasn't very good.

"Simon packed a bag for me when we left the trailer behind. I guess Simon doesn't view underwear as a necessity."

I found Simon's point of view quite compelling at that moment.

"So, what's the plan?"

I tore my eyes from the front of his jeans. Truly, a decade of celibacy had turned me into an outright pervert. I decided the plan was to prove Sera innocent, then lock the Airstream door and refuse to open it for at least a month. We could deal with healing our weird connection once we actually wanted to be more than a hundred feet away from each other for any length of time.

Unfortunately, step one of that plan was something of a doozy.

"I'm trying to figure out what's going on. Vivian has the list of everyone on the island, and she's looking into it, but I don't know if she'll be fast enough. There was another body this morning. Someone I knew."

He didn't hesitate, just stepped to me and wrapped me in his arms. If I let myself go, stopped trying to hold myself up while the world fell apart around me, I knew he'd catch me.

Whatever else was between us, whatever tension and strain our magical bond might bring to our relationship, I wasn't alone. It was the one thing I knew.

"Are you okay?" His chin brushed my temple, the stubble rough against my skin. I felt the words more than heard them.

"Yes." I pulled back to meet his skeptical expression. "Okay, not really. Not even a little. But I can't fall apart, not yet."

He nodded, his face thoughtful. I wanted to stay, to discuss everything that was happening, everything that was changing, but it wasn't the time. Not yet.

Some day, it would be our time. I'd just keep telling myself that until it was true.

CHAPTER 11

As I approached my mother's house, my mind remained fixed on a houseboat drifting miles to the west—at least until I noticed who was standing on her porch. Lana Pond was happily chatting to two others, her hands moving gracefully through the air to emphasize her point. I couldn't see the faces of her companions. One was tall and blond, like most of the island. The other had dark hair and a compact build. Josiah was talking to the woman who could unknowingly doom me.

I picked up speed until I was damn near running. I'd managed to fob Josiah off on my mother, somehow forgetting I should be doing everything in my power to keep him and Lana from speaking. She had information that could end my life. He had a bad habit of killing people who threatened me. It was a rather large oversight on my part.

"And that's how you build a wind chime from coconut husks." Lana triumphantly finished her story, and I made no attempt to disguise my relief at finding them discussing something so innocuous. I also felt no small amount of happiness that I'd missed that particular tale. "Aidan! I was going to visit you today, but everyone told me if I did, your roommate would kill me. I didn't believe them, of course. Well, not entirely. But still, I must say I'm glad you've come for a visit instead. You know my aunt, right?"

I turned to the other water on the porch and, using

reserves of control I didn't know I possessed, managed not to drop several loud and heartfelt f-bombs. "We weren't ever properly introduced." I tried not to squeak the words.

Lydia Pond inclined her head, offering me a gracious smile.

I'd assumed Lana and Lydia Pond knew each other. They shared the old surname, which indicated a relation, but not necessarily a close one. There were plenty of Brooks I'd never met, so I'd rather hoped the woman who could out me as a dual magic and the woman who could order my death were sixth cousins, twice removed.

"Lydia takes such wonderful care of my family. My mother and grandmother are a bit flighty, you know. My family would fall apart without her help."

Her aunt waved off her niece's gushing praise. I forced a frozen smile, afraid to believe there were waters flightier than Lana.

Josiah turned to me, looking bemused. "Aidan," he said in greeting. "I've just been speaking to this... lovely young woman."

Lana missed Josiah's doubtful tone. "It's been wonderful. I've never met a fire before. You should have introduced me to Sera, you know, with us living so close to one another."

I offered some sort of non-committal grunt. "Lana, Lydia, I'm sorry to interrupt, but I need to speak to my—" I caught myself in horror, and Josiah's lifted eyebrows told me the slip hadn't gone unnoticed. "To Josiah for a bit. I have some questions about fire elementals that might help clear Sera."

Lana nodded happily, her head bobbing on her thin neck giving her the distinct appearance of an exotic bird. "I'll go make some tea. Come in when you're ready." She wandered inside, humming to herself.

Lydia remained. "Do you really believe your friend is innocent?" She sounded more curious than skeptical.

"I'm certain she is."

"Despite there being no one else on the island with both access and motive?"

I wasn't about to mention the dual magic possibility to a member of the council. Best to keep that particular elephant far, far from the room. "I'm looking into other options."

"Hmm. I wish you luck, Aidan Brook. I don't quite understand what is happening on this island, so I would be grateful to anyone who could make sense of it all." She glanced through the open door and eased backwards down the stairs. Her movements were furtive, a woman who didn't wish to be caught. "Er, can you tell Lana I had to be... somewhere?" She offered a weak smile. I suspected it was the same one on my face when I was trying to disengage from a conversation with Lana.

"Of course."

She hurried away before I finished responding, bound for my Grams' house, where she and the rest of the council were staying.

"Walk with me?" I asked once I was alone with Josiah.

"Absolutely."

We strolled to the shore behind my mother's house. Anyone peering out a window would see us, but there was no risk of the conversation being overheard. I perched on a picnic table, my feet on the bench. Josiah paced along the water's edge, staring out to sea.

I studied him, this man I didn't trust even a little. And yet, this time we were on the same side. We might have different ways to go about it, but we wanted the same thing: Sera safe.

I just couldn't believe his presence would make anything easier.

"I assume you have a reason for sticking around. Do you have an evil plan you'd like to share?"

He smiled, amused as ever at my attempts to insult him. "Why are you surprised I'm here? You know I'd do anything to protect my daughter."

I wondered if he ever said anything that didn't have at least two layers of meaning. "Seriously, though. I assume you've figured out by now there's another fire on the island. Unless you torched Edith Lake and Robin for some mysterious reasons?"

"The fact that she was about to announce some unprecedented punishment on my oldest daughter is hardly a mysterious reason. I suspect she deserved to burn, so I won't waste both our time feigning shock or horror. However, I was not the one who did it, nor did I kill the other one."

"So, if it wasn't you, it was someone else, and they're still on the island. No one's left since the murders."

He waited, the picture of saintly patience. He wasn't going to make this easy for me.

"Obviously, I can't go around, testing for other fires, but you can. I thought you might already have done so."

"Are you asking for my help, Aidan?" His expression was mild, as if he inquired about the weather, but only a fool would have missed the sharp eyes. "The last time we spoke, I was under the impression you never wished to have anything to do with me."

That impression might have been due to the shotgun blast I'd sent into his shoulder. That encounter was rather difficult to spin.

Still, I tried. "This isn't about me. This is Sera, and you'd have done this whether I asked you to or not."

He inclined his head, acknowledging my point. "You are overlooking one key detail. This may not be entirely about

Serafina."

I offered him a blank look, and he groaned, as disappointed as any father with an especially thick child. "So far, two women have died. One before announcing your mysterious sentence, the other a woman you spoke to earlier, who I believe was visiting your cottage with information. You may not be accused of these murders, but you are every bit as involved as my daughter. So I repeat: are you asking for my help, Aidan?"

My face contorted into a grimace. Josiah spoke the truth. I'd known it since Edith burned, and the only reason I'd been able to overlook my own possible role in these events was that Sera needed my immediate help. I figured I could worry about what it all had to do with me much later, when Sera was cleared and we were lounging on a deck somewhere, preferably while holding very large margaritas.

Josiah studied his fingernails and picked at a few imaginary specks of lint on his suit. He would wait all afternoon, if that's what it took.

"Fine." The word was bitten out, a reluctant concession. "I need your help."

His entire posture changed, his body filling with energy. "Splendid! I will do as you suggest, though you know we can only identify another fire user when they access the magic. Though life would be easier if we were dealing with a complete idiot, I fear that is not the case, and the true killer is unlikely to burn anyone else if he spots me nearby."

"Can't you be unobtrusive? You must have some spy skills."

He stared at me in wonder. "Aidan, what reason would I ever have to hide? No, I fear searching for another fire must be a backup plan." Josiah withdrew his phone and dialed a number from memory. "Ms. Strait? Josiah Blais. I would like a word with you and the rest of the council. I require a better understanding of the evidence you possess and the proof you require before my daughter will be cleared. Meet me at the court in fifteen minutes." His tone allowed for no disagreement. The council was powerful, but with the possible exception of Deborah Rivers, none were half as old as he was. Though I couldn't make out the words from the other side of the conversation, the obsequious tone was impossible to mistake.

Josiah punched the end button with a flourish. "Excellent. Two birds with one stone, then."

I had no idea what he meant. "What, David?"

"Who? Oh, the strange girl's plaything? No, no. Just a turn of phrase, though I assume you're looking into him, as well?" I nodded my confirmation. "I simply meant we can accomplish several things at once. I will establish what the council requires to prove Serafina's innocence, and you have one hour to search their rooms. Perhaps one of them is our killer."

He wandered off, whistling, and I headed toward Grams' home to add "shameless snoop" to my ever-growing list of dubious skills.

THOUGH GRAMS' HOUSE wasn't quite the monstrosity my great-grandmother's was, that was due more to its sedate architecture than its size, as it still possessed eight bedrooms, a study, a library, and even its own billiards room no one ever used. It deserved to be called a mansion, though no one ever did. They thought that sounded gauche.

Whatever it was called, it was only two houses east of my mother's house, so I made it in plenty of time to see the entire council, including Grams, head toward the beach and the meeting spot Josiah assigned. The moment they were out of sight, I strolled to the front door, making no effort to hide myself. I was just a dutiful granddaughter paying a visit to a beloved relative.

The front door was unlocked, of course. I stopped only long enough to set an alarm on my phone, giving myself plenty of time to get out of the house before anyone returned, then headed for the stairs and the guest rooms on the second floor.

Grams kept a spotless house, and her guests seemed to have absorbed that trait while visiting. Each room was in perfect order. The beds were made, the towels hung, the desks clear. Sadly, there were no neon arrows that read "Clue!" and pointed to suspicious objects. I was going to have to do some actual investigating.

I started in the green guest room, where the suits hanging in the closet told me this room belonged to the council's sole male member. I looked under the bed, rifled through his pockets, and opened every desk drawer, but the room was pristine, not even an old grocery receipt to be found.

I repeated my search in the blue and ivory guest rooms and had as much luck as I had in the first one. The rooms were so impersonal as to be interchangeable. I knew they belonged to the female members of the council but couldn't have told you which. One woman kept what seemed like a vat of body lotion in the bathroom, while the other had a preference for baby powder, but otherwise the toiletries were almost identical. The shampoo was the same brand and the makeup was all in the same general color palette.

When I entered the gray room, it took me a moment to understand why it was different from the others. It was as tidy as the first three, with one key difference. The closet was empty, a suitcase filled with clothes rested on the bed.

My first thought was that a council member was preparing to flee, but the luggage tag corrected me. This room had briefly housed Edith Lake.

I stood in the middle of the room, eyes closed, and inhaled deeply. The room still smelled of her perfume, a soft jasmine blend. I pictured Edith, her height and delicate coloring, but it wasn't enough. I might as well have been visualizing any water.

I dove deeper, seeking the essence of the dead woman. Her deliberate gaze and the movements that were both precise and graceful. Her intensity, so rare for our kind. She wasn't a welcoming woman, the sort that easily inspired positive emotions. She was cool, an arctic sea rather than a tropical ocean.

Till now, all my focus had been on proving Sera's innocence, rather than finding possible reasons people would murder this woman. Perhaps this was never been about me or Sera. Maybe our presence just made it more convenient.

I needed to understand Edith to discover why someone might wish her dead.

The bathroom still contained all her toiletries, spread out on the counter. Expensive cosmetics with exotic names. Makeup brushes so soft I wanted to cuddle them. All signs pointed to a woman who valued luxury and beauty. Or possibly just a woman who spent lots of time in France.

In the bedroom, I ran my fingers along the woman's clothes, neatly folded in the suitcase. She favored the same colors most waters did, the greens and blues and grays of the sea, and she had the same preference for natural fibers, though most of hers were silk.

Once, these clothes draped her body, carried her scent, had been an expression of her taste and personality. Now, they were just empty pieces of fabric with no purpose. That's what death did. It made things meaningless.

I was so lost in my own thoughts I forgot where I was, at least until I heard footsteps padding down the carpeted hall.

Panic rose in my chest, and the fire along with it. No one should be here. I'd counted the council members as they left, and everyone was accounted for, even Grams. I'd been distracted, but not so much I'd have missed the front door opening and the sound of Italian shoes on the marble floor of the foyer.

I scanned the room. The closet offered a hiding place, as did the heavy curtains. I'd be trapped in either spot, but they were the only options. Choosing quickly, I stepped behind the charcoal drapes and desperately tried to think of plausible explanations for my presence.

The steps grew closer, but there was something off about them. They were quick, light, and close together, more the steps of a small child than a full adult.

The footsteps paused in the doorway. I stopped breathing, all my attention straining toward the sudden silence. The wait felt eternal, one long moment following another. I squeezed my eyes shut, willing my body to find previously unknown reserves of patience, and I reached for my magic, anything that would help sustain me.

I touched the water first, felt its familiar greeting, then skipped over it to the fire. It wasn't a conscious decision, but as soon as I did it, I knew it was the right one. The fire filled me with energy and focus, narrowing my world to nothing but the quiet breathing of the person in the doorway.

"You know I can see your shoes, right?"

My breath expelled in a rush. I flung the curtains aside, the better to glare at the naked cat shifter looking back at me.

"What are you doing here? Sneaking around the hallway like some thief? I was inches from burning you in a panic."

Simon shrugged, unconcerned. "I was not trying to

sneak. I can't help it. I'm slinky by nature. And you should not be burning anyone, as we both know."

My heart began to calm, though my brain was still trying to send the message to my adrenaline that it was safe to resume normal activity.

"Fair enough. Still, what are you doing here?"

"The same thing as you, I suspect. Plus, the island has the distinct advantage of not being a boat. I am attempting to prove Sera's innocence immediately, so we can all resume living in houses that are not surrounded by water." He wrinkled his nose, disgusted by the mere existence of houseboats.

"I won't turn down help, even if I owe you major payback for scaring the hell out of me. Something involving a big dog, I think." I glanced at my phone. "But we only have about twenty minutes before they return, and I haven't found a damn thing yet. Do you have clothes you can wear?"

He gave me the exasperated look he always did when I suggested there was any problem with him parading around in his birthday suit. As usual, he ignored the question. "This is the room of the dead woman?" I nodded. "We must assume they would have found any incriminating evidence already, if it existed."

Reluctantly, I admitted he was right. The room held nothing but the possessions of a woman who was never coming back for them.

I led him to the last bedroom, this one decorated in lavender, both the color and the plant. Much like the others, it was pristine, though this one at least held a laptop computer.

I recognized one outfit hanging in the closet, the linen pantsuit she'd worn yesterday while dealing with Robin's murder. We were in Rachel Strait's room.

With only one laptop in all the rooms, it seemed likely this was a shared computer for the council, rather than a personal one. Rachel probably claimed it the same time she claimed her new role as council leader.

"We need to get those files." I hadn't finished the sentence before Simon opened the laptop. The computer hadn't been shut down, but it was password-protected. "Damn. I don't suppose you can channel Vivian?"

His face darkened for a moment. Simon had a unique bond with Vivian, and I suspected he missed her even more than the rest of us did. "Is she answering calls yet?"

"Barely. She says she'll help until Sera's safe, then she's out."

Simon closed the computer, returning it to its original position. "If we can get the IP address, that will give Vivian a place to start."

"Vivian is already looking into something, and she didn't seem too enthusiastic about even doing that. It's that whole space thing, you know."

"Sera's life is on the line. Perhaps we can worry about Vivian's boundaries after we learn what is happening here." There was an uncommon bite to his words, and it wasn't directed at me. Simon had asked for space, too, but he'd given it up the moment his friends needed him. I suspected he would have some strong words for Vivian the next time he saw her. "Now, the IP address?"

I gave him my best blank look. My friends knew, if they were going to talk computers around me, they had to use small words that could all be found in a dictionary from the mid-90s.

"All computers have one. It is a way of identifying the various machines. A variation on the same address will be used by any computer accessing the internet through the same modem. Does your grandmother have a computer?"

Grams still referred to microwaves as "those new-fangled devices" and refused to have one in her house, so I wasn't optimistic.

Much to my surprise, I was wrong. We had to explore several downstairs rooms before we found it, but there was a desktop computer tucked away in a corner of the library. It was only a few years old, and the spotless screen and keyboard suggested it hadn't seen much use. Still, it was a computer.

Simon booted it up while I perused the shelves. For a woman who still considered the Roaring 20s the height of modernity, she'd managed to acquire an impressive collection of books from the last century. Though the lower shelves were filled with respectable classics and award winners, the higher shelves, the ones reached only by ladder, contained a more varied selection. I snagged a couple that caught my eye, dropping them into my purse.

"You may not want to do that. It appears she uses this computer only to catalog her books and might notice they're missing."

"I'll confess the next time I see her. Is it connected to the internet?" I stood behind him, watching him navigate various computer programs.

Simon double-clicked the internet browser on the desktop. It opened to the homepage for the Elliott Bay Book Company, and we both sagged in relief. "Fortunately, your relative has accepted that the modern age has benefits for the book lover." He closed the browser window and opened another program full of information I didn't understand. "Paper?"

Grams kept the surface of her desk as tidy as the rest of the house, but the drawers were far less organized. I rifled through one of them and found several unopened envelopes, most of which were intent on offering her fabulous and improved cellular phone service. I sliced one of these open with a letter opener and handed Simon the empty envelope, then returned the junk mail to her desk, just in case she was saving it for some reason.

Simon scribbled a series of numbers on the paper, then glanced down, as if looking for a place where he could store it.

Rather than ask him to carry it in an unpleasant location, I took it from him and tucked it into my jeans pocket.

"Is there anything else you still need to look for?" Simon asked.

I looked at my phone. Only ten minutes to go. "We better leave. Let's just hope Vivian finds something good on the computer."

We started toward the foyer but pulled up short when the front door silently slid inward.

CHAPTER 12

I didn't wait to see who it was. Instead, I lunged for the window and pulled the floor-to-ceiling curtain closed. It was a bay window, so I perched on the ledge, remembering to lift my feet this time.

Simon wasn't next to me. I risked a peek around the curtain in time to see a black cat scramble up the ladder and settle himself in a dark corner of the highest shelf. Other than the glint of his green eyes, he was practically invisible.

I strained my ears, trying to discover who'd entered the house. I thought I heard more than one pair of footsteps in the foyer, which was confirmed when several voices reached the library.

They were two steps inside the door before they started arguing. "I don't understand why he's still here. Who does that man think he is?" Michael Bay asked.

"He thinks he's one of the oldest and most powerful elementals in existence. He's not wrong, either." I recognized Lydia Pond, as usual sounding like the resident voice of reason.

No one made any effort to move from the foyer. One by one, they allowed their words to pour forth, arguments that had likely been growing and gathering weight and rage ever since they parted from Josiah.

"Not more so than Deborah. He's just one man. Why should we jump through his hoops?"

"Perhaps we are of an age," said Deborah, "but I would not wish to pit my power against his. Do we even have any notes on this case?"

"We hardly thought we needed them. It was clear to everyone in attendance that his daughter caused the fire." There was no mistaking Rachel Strait's imperious tone. "I will write something up this evening and deliver it to him. We will not have him arguing this was improperly handled. The girl's trial is tomorrow, and then we can return to the issue of the Brook child."

"And then we can get off this island, right?" Michael asked.

"Are we really in such a rush to convict? Our verdict will lead to a death sentence. We can't take that lightly. Don't we owe it to ourselves, to the elementals for whom we are responsible, to treat our duty with the weight and honor it deserves? To truly consider what we plan to do to Aidan Brook?" Lydia Pond spoke quietly, but there was no missing her beseeching tone.

Blood rushed to my face at her words. I fought to remain still when every muscle in my body yearned to jump out and demand they explain what, exactly, they had planned for my future.

Grams couldn't be with them. They'd never talk this way if she was there. It was just the four remaining council members.

With every mention of my intended sentence, I became more certain it was something to be avoided at all costs.

I thought of Edith and wondered if my fate had been something worth dying for.

My fire stretched, reminding me of its presence, reminding me that I didn't need to meekly accept whatever punishment they had planned. My core warmed, filling with the power and strength of forbidden magic.

Impatience colored Rachel's words. "We've had this discussion, and we voted. We voted with Edith, and we voted again after she was killed. The decision was made, and it is past time you accepted that, Lydia. We all know this is our best chance to do this."

Before, I'd been concerned. Rachel's words pushed me into "downright disturbed" with the needle edging toward "really fucking pissed." Whatever they were planning, all my instincts screamed that I needed to stop them, any way I could.

There were murmurs and a bit of grumbling, but no one argued. No one fought against this mysterious sentence. No one stood up for me, not even Lydia.

My fire side was not impressed.

It growled and spat, no longer quiescent. In the face of a perceived threat, it wasn't content to rest until I called on it. It whispered a solution, one so foreign and impossible I wanted to believe it came from elsewhere, from someone else. I couldn't be the one thinking this.

And yet, I was.

I could end this, right here. All I needed to do was give the fire free rein to attack Rachel. I could blacken her heart, roast her lungs, turn her insides to ash. I knew I could. Just the thought was enough for the magic to roar in triumph.

I gasped at its power and fought against it for the first time in weeks. I imagined the box where I used to trap it, where I would keep my fire separate, and I demanded it return.

It refused.

The fire knew exactly what should happen. It would only take one dead body. If Rachel fell while Sera was safely tucked away on the other side of the island, no one could say she was guilty.

If Rachel fell before my sentence was read, they wouldn't

have the numbers necessary to complete my farce of a trial.

It would solve all our problems. All I needed to do was kill one unpleasant woman.

I narrowed my focus on Rachel's voice, following her as she moved toward the stairs and dropped first one foot, then another onto the marble. It would be so simple to end her life. I'd need to be fast, before anyone understood what was happening and attempted to heal her, but I could do that. Though I tried to deny it every day, I knew I was a strong fire. I was Josiah's half-blooded daughter, after all.

I felt the magic uncoil, greedy and willful. It wanted release. It wanted payback for a lifetime of being ignored, for being denied access to its element. More than anything, it wanted to burn, and it agreed that Rachel was a damn good place to start.

I thought I'd found some measure of peace with my magic. I thought I might control it.

I was wrong.

The magic poured forth, freeing itself from the confines of my body. A small voice whispered that I needed to stop, to consider what I was doing, but that voice was no longer in charge. Fire ruled me now, and it had no interest in debating its plans.

The magic was not subtle. It did not flow toward Strait along a gentle path, as the water might. It surged toward her, hungry tendrils seeking their target. She was twenty feet away, then ten, then only inches from the fire.

I wanted the flames to consume her. Fire is heat and life, but it is also change and destruction, and I longed to watch and laugh while Rachel succumbed to its power.

I exhaled in pleasure.

I was so lost in the moment, the noise hit me like a physical assault, bludgeoning me with its high-pitched demand for my attention. My alarm, telling me it was time to get out of the house.

Though it couldn't have been more than a few seconds, I felt days pass, time stretching to impossible lengths as I was torn from my fire-induced stupor. I blinked and drew in a long, shaky breath.

My water side surged and rolled, demanding my attention. It was almost enough to remember who I was. I yanked on the fire magic, pulling it hard to me. It resisted. It still wanted to feed.

A shadow dropped over my mind, its inky tentacles threatening to consume the light I knew.

I called to the magic again, putting the entirety of my will into the action. All my determination, all my stubbornness fed the command, ordering the fire to return. At last it came, sullen and reluctant, but it refused to be put back into its neat box. It whispered through my core, unwilling to be silent. It dared me to believe I'd ever been in control.

The fire mingled with the water, the two magics speaking to each other in a language I didn't understand and could not trust. I wrenched them apart. I called on memories of my friends and home and even my family, all the reasons I needed to fight, and after the longest moment of my life, the magic settled.

The shadow receded. I felt myself return. I was still me, and I wasn't a murderer. Not this time.

I swiped the screen, silencing the beeping tone, but it was too late. Footsteps turned toward the library, the clack of heels telling me Rachel was leading the parade of council members. It wouldn't take more than a cursory search for them to find me.

Maybe I could have justified visiting my own relative's house while she wasn't there. It would be a fair bit harder to explain why I was hiding behind a curtain while doing so.

I rifled through my brain, looking for any possible excuse for my presence. I made it as far as bay window fetishist before I was spared the need to defend myself by a black cat hurtling toward the council members.

Though I dared not peek around the curtains, the sound effects were more than enough to fill in the missing visuals. The high-pitched yowl of an angry cat, starting from high in the shelves and arcing down to the floor. The startled exclamations from the four people in the doorway as the small body darted between their legs, escaping the room and fleeing upstairs, all the while making high pitched noises one might confuse for the beeping of a cell phone.

The council questioned where on earth that cat had come from, but already they were laughing at their surprise. The clack of high heels was no longer in the library, and as I waited, the council members headed upstairs to their rooms.

A few seconds later, I peeked around the curtain to confirm I was alone, then raced to the front door. I don't think I took a single breath as I crossed the foyer, my rubber-soled sneakers far quieter against the marble than Rachel's heels.

I opened the door just enough to slide through and closed it gently. Even so, the click of the latch sounded impossibly loud, and I pressed myself against the house, fearful someone would look out an upstairs window and see me fleeing. I counted to five, then slid to the west side, where the only windows were in the garage and the billiards room on the second floor. I had to trust that a meeting with Josiah wouldn't inspire a sudden need to play pool.

I strained my ears toward the house, but all was silent.

At last, I stepped away from the house. With each step, I grew more confident as I made the effort to look like I belonged there and absolutely had not been up to any sort of breaking, entering, or attempted murder on that particular day. At some point, a small black cat appeared at my side, and together we strolled along the northern shore, doing our best to look perfectly innocent.

I was anything but.

With each step that took us closer to the cottage, some facsimile of calm returned. My magic felt just as it had an hour ago, but I knew. I knew what it was capable of now. I knew what *I* was capable of doing.

That was the woman I was edging closer to every day. Cruel, unrepentant, and more powerful than she had any right to be.

It was why there was a death sentence imposed on all dual magics, and I couldn't blame them.

I wanted to find a dark corner, curl up in a ball, and give in to the fear and panic threatening to consume me. I didn't know how to paste on a smile and pretend everything was okay, but I had to figure it out damn fast. Sera still needed me, and Mac. I could go crazy later. First, I had to save them.

And maybe, just maybe, if I did that, everything would be okay.

At least, that's what I told myself as I walked to the cottage, clutching the tattered shreds of my sanity the entire way.

WHEN WE NEARED the cottage but before we were in camera range, I placed my purse on the ground for Simon to jump into. Though the look he gave me was scornful as only a cat's can be, he didn't argue, so there was no photographic evidence that a small black cat entered the house along with me.

His reunion with Sera was brief but sweet, though I was certain they'd both reject that adjective. They lifted the corners of their mouths slightly and nodded, acknowledging the other's presence.

"I knew you couldn't stay away," Sera told him.

Simon grabbed a blanket and spread it on the sofa before curling up, a small concession to us weird elementals who preferred not to have butt sweat on our furniture. "I'm fairly certain it's the other way around. You lot are useless without my help."

After the last twenty-four hours, I couldn't even argue that point.

I handed them the IP address. Vivian didn't answer when they pinged her in chat, and she didn't pick up the phone, so they sent her an email, arguing the entire time about what information they should include and how much grief they should give her about her continued silence. I figured, so long as they were the ones contacting her instead of me, I was sticking to the letter of her request for distance, if not the spirit.

Neither noticed how quiet I was. I watched them, these friends I loved, and tried to burn their images into my memories, a reminder of something good and pure to cling to when my mind had little interest in being either good or pure.

It was starting. The fire was done being quiet. I'd called on it too many times, granted it too much freedom. The schism was forming in my mind, the use of both magics creating a dual self. For now, it was just the fire side that lacked a conscience, likely because I'd never learned to control it, but it was only a matter of time before the damage seeped into my water side, as well.

I'd dared believe I had it under control, but this afternoon exploded that particular self-delusion. I didn't control the magic. The magic was beginning to control me.

I needed to tell someone. I'd vowed to give up that

whole "no man is an island" thing right around the time I burned down my house in Oregon. I just had no idea where to begin.

If I told either of my parents, they'd lock me in a padded room for the rest of my life, safe from anything that could ever harm me, including myself.

Josiah might be more creative. He would move me to his Hawaiian compound, as he'd tried to do on more than one occasion, where I'd be subjected to all sorts of tests intended to save me, if I didn't mind being a lab rat for centuries to come.

Once Mac knew what I was becoming, I'd lose him, and I wasn't ready for that. I wasn't ready for whatever we were to end before we'd truly begun.

Mac was the last one. He was the last man I'd know, that I'd care for, that I'd be with, before the crazy fully took over. Fair or not, I needed that. I needed one night with him, one night when I could pretend forever was still an option, and then I'd tell him. And if that was playing dirty, I'd happily roll in the muck with the pigs to have just a few more days with that man.

Sera's trial was the next day, and I refused to give her more reason to worry. When she was safe, I'd tell her. It was a place to start, at least. I could wait one more day.

And while I waited, I'd save my best friend this one time, to make up for all the times she'd been there for me. If my sanity was burning out at an accelerated rate, then I was going out in a blaze of glory. Fixing Mac. Saving Sera. Hell, give me enough time and I'd cure the common cold and find out who took the Lindbergh baby. Whatever happened, I wasn't going quietly into madness.

"I'll be back in an hour," I announced, and exited the cottage before either could ask where I was going.

If I was running out of time, there were a few loose ends

I needed to tie up first.

When I felt like this, felt the desire for action, for movement, for something concrete I could touch and understand and change, I knew that was the fire side speaking.

It didn't matter that my fire and water magic were equally strong. I identified as a water. It was how I was raised and what I saw in the mirror. It was the identity of the family that surrounded me. I could never see the fire as anything but an interloper.

So I did the one thing that always worked for me, a quiet, calming activity I associated with my water side. I found a rock overlooking the ocean on the south side of the island and pulled out my notebook. I might not feel safe putting my recent personal problems in writing, but I could at least outline everything I knew about the recent murders.

It didn't take long. I knew the council had a plan, and based on all available evidence, I was fairly certain it was a nefarious one—and not just because nefarious is such an awesome word. In my experience, when people are keeping secrets at the same time bodies start falling, the two things tend to be related.

It wasn't much to go on.

Next, I listed everyone I'd seen on the island since arriving. For the most part, it was one Brook after another, the people I'd grown up with, but I knew better than to discount them outright. After all, none of them knew I was part fire, so there was always a chance they were keeping the same secret. It was a teeny, tiny chance, but I was a desperate woman. I couldn't afford to ignore any possibility.

I wrote Lana's and David's names, and the four remaining council members. They were all strangers to the island, and smart money was on the hidden fire being somewhere in their midst. If it was Lana, we'd need to hand over the island to her, and possibly the keys to the entire world, because anyone who could hide her villainous intentions under such a ridiculous exterior was a criminal mastermind the likes of which the world had never seen.

I knew little about David, which was reason enough to suspect him. It was a shame, because I liked the quiet stone, but I'd liked a couple of other murderers before I learned what they were. I underlined his name on the list, then studied the remaining four names.

Four council members. Four powerful waters from old families. Four people in obvious disagreement over, well, something. I didn't know what it was, but I was certain it was important.

My phone buzzed. To my surprise, Vivian's number came up on the caller ID.

"You know, asking Sera and Simon to email instead of you doesn't let you off the hook on the whole distance thing," she said in greeting.

"They volunteered. You said you'd help till Sera was clear, remember?"

"I should know better than to ever give you lot an inch." The words contained no small amount of frustration, but there was also an unexpected hint of laughter.

"Well, they miss you." She didn't respond. "What's up?"

"I need to know what the priority list is. Computer files or info about the islanders?"

I weighed the options. "Computer files, I think. Those bastards are up to no good."

"Got it. And so you know, I've already gone through half the list. Other than finding some possible contenders for a wine rehab program, I'm not uncovering much dirt."

Another dead end. This wasn't the news I'd wanted.

"Except there's some stuff on the councilman who ruined the Transformers movies."

I perked up. "Not the same man. We can't blame him for

those. What'd you learn?"

"He's broke."

"Is that even possible? You know all the old ones are filthy rich."

"Well, numbers and offshore bank accounts don't lie. He invested eight hundred million dollars in some seven-star hotel being built in Dubai, all of which vanished when the entire building fell into the Persian Gulf. Apparently, there are reasons one shouldn't hire workers just a step above slave labor to build a luxury hotel on a man-made island."

"No insurance?"

"Not a cent."

I wasn't surprised. Being a flighty water had its downside.

"That's interesting, but I'm not sure if it helps us."

"I'm not done. Guess who his business partner and co-investor was? One Edith Lake."

My eyes widened. "Seriously? Am I correct in thinking she bought insurance?"

"Made a tidy profit, while he was ruined. Sounds like a nice revenge motive to me."

"It sure as hell does. Vivian, you are a rock star."

"Keep your flattery. Just save Sera, okay?" Though she didn't say it, the implicit meaning was hard to miss: clear Sera so we could once again leave Vivian alone. We hung up on her promise to get me the council's files that night.

While I waited for Vivian to hack the council's laptop, I could manage a bit of legwork. I tucked my notebook into my purse and headed toward town.

It seemed the people ran as soon as I approached. I felt like the villain entering the center of town in an old western, riding his black horse while all the townspeople hid, desperately hoping the bad guy would ride away without stopping to shoot any of them first.

I couldn't help it. I looped my thumbs into my belt loops and stared at the handful of storefronts while attempting my most menacing expression. Experience had taught me that my version of menacing is similar to most people's expression of vague discomfort, but it was the best I could do. Curtains twitched in the windows, distant cousins and great-aunts and uncles all hiding from me.

I didn't belong here anymore. Not on this tiny island, with these people who managed to be simultaneously kind-hearted and close-minded. Though I stood beneath the open sky, surrounded for miles by my element, I felt as if walls were tightening around me, and I fought for breath. The fire stirred, rebelling against the feeling of entrapment. I beat it back.

On the plus side, for that moment I was pretty sure my menacing stare improved exponentially.

I headed toward my great-grandmother's house, hoping to find news there. Night was falling at last, the stubborn light of the long summer day finally giving way to a blanket of stars. I resented its approach, the reminder that I was rapidly running out of time to exonerate Sera.

The house was well-lit, and the curtains were open, allowing me to easily see inside. I leaned against a large maple in the yard, taking stock. Georgina, Marie, and Tina sat at the dining table, playing Scrabble and, of course, drinking wine. I'd watched many such games as a child, though I'd long ago given up attempting to participate in them. If I was closer, I'd be able to say how many bottles they'd already drunk based on the quality of their spelling and the number of proper nouns allowed on the board. Usually, by the third bottle, the game would descend into alphabet anarchy, a chaotic rule of letters none but the three of them could understand.

David and Lana were in the living room. Like any good

stone, David was slouched on the sofa, looking like he might not budge for another week or two. He watched TV while Lana stared at him with a dopey expression that was visible even from a distance. My mother, bless her heart, was sitting nearby, keeping her promise to supervise Lana.

"I've been waiting for you." I jumped as my father appeared out of the darkness.

I placed a hand on my heart, willing it to calm. "Why? To test my fight or flight response?"

"I wanted to discuss what happened earlier today," said Josiah.

Recently, I'd had a lot of occasion to practice my innocent face, and I desperately hoped it had improved since the last time I tried it. If Josiah had picked up on my fire usage earlier that day, I'd quickly find myself hauled off the island with a reservation for a padded room, party of one.

"The council are really an unreasonable bunch. Aren't you waters supposed to be easy-going? They attempted to block me at every turn."

"Oh, that. Yes," I tried not to look happy about the stonewalling council, but I was too relieved my fire use had gone unnoticed to hide it.

Josiah quirked an eyebrow. "My failure amuses you?"

It did, actually, but that was beside the point. "No, it's just that I overheard them discussing you. They might like you even less than I do."

He laughed, feelings entirely unhurt. I filled him in on their discussion and what little I'd discovered in my search of their rooms.

"So, you learned nothing from the council?" I asked. His failure might amuse me, but it was also out of character.

He shrugged, shoulders moving up and down in an exaggerated movement. "There were too many others nearby. Everyone wants to see the spot where the island's first murder in centuries occurred, particularly as this one is a safe distance from the accused. You waters are a morbid lot, aren't you? Sadly, so many witnesses severely limited my ability to question them."

He said "question" the way an interrogator would say "threaten."

"Who was there?" I knew there was an old chestnut about returning to the scene of the crime. I could always hope someone had been lurking about in a suspicious manner, possibly while rubbing their hands together with glee.

Josiah looked at me in confusion. "There were fifteen tall blonds on a beach. Does that help?"

"You saying we all look the same?"

He rolled his eyes, for perhaps the fifth time in this conversation, and was smart enough not to answer.

"We should focus on Michael Bay." I relayed the information Vivian had uncovered. Josiah appeared downright pleased, and I imagined he was hoping the killer was a council member. The man didn't react well to being thwarted. "Also, I haven't had a chance to look into David and Lana yet. The stone and the odd water," I clarified. "They arrived on the island just as the murders started."

"Of course, of course," Josiah answered. "Ah, this doesn't require talking to the Pond girl, does it?"

I hid my smile, pleased to hear he intended to avoid Lana as much as possible. The woman might be a nut job who hovered just on the wrong side of annoying, but I had no desire to see her dead because of my father's paranoia. "No, just test her to see if somehow, against all laws of nature and common sense, she's a dual magic. Him, too."

"I'll light a fire tonight, then exit to the garden and wait to see if anyone accesses it. Perhaps I will pay a visit to your grandmother and submit Mr. Bay to the same test." My father was practically bouncing on his toes, eager to catch the killer.

I shut my eyes, bothered that I was thinking of him as my father. I'd rejected him. Hell, I'd shot him. Just because we shared a goal didn't mean we had anything else in common. He was an awful man who would happily murder anyone who knew what I was if he thought it would help keep my secret.

I felt a light hand on my arm, a gentle squeeze. "We'll find this person, Aidan. You know that." I nodded, eyes still closed.

He might be an awful man, but he was also my father. Some things are easier to deny than others, and family lives in your very blood, impossible to erase through pure force of will. I wasn't ready to stop trying, though.

I waited until Josiah's footsteps disappeared in the direction of Grams' house, then finally opened my eyes. I withdrew my phone and dialed, watching as my mother picked up.

I glanced toward the west, to a houseboat I couldn't see. "I need your help."

CHAPTER 13

When you're a half-blooded water elemental and need to reach a boat half a mile offshore, you jump in the water and let it do all the heavy lifting. There's no swimming involved, and no muscles need to be worked.

If you're a full-blooded water elemental who doesn't feel like getting her clothes wet, you bring the boat to you.

It was dark, the western side of the island still deserted, so my mother simply pulled the houseboat through the water at a pace that would earn a sailing medal in the summer Olympics, returning it to the cottage where I'd originally found the boat.

"Quickly, then." She strode forward with long, deliberate strides. Her posture was flawless, as ever, her movements efficient and focused.

Growing up, I'd always thought she was different from my aunts because of her age. She was the oldest, and every pop psychology article I'd ever read insisted oldest children were the most responsible. Now, I wondered how much of her discipline came from decades of striving to keep me safe, to guard my secret from a world that would kill me if it learned what I was. She wasn't like other waters I knew, but she was still my mother.

Right then, I needed my mommy, or at least Mac did—and she'd be able to help him as soon as we convinced the glowering otter to stop blocking our way onto the boat.

"What the fuck do you want?"

I stepped forward into the light cast by houseboat's interior. "It's just us, Miriam."

She glared at me. If she'd been less adorable, it might have been scary. "Brook, you need to stop this habit of dragging me through the water. We could have brought it in ourselves, you know."

"This was faster. Miriam, meet my mother, Fiona. She's here to help Mac."

Miriam didn't look impressed, or even surprised. Of course, she'd seen my mother plenty of times at the Tahoe cabin, though my mother likely hadn't noticed the otters drifting in the Truckee River during her visits.

Because of their proximity to the cabin and tendency to be nosy little buggers, the otters had learned things I'd prefer them not to know. Based on Miriam's reaction, I suspected one of those things was, while my mother tolerated shifters more than most old ones, and could manage a respectable show of politeness, that didn't mean she had warm, fuzzy feelings for them.

"Didn't she already try to figure out what was wrong with him? I thought there was nothing she could do."

"That was weeks ago, before he started getting ill. We have to try again."

Weeks earlier, my mother erred on the side of caution, preferring to wait and see how the shared magic affected us. She could have explained her reasoning to Miriam and perhaps lessened the otter's glare, but she had no interest in justifying her choices to the shifter.

The two women engaged in a staring contest that made me glad neither was looking at me. Miriam's was full of scorn and challenge, while my mother's was distant and patient.

"We don't have a lot of time, so stop wasting it," I told

them. "If we finish early, you can both whip them out then."

"Please don't be vulgar, Aidan."

Miriam laughed. Vulgar was where she lived. It was enough to break the tension, and she turned sideways, creating enough room for us to slip onto the houseboat.

"Wait here," my mother ordered. "In fact, leave the beach entirely. I'd like to examine him without your magic interfering."

I grumbled, partly because I already missed Mac and partly because I feared leaving him alone with my mother for any length of time, but I accepted the necessity.

Miriam looked between us, trying to decide whether it was more important that she supervise my mother or that she fill me in on her day's activity.

"She won't hurt him."

My words helped make her decision, though she still looked uncertain. Elementals really haven't given shifters a lot of reason to trust them. For that matter, some of the Tahoe shifters haven't been on their best behavior of late, either, what with their whole "control shifter families so they'll help us kill elementals" supervillain plan we'd only just prevented.

Basically, we had thousands of years of animosity between us and little access to media tolerance campaigns or school assemblies intended to educate us about each other. So we kept hating each other, and no one showed any interest in stopping.

My mother stepped inside the houseboat. Through the windows, I watched her disappear into Mac's room, shutting the door behind her.

Once again, a shifter needed an elemental's help, and while neither was happy with the situation, they were willing to accept it. Peace was possible between our races. We just needed a lot more practice to get it right.

"I suppose she's slightly less asshole-ish than the rest of you lot," Miriam observed.

"That's on our family crest. 'Slightly less asshole-ish than other elementals.' But yeah. She'll at least acknowledge you exist."

Miriam and I stepped away from the boat, just far enough to keep my magic from interfering with my mother's examination of Mac.

"I spent today in your canals. You all don't think about much besides yourselves do you?"

"Hey!" I attempted to appear indignant. It would have been easier if she wasn't right. "We're a bit insular here," I acknowledged. "We don't really have much to distract us from ourselves. It's easy for the old ones to maintain their belief that shifters don't actually exist."

"Which makes me think you're either deluded or stupid. You know you're surrounded by shifters, right?"

I blinked. I hadn't known shifters existed until recently, and I certainly had no idea I'd grown up near them.

"What, birds? Fish? Are there fish shifters?" I was horrified, imagining all the sushi restaurants in Seattle.

"Brook, you still have a lot of ignorance we need to correct. Has no one explained shifters are mammals only? I'm talking sea lions and otters. I spent the day getting to know them. Good group. A bunch of them own a bar in Friday Harbor, but they travel up and down the islands, taking stock."

"You were careful of the orcas, right?"

She waved a dismissive hand. "Those bullies? We keep an eye out. Don't worry about us."

I wasn't convinced, but I knew I couldn't insist Miriam stay out of the water. I just wasn't used to worrying that my friends would be eaten by Shamu.

"If you insist. Wait, are there orca shifters? They're

mammals, after all."

"Again with the ignorance. You know our history. The original magical creatures transformed themselves and mated with animals, creating a race that was both human and animal."

"And?"

"Why the hell would they choose to transform into a killer whale? First, they'd have to get in the water, cause if they shifted on land they'd beach themselves. Then they'd need to hunt down an animal constantly on the move, all for a little nookie? I'd hope they had better things to do with themselves. So, no. There are no dolphin or whale shifters."

"Damn, Miriam. You're better than Wikipedia. So, did you learn anything from the otters? Anything that could help us?"

"They gave me a bunch of gossip. Not sure if it's useful, or if it's even true."

"Give me whatever you've got."

"According to the shifters, they could film a soap opera on this island. One of your aunts spends a lot of time in video chat with some water from the East Coast. Cape Cod, they think. Your great-grandmother leaves the island all the time these days, so her absence right now may not be about you. Lydia recently moved from her family's enclave to a small town in Texas, right on the Gulf of Mexico. That stone guy, he looks all stoic and such, but every evening he's down at the water, crying about something or other. Won't tell his girlfriend what it is, either. Nothing on the others, but give me another day."

While she spoke, my jaw dropped steadily toward the ground. We always called Simon our ninja, but I was beginning to think the otters were the spies of the shifter world. Everywhere there was water, they seemed to know a little too much about what was going on. Even so, it wasn't enough. Not yet.

"Another day is all we have," I reminded her. "But seriously, well done. I'm impressed."

"Someday you're gonna learn, there ain't much I'm not good at. Think the agents will hire me next? I'd happily go for a swim with that Johnson fellow, if you know what I mean. So, will any of that help Sera?"

I turned over each individual fact, weighing their many possibilities and potential hidden meanings. "I have no idea. But it's more than we knew this morning. Keep it up, and maybe I'll put in a good word for you with Johnson," I teased.

"Like I'd need your help." Miriam stretched, a movement that only highlighted her lush body. The glint in her eyes told me she was well aware of this. "You're not the only one around here who can bend men to your will."

I wasn't sure Mac had bent to anything just yet, but it was a nice thought. "Speaking of…" My mother appeared on the houseboat's deck, gesturing for us to join her.

She didn't bother with small talk when we reached her. "How long has it been since you saw him?"

"I stopped by this morning. He was fine when I left. How is he?" I didn't wait for her to answer, already moving to the bedroom.

Mac was swinging his legs out of bed. Though there was a thin sheen of sweat on his forehead, he otherwise looked healthy.

"He's fine now," he said with a pointed look. It really wasn't easy having a private conversation when half your friends had shifter ears.

"Cause I'm here," I finished. He nodded, mouth set in a grim line.

I turned to my mother, who'd followed me to the room

and watched us both with worried eyes. "What the hell is happening? How do we fix this?" I tried to keep the panic from my voice, lest I give Mac even more reason to worry, but it was too close to the surface, too alive and desperate to stay hidden.

I expected my mother to look as helpless as I felt, but her face revealed only sadness.

"You know. You understand what's happening."

Mac looked between us, uncertainty and a wary hope battling across his broad features.

"Only to a point. There is no precedent for this. I can make an educated guess, based on what little we know."

Miriam crept into the room while we spoke, and my mother stopped speaking.

"She already knows what I am, mother."

She squeezed her eyes shut. "That is unfortunate."

I shook my head, the movement sharp. "It's not. Hell, my friends are the reason I'm fighting to stay sane." She winced, but it was too late to withdraw the words. I loved her, but it was different from the love I felt for my friends. My mother offered comfort and security, but my friends gave me a place to belong.

My mother was blood. My friends were home.

"Josiah can never know," I insisted.

She cast an exasperated glance at me. "I tell that man as little as possible. I still have no idea what I was thinking, all those years ago. I suppose, on occasion, the daiquiris do the thinking for you."

I barely refrained from putting my hands over my ears and singing "La la la" at the reminder that my mother once had sex with Josiah.

Mac saved me from the visual, drawing us back to the matter at hand. "So, what went wrong when Aidan healed me?"

My mother glared at him. "You died, and my daughter risked her health and sanity to save your life. Now, your magic is tied to hers and you are whining about it like a small boy."

Apparently, we had a ways to go before Mac would be invited to family dinners.

I moved to the bed, sitting at his side and taking his hand. "How do we fix it?"

My mother sat in the room's only chair. To look at her, she was a vision of control, but the tension in her clasped hands told a different story.

"You sent your magic into Mac. Both your magics."

I still remembered it, the fire's strength fueling the healing properties of the water. I'd known joy as I felt Mac heal beneath my touch, as his heart remembered to beat again and the blood began to flow through his veins, but there'd been more. I'd felt whole, my magics working together for the first time. For a few minutes, I'd been pretty certain that, left to my own devices, I could take over the entire world.

"When you drew them back to you, you left some behind. We already knew this, based on my examination after the events with that wretched woman. Also, there was the fact that, after Mac healed, he could control a small amount of water."

"But not fire," I added. "He hasn't been able to do anything with that."

"Have you tried?"

He nodded.

"Stop it, you fool. Aidan was perfectly healthy for years, unaware of her fire side. Unless you want to face the same battle with sanity as my daughter, I suggest you leave it alone."

My insides turned to lead. "You're saying he does have

fire magic?"

"Fucking hell," whispered Miriam. I couldn't have said it better myself. I thought I'd only broken him a little. I might have ruined him.

And yet, he was still alive, still sane. It beat the alternative, in which he'd died weeks ago.

"Of course he has fire. Your magics were working together as one, and so you left them both behind. Before, he seemed stable, as far as I could tell, so I felt no need to worry you with information about the fire magic."

I closed my eyes and counted to ten, then to twenty. "Stop trying to save us from ourselves." The words came out covered in grit.

Mac squeezed my hand. I returned the movement, seeking reassurance and calm when I knew we both wanted to scream at my mother. Perhaps we would, but not until she'd delivered the entire diagnosis.

"I was merely trying to spare him the same struggles you experience, Aidan. I thought you would be grateful. Regardless, this time I focused on how his shifter side was reacting to the elemental magic you'd left behind. It wasn't easy. Shifter magic is far more chaotic and difficult to understand."

Miriam nodded. "Damn straight." For some people, chaotic and difficult to understand are compliments.

My mother had the look of a doctor preparing to deliver a terminal diagnosis. I gripped Mac's hand even tighter, anchoring him to me.

"Tonight, I discovered something different from when I studied him in Tahoe. Mr. MacMahon—ah, Mac—your shifter side is rejecting Aidan's magic. It is still within you, still a part of your makeup, but it no longer belongs to you. It is Aidan's magic, not yours. And, just as she needs regular access to her element to survive, you need regular access to my daughter."

"Are you saying…" I couldn't finish.

Mac did not share my avoidance. "You're my element." He stared at me, wonder and fear battling across his face.

It was impossible, terrible, beautiful. A connection I longed for, and one that needed to be shattered before I destroyed him. "We can't live like this." It was a statement, a plea, and a question.

"You may have to." My mother stood. "Aidan, can I speak to you in the other room?"

"There's no point. They'll hear anything we say."

Annoyance crossed her face. "Very well. If you reclaim your magic, this will be over. It will be difficult, but I believe it can be done."

Mac's gaze snapped to my mother's face.

"Then why don't you look happier?" I asked.

"Because difficult is an understatement. You must essentially complete the procedure in reverse, without killing him, and this time you would need to work around his shifter magic. When he was dead, that wasn't an issue. The last time you did this, you were highly motivated, willing to do anything to prevent this man from dying. You'd need to achieve a similar state of highly focused intensity. You must want nothing more than for your magic to return to you."

Mac didn't say a word, but I knew what his independence meant to him. He wouldn't pressure me or even argue with me on this point, but I knew what he wanted to hear. "I can do that," I said, hoping I spoke the truth. "Somehow. Meditation or chanting or drugs, whatever we need to do. We'll find a way to get me focused."

"You would do that for him?"

I studied his face. The high cheekbones, the dark brows, the wide lips, the warmest brown eyes I'd ever seen. "I'd do pretty much anything for him."

"And that, my dear, is the problem."

We turned to her in confusion.

"Your magic isn't just keeping him healthy. It's giving him the benefits that come from being an elemental. As long as he has your magic, he has access to your lifespan. Mac may no longer live and die as shifters do. He could live thousands of years at your side, and the only downside is that he would need to recharge through you on a regular basis."

Miriam looked shocked, and for once she didn't seem to have a ready joke. Mac's shoulders drooped, the tension he carried exiting his body in a rush. His squeezed my hand once in silent reassurance, then released it, leaving my palm empty and cold.

"Aidan, you can heal him, but to do so you must have no doubt this is what you want, and that is why you will almost certainly fail. You cannot heal him *because* of how much you care for him."

Miriam whistled, long and low. "Another thousand years of life? That's one hell of a trade-off, bear-man."

Mac closed his eyes, hiding his thoughts. "It's an interesting option, assuming..."

He didn't finish. He didn't need to. I heard all the unsaid words. It was an interesting option, assuming we wanted to stay together for a thousand years. Assuming he could ever know peace, with his health dependent on another person. Assuming he wasn't in danger of attaching himself to a crazy woman for the rest of his life.

"I need a minute," he murmured. He left the room, and I let him go. The sound of grinding metal filled the room, followed by a splash. I made a mental note to pull the houseboat's dining table from the ocean floor the next day.

"I'll fix this, Mac. Somehow, I'll fix this." I didn't raise my voice, but I knew he heard every word.

CHAPTER 14

I returned to the cottage well after midnight. I was unused to Sera heading for bed before I did, but her door was closed and no light shone from underneath. Her music still played, but instead of the bone-jarring noise I'd come to expect, the volume was low and one of Elvis Costello's quieter songs drifted through the living room.

Simon was stretched before the dying fire, furry black stomach exposed to the small embers that clung to life. He raised his head when I entered and blinked once in greeting, then returned to his prone position.

I sat cross-legged behind him, feeling the warmth on my skin. A tendril of magic stretched toward the flames, seeking to recharge, and I was almost too exhausted to stop it.

"You're not going back tonight?"

In answer, he only scooted closer to the flames. There wasn't a fireplace on the houseboat, after all.

"It's probably for the best. I can't imagine Mac's in a very good mood right now." When Mac started throwing things, it was best to get out of his way until he calmed down. A houseboat didn't provide many escape options, particularly for a cat who viewed the ocean as the devil's work.

I held out my hand, fingers curled into a loose fist, and Simon stretched until his cheek rubbed against my knuckles. He twisted his head to give me access to both cheeks, his chin, and his nose. Content, he dropped his head onto his paws, his permanent cat grin slightly larger than usual.

I'd discovered that different rules apply with shifters. While I'd never dream of wandering up to Simon and scratching his face when he was in human form, I had no problem petting him when he was a cat, and he never seemed to mind. I moved my hand along his black fur in slow, deliberate motions and was rewarded with a soft purr.

My world might be going to hell, but at least I had a warm cottage and one happy friend. It was a place to start.

"I think I screwed up again," I told him. "I didn't mean to, and the screw-up saved Mac's life, but it won't be easy to fix." He rolled over, belly wantonly displayed, and fixed sleepy green eyes on me. I wasn't telling him anything unexpected.

"There's more," I whispered. "And I can't tell anyone. Sera will worry about me, and I need her to worry about herself right now. My parents will lock me up. Mac will pull away. But I don't want to bear this alone."

He rolled to his feet and sat on his haunches, waiting patiently.

"I'm starting to lose control. I almost hurt someone today." I spoke in a whisper. If no one heard me, maybe the words wouldn't be true.

Simon said nothing. He didn't shift, either, only continued to gaze at me with intent green eyes in a serious feline face.

"Everyone's looking to me right now. I'm supposed to free Sera and cure Mac. I don't know how I'm supposed to do that when I can't even fix myself. When I'm just going to screw up again, and I don't know how much damage I'll do the next time."

Simon padded toward me, stepping into the lap created by my crossed legs, and gave my shoulder a good swipe with his paw.

I laughed, jolted out of my self-pity. "Good point. I should listen to you more often."

He seemed to nod, then curled up into a ball. He was asleep within minutes.

I rested my left hand lightly on his body, feeling the slow rise and fall of his rib cage, and I tried to find peace in the moment. It was all I could do.

I GAVE IN to sleep, eventually, grabbing a throw pillow for my head and wrapping myself in a knitted afghan. When I rolled onto my side, Simon grumbled and withdrew to the sofa. That's how Sera found us the next morning.

"You know he's only ten pounds, right? Even you could fight him for the sofa and win."

I stretched, working out the stiffness from a night spent on the floor. For good measure, I sent my magic to the ocean, gathering its energy. It revived and grounded me, reminding me that, whatever else I might be, I was first and foremost a water and a daughter of the old ones.

The rest of it—Mac's connection to me, my growing problems with control—that was all an accident, a strange quirk of fate. I'd had my pity party of one the night before, and that was enough.

I needed to fight for everything I cared about, and I included my own sanity on that list. I would be conscientious. I would be diligent. And I would possibly keep a small bucket of water with me at all times.

I glanced at Simon, still in cat form, stretching his own way back to wakefulness.

"He just looked so cute, all curled up in a ball." Simon didn't look indignant at my teasing. In fact, I suspected he shared my opinion. I stood, keeping the afghan wrapped around my shoulders, and sat next to him. He ignored me, the easy friendship of the night before less important than the need to clean his face. "Did you put the kettle on?"

Sera threw herself into the room's only armchair and simultaneously nodded and yawned. She was wearing a black t-shirt and black sweats. Normally, the dark colors set off her bronze skin perfectly. Now, she looked drawn, her skin noticeably pale.

She looked like a woman facing a trial for her life.

"Any word from Vivian?"

The air next to me changed as a small black cat was replaced by a slim man of average height. "She got back to us eventually," he muttered.

I'd never heard Simon mutter before. I glanced at him in surprise and saw far more than I intended to. Silently, I handed him my blanket. By that point, I'd seen Simon's naughty parts so often I could draw them on command, but I felt I should at least have a cup of tea before getting an eyeful of my friend's genitals.

"Did it take her time to hack the files?"

Sera shook her head, her eyes sharpening. "It took time for Olivia to go to bed so Vivian felt she could help us. She was still working on them when we went to bed." The kettle whistled. Sera bounced up, the movement far too energetic for someone who hadn't yet had coffee. She walked into the small kitchen and prepared a cup of tea for me. She waited for the coffee to finish brewing for approximately two seconds before giving up and pouring herself a cup from the half-full carafe.

I took my mug with a grateful nod. Truly, there are few pleasures in this world more satisfying than having someone else deliver your morning caffeine.

"So, is it time for us to make Olivia disappear? We know people, you know."

I was joking, mostly. Sera's considering expression made

me wonder if she realized that.

"Sadly, we cannot," said Simon, sitting upright. "It will only turn Olivia into a lost love, the one that got away. Vivian is choosing to be with her. We must wait until she chooses not to be."

"What if she doesn't?" I asked. "What if she chooses to spend the rest of her life in domestic bliss with Olivia, knitting and watching reality TV?"

"Then she's not the woman we all thought we knew, and we let her go so that she can be happy," he answered. In his early twenties, Simon was the youngest of all of us, but he had an unsettling habit of dropping words of wisdom when they were least expected.

Sera grimaced. She saw little reason to let things remain as they were when she could change them to her liking. "Is that what happened with you, Simon? You decided on your own that you'd rather be with us than with Carmen and her brood?"

I buried my face in my mug, inhaling the steam. I still wanted to beg him to stay and never, ever leave us again, but I was trying to take the high road here. Simon once told me he needed to choose his own future, and he needed to do it on his terms. Pressuring him to stay wasn't playing fair.

"Mac is my friend," he said, as if that explained everything. I supposed it did.

"About Mac..." I filled them in on my mother's diagnosis.

Sera gave a low whistle. "What are you going to do, Ade?"

"Only thing I can. I'll draw the magic out of him, somehow. Maybe all those meditation exercises Vivian taught me will help me focus. It's the only option. He'd be miserable, so dependent on me. We all know it."

Sera didn't argue the point. Not that one, at least. "But it sounds like it's a risk to you, too, if you aren't one hundred percent committed to this. Are you really willing to take this away? To make him mortal?"

"If it's what he wants." Last week, I'd have fought him on this. I'd have insisted he at least consider the option, consider the possibility that our relationship didn't need to have a built-in expiration date. Yes, we'd be more or less joined at the hip for centuries to come and would become the poster children for Co-Dependents Anonymous, but at least we'd be together.

Last week, I'd have fought for us.

But Mac deserved more than what I was becoming. He couldn't spend the rest of his life with a violent nut job. I'd try my damnedest to remain sane, but rumbling just below the morning's newfound resolve was the knowledge that I could fail. No matter how hard I tried, I could lose myself, and if I waited too long to recall the magic, I would lose him, as well. That wasn't an option.

"I'm going to do it tonight, once your trial's over and you're in the clear." I stated, so positive I could be mistaken for Pollyanna. "The longer I wait, the more Mac will suffer. Now, tell me about the files. How far did Vivian get last night?"

They exchanged a look at my blatant attempt to change the subject, but they went along with it. "She retrieved the files from the council's computer, but they were encrypted."

On cue, Sera's phone chirped, the sound of an incoming email. She opened it, then stared at her phone for much longer than it ought to take to read a single message. Her absolute lack of reaction told me the message contained news I needed to know.

"What?"

She put down her phone and looked between me and

Simon several times. "It's not good news." Her voice, pitched low, suggested this was a massive understatement. "Aidan, after Fiona cured the shifters and removed the magic-nullifying drug from their system, what did she do with the drug?"

I stared at her, shock written across my face.

Months ago, someone we knew injected me with a drug capable of blocking an elemental's access to their magic. It was terrifying to lose touch with such a vital part of myself, but it lasted only a few hours with no apparent side effects.

Then it fell into a shifter's hands, and she adapted the formula until it was more a weapon than a drug, a long-lasting solution capable of destroying both elementals and shifters. My mother was attacked, and she fell into a coma that lasted for days. The shifters given the drug were unable to take animal form, forcing the beasts within to rail against their confinement and slowly strip away the humanity that kept them balanced.

In other words, it was the sort of thing that should be thrown into a deep, dark well and never spoken of again. When we subdued the last woman who used it, I thought we'd gained control of the drug.

"I don't know." I searched my memory. "She took some blood samples, I think. She wanted to understand what it was, to create a faster cure or even a vaccine."

"Did she give it to anyone?"

I pressed my lips together and gave a curt nod. Of course she had. She would have needed the blood broken down for analysis, and we didn't have a forensics lab on the island. "She swore they were people she knew. People elementals could trust."

Sera stood and began pacing. The living room wasn't large, and the energy that vibrated around her made it feel even smaller than it was. "Well, unfortunately the council are elementals, too. They learned about the drug, Ade. That's your punishment. They're going to take your magic."

Simon and I shared matching horrified looks. "But that's barbaric," I said. "We can't exist without magic. I'd be in a coma, like my mother, and that's probably the best case scenario."

"Maybe it's a new formula, another variation on the drug Brian created. Maybe it's the same version, or something worse. I don't think it matters. If something goes wrong, no one would ever know. You'd still be banished. Once they got you off the island, no one would ever know how the drug affected you longterm. You'd become an example to elementals for centuries to come: step out of line, lose your magic."

"They're going to make me into a cautionary tale for misbehaving elementals? A bedtime story for naughty children?" I watched Sera pace the room and wanted to join her, to release my anger and the pulsating energy flowing through my body. "That case. At the trial, Edith kept one hand on a slim black case. I thought it was a fucking clutch purse, but it was the drug, wasn't it?"

I didn't move. I clung to my water and, with it, my control. Another piece fell into place. "You realize they just gave you a motive, right? It never made much sense, you killing someone to prevent my banishment. I mean, we already live outside the elemental world. But killing someone to prevent me from becoming a magic-deprived zombie? That might hold up."

Sera froze in place, considering my words, then began moving again, faster than before. "But I didn't know. They can't prove I did."

"I'm beginning to think this council isn't so interested in proof. They came to my trial with a plan, and they intend to execute it. They're going to announce it today, after your trial."

Somehow, Sera managed to pace even faster. She was practically leaving skid marks on the rug. "Lydia. She knew, didn't she? She looked disgusted the entire time, and someone cast an innocent vote for you. She doesn't want the council to resort to this. Maybe she can give us more information."

"I'll talk to her first thing. I can be very persuasive." Simon and Sera stared at me, and I gave them points for not bursting into laughter. "Okay, no I can't. But I can talk at her until she tells me something to make me go away."

They nodded, finding that scenario more believable. I wanted to be indignant, but they weren't wrong.

"I'll head over this morning. I'll stop at my mother's first, just to confirm what she did with the blood. I'd really like to know whose idea this was, particularly as we only need to change one council member's mind. We do that, and we're both free. You," I said, turning to Simon, "need to head back to the houseboat. Someone should be near Mac at all times, and I don't know what Miriam has planned for the day."

Simon winced. "You want me to use the rowboat?"

"Of course. How else have you been getting back and forth?"

He tensed, and I recognized the expression. It was the look of a cat that fell off a piece of furniture and was trying to recover its dignity. "Simon?"

He sat up perfectly straight, willing his faux dignity to become the real thing. "I had a ride over."

Sera studied him through narrowed eyes. "So what's the problem with using the rowboat now?"

"I didn't ride a boat. I rode an otter." He met our gazes defiantly, daring us to make any comment. "It was faster, and I wanted to spend as little time on the water as possible."

I was too busy picturing how freaking adorable they must have been, a nervous black cat clinging to the back of a river otter, to have anything insulting to say.

Sera grumbled, and it wasn't difficult to read her frustration. She needed something to do. Anything.

"Check with Vivian again," I told her. "See if she's learned anything else from that list of names I gave her."

"If she answers." Sera and Simon spoke together, in the same irritated tone.

"Yeah. If."

I nodded to both of them and headed for the shower, needing five minutes of quiet time with my element before facing the day's growing list of ifs and maybes.

I had less than twelve hours to figure out how to save Sera and keep myself from being drugged. It was time for my favorite investigative technique: throw everything at the wall and see what stuck.

CHAPTER 15

When I emerged from the shower, clean and dry and almost ready to face the day, Simon and Sera's long faces told me Vivian was still ignoring calls.

We couldn't afford to wait any longer. We needed to do this without our earth friend's help.

There was a second option. It wasn't ideal, partly because no one else could dig up information like Vivian could and partly because I was still giving the second option the silent treatment.

To be fair, he did kill Mac. I had good reason to be mad at him.

The phone only rang once before he picked up.

"I'm prepared to offer you a deal. I'll forgive you shooting and killing my sort of boyfriend if you help us solve this new case."

There was silence on the other end. I suspected Carmichael was taking several long, controlled breaths. I did have that effect on the man.

"Aidan?" He knew it was me. I just didn't think he believed it. We hadn't parted on the best of terms, what with the aforementioned boyfriend killing.

"Yeah. Look, we're kind of at loose ends here, and we need your help."

"Does this mean we're good? He didn't stay dead, after all."

"It means we need your help. Beyond that, I have no idea. But let's start here, okay?"

I'll give Carmichael this—he doesn't waste time on pointless questions, particularly when a shiny new case is waved under his nose. "Fill me in."

Sera watched me. I thought she was trying to determine if contacting the man who shot Mac was a sign of increased maturity or decreased sanity.

I covered the mouth piece. "I'm taking the high road," I informed her, doing my best to look like the saint I obviously was. She snorted and sat next to me, close enough to hear Carmichael's end of the conversation.

"Are you talking to Sera? Is she there?" He sounded almost hopeful.

Last I checked, he and Sera were self-declared nemeses, so I tucked this aside for future teasing possibilities. "Yeah. She was accused of murder."

"Again?"

"Hey, you were the ones who accused her the first time, and you were wrong. Show some faith."

"I have plenty of faith. I just have no idea how you two manage to find death and destruction wherever you go."

"It's a gift. You ready to hear the details or what?"

"Yeah. No, wait." The background noise changed. "You're on speakerphone now. Johnson is here."

"Hi, Aidan."

I returned his greeting with none of the ambivalence I felt for Carmichael. After all, Johnson hadn't shot Mac. "I'm doing the same so Sera can hear."

We spent the next thirty minutes explaining the case. Carmichael and Johnson mostly listened, only asking questions when a point needed clarifying. They were thoughtful men, and I could practically hear their brains churning as we spoke. Simon listened to the entire conversation but remained silent. I thought he might also harbor a grudge against Carmichael.

"Who are your suspects?" Johnson asked.

"That's the problem. We have one possible revenge killer, but that's it. No one else seems to have a motive. I'm guessing Robin died to cover something up, probably someone coming to or leaving the island, but I have no real idea why Edith is dead."

He grunted, and I assumed that was agreement. "What about your family? Are any of them like you?"

I shook my head before remembering they couldn't see me. "No. Dual magics are quite rare. Even if any of them were like me, they're all so old they would have given themselves away by now. It's not easy to hide." Because madness will out, I silently added.

The pen stopped moving and Johnson spoke up. "You're forgetting what we taught you."

I worked to remember our previous conversations, but Sera got there first. "Motive doesn't matter."

"Exactly. People have all kinds of reasons for killing, and you'd be surprised how rarely they make sense. Follow the evidence. Follow the clues. What do you have there?"

It probably would have been more impressive if we hadn't answered that question with complete silence.

Carmichael's response was bone dry. "Well, I suggest you work on that. Find whatever clues you can, then put them together. You've done it before, so just do the same thing again. Call us tonight and let us know how it went."

"I can't."

"Oh. I understand."

"No, I mean I can't. I have plans. I'm either helping Mac or I'll be on the run with Sera, evading a bunch of elementals who want her dead. So, you know. Busy. But I'll call when I get the chance, okay?"

We started to say good-byes, but Carmichael interrupted. "I am sorry, Aidan. I already said it to Mac, but you warned me before I went in. You told me I was out of my depth, that I had to be careful, and I ignored you. I shouldn't have done that. I am, well, I'm sorry," he repeated. There was no doubting his sincerity.

"I know." There didn't seem much else to say, but just before I hit the end button, Carmichael spoke again.

"Wait, one last thought. You've been looking for a dual magic like you, right? Someone who can control both water and fire? Is it possible you're looking for someone in disguise? A fire who has disguised themselves to look like a water?"

Sera smacked herself on the forehead. I leaned toward her, letting her smack me next.

"That's not a bad idea, Carmichael. We might let you back in the gang after all."

"Do we get satin jackets this time?"

"Don't push your luck."

We hung up, and Sera and I stared at each other, considering the possibilities Carmichael's words had raised.

"It can't be one of the waters," I said. "They're all too tall and skinny, too blond. Any fire trying to disguise themselves would need a mountain of bleach for both skin and hair. Also, stilts."

She stood, already reaching the same conclusion I was. "But a stone isn't too far off from a fire. A few months of hard work in the gym, some hair dye…"

"Colored contacts," I finished. "And a crazy water girlfriend you have nothing in common with who can provide access to the water council."

Her excitement fell, though only slightly. "But why? What vendetta could a fire possibly have against a member of the water council?"

"Hell if I know, but we should go with Johnson on this one and say screw the motive."

I didn't even bother to say goodbye. I just wrenched upon the front door and rushed out, ready to discover if a stone was really a stone.

WHILE WE'D SLEPT, the weather decided it wasn't fully ready to commit to summer. The sky was filled with charcoal clouds promising rain, and I smiled to see it. The more water that surrounded me, fueling the happy, non-murderous side of my magic, the safer we all were.

I paused on the stairs just long enough to pull on a hooded sweatshirt. As my head popped out, I squawked.

David stood right in front of me.

"Did you teleport?" I asked, calling to the water to calm my nerves.

"I didn't mean to surprise you. I was standing next to the stairs. You'd be surprised how often that happens with stones. People just don't notice us."

I grumbled, not ready to accept his explanation. "What are you doing here?"

"Lana and I had a fight. I thought you might be able to help."

"I'm kind of busy right now, David," I stepped off the stairs and headed for my mother's, expecting he would follow. I'd planned to check in with my mother and investigate David. If he was going to throw himself into my path, I could do both at the same time. I was on a tight schedule that day, after all.

He kept up with my long strides, though he never seemed to rush. Everything he did was slow and steady. We followed the canal that led to the northeast side of the island.

"I understand. But Lana seems to like you. I thought you might convince her to see things my way."

I stopped. "And what way is that, David?"

If he noticed the bite in my voice, he gave no sign. "We need to get off the island. One body was bad enough, but two? It's not safe. And I know there's a ban on travel, but Lana could get us to Friday Harbor, at least. She's strong enough. But she refuses, says she won't leave in the middle of a crisis."

I thought of several choice words for his cowardice. I only shared a few of them out loud.

"It's not about me," he insisted. "I don't mind being in danger. But Lana…"

"Can handle herself, and she knows her own mind. Hell, she's probably the only one who does."

His jaw locked. "You know she didn't do it. There's no reason for us to stay."

"Do I? Maybe. I don't know about you, though, and the fact that you're so eager to run really isn't helping your case." It probably wasn't a good idea to antagonize our number one suspect, but as usual, the words were out before my brain had a chance to approve them. "Why are you here, David?"

"I told you. To ask for help with Lana."

"No, on the island. Why did you come here?"

His forehead creased. "You know this already. Lana and I are traveling together. We'll go to my family's home next. What's this about, Aidan?"

"It's about you being a stranger who showed up the day before my best friend was accused of murder."

"That's been true since Edith Lake's death. Why are you only acting suspicious now? I don't understand where this is coming from." Though his tone didn't rise above mildly curious, his enormous muscles tightened until he looked much like a slab of granite.

I wasn't ready to accept that, not yet. I had a perfectly good theory I still wanted to explore. "At the moment, I'm suspicious of everyone on this island, David. Particularly those with some physical similarities to fires." I winced, fearing I'd said too much.

He laughed, an incredulous sound rather than an amused one. "Are you asking if I'm a fire in disguise? Do you seriously think that's a more likely explanation than the obvious one? Everyone on this island knows who's responsible, Aidan, and you're just too loyal to see it. Has it never occurred to you that Sera did it? She is Josiah's daughter, after all." His mouth snapped shut, as if he hadn't quite planned to say so much, either.

"What, exactly, does that mean?" I ground out.

"Never mind." he said.

"No, finish. When you installed the camera, you said something felt off. You thought Sera might be innocent. What changed?"

"What changed? A second body. Learning who her father is. Look, it's not my business, Aidan, but you should take a close look at the Blais family."

I laughed. I couldn't help it. One single astonished snort, followed by a handful of chuckles that led into an outright guffaw. He wasn't wrong, I'd give him that. He was just looking in the wrong direction.

David's eyes hardened, becoming the flint from which he took his name. His fists clenched at his side. "What's so funny?"

With effort, I suppressed the laughter, though a few giggles still snuck out. "You had to be there."

"You think this is a joke?" The words came out on a low hiss, and that's when I knew how to find the answers I needed.

It was a bad idea. Sera, Josiah, and my mother could all yell at me later. For now, I had an enraged maybe-fire before me, and one surefire way to confirm what he was.

I reached my magic toward him.

No fire could be as angry as he was without accessing their magic, without risking the fingertips sparking.

I wasn't used to controlling the fire. I asked it to seek out David's magic, and it ignored me, choosing instead to reach toward the trees, imagining how pretty a burning branch would look.

I yanked it back, and I swore it laughed.

This magic was different than the water, wilder. It had little interest in polite requests.

This time, I ordered it, forcing it toward David, wrapping it around his arms and legs, outlining each finger.

"It's here!"

"What?" My voice was thick and dull, all my attention on the magic, looking for the familiar touch of fire on David's body. I snapped back to reality right about the time David tackled me to the ground.

"The fire. I think it was here. I felt warmth on my hands. Are you okay?"

I blinked into his concerned face and watched a perfectly good theory go up in smoke. He hadn't budged, still protecting my body with his own. I almost felt bad for thinking he was a coward earlier. "Yeah. You?"

"I'm fine—" He didn't finish the sentence. It's hard to speak when an otter shifter emerges from the canal next to you and hauls you to your feet.

"Now this just isn't right, a big guy like you attacking Aidan. You've noticed she doesn't have any actual muscles, right? If you want to pick on someone your own size, hey, I'm right here." Miriam grinned, altogether too pleased at the prospect of a fight. David was stronger than she was, but she was several inches taller, and I suspected she fought dirty. I would never bet against her.

David looked like he was coming to the same conclusion. He tried to speak at least three times, unsure how one was supposed to react when a naked woman appears out of nowhere and offers to deliver a beatdown. At last, he gave up and turned to me for aid.

"It's okay, Miriam. He wasn't hurting me. Let him go."

She did, quite slowly, daring him to give her any excuse to change her mind.

"So, are you one of the shifter-deniers?" I asked. "Cause if so, your reality is about to get messy."

"What? Um. No. My mother spoke well of them, so I guess I wasn't raised like other elementals." He paused. I thought he might still be recovering from being threatened by the one of the cutest women in the world. "After she died, I guess I just never thought about them much."

"Not even when Lana told you about the horse?" The devil made me say it. That was my excuse, and I was sticking to it.

"The what? No, that's not... Look, can you not mention this?" With one last uncertain look between me and Miriam, David turned and walked away, bound for my mother's and Lana.

"I think you broke him," I told Miriam.

"Brook, if I'm going to break a man, we're both going to have a lot more fun getting there. Speaking of which, if he wasn't attacking you, why were you lying underneath him?"

"Long story. You didn't actually have to assault him, you know. He was trying to protect me, I think."

"I figure it's better to be safe than sorry. Plus, it was fun."

Miriam and I did not have the same definition of fun.

I cast an eye over her naked body. She'd obviously been

swimming through the canal in her other form. I chose to give her the benefit of the doubt that her presence at that moment was a coincidence, rather than the direct result of more otter spying.

"Did you just come from the houseboat? How's Mac?"

"Irritable, but hanging in there. He only threw two plates and one coffee mug before settling down, so I think he's coming around. He did start getting ill a few hours ago, which is normal. Well, the new normal. He's stable, in his way."

"Do me a favor? Simon should be heading over in the rowboat soon. Do you mind giving these to him, for Mac?" I pulled the books I'd grabbed from Grams' library, dog-eared paperbacks by Agatha Christie and Dorothy L. Sayers that I knew he'd love. "He can tell Mac... just ask him to say they're from me."

"I'll deliver the message myself, and I'll tell him more than that. This isn't your fault, and I won't let that damn man act like it is." Proclamation delivered, she strolled away, ass swaying with every step.

She was right. This wasn't my fault, most of it. It didn't matter. So long as I could help fix it, it was still my responsibility.

One way or another, things were going to change that day.

CHAPTER 16

My mother's house was empty, so I headed next door. Though it was early, most of the island was already gathered, not wanting to miss any part of this momentous day. They might not be certain what would happen, but they planned to tell stories about it for decades to come. Nervous excitement filled the rooms, my family and the visitors counting down the hours till the trial.

To my surprise, my aunts hadn't started on the wine yet. I found them on the back porch, in swings and rocking chairs, watching the rain that had begun to fall on my walk over.

Music followed me through the back door, an old Patsy Cline song. Tina was the aunt who'd turned me onto country music, and normally few things made me happier than a cup of tea, a rainy day, and a bit of twang on the radio. I wished I was in any position to enjoy it now.

"Aidan!" called Marie. "We've scarcely seen you. Sit, sit." She patted the open space next to her.

"Sorry, Marie. I've been busy. The whole best friend accused of murder thing, you know."

"Is that still happening? Goodness. Perhaps they should just flip a coin. It would be simpler."

Tina shook her head. Being the youngest, she was slightly less odd than the others. "That wouldn't be right. They need evidence. Show us your evidence, Aidan."

"That's kind of the problem."

Tina stared at me, confused. "But you've had three days. That's enough time to scour this entire island. What are you still hoping to find?"

Georgina shrugged. "Perhaps there's nothing to find, dear. Have you considered that the reason you're unable to exonerate your friend is that she's guilty? It really is the simplest explanation."

Her words echoed David's, and I wondered how many others shared their belief. "Simple isn't always right, Georgie. Is my mother around?"

Marie nodded. "Upstairs."

I thanked her and moved toward the door. "Aidan." Georgina's voice stopped me, the tone far too serious for my light-hearted aunt. "She's barely recovered from the last decade. We both know she's not the same woman she was before you disappeared. Whatever happens, you can't do that again."

There was nothing to say, no answer I could ever give that would satisfy my family. Ten years in elemental time might not be much—unless it was time spent in hiding, letting no one know whether I was alive or dead. Those ten years would always feel like a small eternity to my mother, I knew, and based on the three somber faces looking at me now, she hadn't been the only one.

And yet, I couldn't promise I wouldn't disappear again, so I only nodded and stepped inside.

My mother was sitting on one of the guest beds, folding sheets. She always liked to organize when life became too complicated.

"Did you know that David is trying to leave with Lana?" I asked in a low voice.

She shook her head. "I wish he could. If I had my way, I'd put that Pond girl on a boat and send her to Alaska. The poor dear babbles so much, and I live in fear of what's going to come out of her mouth next. But I can think of no way to remove them without inviting the council's suspicion."

"Too bad. I'm pretty sure they're both innocent."

"I'd be inclined to agree. Josiah informs me that neither of them accessed fire magic last night. Nor did anyone staying with your grandmother."

"There's got to be someone, though. We're missing something."

She shook her head. "Perhaps we're looking at this all wrong, Aidan. It may not be a dual. They really aren't especially common."

That was an understatement. Despite decades of searching, Josiah knew of only three living dual magics besides me. There was Trent Pond, still locked away in the hospital in Eureka. The other two were mysteries. We only knew that one lived in the deserts of the southwest US, and the other lived on the Prince's Islands in Istanbul.

I'd seen no evidence that a half-desert or a Turk were anywhere on the island at the moment.

"Well, a dual magic may not even be our biggest problem anymore." I shared what I knew from the council's files. As I spoke, two angry red splotches appeared.

"How dare they? They have no right. That drug would ruin you."

"Why did you even tell them about it?"

She set the folded sheet to the side. "I informed the council of the problems we had with that shifter woman who sought to destroy elementals. I believed they needed to be aware of the growing shifter threat in Tahoe, and the discovery of the magic-nullifying drug was an integral part of the story. It was perhaps the wrong call."

I groaned, thought of five different names I wished to call her, and bit them all back. She'd done exactly what she was supposed to do. She'd trusted the people whose job it was to protect elementals. It wasn't her fault they were terrible at their job. "Only because the council are a bunch of insensitive morons. How do we get rid of this drug, once and for all?"

She shook her head. "It's too late for that. It has gone too far, too fast. There's no telling who has access to the formula now. You can't keep this kind of lightning in a bottle, Aidan."

Maybe not, but if the most powerful weapon one could use against an elemental was on this island, it needed to be in my possession.

Better to be the one to wield the lightning than the one to get struck.

THIS TIME, GRAMS' house wasn't empty. Through the ground floor window, I could see the council in the library. The three female members sat on the armchairs and the soft green love seat, though they appeared far from relaxed. They gestured emphatically, using sharp, pointed movements, and their faces were animated with frustration and anger. Michael Bay showed little interest in joining the debate. Instead, he paced along the shelves, running his fingers absently along the spines. Seeing the casual movement set my teeth on edge. He shouldn't be here at all, let alone staying long enough to get his cooties all over my family's books.

They hadn't come the the island just to dispense your regular, bog-standard elemental justice. They'd arrived with a plan already formed, a plan that would ruin my life faster than being a dual magic ever could.

I had a good idea where I needed to look. Rachel Strait's room was the only one I hadn't examined in detail. At the time, I'd been distracted by Simon, the discovery of the laptop, and the need to find the IP address.

This should teach me a valuable lesson about leaving a job half done.

I studied my grandmother's house, looking for a way to lure the council outside so I could finish searching Rachel's room. There was no fire alarm I could pull, no stink bomb I could lob into the library.

I circled to the kitchen door at the back of the house. The screen door opened with a high-pitched whine, and I grimaced.

"Aidan Brook! What are you doing here?"

I jumped, releasing an undignified squeak.

My grandmother stepped from behind the pantry door, and I did my best to only look a little bit shifty.

"Grams! I didn't see you there."

"Shh." She sent an admonishing glare my way. "If they know you're here, they'll... well, I've no idea what they'll do."

I strained my ears toward the library. I couldn't make out any individual words, but the angry tone was impossible to miss.

"What are they discussing?" I whispered.

She shook her head as she moved around the large kitchen, gathering items for tea service. "I've no idea. Every time I get within twenty feet of them, they clam up. They're acting like I'm not even a member of this ridiculous council. I'm older than half those fools," she huffed, spooning loose leaf tea into a strainer. "I understand why I was removed from your case, but they're now saying I can't be impartial about your friend's situation, either. I have been completely cut out, and in my own house. It's lunacy. Ill-mannered lunacy." Her final words were directed toward the library, and though they were delivered in a quiet hiss, her indignant glare spoke volumes.

"Even Lydia? She seemed relatively sane and willing to listen to something other than her own voice."

"Well, yes, she's been the one exception. Quieter, as if there's always something going on behind her eyes. Rather the opposite of her niece, in fact."

I didn't say anything, but I gave Grams a mental high-five for that one. Based on the sly smile that curved her lips, she knew it.

Grams opened the fridge, took out cheese and mayonnaise, and placed them on the kitchen island alongside bread and tomatoes. "I'm making you a sandwich. You're too skinny." My grandmother only looked about thirty years older than me and was every bit as thin, but I've learned not to protest when someone offers to make you food.

Besides, I was starving. I was running all over the island and only fueling myself through the ocean and canals. I could exist for weeks on just my element, with no food and sleep, but existing was a far cry from thriving.

"Grams, are you hiding in here?" I asked. "Tell me you haven't been booted out of your own library."

"Booted, no. Given a bunch of irritated looks that stated as clearly as words that I wasn't welcome? Perhaps. So I said I'd make them tea. Which I will. Eventually. When I decide I don't mind feeding a bunch of discourteous moochers." Again, she lifted her chin to direct the last words to toward the library.

She slapped two fat slices of tomato onto the white bread and added no small amount of mayonnaise to the other side. She positioned the knife against the block of cheese, preparing to slice off a piece that could feed an army of mice for a month. "I'm wrapping this for you to take away. It really won't do for them to find you here."

I snagged a leftover piece of tomato, salted it, and

popped it in my mouth. "I can't. I need to look for something upstairs."

She set down the knife and waited.

"I shouldn't tell you what. Plausible deniability and all that."

"Aidan Brook, I am nine hundred and thirty years old. Unlike some people I might know, I am capable of telling lies without the entire world knowing. Now, spill."

"It's complicated."

"Then it's a good thing you got your smarts from me, isn't it? I'm fairly certain I can wrap my brain around whatever information you've managed to uncover."

Hey, she asked for it.

"Okay, but you're not going to like this. And don't ask me how I learned any of it. There's a drug that interferes with magic. I knew the man who created it. He used it on me once, and I've seen its effects on others. The council discovered its existence when my mother freaking told them about it, so maybe you're right about where I got my brains. Don't tell her I said that, please. The council was planning on injecting me with the drug as part of my punishment. I think it's in Rachel's room, and I need to find it, either to show everyone what the council has become or to destroy it. I haven't thought that far ahead yet. Actually, I just found out about the drug and rushed over here. That's pretty much the entire plan so far." I took a big bite of the sandwich, mainly to shut myself up.

Grams listened to the entire story without appearing to blink, let alone move. When I finished, she said nothing.

Instead, she carried the knife to the sink and opened a drawer next to the fridge. It looked like it held rows of spices. She moved several glass bottles out of the way and held up a few more, inspecting the contents. At last, she placed a small blue bottle with a dropper lid on the kitchen counter. It was half filled with a dark liquid.

"Grams! You have it? How? Why?"

"Of course I don't. I've never heard of such a terrible thing, let alone kept a vial of it. But you need to search the upstairs without witnesses, and I can hardly lock the library door, or tell everyone to stand outside for the next thirty minutes because it's such a pretty rainstorm." She shook the bottle, then deposited ten fat, dark drops in the teapot. "Fortunately, this isn't the first time I needed a break from an unwanted guest. Someday, ask me about the wretched Martha's Vineyard branch of our family tree."

"You're going to drug them?" I was both horrified and impressed.

"Oh no. That sounds so dramatic. I'm merely giving them a respite from wakefulness."

Grams plucked the kettle from the stove and poured water over the tea leaves, humming the entire time. I supposed it was good to know I couldn't ascribe all my crazy being a dual magic. Some of it appeared to be good old-fashioned genetics.

When the tea had steeped just the right amount of time to disguise an illicit sleeping potion, she carried the tray into the pantry with a cheerful "Be sure to finish the sandwich, dear," thrown over her shoulder.

I stared at the pantry door for a full minute, waiting for her to reappear. When she didn't, I peered inside. The pantry held dry goods, potatoes, and a basket full of spare batteries, but no Grams.

If someone in the family knew how to teleport and forgot to tell me, I was going to be seriously pissed.

I ran my fingers along the wall, looking for the seam of a door. I found nothing until I hit the back wall. Behind several stacks of clean dishcloths, there was a small latch, about the size one might find on a cabinet door. I pressed it and watched in awe as the wall fell backwards, revealing a dark hall.

It wasn't pitch black, though. Small holes and vents were cut into the walls, allowing in light from the other rooms. Vision was still limited, but it was enough to see a few feet ahead. With my right hand against the wall to guide me, I followed the hallway until I hit a dead end.

This time, I knew what I was looking for. I felt for the latch and released it, catching the wall as it swung backwards. No, not a wall. A bookcase.

I emerged into my Grams' study, a classically decorated office just across the hall from the library.

On the one hand, it was a stressful day filled with all kinds of deadlines I wasn't certain I could meet. On the other hand, I'd just discovered a secret passageway in Grams' house, complete with a false bookshelf. That almost evened things out.

I could hear the council talking, though their voices were civil now that Grams was in the room. As much as I wanted to confirm they were drinking the tea, the risk of being spotted was too great. Reluctantly, I withdrew, walking back along the corridor and emerging in the kitchen a minute later.

Lacking any other options, I did as she told me. I sat at the kitchen island and ate my sandwich.

The clock on the stove said she'd been gone ten minutes, but I was fairly certain I'd been sitting in the kitchen for hours, waiting to hear a council member accuse my grandmother of doing exactly what she was doing.

Even if the potion worked, it needed to put the council members to sleep simultaneously, before anyone became suspicious. There was no way four different people would drink their tea at the same rate. Someone would down it as soon as it was poured. Someone else would let it cool.

This was a horrible plan. Absolutely awful. Any moment now, Grams was going to step through the kitchen door and tell me it was a valiant effort, but the council had decided our entire family had gone off the deep end and would be tried as a group.

Instead, when she stepped back through the pantry door, she was still humming. "Works every time. Bless that handsome young herbalist with a preference for well-preserved blonds. You'll have about an hour, though I've seen it wear off in half that time with the more stubborn full-blooded elementals. I'm going to wash out this pot and stay here, just in case that whole plausible deniability thing becomes an issue."

"Thirty minutes is all I need. By the way, how long has that shortcut been part of the house?"

She looked flummoxed by the question. "Always, of course. What's the point in building your own home if you don't add a secret passageway or two?"

She had a point. "I like it. Thanks, Grams." I took a second on my way out to kiss her cheek.

The house wasn't quiet, not entirely. I could hear quiet snuffles and snores from the sleeping elementals in the library. I risked a peek into the room. Lydia was sound asleep in an armchair, while Michael and Deborah were on the love seat, his head on her shoulder. Rachel never even made it to a chair. She was curled up on the area rug, knees tucked into the fetal position. She almost looked sweet.

I wasn't ready to trust the thirty minutes Grams had promised—elemental metabolisms are far from reliable—so I ran upstairs and tore through Rachel's room as quickly as I could.

It took longer than I expected, because after I tore through one section of the room, I had to put everything back where I found it to keep my presence a secret. If police searches were conducted by neat freaks, it would look very similar to what I was doing.

I lifted her mattress and checked under the bed. When that turned up nothing, I lifted the sheets and rugs. I picked up stacks of folded clothes, looking for hidden items in all the drawers, then looked between each item of clothing. I ran my hands over the linings of Rachel's suitcases. I even poked my head out the windows, in case an enterprising council member had duct taped a vial of the drug to the shutters.

Fifteen minutes were already gone, and I hadn't found a thing.

I couldn't afford to panic, not yet. I was missing something, that was all. I spun in a slow circle, relaxing my eyes and trying to see the room for the first time.

On the second rotation, I lowered my eyes to the floor, and I saw it. The air vents. I dropped to my knees and peered through the slats. I saw nothing, but I needed to be sure.

Twenty minutes had passed now. I grabbed a nail file from the bathroom and inserted the flat end into the screws holding the vent in place.

My nerves were frayed, and I dropped the nail file twice, but eventually the screws loosened and sprang free. With careful hands, I pried the vent from the wall and checked inside.

It was empty.

I sat back on my heels, defeated. If the drug was on the island, it wasn't in Rachel's room. Maybe they hid it elsewhere in the house, but my gut knew that wasn't true. They'd never leave such an incendiary item where anyone might stumble upon it.

It was on their person, damn it. I'd just wasted Grams' potion searching the house when I should have been frisking the people.

"Looking for something, Ms. Brook?"

I spun, dropping the air vent cover. It clattered to the floor. I raised my eyes to find Rachel Strait standing in the doorway, looking at me like something she'd scrape off her shoe.

CHAPTER 17

I rose to my feet as slowly as possible, buying time to think of an explanation for my presence in Rachel's room.

Rachel fought a yawn, and her lids remained heavy. Grams' potion had worked, just not long enough. I imagined Rachel was the sort of woman who'd fight against drugs on principle, refusing to let anything else control her. She's probably been struggling to rise from the moment she fell into a Grams-induced slumber.

"Grams said she was having problems with her air conditioning. With August around the corner, I told her I'd have a look." I smiled brightly. I probably would have been more convincing if I hadn't been casting nervous glances over her shoulder as I spoke.

"Really? I hadn't realized you were so capable." She glanced at my hands, still clutching the nail file rather than a flat head screwdriver, and somehow managed not to laugh outright.

The irony was that I actually could fix the air conditioning if it was broken. I'd lived alone in a worn down farmhouse for a decade and been determined to avoid humans as much as possible. I ordered the entire *Time-Life* home improvement book series and eventually learned which end of a hammer to hold.

But Rachel knew none of that, and she clearly didn't believe a word I was saying.

Of course, being drugged against her will was a good reason to be a bit suspicious.

"I didn't mean to intrude. Grams said this was a good time, that you were napping in the library." I met her gaze, my own more defiant than was probably wise.

She returned my stare. Hers was impressive, I had to admit. She had centuries on her side. I had a secretly pissed-off fire on mine. I thought we could call it a draw.

"Yes, napping," she said. "I'm not sure I've done that since I was a child. It is surprising that, when the mood struck me again, centuries later, it did so at the same time it afflicted my fellow council members."

She made no attempt to hide her scorn, and I saw little point in claiming innocence. It's not like they could sentence me to a worse punishment than they already had planned.

"I put the drops in the teapot when Grams wasn't looking. She had nothing to do with it." Of course, she believed that lie when she scoffed at the idea that I was a secret handyman. As transparent as my face is, sometimes people still only see what they expect to see.

Rachel stepped into the room and examined her belongings, looking for evidence that I'd searched through them. She kept her back to me as she spoke. "Last I checked, elementals have no laws against forcing someone to sleep, though at the moment that seems like a gross oversight. Your crimes, however, have been established. Everyone on this island seems to forget you were already convicted, Ms. Brook, but I have not. Edith's death delayed your sentence, but it will be delivered when the council reconvenes this evening. Please tell me you are not attempting to delay the trial."

"Actually, I was looking for evidence that proved the council has lost their ever-loving minds." I kept my voice mild.

Rachel's eyebrows twitched toward each other. She possessed too much control to show surprise, but it was pretty damn close. "I'm not certain I know what you mean."

"And I'm quite certain you do. How about this. We'll flip a coin. If I win, you tell me where you're keeping the medicine that would put me into a magic-deprived vegetative state. You really weren't kidding about needing laws that forbid drugging other elementals, were you? And if you win, then I'll rip this house apart until I find it, since it looks like I don't need to worry about secrecy anymore. Those are your options, Rachel. You're in my family's house, on my family's island, threatening one of their daughters with an unspeakable punishment. Perhaps you should recognize that your position isn't as strong as you believe it is."

Even as I accused her of threatening me, I did the same to her. The council's power was formidable. It had been designed that way, to have the strength necessary to govern the water elementals. Six of the most powerful waters in the world could battle their way out of any potentially hostile environment.

Except there were only four now. Even with Deborah Rivers on their side, they were weakened. Or, to put it in slightly blunter terms, they were screwed, and Rachel knew it. Though color rose in her cheeks and her lips tightened, she didn't argue with my assessment.

Instead, she reached one hand into the inside pocket of her jacket and withdrew a small black case. She placed it on the desk, several feet from me, and cracked it open. Ten syringes were tucked neatly into each side, for a total of twenty. They were all full.

"This is what you wanted." Her voice had little inflection.

I didn't glance at her. I couldn't look away from those

vials intended for me. "How was it going to work?" I asked. "I've seen the effects before. Without some sort of time release, each vial would only last a couple of days."

"That's all Edith intended. Three days per vial, for a total of two months' punishment. She believed being banished wasn't enough incentive against others committing your crimes. She wanted to make an example of you."

The words confirmed my and Sera's suspicions. Sometimes, it sucks to be right.

I still couldn't take my eyes off the vials. I remembered how terrible my mother looked when she'd been drugged. For several days, she'd been, for all intents and purposes, in a coma, and that had only been one vial. There was no way of knowing what multiple vials would do. How week upon week without access to my magic would change me.

They'd planned to use me as their living experiment.

With that realization, the fire awoke.

"It doesn't make sense," I insisted, fighting for calm. "I understand what I did was problematic from the council's perspective, but I don't know if I'd have lived if I hadn't tilted the lake. The evidence was immediately erased. Why is it so important to make an example for something that will never happen again?"

"It wasn't the lake. Or the agents, for that matter. We're aware the FBI knows about us. We've worked with them in the past."

At last, I tore my eyes from the vials and looked at Rachel. "Then why?" She appeared pained, but she didn't answer. She didn't need to. "The shifters. This is about me being friends with shifters."

"Edith wished to discourage more people from following your example. We are not the same, Ms. Brook. Though we were born from the same source, theirs was a corrupted form of that magic. We should not be friends with them any more than you would be friends with a pig or a rat."

I'd rather be friends with a whole zoo full of rodents than think the way the old ones did, but I doubted such an argument would help my cause. "You keep saying Edith, as though she was the only one who believed this. You all knew what she had planned, and only one council member voted against it."

"Edith believed it most firmly, yes, and she was quite persuasive. Now that she is no longer available, we will vote again." I winced at the euphemism. Rachel pretended not to notice. "Perhaps the vote will be different this time." Nothing in her voice suggested she believed her own words.

"Is this what you were arguing about downstairs?"

"The council's business is its own, Ms. Brook. We do not answer to outsiders."

"What else could it be? Is Lydia still trying to convince you? I know it's her. The rest of you look through me. She's the only one who seems to take her responsibility seriously."

"Insult us if it makes you feel better, but it changes nothing."

I'd known ices and stones more flexible than this woman. The discussion was over.

I could back out of this room and wait for my sentencing and Sera's trial. Sera would be convicted, and just when I needed to help her, when I needed my magic the most, I'd get jabbed with one of these needles and be incapacitated. By the time I woke, my entire world would be broken. Sera would be dead or in hiding. I couldn't even imagine how Mac would be affected if he couldn't feed on my magic.

There wasn't a single part of that scenario I was okay with.

Rachel stepped back, leaving space for me to exit the

room. I laughed at her. The fire joined in, turning incredulous laughter into something raw, ragged, and oddly joyful.

"All because you hate shifters this much. You would torture me, just to keep our races from mingling. You should be ashamed of yourselves. Every single one of you."

She paled at the insult. "That's enough."

"I haven't even begun. You're making choices you have no right to make, creating barriers and rifts where none should exist. Do you have any idea how much shifters hate us?"

Rachel bristled. "After the recent events in Lake Tahoe, it is difficult to pretend otherwise. For centuries we have lived separately, never intermingling with their kind, but that is no longer the case. You and your friend involved yourselves in the affairs of shifters, and soon thereafter one of them made what amounted to a declaration of war. It does not matter that she failed. Her actions revealed the truth. Shifters no longer desire peace. It is time to remind our kind why we belong apart."

"Is that supposed to prevent war or hasten it?"

She thinned her lips and refused to answer.

"It doesn't matter. We keep heading the way we are and something's going to give. I'll tell you this, these days I see no reason to fight on the elementals' side."

I might as well have told her I was thinking of waging war on Canada. She couldn't have been any more shocked. "How can you say that?"

"After everything I've learned today, after what you planned to do to me, how can I not? What reason have I been given to feel loyalty to elementals?"

As I spoke, I stared at the case full of syringes, still several feet away. I wasn't faster than Rachel. I wasn't a more powerful water. In every visible way, I was weaker.

Fortunately, I had a few invisible tricks up my sleeve.

"I don't care what you had planned. It will not happen. You will never control me." I paused between each word of the last sentence, letting the weight of my words build until they hung in the air, an overt challenge.

For the second time that day, I called to the fire. I encouraged it, grateful for its warmth and power, its hunger for destruction. It responded like an eager child, thrilled to be recognized at last.

All this time, I'd been wrong. The fire wasn't the enemy. The enemy stood in front of me.

The heat soared from me, arcing through the air toward the glass vials. I knew Rachel watched me, that she saw my gray eyes turn hard and dark, but I didn't care. All my attention was on the vials. I stoked the fire, raising the temperature until it would burn everything it touched, then made it hotter still. It wrapped around each small tube, and it squeezed. The heat contorted the glass, forcing it to bend to its will until, one after the other, the syringes exploded in a shower of glass.

The contents fell to the ground and soaked into the rug.

There was no relief. I was safe, but my friends were not. There would never be peace between elementals and shifters so long as women like this fueled the hate. She was poison to us all.

Without the drug, I might be again facing only banishment, but Sera was about to receive a death sentence. I'd run out of time. Whoever the killer was, I wouldn't find them before dusk.

The only way to prevent her death was to delay her trial. The only way to do that was to kill the woman before me.

The fire grinned. On this, we were in perfect agreement.

I thought even my water side might want to watch Rachel Strait burn.

"How are you doing that?" She stared at me, her eyes a

mix of fear and wonder. "You can't be…"

"Aidan? Aidan, are you still up here?"

The fire created tunnel vision. It always had, and it fought against the familiar voice trying to pull me from from that narrow, wonderful world where everything made sense.

"I just looked, and I didn't see Rachel. Perhaps you should come downstairs. Oh. Oh my."

My grandmother stood in the doorway, and I didn't even think she saw the councilwoman. All her attention was on me, on the eyes I knew were far darker than they should be. On the intense expression no water ever wore. On the fire sparking from my fingertips. "Oh, dear," she said, and ran.

Somewhere, I knew my life had just taken a most unwelcome turn. I should run as fast as I could to the cottage and grab Sera. We would break a window and jump into the ocean and start swimming, and we wouldn't stop until we reached Japan. It was a more sensible plan than staying here while Grams told the whole island what I was, and then waiting for death to find me.

Maybe I would have done that. Maybe sense would have ruled the day, if Rachel hadn't tried to flee along with my grandmother. That, I could not allow.

I lit the doorway on fire, trapping her in the room.

She turned to me with wide eyes, but she was still a full-blooded water. She might be terrified, but she would fight. She extinguished the fire, and the one I set after that, and the next one. Soon, I was sending hundreds of flames toward her, small bullets of fire. She put them all out. Minutes passed as we engaged in this dance, and my anger only sharpened and focused. She would not win.

She had wet her clothes and hair, so there was no way to set her on fire. Not her outsides, at least. I felt it then, the smile pulling at my lips, the maniacal glee infusing my body and possibly my soul. If I couldn't set her outsides on fire, well, there were always the insides.

I knew how the body was formed. I understood how the organs worked together, how the heart pumped blood and the lungs filled with air. I'd had the same lessons in healing as the rest of my family, but I had no recollection of any Hippocratic oath. My knowledge could heal, but it could also destroy, and this time I was picking the second option.

I stretched the magic toward Rachel, sent it crashing through the layers of her skin. I pushed the fire toward her heart and lungs. I let it grab onto the blood vessels and the bone, and I took one long second to find joy in its power. In my power.

Rachel's eyes revealed no understanding, a child on the verge of blind panic when the world refuses to make sense. A voice whispered that I shouldn't enjoy her fear so much, but it was a tiny voice and the rest of me scoffed at its weakness. Rachel felt fear because her illusions of power had been stripped. She was an old one, and a member of the council, and centuries had likely passed since the last time she didn't feel in control.

I would take her control away, forever, and I would smile as I did so. I reached for the magic, and I let it burn.

"No!"

It wasn't a scream, but it was close. The voice was firm and determined to the point of desperation, and as it rang through the room my magic was forced from Rachel's body. When I tried to re-enter, there was no room. Someone else was already there.

"You cannot do this, Aidan." Josiah stood at my side. He appeared agitated, his body almost vibrating, but his voice was measured and calm even as he began to burn Rachel's life from her body. "It will be hard enough to keep you sane as is. If you murder this woman, it'll be over. You'll be a lost cause. You know this is the truth."

I stared at him, a low growl emerging from my throat. The fire tried again to attack Rachel, and again it was swatted back.

"I will handle this. She must not live, not now. Go with your grandmother. And if you don't mind a suggestion, please don't kill her, either. You'd feel quite guilty about it once the fire receded."

His calm voice penetrated my rage as shouts or fear never could. No, I did not want to kill Grams. That would be a bad idea.

That wasn't the only bad idea. I looked at the councilwoman, at her face frozen in a permanent scream, and a distant part of me knew I should try harder to stop this. I shouldn't let Josiah kill her.

I shouldn't have forced him to kill her.

There was a hand on my waist, guiding me out of the room, and I was spared the sight of Rachel's desperate face as she gasped her final breaths. It was a gentle hand, but insistent, and I suspected if I fought, I'd be thrown over Grams' shoulder in a fireman's hold. "Where are...?" I couldn't finish the sentence. I wasn't even sure what I was asking.

She urged me down the hall and into her private bathroom, where the tub was already filling with warm water. Without stopping to remove my clothes or shoes, she pushed me into the bath and sat on the edge, waiting.

"You'll let me know when you're you again, yes?"

The words circled my brain, and when they at last made sense, I gave a single nod.

It took a long time. The fire rose and fell, still insisting we return to the other room and finish what we'd begun. For a moment, I even sensed the water murmur in quiet agreement. Every time I struggled to rise from the tub, a deceptively strong hand pressed against my chest, urging me back into the bath. The fire hissed and spat, and I felt it turn to Grams with hate.

That was when I began to fight against it. I couldn't be that person. I couldn't lose myself, not yet. There was still too much I needed to do.

The water surrounded me, reminding me there was a way back.

I grabbed the fire, one slippery, angry tendril of magic after another. It took all my will to force it into submission. The rage grew quiet, and as it conceded defeat I reached for the water, tentatively at first and then with greedy certainty, using its power to heal myself, to cure the exhaustion that lingered long after the fire was corralled.

I'd almost killed someone. Again. I'd craved her death, longed for it with every part of my being. If not for Josiah, I'd have committed cold-blooded murder.

I may not have been the one to extinguish her life, but I'd sure as hell been complicit in her death. If I hadn't lost control, if I hadn't revealed what I was, Rachel Strait would still be alive.

Josiah said I'd be a lost cause if I murdered someone, but I thought maybe I already had. I hadn't burned her myself, but only because I'd been denied the opportunity. Instead, I'd made my father kill for me.

I'd caused a woman's death, and this time it hadn't been an accident.

"Aidan?" My grandmother nudged me.

"I'm me," I told Grams, though I was no longer certain that was true.

Josiah appeared in the doorway, and for once I felt no resentment or hatred for the man. He'd just tried to save me from myself, and unless I wasn't seeing the whole picture, he'd done so at a terrible cost to himself.

"Will you dispose of her body?" I asked, my voice dull. Josiah could turn a body to ash and leave no evidence behind.

He shook his head. Normally, this man was energetic and perfectly presented, but I saw none of that now. His shirt was untucked and only half-buttoned, and he wore one brown loafer and one black dress shoe. Grams must have run for him immediately. Whatever she'd said or done when she found him, he hadn't taken any unnecessary time to dress himself.

"How did you know to get him? How did you know what I was?"

Grams reached into the tub and pulled the plug, then handed me a thick towel to wrap around my wet clothes. "Other than he was the strongest fire on the island and the only one who might stop you? I guess I've seen the puzzle pieces my whole life, but somehow they never matched the picture on the box. It wasn't until I got the last piece that I finally understood. It really was a doozy of a piece, Aidan." I looked at her, expecting fear or revulsion, but all I saw was gentle chastisement, sadness she had to find out this way.

There were so many questions I wanted to ask that my brain tripped over them, and in the end we didn't have time. I focused on the biggest one.

"What are we going to do about the body?"

Josiah leaned against a wall and ran one hand through his hair. Without the product he normally used, it sprang free, short but every bit as curly as Sera's. "Well," he said. "I killed her in an attempt to save one daughter. We might as well use her death to save the other."

———

THE THREE STILL-LIVING council members were stirring, the effects of Grams' potion wearing off at last, when Josiah walked into the middle of the library and announced he'd killed Edith Lake and Rachel Strait. While the confounded council blinked and took a few moments for their brains to confirm they had, in fact, heard what they thought they'd heard, Josiah snagged a cookie from the tea tray and sat in one of the plush armchairs, thoroughly unconcerned with their response.

The council members exchanged alarmed glances, uncertain how to react to Josiah's statement. They appeared more shocked than grief-stricken, and I doubted Rachel Strait was the sort of woman to inspire mourning. Though I was still horrified by what I'd done, even I wasn't about to pretend I would miss the hate-filled woman.

Michael broke the silence first, clearing his throat several times in an attempt to force the words out. "Er, why?"

"Why am I confessing, or why did I do it?"

Michael's head bobbed up and down like a nervous chicken. "Yes," he said, grateful Josiah understood.

"I'm confessing because I no longer trust this council to see reason. Despite my daughter being innocent, you lot would have convicted her and sentenced her to death. As I have confessed and you no longer have a quorum, her trial is canceled. She will no longer be trapped in that house and will have access to the entire island. I'll take her place so we can all pretend you have me under control while you arrange for a fourth council member to arrive and begin my own farce of a trial." They looked uncertain about being given orders by a confessed murderer, but no one spoke against him, either. Even Deborah looked cowed by his utter certainty. "Unless you wish the elder Ms. Brook to be reinstated on the council for the trial and Aidan's sentencing? I didn't think so."

Deborah found her voice at last. "Josiah, we have both walked this earth a long time and had, I thought, earned a certain degree of wisdom." She focused briefly on his mismatched shoes before continuing. "I admit to being somewhat unsettled by your rash actions. Rachel was no friend of mine, but she was an old one, and this death is unacceptable. If elementals begin killing each other, what will our race become?"

"I'm not sure, Deborah. Will we even have a race if we start removing each other's magic?"

He spoke lightly, but the words fell like a bomb on the room. A big, awkward bomb.

"Does that answer the question of why I did it? Good, good. I'm sure we can all come to some nice compromise in which no one else dies and no one is deprived of their magic in order to prove some ridiculous point. Though, really, the latter is no longer an issue. It seems I broke all the syringes. Such fragile things, they are."

Waters weren't especially prone to rage, but you'd never guess it to watch the faces of the three remaining council members. Deborah, Michael, even Lydia glared at Josiah. If they'd been capable of harming him at that moment, I don't think they would have hesitated.

Josiah leaned back in his chair and nibbled the cookie.

Michael was either the bravest or the most foolish of the bunch. "But you weren't even on the island when Edith died. How can your daughter be innocent?"

Josiah pinned him with a stare that would cause a weaker man to lose control of his bladder and possibly a few other bodily functions. "Of course she's innocent. I just told you I did it. Are you calling me a liar?"

Michael blanched. I was accustomed to Josiah's unpredictable moods, and even I was getting whiplash trying to follow along.

For all intents and purposes, the council was now toothless, and everyone in the room knew it.

Josiah inclined his head, the barest of nods. "I will head directly to the cottage, where you will find me until this is resolved. You have my word I won't run. At least, not without giving you fair warning." He smiled, believing he'd told a joke. The others looked less certain, but they all nodded. His proposal wasn't ideal, but at least he wasn't attempting to set any of them on fire. They had to be grateful for small favors.

Josiah stood. "Your lovely hostess and the young Ms. Brook will escort me to the cottage. The three of you can use the time to discuss what you believe my punishment should be for murdering a woman who planned to inflict torture upon one of your own." The words were lightly spoken, but they were underscored by a current of rage. He walked away, only turning at the door to deliver a parting shot. "I suggest you remember why I was so angry with this particular council. The more extreme your decision regarding my sentence, the more inclined I'll be to share your novel approach to law and order with our fellow elementals. I'm sure at least one or two of them will understand your choice. As for the rest..." He let the unspoken words hang in the air. The council knew, if their actions became common knowledge, they wouldn't just have one powerful enemy on the island. They'd be hated by elementals across the world. It was one thing to quietly give me the drug, then ask for forgiveness once the effects were known. It was something else altogether to knowingly set a dangerous precedent.

He walked out of the library, and for the first time in my life, I willingly followed my father.

———

We walked along the southern shoreline, trying to avoid the rest of my family. There'd be time for explanations later, but right now I didn't think I could handle a single innocent question from a well-meaning relative.

I walked between my grandmother and my father, both of whom had just saved my life in one way or another, and tried to think of a way to broach the enormous, flame-colored elephant in the room.

As usual, tact was powerless against my gift for babbling. It might be highly inappropriate, considering what I'd just done, but it was either that or start screaming, and I thought if I started screaming I might not stop for several weeks.

"So, I'm going crazy and nearly killed a woman, a father I disowned less than a month ago stopped me at no small cost to himself, and my grandmother has learned the biggest secret of my life. How are things with you?"

"Don't be so modest, dear. This is likely the biggest secret among all elementals. Dual magics are the stuff of nightmares to us old ones. They wouldn't take kindly to knowing there's one among us."

"Will you tell?"

She snorted, a most unladylike noise. "And condemn my granddaughter to an instant death sentence? Don't be foolish. Did you kill Edith, by the way?"

I stopped walking and stared at her. "You're ready to protect me, and you don't even know if I'm innocent?"

She looked at me as if I'd gone a bit soft in the head. "You're family, Aidan. Family protects each other."

My throat tightened. Such faith was more than I deserved after staying away as long as I had. More to the point, it was more than I deserved after my part in Rachel's death. I wasn't sure I was worth protecting anymore, but I was glad she was willing to try.

Josiah threw his hands in the air. "That's what I've been

saying for months, but you tear up for her?"

I turned to study my father. He'd killed innocents to protect me, and he seemed to feel not the slightest shred of guilt for murdering Rachel. He was controlling and manipulative and, in general, possessed every single personality trait a good self-help book would tell you to avoid. I hated him.

At least, I was supposed to hate him, but right then I only remembered the way he'd forced my fire magic to return to me. If he hadn't done that, I wouldn't have only triggered the death, I'd have been its direct cause. I knew I wouldn't have stopped in time, just as I knew I couldn't cross that line without my tenuous grip on sanity disintegrating.

I was full of regret and horror for what I'd done, and I was terrified of how fast I was changing. I could no longer pretend I wasn't dangerous, but most of the time I was still sane.

Once I killed, I didn't think that would be true.

I knew Rachel's death was on my conscience, and I wouldn't forget that. I'd be haunted by what I'd done for as long as my sanity held. But in the end, it hadn't been my magic that killed her, and I thought that small detail might make a difference.

I was still me. I still had a chance.

Josiah's actions didn't just save me from myself. They bought me time. I didn't know how much, but I wasn't going to waste a minute of it.

"I need to go." They both looked surprised, and I knew I only had a second before they began making reasonable arguments why I should stay with them. I didn't give them the chance. "You don't need me. Besides, this way you'll have privacy to better plan my future, which I know you're both dying to do." Neither could argue with that.

I took off running for the western side of the island and

the houseboat that was anchored half a mile offshore.

I ran to Mac.

CHAPTER 18

The rowboat wasn't tied to the cottage. Simon or Miriam must have returned to the houseboat, and I wasn't going to waste time phoning them to bring it back. I left my shoes on the rocky beach, my cell phone tucked into the toes, and I jumped into the water fully dressed.

My water magic came eagerly. It was stronger than I'd felt in a long time, as if seeking to obliterate the memories of the fire. I welcomed it, wrapping myself in its power and asking it to speed me toward the boat.

It didn't take long before the houseboat came into view. Though it was afternoon, thick clouds covered the sun, leeching color until the sky and sea appeared to be the same shade of gray. A few interior lights were turned on inside the boat, beacons calling me to Mac.

I hauled myself up the ladder and stood dripping on the deck. It had stopped raining, but the open sea offered little protection against the breezes whispering against my damp skin. I pulled the water from skin and clothes. Once I was mostly dry, I stepped into the houseboat's sitting room.

Simon and Miriam played cards at the dining table. Based on Simon's intent expression and the fat pile of chips in front of Miriam, I guessed she was winning.

There was no sign of Mac.

They glanced up when I entered and nodded. "Any news?" asked Miriam, placing a card on the table.

"Um, yeah." I barely looked at them, my attention already fixed on Mac's door. A light shone from underneath. I walked toward it, calling over my shoulder. "Josiah killed Rachel Strait and confessed to all the murders, so Sera's trial is canceled and she's being released. And my sentencing will be delayed till the council again has a quorum. Also, we destroyed the drugs they planned to use as my punishment."

The silence behind me was heavy. If I turned, I suspected I'd see two confused shifters.

I would fill them in on the details later. Right now, I had better things to do.

I didn't bother to knock. I simply strode through the door and closed it behind me before Simon and Miriam had a chance to find their voices.

Mac was sitting up in bed, one of the mysteries I'd snagged from Grams' library in his hands.

I reached one hand behind me and locked the door, never taking my eyes from him. He closed the book but kept his thumb holding his place, as if he would return to reading soon.

It only took three steps to cross the small room. His eyes followed me, dark and curious, but still he said nothing. I plucked the book from his hand and set it on the bedside table.

"I know you're upset. I know you've spent a lot of your life fending for yourself, and you don't want to be dependent on anyone."

He watched me with cautious eyes, but he didn't interrupt.

"And maybe it's worse when you have no way to fix this and no one to blame. Hell, I've been mad at Carmichael for weeks, but we both know he was trying to protect me. We also know, if I hadn't saved you, you'd be dead now, and don't you dare tell me that's a better option than being tied to me."

He shook his head, a minute movement.

"But I've got enough going on right now, and my brain is full of more than I know how to handle. I can't deal with you being distant on top of everything else. As soon as I feel anything close to stable, I'm going to find a way to fix you. You know I will. So, and I mean this from the bottom of my heart, whatever anger you're feeling, get over it."

At last, I stopped speaking, waiting for the rage I knew lay just beneath his skin to erupt.

Instead, his mouth curved into a warm smile, and I swear I felt my soul lighten. "Okay."

"Okay?"

"Okay. I know you didn't do this, and I'm sorry if I was an ass. I just needed to work things through for myself. And hell, I've been sick off and on for the last week. I haven't really been at the top of my game. We're okay. We've always been okay. I just needed to sulk for a while."

I exhaled in relief. "Good. Look, today was a doozy and then some. I don't dare try to focus the magic. Tomorrow?"

"I can wait. Want to talk about it?"

I sat next to him, my hip brushing against his thigh, and I forced the memories of Rachel's death from my mind. I'd have plenty of time to relive them later. "I really don't. So I was thinking. You must be going stir crazy trapped on this boat."

He gave a rueful laugh. "You have no idea."

"You probably want to throw some more things, feel your muscles working. You haven't shifted in days, and you have all kinds of energy you need to release."

He raised an eyebrow, wondering where I was going with this.

I leaned toward him, letting every wicked impulse show

on my face. "Want to release some energy?"

Our eyes locked across the small space. We let the aware-
ness build, the knowledge that it was just the two of us,
alone in a room with a double bed. His nostrils flared, and I
knew his shifter nose picked up my desire. We were barely
touching, and already it was building, electricity humming
across my skin.

"What are you up to, Aidan?" His voice was low, with
more than a hint of a growl.

I'd said all the words I had to say, and I didn't want to
talk anymore. What was the point in dating a strong, silent
type if he didn't know when it was time to shut up? Instead
of answering, I placed my hands against the headboard, on
either side of his shoulders, and pulled myself onto the
bed, straddling his legs with mine. I drew my thigh muscles toward each other, gripping his body. It was a promise
of what was to come.

Mac's breath caught, and I watched the expressions
dance across his face, lust and uncertainty and something
so warm I dared not name it. His brown eyes heated, but
they stayed locked on my face, and we held the gaze as I
reached forward, running my hands from his broad shoulders down his arms.

I threaded our fingers together and stretched my legs
behind me, leaning forward to balance on top of him. I
aligned my body against his.

I paused, almost afraid to move. Already, I was flooded
with sensations that were distinctly Mac. He was the strongest man I'd ever known, his body offering a safe harbor.
There was little give in his chest muscles, his abs and
thighs, but his skin was soft and warm. I took a deep breath
and imagined I could scent his need. Not that I needed
to imagine much, with some mighty compelling evidence
pressing against me.

"What are you doing, Aidan?" Mac asked again, his voice thin and strangled.

"I'd think that was obvious." I unwound our hands and reached up, gripping the thick muscles of his shoulders. I pulled myself along his body, one slow inch after another, until our faces met. I smiled then, a smile as full of promise and hunger as any I'd ever allowed him to see. He strained toward me, but I pulled back, dropping my face into the curve of his neck.

I inhaled the warmth, the scent that belonged to Mac alone, and skimmed my lips across the skin. My tongue darted out, tasting, but it wasn't enough. It was too slow, too deliberate for the hunger claiming me. One nip, then another, then I sank my teeth into his skin. He gasped, a mix of surprise and pleasure, and I fought the voice telling me to deepen the bite. To mark him.

Reluctantly, I released his neck, soothing the teeth marks with my tongue. I lowered my head until my lips met the neckline of his white t-shirt, and I tugged it with my teeth. I wanted nothing between us. I needed to feel his skin, warm and sweaty, pressed against mine.

"Take it off," I said.

His voice was strained. "I don't want you to think I'm complaining, but what brought this on? Are we done waiting?"

"Fuck waiting," I told him. "Off."

I watched the smile spread across his face, the slow grin I sometimes hoped would be the last thing I saw before I died. He placed one enormous hand high on my chest and pressed gently, lifting me off his body.

I reached out to him, resenting the distance. The whole time, Mac watched me, his gaze intent, loaded with thoughts I could only begin to guess.

"Aidan, I'm not sure this is the best idea."

"I am." I tugged at his shirt again, wondering why it was still on his body. "I'm tired of thinking, Mac. I'm tired of waiting for some perfect moment that seems unlikely to ever come. I know this isn't it. I know I still need to undo the magic. But that's in the future, and I'm so tired of waiting for the future. We only get so many chances in life. Can we stop screwing this up?"

I had no warning. One moment I was straddling him, my hands sneaking underneath his t-shirt to feel the heated flesh. The next I was on my back, my wrists held in one of his hands and pinned above my head. He braced himself on his other forearm and his knees, sparing me most of his weight, but I still felt the press of his body, a welcome heaviness pushing me into the mattress.

"I don't plan on screwing anything up," he said, lowering his head to my neck and speaking the words against my skin. I squirmed, trying to get even closer to him. If I could have climbed inside him, I might have tried.

I arched my neck, giving him better access. "Do you plan on screwing anything else?"

I felt the rumble of laughter that started deep in his chest and moved outward, ending on the lips now pressed against my collarbone. "Classy."

My wrists were still pinned, and I fought against him, wanting his skin beneath my hands. His grip didn't lessen, but the effort raised both our shirts, pressing an inch of my bare skin against his.

"You know me. I'm classy lady." I undulated, urging our bodies closer together, the heat from that small contact moving through me.

Mac's lips slid upwards along the column of my throat. He grabbed my jaw between his teeth, holding my face in a soft bite. At last, he released my hands, running his own down the length of my arms, a slow caress from wrist to shoulder.

One hand moved to my face, cupping my cheek, while the other slid along my ribs, When he reached my waist, I fought for breath, unsure how much lower he'd send that hand. Instead, he slid it underneath me and lifted me toward him, fitting me tighter against his body.

He stared at me the way only Mac did, as if he saw things no one else ever would. I refused to look away. Whatever he saw, it was his, if he wanted it. I wouldn't hide from him.

"This isn't…"

I didn't let him finish. Whatever protest he was about to make, I had no interest in hearing it. I covered his mouth with my own, silencing all doubts.

The kiss radiated through my entire body until all I knew was Mac. I met his tongue and rocked my hips against his, wanting him more than I'd ever wanted food or warmth or air. His body and his touch, his lips and tongue and breath, they were everything. Absolutely everything.

When he pulled back, I chased his lips, a whimper escaping as my head rose off the pillow. Again, he captured my wrists, preventing me from touching him.

His breathing was ragged, his body as desperate as mine, but he fought to regain control. I writhed against him, reminding him how overrated control was in this particular situation.

He groaned, a low sound of pain and regret, and rolled off me in a single motion. He leaned against the closed door, putting painful distance between us.

I sat up. Frustration coursed through me, and it gave my words a sharper bite than I intended. "What? Seriously, what the hell is it this time?"

He didn't look offended by my anger. If anything, he seemed to share it. "I think you've forgotten something," he said. He shut his eyes tightly, as if even the sight of me was too much.

"Condoms? You know full-blooded elementals aren't that fertile." It wasn't the most compelling argument, I had to admit. Teenage boys in the back seats of their cars had come up with more convincing excuses. "But if you're worried, there are plenty of other things we can do." I let my eyes drop to the front of his jeans, where there was still evidence that part of his body was open to hearing arguments.

Teenage boys had nothing on me.

His face contorted at my words, the battle for control still being waged. "No, not condoms," he said. "We're on a boat. Rather close quarters."

"I can be quiet," I said, lying through my teeth.

"Well, I can't be. And even if we could, that's not the problem. We'd still have to deal with, you know." He jerked his head toward the door.

"With what?"

"Shifter ears," said Simon, as clearly as if he were in the room with us.

No cold shower had ever been so effective. I flopped backwards on the bed and pulled a pillow over my face, hoping that would hide my humiliation. "They heard everything?" I whispered.

"Yep." Miriam sounded far too amused by my pain and suffering.

That was it. I didn't want much in life. A pony, sure. World peace, okay. But right then, more than anything in the world, I wanted some quality naked time with Mac before the madness consumed me, and this was one obstacle too many. I jumped to my feet and flung the door open, glaring at the two friends I kind of hated at that moment.

"Can you please leave us alone for an hour?" Mac muttered something behind me. I was underestimating his prowess. "Two hours?"

Simon looked at me, expression wry. "Let me be sure I understand this. You are asking me and Miriam to take the rowboat out in orca-infested waters just so you and Mac can finally consummate your relationship? This despite the fact that the two of you spent weeks actively *not* having sex when you could have done so in relative privacy?"

I nodded. "Exactly."

Simon gave me the look I probably deserved. "No."

Miriam shrugged. "Sorry, Brook. I hate to cock block you, but the cat has a point."

I grumbled, loudly. I could accept their reasoning, but that didn't mean I had to be gracious about it.

"We can take off for a bit tomorrow," Miriam volunteered. I resisted giving her a grateful kiss. Just.

My joy was short lived as reality came crashing down. "We can't. Tomorrow night, I have to try to cure Mac. This has gone on long enough. And during the day I should probably try to clear my father." I was surprised to discover I meant that, too. Our relationship was complicated, to say the least, but Josiah had saved me today. I needed to try to repay that gift.

"Care to fill us in on just what happened today?" Miriam looked at me a little too closely, as if wondering which parts of the story I'd omitted.

They deserved to know. They should know, for their own safety and for mine. I needed people I trusted watching my back.

I didn't want to tell them. I didn't want Simon to decide it was safer to permanently live with Carmen. I didn't want Miriam, my newest friend, to figure out I was more bother than I was worth. More than anything, I couldn't stand for Mac to put distance between us again.

But those were my worries, my insecurities, and I couldn't let them make the decision for me. I opened my mouth to tell them what I'd almost done to Rachel.

I didn't get one word out before the three shifters covered their sensitive ears. Even I winced at the noise.

It took me a second to understand what I was hearing. I'd only heard such a sound once before, the day of my trial. The day Edith was killed.

Horror flooded me as another explosion assaulted our ears. The deafening noise came from the island.

CHAPTER 19

I didn't wait to see how the others reacted. I dove into the sea and called every bit of magic I possessed to push me toward the shore. I didn't need to guess where the explosions originated. Despite the distance between the houseboat and the beach, my fire instinctively knew, and it urged me toward the western side of the island.

When the shore was in sight, a third blast, even louder than the first two, fueled my panic. My ears rang, but I refused to spare any magic to speed their healing. I needed to reach the house. I needed to reach Sera.

I didn't beat the crowd drawn to the western side of the island by the explosion. I dragged myself from the sea and stumbled across the shore, feet churning in sand that seemed determined to trap me.

Fire, Sera could survive. It only made her stronger. It's what fueled her, what defined her. She could stand in a bonfire and only have a healthy glow to show for her troubles.

An explosion, however, would have an entirely different effect. Sera couldn't repair her body if it was blown into hundreds of tiny pieces.

I crossed the hundred feet or so to the small cottage. It was even smaller, now that everything except the back wall lay in pieces on the beach.

The house was completely obliterated. Wood and plaster were strewn across the ground, along with chunks of furniture and broken glass. Stubborn flames clung to the wreckage, and black smoke rose against the darkening sky.

My fire reached toward it, curious and greedy, and I didn't try to stop it.

I studied the debris with panicked eyes, looking for any sign of Sera or Josiah buried beneath the rubble. A single shoe rested near the gathered waters, a beat-up old boot Sera had worn the day before. I froze, unable to move any closer lest I discover the shoe still held a foot.

Though the others could have easily put out the flames, they chose to stand quietly, murmuring amongst themselves as they watched the house burn.

"What happened?" I demanded of no one in particular. "Where's Sera?"

Many chose not to meet my eyes, and those who did looked at me with pity. No one answered, until Grams stepped out of the crowd.

"I haven't seen her. We only arrived a minute ago."

I inched toward the burning remains that had once been a house, dreading what I might find. There were no steps to climb, but I grabbed onto the scarred floor and prepared to boost myself up. Strong arms grasped my arms, Grams and my mother pulling me back.

"Think, Aidan." My mother spoke in a whisper no one else could hear. "You can't go in there. The fire would kill you."

It wouldn't, of course, but it was a necessary reminder that the others would be mighty surprised to see me walk unharmed through the flames.

They'd have no idea if I accessed that part of my magic, however. I turned away, hiding my expression as I ceded control to my other half, and I sent the fire across the island.

I moved it in a radius, one hundred feet in every direction, looking for any sign someone else was accessing their magic. When I found nothing, I moved further down the beach and tried again, and then again, until at last I felt it. It was weak and fading, but it was undoubtedly a fire elemental.

I felt no anger right now. Shock and fear and horror, but no anger, so when it was time to release the fire and call my water back to me, it didn't fight. I sent my magic into the ocean, where I'd picked up the signal, and asked it to grab hold. One thick wave after another fell across the shore, dousing the fire and sweeping the pieces that had once been a house out to sea. Even when the flames were extinguished, I kept going, ordering the ocean to the beach time and again.

The eighth wave I called returned a water-logged computer to the land along with two fire elementals.

"Sera!" I ran toward her limp body. She looked awful. Her clothes were torn and blackened, and while she appeared to have four limbs and a head, she wasn't moving.

She wasn't breathing, either. I thought I'd been panicked before, but that had only been a teaser. It was like the sand and my own body conspired to keep me from her, every movement pained and sluggish.

Josiah lay next to her, flat on his back and staring at the stars.

After what felt like a small eternity, I reached Sera and roughly pulled her upright. "Hold on," I told her. With no other warning, I launched my magic into her lungs, grabbing hold of the water she'd inhaled and forcing it upwards, out of her body.

It wasn't enough. I repeated the action, expelling every last drop until her lungs were empty. She was alive, damn it. She just needed to breathe.

I knew I couldn't bring a second person back to life

without ruining myself. I also knew, if it came to that, I would do it anyway. This was Sera.

I didn't look behind me, but I sensed my family circling us. While their silent support was better than nothing, it still wasn't enough.

I focused inward, trying to recreate the anger and desperation and clarity of the night I healed Mac. Maybe I would have found it, had my mother not grabbed my hair and yanked my head backwards, distracting me. Her message was clear: whatever the cost, she would not let me destroy myself.

That day, at least, it didn't prove necessary.

There was no space between death and life. One moment she was limp and still. The next, her eyes flew open and her body convulsed, retching and coughing, attempting to reject the intrusion of the water and my magic.

"Oh, thank you. Thank you." The words came out in a sob, gratitude and relief battling the slow anger I allowed myself to feel, now that I knew she would live.

"Serafina." A hand reached out to grab hers. Josiah, looking weaker than I'd ever seen him, stared at his daughter. When he met my eyes, I saw the same potent mix of emotions that coursed through me.

If someone didn't die for this explosion, it wouldn't be for lack of trying on his part.

Even so, our priority was still Sera, and we watched her closely, needing confirmation that she was unharmed.

She looked between us. I was used to seeing her black eyes glowing with intelligence and energy, but at that moment she only looked tired. Tired, and a tiny bit amused. "This is what it takes to make you stop fighting? You two are hard work."

Somehow, I found a way to smile around the sobs that threatened to burst from me. "Still more pleasant than a group therapy session, right?"

She started to laugh, which turned into a cough. Josiah patted her back, ignoring her dark glare and mutters about not needing to be burped.

At last, she sat up on her own. Color returned to her face, and I thought she was reaching out to the few small flames I hadn't succeeded in putting out, feeding on them as best she could.

Josiah stood. Though he was unsteady on his feet, he already appeared mostly healed. The waters all took several steps back as he moved around the shore. He paid them no attention. They meant nothing to him.

Instead, he picked up the largest piece of wood he could find and fed the flame, building it into a respectable bonfire and placing it next to Sera.

I closed my eyes, hoping "out of sight, out of mind" applied to magic, as well. I could still feel the fire's warmth, even feel Sera's magic reaching toward it. Several deep breaths later, I was as controlled as I was likely to be, and I opened my eyes to see Josiah, Sera, my mother, and Grams all staring at me in concern.

"I'm fine," I muttered, irritated. "Can we just once not worry about me going off the deep end?" My aunts looked at each other in confusion, but I was too exhausted to speak in code. "What the hell happened here?"

Josiah stared at what had once been a house, his face ricocheting from anger to confusion to doubt, none of which comforted me. If Josiah didn't know what was happening or why, there was little hope for the rest of us.

Sera stood shakily, but once she was upright she gained strength by the minute. She continued to feed on the fire, walking in slow circles around the flames. Sera always thought best when she was moving, so I took this as a good sign.

"It happened so fast. I was in the kitchen, getting something to drink—"

"The wine!" Marie interrupted, her face horrified at the loss of so much quality booze. "Is it all gone?" Tina wrapped a consoling arm around her in a moment of shared and inappropriate grief.

"—And there was a loud noise. I thought it might be a gunshot at first." She swallowed, and she wasn't the only one who looked nervous. Elementals lived exceptionally long lives, but our magic had its limits. We'd been born from the union of magic and humans. It was our origin story, and our weakness. It was why we looked human, and it was why a gunshot or knife wound or explosion would kill us as easily as it would any human.

Suffice it to say, elementals donated a lot of money to gun safety groups and spent little time at firing ranges.

Sera shook her head to clear it. "My father was in the living room, and the blast threw him backwards. He slammed into the kitchen counter."

Josiah rubbed the base of his spine. "The force was strong enough to break my back." He said this the way a human might say they stubbed their toe. "Fortunately, by this point the house was already catching fire, so I was able to heal it before the second blast."

Sera looked at the ruined house. "The second was in the bedroom."

"Which one?" I interrupted.

"Yours." We exchanged a long look, one full of questions. We didn't know if the bomber thought I was still there, or if they'd been informed Josiah would be staying in the house. Though someone new might be trying to kill me, I felt only relief that Sera wasn't the target.

Josiah didn't share my relief. His face darkened at the mere possibility that someone might want me dead. "We didn't want to see if the third time was the charm, so I grabbed Sera and jumped through the new hole created in the living room floor. We landed in the ocean, and I tried to swim toward the shore, but the third blast pushed us the other direction."

Sera stopped pacing, and her voice was so tightly controlled I could only guess at the turmoil below her words. "And then I don't remember anything. The third one knocked us out, at least until you found us."

I released a ragged breath. She was alive. Logically, I knew this. She was right before me, breathing on her own, her wounds from the explosions already healed by the fire. Somehow, it wasn't enough. Part of me, that place far below the conscious mind, the part that rejected rationality and empirical facts, refused to believe Sera and Josiah were safe.

If they'd been in the bedroom when it exploded, they wouldn't be. If I'd been a few minutes later, they wouldn't be. If I hadn't accessed my fire side to find them, they wouldn't be.

It was pure dumb luck that they were still here, and I wasn't ready to count on our luck holding.

I stood and faced the island residents, looking at each one in turn. Everyone was present. My extended family. Lana and David. The council. Whoever had done this, they were here, watching.

One by one, their gazes dropped. I doubted it was guilt that caused them to avoid my stare. I could feel the rage and anger in my eyes, the gray hardening to steel. My face didn't feel fluid and expressive. It might as well have been sculpted from granite. I didn't show them anger, for that's not what I felt. I felt cold.

"Someone on this island did this." My voice was clear, the words carrying with no effort to every witness. "Someone attempted to kill my best friend and her father. I do not care that Josiah confessed to all the murders. I do not care that the fire elementals are strangers to most of you. I really don't care about anything right now, except finding the person who did this and making them pay. You may think Josiah had it coming, but you are wrong. He is innocent, and only confessed to spare his daughter. I am absolutely certain of this." The crowd started at my proclamation, and behind me Josiah protested. I ignored them all. I was so tired of lies and half-truths and secrets. "If you take two seconds to think about it, you'll know I'm right. This was an explosion, same as the one that killed Edith Lake. Whoever created that explosion did this one, as well, and Sera and Josiah sure as hell didn't try to blow themselves up. Someone else did this, just as someone else killed Edith."

I paused letting my words sink in.

"What about Rachel?"

I sought out the speaker, finding him standing between the two remaining council members.

"Do you really want to discuss why Josiah killed Rachel at this particular moment, Michael?"

He held my gaze for only a second before dropping his eyes in defeat.

The crowd murmured questions, and I spoke again, refusing to allow them to be distracted.

"Sera and Josiah will be staying with me tonight, on a houseboat anchored to the west. I am giving no one else a chance to hurt them."

I stared at the three remaining council members, daring them to disagree. They no longer looked like powerful representatives of one of the elementals' oldest bodies. They looked scared and uncertain, willing to hand over control to someone else if it meant they could live long enough to get off this island. One by one, they nodded.

"No one on this island is safe. We may not understand what is happening, but we know that much. Don't be alone. Call on your element often, to stay strong." As I spoke, I sent out my own magic, knowing every scared water on the island was doing the same. My magic intertwined with my aunts', my mother's, my grandmother's. It found Lana's, splashing in a nearby canal, and circled to my extended family, people I hadn't seen in years but whose magic I still knew. I even sent it toward the council. I danced between them all, reminding them what we shared.

It was what connected us to the land and the water, but it was also what connected us to each other. As our power greeted one elemental after another, tension disappeared from shoulders and faces lightened, distrust easing with the reminder of what we meant to each other.

When I spoke again, I found my anger and coldness had vanished. "We will solve this, but we must work together. No more secrets. If you know anything you believe will find the person committing these awful crimes, you must tell me. For all our safety, we must end this."

The group nodded. I knew there were holes in my argument, and it wouldn't be long before people thought to ask questions to which I didn't have the answers. For now, though, they were caught in the spell of shared magic and my absolute certainty.

Then, the spell broke.

"Who are they? What are they doing here?" Michael Bay pointed one shaking finger toward the water, and the entire island turned to watch three shifters pulling to shore in a battered old rowboat.

CHAPTER 20

"A welcoming party? How thoughtful of you." Simon sounded entirely sincere, and only the glint in his green eyes gave any hint that he sensed the animosity rolling off the elementals in waves.

He stepped lightly from the boat, every movement precise. Simon was always graceful, but I thought he was emphasizing it now. The slit pupils he'd learned to hide during his time with Carmen had returned, and even his canines appeared a bit longer than usual.

He would not hide what he was, and he would not apologize for it.

Miriam stepped out next. She didn't possess Simon's grace outside the water, but she had at least twice his attitude. She looked at the elementals lined up before her, pale and reed thin, and the devil's own grin appeared on her face. If I was translating otter to English, I'm pretty sure the message would be "bring it."

Mac was last, and there was an audible gasp as he unfolded from the boat. Waters might be a tall group of people, but we had nothing on bear shifters. While anyone standing on that shore was powerful enough that, if unopposed, they could send him out to sea on a large wave, it was hard to remember one had the upper hand when faced with a man-shaped wall of pure muscle.

Part of me wanted to throw them into the boat and send

it careening back to the houseboat. I was sure the waters would all be happy to pretend this visit had never occurred.

A bigger part sighed in relief, both at the sight of my friends and at the knowledge that one more secret was revealed. Besides, their presence posed no real danger, other than to the elementals' understanding of the world—and if there was one group of people in the world that needed their preconceptions challenged, it was the people on this island.

Michael found his voice first. "What is that?" He pointed at Mac. I could practically see Mac's hackles rise. I wasn't sure if I had hackles, but if I did they were rising alongside his.

Josiah, Sera, and my close family stood behind me, lined up where the water met the shore. The rest of the island stood to the east in a large clump of prejudice and fear. The three shifters had landed about fifty feet to the north.

I stood between them all.

I suppose I made a choice, though I don't recall doing so. I only knew that I walked to Mac, taking long, confident strides, until I was at his side. "I guess the council isn't invited to the wedding." I winked at him, letting him know I was teasing, but I saw no humor in his eyes. Only heat mixed with relief and something close to gratitude.

The rest of the island didn't find the joke funny, either.

A moment ago, they'd all been ready to link arms and sing songs in the name of magical unity. Now, they looked like they were ready to fire up some torches and go in search of pitchforks.

Not all of them. A few looked surprised, even curious. My aunts studied the newcomers as if they were an unexpected specimen in a biology textbook. Grams glanced between me and Mac, likely making all the right connections.

I was thankful my great-grandmother wasn't here to witness this. She was the one who'd raised me to believe shifters were nothing but myths, and I doubted her presence would have smoothed the current tensions.

"Everything okay?" Mac asked in a low voice.

"More or less," I assured him. "Everyone's alive, at least."

I turned from him, needing to calm the side of the island that looked like they shared Great-grandma's opinion. "So, these are shifters. They exist." It seemed obvious to me, but there were still so many doubtful expressions I wanted to be extra clear. In addition to doubt, I saw anger and outrage, shock and disbelief. Basically, all the shades of horror one would expect from a group who would rather deny shifters' existence than acknowledge we shared our magical heritage with those who possessed animal DNA.

"It's bad enough that you allow three humans on the island, Ms. Brook. To lie about their origins is a step too far. We all know shifters are a myth." Deborah Rivers wouldn't even look at my friends, addressing her words to the waters gathered around her. Still, no one watched her. They couldn't take their eyes off our visitors, trying to reconcile years of lies and denial with the counter-evidence standing on their shore.

They might have clung more stubbornly to their disbelief if Simon hadn't chosen that moment to turn into a cat.

As one, the crowd gasped, then subsided into silence as the small black creature walked toward them. He kept his distance, giving himself space to run if necessary, but to look at him, he was the pinnacle of feline confidence. He strutted down the line of gathered waters. Once he was convinced they'd all seen him, he returned to human form and strolled buck naked back to the clothes that had fallen from him when he changed to the smaller form. In no hurry, he pulled his jeans back on, then turned to face everyone with a smug, close-lipped smile.

While the elementals gaped, Miriam smacked Simon's ass. "Drama queen," she said with a chuckle, loud enough for everyone to hear.

That broke the spell. At once, everyone had something to say, a question or protest or, in some cases, panicked non-sense. I let it go on for a few minutes—sometimes, waters just need to get the words out before they explode—then nodded to Sera.

She put her fingers to her lips and gave a loud, piercing whistle, the kind I'd never figured out how to do myself. It caught everyone off guard, and I stepped into the silence.

"Once again, for the record: these are shifters. They exist, and despite what some will try to tell you, they are not our enemy. We have people and houses exploding, or being burnt to a crisp, and that happened long before these three stepped foot onto the island. So, you know, deal."

It didn't seem worth mentioning that Miriam and Simon had been hanging out on the island for days.

Sera snorted. It seemed she was improved enough to find my tactlessness amusing.

"This isn't the big deal you all seem to think it is. There have always been shifters, and if you were unaware of their existence, you should probably make more of an effort to get off the island from time to time. So go home, open a bot-tle of wine, and know that reality hasn't actually changed. Just your knowledge of it. Sera, Josiah, the shifters and I will all be heading out to the boat, unless someone offers their guest room to two fires and the three shifters you want to pretend are figments of your imagination. Anyone?" I finished with a bright and wholly insincere smile.

To no one's surprise, my offer fell flat.

"Fine. We'll see you in the morning." With that, I turned

my back on the waters who'd once called me family.

Tomorrow was going to be a bad day. Once the island had time to process what they'd seen, to fit it into their understanding of the world and start looking for someone to blame, things would get complicated. That was tomorrow, though. Tonight, we all just needed to sleep.

Sera and Josiah climbed into the boat with the shifters. That left no room for me, particularly as the tension that still existed between my father and Mac practically required its own seat.

Miriam glanced at the overcrowded boat and started undressing. "I'm counting on you to be on orca patrol, Brook. I don't plan to meet my maker anytime soon, and I intend to do so while riding some pretty young thing, not as a midnight snack for some fucking oversized fish."

I grinned, taking a moment to let go of all that day's horrors. "Like I'd deny any of those pretty young things the glory of your presence, Miriam. Let's go."

She stepped into the surf, and a second later an otter poked its head above the water, waiting.

For the final time that day, I jumped into the surf and headed toward the houseboat, pulling a rowboat and its motley crew behind me.

It wasn't late, the sun only just setting, but no one seemed interested in staying up and talking. It had been a long day, and we were too exhausted to do anything but sleep.

The houseboat didn't have room for all of us, particularly as I was unwilling to share Mac's bed with Josiah nearby. Shifter ears only meant we risked embarrassment. Having an overprotective father on board meant we risked Mac being set on fire if Josiah felt he crossed some line.

Instead, Simon and Miriam took blankets to the roof.

They muttered something about a clear night and the stars, but since the sky was still covered with heavy clouds, I suspected they really wanted to put as much distance between themselves and Josiah as possible. Josiah was many things, but a paragon of elemental tolerance wasn't one of them. He would always believe shifters were inferior to elementals, and he made little effort to disguise this fact.

Sera and I agreed to share the second bedroom, leaving Josiah to the couches.

Silently, we prepared for bed, washing our faces and raiding the houseboat's limited food supply. Despite everything that happened that day, I felt no desire to sleep. I was too wired, too aware of Mac's presence just a few feet away.

At least I had an excuse to visit him once before bed. I closed the door to his bedroom, needing at least one private moment, even if I had to resort to mime to get my message across without anyone eavesdropping.

"Do you have a t-shirt I can borrow?" All our belongings were either burnt or in pieces, so it seemed a reasonable request. At least it did, until he removed the shirt he was wearing and held it out to me. Reason pretty much disappeared altogether.

"Thanks." I took it and pressed it against my chest, as much to feel his warmth as to create a highly ineffective barrier between us.

His eyes slid toward the door. "Why is Josiah here?" He pitched his voice low. The shifters above us might be able to hear, but elementals were stuck with standard human hearing.

I shook my head, trying to clear it of the fog caused by his half-dressed status. "His house exploded, and no one else would take him. Or if they did, that house might blow up next. I couldn't very well leave him to sleep on the beach."

"Why not? You hate him."

"It's complicated."

"And yet, I'm capable of holding more than one thought in my head at a time. What's going on?"

"It's not that you won't understand. It's more that they're words I'm not ready to say out loud." I stared at him, begging him to allow me this moment.

He shook his head, and though his voice remained quiet, the words held an edge they hadn't before. "That's not good enough. You're off, Aidan. There's this energy coming off you, this manic desperation. It was there earlier, when you came to me. I wanted to believe it was because you stopped fighting this thing between us, but there's more to it, isn't there? A man you're supposed to hate, a man who actively despises me, is just outside that door, and you're acting like you're okay with this."

"I'm not." I was glad we were whispering. The words and thoughts crowding my head were too unbearable to be spoken at full volume.

I stepped toward him, laying my hand against his chest. It wasn't a lascivious touch, nor one of invitation. I only wanted to feel the steady beat of his heart. I wanted to believe the connection we shared went beyond magic and desire and the friendship we'd built over the past months. I wanted his heart, and I didn't know if I'd have it once I spoke the truth.

"I lost control today. Josiah stopped me from killing a woman by killing her himself. I set it all in motion, Mac. She's dead because of me." I paused, just long enough for the words to sink in. I watched his face closely, seeing the shock and the brief recoil. He recovered quickly, but it was there. "The madness is starting. We're not meant to hold two magics, Mac, and the schism has been forming in my psyche since the first time I touched the fire. Earlier, even the water wanted Rachel's death, and that's never happened before. Soon, I won't be the person I am now. The woman you want to be with, she'll be gone. So yes, I'm desperate. I want everything I can get before it's too late, and that includes you. It may not be fair, but I want you. Sometimes, it feels like that's the only thing I want in this world."

When I finished my speech, Mac opened his mouth to reply. At that moment, I knew more fear than I had when I heard my sentence, when I saw Sera accused, when the fire blazed through me. His words could change everything, and I wasn't ready for that. Maybe in the morning, when the sun was bright and full of the day's promise, and the blue ocean stretched all around me, I could handle whatever he needed to tell me, but the night felt dark and full of quiet monsters ready to steal my last hope.

Instead of letting him speak, I backed away. I tried to smile, but even I could feel how false it was. "Tell me tomorrow." I gestured upstairs, where Simon and Miriam were certainly hearing every word, and past the closed door, where Josiah was likely making a list of all the reasons I shouldn't date any man, ever, and certainly not a shifter. "Tell me when we're alone, and when we've cured you. When you aren't bound to me anymore, tell me then if you think you can handle being at my side."

He only watched me, and whatever he was thinking, it didn't show on his face.

My throat began to close, and I stepped through the bedroom door before he noticed.

I kept my face down, avoiding Josiah and Sera's eyes, and rushed to the second bedroom. With Mac's shirt wrapped around me, I crawled into bed. When Sera entered soon after, I feigned sleep.

Long after she'd fallen asleep herself, I remained awake,

taking long breaths, trying to absorb Mac's scent and, in some small way, keep him with me always.

CHAPTER 21

Though I fell asleep with my thoughts muddled and my general sense of well-being threatening to pitch itself into the pit of despair, I woke with excess energy and a clear mind, my plan for that day worked out during the wee hours by my subconscious.

At some point during the night, my brain found space for the previous day's events, for Rachel's death and my loss of control. It wrapped the memories in fragile tissue paper, a delicate container that would crumble at the slightest touch. It wasn't much, and it wasn't a permanent solution, but it might let me get through another day.

Truly, there's a lot to be said for a good night's sleep surrounded by water.

My optimism lasted as long as it took me to reach the houseboat's tiny kitchen and discover there was no caffeine to be had.

Sera was already there, opening every cabinet and drawer in search of anything that might resemble coffee.

Josiah's couch was empty, and the rowboat was missing. His presence tended to complicate matters, so I wasn't sad to see him gone.

"Screw this," Sera announced, not bothering to lower her voice. "We're making a break for it. If there's no morning coffee, there's nothing to live for, anyway."

At her words, I gathered water behind us and started

pushing, urging the boat closer to the island. Now that the secret was out, there was no reason for me to keep swimming back and forth. Besides, I was fairly certain my fire side enjoyed the physical activity, and I was determined to do everything in my power to keep the fire sullen and unresponsive—and if that meant not burning a single unnecessary calorie then, by jove, I'd do what needed to be done.

There was rustling on the roof, and it was only a matter of time before the shifters joined us. Miriam's phone lay on the table. As mine and Sera's hadn't survived the explosion, we needed the loaner for the day. I shoved the phone into my pocket, then scrawled a quick note apologizing for the theft.

As the houseboat approached the shore, I stepped onto the deck, knowing Sera would follow. Together, we jumped into knee-high water and walked toward dry land.

Some might say I was avoiding my shifter friends, now that they all knew what was happening to me. I preferred to think of it as working for truth and justice in a way that didn't involve me answering unpleasant questions. But the emphasis was totally on the truth and justice part.

As soon as we were on shore, I rang my mother, hoping the cameras had managed to catch something this time. I knew what she'd say before she answered. There was nothing to see. The camera had exploded along with the rest of the house, and the backup file had been wiped clean.

"So, what's the plan?" asked Sera when I hung up. I faced my best friend and got my first good look at what she was wearing. While I still had the clothes I'd worn the day before, hers had been victims of the explosion. Lacking anything of her own, she'd been forced to borrow from Miriam, who was several inches taller than she was. She'd picked an old concert tee featuring The Who, probably because it was the closest she could come to her beloved punk, and had knotted it at her waist so it mostly fit, though the sleeves neared her elbows. The pants were cinched with a belt, keeping them from pooling at her ankles, but the thighs bagged and the legs had been rolled up several times. The end result looked like a child playing dress-up while on her way to a classic rock clambake.

"Don't even laugh. You know I'm totally making this work."

"I'm sorry. I hadn't realized your brief imprisonment affected your mind so much." Silence greeted my jab. Sanity jokes just didn't land like they once did. "So, Josiah told you?"

"That you tried to turn Rachel into a sparkler for the Fourth of July? Yeah, he might have mentioned something."

"Come on. As uptight as that woman was, you know she'd explode like a bottle rocket." Sera didn't say anything. Instead, she studied her shoes, avoiding my eyes. "Don't do that. Don't you dare do that."

"Do what?"

"Start acting awkward, or trying to say the right thing. There is no right thing here, and even if there was, we've never been the people who find the right thing to say. See exhibit A, that completely insensitive bottle rocket comment. You think you'll help me by acting like someone else? I'm barely keeping it together as it is. Just be the same person you've always been."

"You mean the sort of person who makes inappropriate jokes while her best friend slides toward insanity? That's who you want me to be?"

I nodded vehemently. "Yes. God, yes please. I seriously can't handle another soulful and worried gaze from someone who claims to only want the best for me. I'm worried enough about myself. I can't be weighed down with everyone else's worries on top of that."

She was quiet again, but it was the silence of thought rather than avoidance. Finally she shook her head, clearing it. "If you're getting more in touch with your fire side, does that mean you'll stop listening to that country shit one of these days?"

"Please. The day you catch me listening to the Cramps is the day you'll know I've lost my mind. Just stick me in a padded room. A non-flammable one, of course."

"Of course." She reached up to tug on her curly hair, the agitated movement showing she wasn't as glib as she wanted to appear. "I am worried though. You can't tell me not to be."

"I know. Me too. I just don't know how much good that will do either of us. And until we come up with a better plan, I need my friends. I need my sister. I need to not be the pariah and the freak. Please, Sera."

Her face was immobile, the surest sign that her emotions were in turmoil. "You know I'm here. I'll always be here. Though, really, you were always a freak. Let's not pretend this is a recent development."

I pulled a small ball of water from the air and dumped it on her in response. She gave me an impressive side eye, but she didn't protest. Any sign that I was in touch with my water side was welcome, it appeared. The shower broke the tension, and we walked for several minutes in companionable silence.

I broke it when we were half a mile from the Brook family estate. "You sure you want to come with me? Josiah may have cleared your name, but I'm guessing you're going to get the stink-eye from most people just for being his daughter, and you know some will still suspect you."

"One near death experience and you think I've gone soft? I can handle a bunch of waters. There's not a single person on the island who can out-stare me."

"Only cause Great-grandma's scaring the bejeezus out of everyone in Martha's Vineyard." She couldn't argue. She'd met my great-grandmother.

We strolled along the back streets, working our way to the house. We didn't pass anyone, and I was glad of it. There'd be plenty of confrontations soon enough.

Sera seemed to pick up on my train of thought. "So, what's the plan? Start accusing people until someone snaps and tries to set us on fire?"

"Amazingly, I've heard worse plans. If we are dealing with a dual magic, we have to assume they've been riding the crazy train longer than I have, to be using the fire magic so cruelly. But we should probably save that one as a last resort."

"You're still thinking dual magic?"

I held my hands up, palms out, showing just how little idea I really had. "It makes the most sense. You and Josiah are the only fires we know about, and the island isn't big enough to hide another one for so many days, particularly when everyone is paranoid and paying extra attention. Plus, Josiah's been testing for magic pretty consistently, and he hasn't found any yet. A fire pretending to be a different elemental would need to tap into their magic by now, but dual magics don't. Hell, I went most of my life just accessing water. So if there's another answer, I haven't thought of it yet."

"I still think something's off with David. He's not just here as Lana's guest."

"Maybe. He did get more upset than a stone should when I wouldn't help him escape from the island."

"There you go. How can you not think he's suspicious? Everyone else on the island is either a local or from a seriously old family. They wouldn't be able to keep such a secret for long." I pointed to myself, noting out the error in her logic. "Yes, but we've already established you're a freak. And we can't really say you're doing great with that whole secrecy thing, either."

She was right. Grams knew, and I had to trust she'd never tell. The Tahoe shifter contingent all knew. Hell, even two FBI agents knew what I was, and they were human.

"I forgot to ask, with everything going on. Did Vivian get back to you with info about the rest of the names? My phone is currently buried in the rubble from the explosion, so she can't call me." As I spoke, I pulled Miriam's from my pocket. I hadn't memorized Vivian's number, so I couldn't text her, but I logged into an email program and sent her a short message, telling her how to reach us.

"No. Though my phone also blew up, so she'd have a really good excuse for not contacting us. Maybe we should get the agents working on that list of names Robin gave you. I know they're not as good as Vivian, but they at least want to be part of the gang."

I stopped dead, the name triggering a thought I should have had days ago. "Oh."

Sera waited for the gears in my head to slowly turn.

"Oh hell. We might have been idiots."

"How so?"

"Robin. All this time, we've been thinking she knew something about a person who came to the island, or maybe left it. What if she was coming to tell me about a delivery? Not someone, but something that wasn't included in the manifest she photocopied for me."

It only took a second for Sera to catch up. "You're thinking someone shipped explosives to the island."

"I think we've been as narrow-minded as any old one, focused all this time on magical solutions instead of human ones. If it was explosives…"

"It changes everything," she finished. "It could have been anyone. Water, stone, fire, even shifter. It could be a human. They wouldn't have even needed to be in a hundred foot radius. They could have detonated it from anywhere on the island. Hell, they could have done it from a boat anchored offshore."

She sounded disgusted, either by how slow we were to consider this option or by the way our homicidal pyromaniac played dirty.

My excitement at finding a new theory was short-lived. "It doesn't explain Robin. She was still in one piece when we found her. No one blew her up."

"Maybe it doesn't explain everything, but it's at least a place to start."

I was sick of this. I was sick of being stuck on a small island with small-minded people, waiting to hear my sentence. I was tired of being stared at by the people who'd raised me as if I was a stranger. I was tired of watching people die.

Not today, though. Today, I was going to stop it. I didn't have much investigative experience, but I was stubborn, and I was homesick, and that would have to be good enough.

ROBIN'S POST REMAINED abandoned, the seaplane and boats still sitting neglected in the water. Despite the previous night's explosion, no one was attempting to leave, though that didn't mean they felt safe. Our walk across the island had been a silent one. I saw a few curtains twitch as we passed, but no one greeted us and doors remained resolutely shut. Whatever sense of unity I'd created last night, it lasted only so long as it took people to remember their lives were in danger.

"So, what are we looking for?" Sera asked.

There wasn't much to see. Robin's desk outside. A shed converted to an office where the files and copy machine were kept. A metal table that held a microwave and a coffee maker so old the brand name had rubbed off.

"Suspicious stuff." I closed my eyes and breathed deeply, trying to clear my mind of its preconceptions and see the scene afresh. "You know, murder weapons, confessions written in blood, that sort of thing."

"Or a leftover crate of C4?"

"Now you're talking."

The entire area was pristine, not a single package waiting to be picked up.

Robin's desk was spotless, more than it had ever been while she was alive. There were no half-full mugs, no disorganized piles of paper, no romance novels with their spines cracked at the juicy parts. My throat tightened at the sight. It made Robin's death feel so sanitized, almost as if the woman had been erased.

I rifled through Robin's papers, looking for any possible information so important it cost her life. Any hope I had was extinguished as soon as I opened the file cabinets. They were too organized. Someone had already gone through them, probably days ago.

Everything was in perfect order, the log maintained in Robin's neat script. The last entry was the same one she'd copied for me.

Except it shouldn't have been the last entry. There was no record of either our arrival on the island or David's trip to Bellingham, though I knew Robin would have noted both flights. She'd been too conscientious for such a large oversight.

No, the last page had simply been removed. I might be a rank amateur with this whole sleuthing thing, but I was pretty sure those in the detecting business would call this a clue. If nothing else, it confirmed that someone was trying to hide information we needed.

Sera gestured at the plane. "It's only a six-seater. Not much room for cargo, right?"

"Not really. How much, um, explosive stuff does it take to blow up a house?"

"Truly, it's a mystery why the FBI didn't fight harder to keep us."

"Hey, they're practically begging to work with us again."

"Probably because we're the only elementals who will speak to them."

"There is that. So, we're not exactly explosives experts, but I've seen enough movies to know they're unstable. They wouldn't have come in on a dinky seaplane. It would be too risky. They would have been locked up on a boat, with all kinds of precautions, and sent separately. The killer picks up the package, and there you have it. Bing, bang, lots of boom."

"We're assuming an awful lot here."

She was right. I pulled out Miriam's phone to call the agents and add "research explosives" to their to-do list. Before I could dial, voices reached me, what sounded like a man and a woman walking toward the pier.

Instinct told me to hide, and I didn't ignore it. I ducked into the small shed Robin used as an office. Sera followed, drawing the door almost closed behind her. We stood close together and watched through the narrow opening as David and Lana appeared around the corner.

It was no wonder we'd heard them from a distance. They were arguing, voices raised and hands moving in sharp staccato gestures, each trying to make their point just a bit louder than the other.

"I told you I wasn't going to leave. Do you even know

how to fly a plane?" Lana's words reached us first, a plaintive whine.

"I took lessons a decade ago. That's not the point. Lana, we have to go. I can't be on this island anymore. It's just… I can't be. And you're not safe." The last sentence felt like an afterthought. His eyes darted in every direction, hands clenching into fists and releasing. He looked more like an addict who'd missed his fix than a stable, boring stone.

"Do you need access to more rocks? I found a nice little outcropping not far from Fiona's house."

"I don't need more rocks, Lana." The words rushed together, frustration and anger speeding them toward their target. He swallowed and tried again, this time speaking with an exaggerated patience that wouldn't fool anyone. "It's just too much. This island is tiny. There's no escape. Everywhere I look—" His words cut off, likely because his nervous eyes had landed on the shed's poorly closed door and spotted two curious elementals staring back.

He turned back to Lana, giving no sign he'd seen us. "But I won't go without you."

Her eyes melted into twin pools of lovestruck goo. "Aw, David. I don't want to be without you either." He had one full second to relax before she finished her thought. "But it's not right to leave my people in danger to save myself, and I won't disobey the order to stay on the island. Now be a dear and stop asking me to be selfish. You'd never have fallen in love with me if that's the kind of woman I was." She bent her head to kiss him on the cheek, then turned and walked away, singing a quiet song as she headed back toward the north side of the island.

David stared at Lana, then looked at the plane with longing. At last, he followed his girlfriend up the rocky path without even acknowledging our presence.

"What just happened?"

Sera shook her head. "Told you he was suspicious. What kind of stone gets that worked up?"

"I can't believe I'm saying this, but it could actually be love. It does make us crazy."

Her only reply was a disbelieving snort.

"Anyway, I don't see anything here, and I need to check in with the council, see how long it will be before the next member arrives. At this point, I'm actually eager to hear I've been banished." I wasn't quite as anxious to get off the island as David, but it was pretty damn close. The longer I stayed, the more it felt like Alcatraz than a home.

Sera didn't answer. I wasn't even certain she heard me. All her attention was fixed on the corner of the shed, where Robin had stored packages while they waited to be picked up. She crouched, inspecting the ground.

I stepped behind her. "What is it?"

She pointed, and I fought the urge to run out of the shed before it exploded.

A thin line of white powder, no more than an inch long, rested on the floor.

"Do we take a sample?" I whispered, as if the volume of my words could affect the explosive.

"You carry forensic baggies with you?"

I moved gingerly backwards until I hit Robin's desk, then slid each drawer open, looking for something to carry the powder. "We have a choice between a plastic grocery bag and a piece of Tupperware that she used to bring sandwiches to work. Sterility's not that big a deal, right?"

Sera stretched her right index finger toward the substance, picking up several grains and examining them.

She sniffed. "Sera, that can't possibly be a good idea." Her tongue darted out and tasted the powder. I debated whether to run for my life or stay to watch my sister and best friend spontaneously combust.

She shook her head, annoyed. "Salt. Just a delivery of dry goods to the island."

I was both relieved Sera wouldn't be exploding that day and annoyed to find ourselves no closer to the truth.

She moved to the coffee maker, filling it with fresh grounds and water. "Call Carmichael and Johnson. Tell them what we know and ask them to email the most likely explosives. Just in case we were right." She rattled off their number, and I was glad at least one of us still bothered to memorize contact information.

I made the call while we waited for the coffee to brew. They had no new information, but they would keep investigating. I was almost starting to feel guilty for giving Carmichael such a hard time.

No matter where I looked, I couldn't find answers. People kept dying. I kept forgetting how to be sane. Mac and I kept doing our best to screw up our relationship before it ever began. It was a mess, and yet I'd keep going. I'd keep trying to fix things.

I just hoped I had enough time left to figure out how to do that.

CHAPTER 22

There was something I probably should have done days ago, but I had a very good reason for avoiding it: I was a wimp.

I wasn't squeamish, but neither did I look forward to time spent with dead bodies. I should have examined Robin's body closely when I found her outside the cottage, but I'd been too happy to go along with everyone else's belief that it was a fire, in some form or another.

Maybe it was. Maybe a seriously powerful dual magic was responsible for both her death and the explosions. I couldn't be sure until I studied the burns.

That didn't mean I wasn't happy to have an excuse to procrastinate, and when I spotted Lydia Pond strolling along the southern beach, I figured I might as well check in.

Lydia walked through the makeshift court still erected along the shore, as if waiting for someone new to condemn. The older woman watched us approach, and though she kept a wary eye on Sera, she didn't seem like she expected to burst into flames any moment.

"Is there any part of this island you haven't seen yet?"

Pond laughed with little humor. "I think I've explored every square inch. I expected to be here for a day. Now, we're all trapped here until another Lake or Strait arrives. I've been told it might take several more days."

"You know, I'm perfectly happy to just accept my banishment and leave. We don't need to make it official."

"Deprive us of an excuse for ceremony? Never." She gave a bitter laugh. "Besides, there's a chance the newcomer won't find you guilty. You must have figured out by now that you have my vote. One more innocent vote will make it tie, and you'll be spared."

"Why did you vote in my favor?" There'd been so many bigger questions over the last few days, I'd never thought to ask that simple one.

"Honestly, I probably would have said guilty, after the trick you pulled with Lake Tahoe, if it wasn't for the planned punishment. That wasn't just cruel. It was inhumane. And they call the shifters animals." She spat the last word.

"Is that sentence still a possibility?"

"No." The single word was terse, and it took her a moment before she relaxed enough to continue. "We only had a small supply of the drug. It's time-consuming for the lab to make, I believe. Josiah destroyed most of it when he, you know." She waved her hand, letting us finish the sentence on our own. "It's no longer an option." She sounded angry it was ever considered.

I thanked Lydia for her time. It was a surprise to discover at least one council member was still in my corner, but not an unpleasant one.

I should have just let her go, but a question had niggled at me for days now, and it seemed as good a time as any to ask it. "Lana said you took care of her family during some tough times."

She waved off the comment. "Someone had to."

"Did you…" For once, I thought about my words before I sent them out into the world, ensuring each one was perfectly neutral and gave none of my own knowledge away.

"She told me her brother was in a mental institution. I can only imagine how difficult that would be for a family. I'm sure they were grateful for your help."

Her face didn't freeze. It locked down. Only her eyes remained watchful, studying my every movement, every expression. "Yes," she said, her voice lacking any inflection.

She knew. She knew exactly what Trent was, and she protected him. It only made me like her more. I longed to tell her what I was, to compare experiences and learn what I could from her time with Trent, but reason asserted itself just in time. She was still a council member, still a member of the governing body that would order my death if they knew what I was. She might be sympathetic due to her nephew's situation, but that didn't mean she'd support me. We did all kinds of crazy things for family we would never do for strangers.

"I just wanted to say I'm sorry," I hurried on, trying to drop the subject. "It can't be easy to watch a family member go through that."

She nodded once, her eyes softening, then she walked away, leaving me and Sera to continue to the ice house where the bodies were kept.

Neither of us was in much hurry to get there.

"Is it time to escape with our dolphin army yet?" Sera asked. She stared at the sea, but I thought she was seeing airport parking in Reno, where her beat-up red Mustang patiently awaited our return. She saw the cabin and our friends and a dream of a quiet, predictable life where people stopped dropping dead and her sister wasn't fighting tooth and nail for her sanity.

I watched the steady ebb and flow of the tide with her, weighing the puzzle pieces in my mind and trying to fit them into a cohesive image.

Despite having so little concrete information, I knew I

was close. I could feel it. I'd been gathering facts for days now, and my subconscious had been busy fitting the information together in different ways. Each time, the picture was almost complete, just missing that final piece.

I let my brain churn through the possibilities. I imagined I was sitting at the breakfast bar in the cabin, writing out my thoughts in the early morning calm. I found the threads and pulled, examining each one on its own and then in relation to each other, until they started to make something akin to sense. It wasn't the complete picture, not yet, but I thought I knew how to get it there.

"You're not going to believe this," I told Sera, "but I think I might have a plan."

THE NEXT TIME I came up with a plan, step one was going to be a long vacation on a tropical island. It would be a vast improvement over the current plan, which began with me studying the burnt remains of a friend.

"What are we looking for, exactly?" Sera picked up the sheet that covered Robin's corpse, giving us both an unpleasant view of her roasted body.

"Anything that might explain why Edith exploded and Robin burned."

I averted my eyes from the corner of the building where Rachel's body has been placed. The sight reminded me too much of how she'd died, and I couldn't afford the distraction. I needed to remain focused on the immediate task.

The island didn't have anything like a morgue. When someone's time came, maybe once every hundred years or so, the residents gathered for a quiet funeral at sea and gave the body to the waves. We had no cemetery, no undertakers. Death didn't touch us often enough for those to be necessary.

This was different though. It hadn't been either Edith's or Robin's time, and even my dingbat relatives had watched enough crime dramas to know the bodies were evidence and couldn't be immediately delivered to the sea. Instead, they'd been placed in an old ice house, a remnant from the days before electricity came to the island, and then ignored until someone could figure out what to do with them.

"Too bad Vivian had to miss this," Sera said.

A small laugh escaped. I wasn't sure if it was disrespectful to make jokes over corpses or a necessary coping mechanism, but I didn't think Robin would mind.

"We'll take notes and tell her about it later," I said, knowing our squeamish friend wouldn't make it one minute before running from the room.

I studied Robin, trying to disassociate my emotions so I could view the woman on the table as a stranger. I registered the burnt hair and skin and the incongruous way the body looked almost relaxed.

"She looks so calm, almost peaceful. If it wasn't for the ruined skin, I mean. Have you ever seen burns like these?"

Sera considered the corpse. "No. That doesn't mean much. I'm often tempted, but I've never actually set someone on fire. I don't know what it looks like."

I did. I'd seen a body crumble to dust under Josiah's flames, and it looked nothing like Robin. When I'd watched Josiah kill, what little skin the woman still possessed had been blackened, almost unrecognizable. Though it was red and misshapen, my friend had most of her flesh.

Plus, there still the question why one woman exploded and the other burned. I looked between the corpses, unwilling to remove the sheet covering Edith. Or, more specifically, the various parts of Edith that hadn't been washed out to sea. I may not be squeamish, but everyone had their limits. Dismemberment was apparently one of mine.

"Different murderer?" Sera asked, guessing my thoughts.

"That, or someone didn't want to deal with the mess of a second exploding corpse."

I bent closer to Robin's body and studied the skin inch by inch. At first, it was difficult to see much through the burns, but I soon grew accustomed to the patterns created by the fire and was able to spot any anomalies.

I ran my eyes along the flesh of her shoulder, neck, and torso, looking for any wounds, any sign she'd been shot or stabbed before being set alight. There was no indication her death hadn't been fire-related.

Grimacing, I placed one hand under her hips. Sera lifted the shoulders, helping me turn her.

I saw it instantly. "There," I pointed.

Sera nodded. The skin at the base of her skull was split in two spots. The fire hadn't done that.

"Someone hit her from behind, twice it looks like. Probably hard enough to knock her out. Maybe even kill her."

"And then they set her on fire and left her on the porch." Sera helped me lay her flat and covered her with the sheet. "To shut her up or incriminate me?"

"Why choose? It could be both."

"You know, when this is all over, we should write a book about all the different ways elementals can kill people. We can go on the lecture circuit."

I forced a smile. It was all we could do right now, keep smiling and joking until the universe gave us something real to smile about.

"Let's head out. I want to see if the agents found anything yet."

"Are you really going to forgive Carmichael?"

"It's under consideration. Mac forgave him right away,

said Carmichael did exactly what he should have if I was in danger."

Sera sent me a wry look. "I'm not entirely sure you deserve that man."

"All evidence suggests otherwise, I've got to say. But until he figures that out, I'm going with it." I shut the ice house door, leaving the dead bodies behind. "And hey, this afternoon I'm going to save his life. *Again.* I get major points for that."

"You really think you can pull it off? That you can get into a mental space where you want to break your connection?"

"I think I have to try."

Sera looked like she wanted to continue the conversation, but I was already dialing the agents. I didn't want to hear any doubts, any reasons why Mac and I should just accept the new normal and be joined at the hip for the foreseeable future.

The phone call to the FBI went to voicemail, and there were no new emails.

"You know, this plan would work a lot better if people got back to us."

"Is it possible it's less a plan and more a desperate hope?"

"Hey, to-may-to, to-mah-to."

We stepped outside, feeling no desire to linger around the bodies. Little warmth awaited us outside, the sun once again dipping behind dense clouds, leaving the day chilly and dull.

I tightened my flimsy cardigan around my body and turned toward the houseboat. "You okay for a couple of hours? I can't take the next step until I hear from Carmichael."

"Do you really have to do this now? It seems it would be safer to wait till we're home to do the whole magic recovery thing. Things are calmer there. Fewer explosions."

"If we had any real idea of the longterm effects, maybe, but who knows what's happening to his body while we wait? I'm at least going to try. Maybe it won't be as difficult as my mother says."

I knew she wanted to push, but in the end she only nodded and followed me toward the boat. I said little else, unsure if I was making the right decision and yet knowing it was the only one I could make.

This was close to being over. I almost had all the information I needed. I wanted to believe, when the murderer was unmasked, they'd blubber a confession on the spot. It would make life a hell of a lot easier.

In my experience, the bad guy was rarely so accommodating and had an annoying habit of fighting back. Lately, when I felt threatened, things hadn't worked out so well. If that happened again, Mac couldn't be the one to pay the price.

I needed to free him before my sanity slipped again, or disappeared altogether. I wouldn't force him to be forever attached to a crazy woman.

I wanted him to be happy, and this was the only way to make sure he was.

We'd only been joking, but even so, Sera was wrong. Most of the time, I did deserve Mac. I just had to set him free before that was no longer the case.

CHAPTER 23

Sera wasn't the only one unhappy with my plan.

"What if you need help?" My mother asked. She and Grams had been waiting for us when we arrived at the houseboat, likely to ask this very question.

"Reclaiming my own magic? What can you do?"

They had no answer, because there wasn't one. This was between me and Mac.

"I'll be surrounded by water," I reminded her. "There is no better way to do this."

I left Sera, my mother, and Grams on the beach and kicked everyone else off the houseboat. When it was just me and Mac, I started the engine and headed toward open water.

Mac took over the steering, and I moved to the stern to watch the shore recede. My mother and Sera stood side by side, wearing matching expressions of concern. Grams stood only a few feet away, her eyes closed. The boat picked up speed, and I knew it was her work. I needed to spare my energy for what I was about to do, and this was her silent way of helping.

Simon and Miriam stood separate from everyone else, the invisible dividing line between the shifters and elementals firmly in place. For once, Miriam didn't look like she was on the verge of bursting into laughter. Even Simon looked concerned.

I raised a single hand to them. None of us knew if this would work. We didn't know the potential side effects. This wasn't the sort of thing that came with its own WebMD page.

The only way we'd know for sure was to try it.

I walked through the boat, returning to Mac and leaving the people on the shore behind.

It didn't take long for the island to fade from view, though I waited until we'd traveled another quarter mile before dropping anchor. There were no other islands in sight, no other boats. It was just me, Mac, and the dark sea as far as the eye could reach.

"How do we do this?" He looked around the boat, which felt smaller with him in it.

"I have no idea." I closed my eyes and took several slow breaths, refusing to let the panic rise. "The last time I worked on you, you were dead. There wasn't much risk of making it worse."

He smiled, and it held so much trust my legs practically buckled from the sight. "Whatever else is going on, my life has only improved since you entered it, Aidan. That's not going to change tonight."

"Except for the part where I made you an enormous freak dependent on my magic?" I kept my voice light, trying to turn it into a joke.

"Small inconvenience," he answered in the same tone, though his eyes were somber.

It seemed we'd made a wordless agreement not to discuss my revelations of the night before, lest they distract me from the task at hand.

I pointed to the bedroom. "You should lie down."

"I'm starting to think you're just looking for an opportunity to get me in bed."

"If it helps, I'll be joining you."

Mac backed into the bedroom with a couple of long strides. He fell on the bed, stretching out and practically filling the entire mattress.

"Take your shirt off."

"Not that I'm complaining, but you know 'Sexual Healing' is a song, not a how-to manual?"

I made a face. "You're feeling mighty sure of yourself. I have to send my magic through your skin, and it will be easier if there aren't clothes in the way."

He removed his top without another word. His hands dropped to the button on his jeans and he looked at me.

"Might as well. Wait. No." His expression turned quizzical. "No underwear, remember?"

"Is that a problem?" His voice was far too innocent.

"You want me to keep my focus, I suggest you leave the pants on." The smile turned into an outright grin. I was glad to see he found my rampant lust amusing. "Scoot over a bit." He moved to the edge of the double bed, creating enough space for me to lie on my side next to him.

I raised up on my elbow and looked down at him. "You know I'm making this up as I go along, right? I'm just relying on instinct."

"I've always found that's the best strategy in bed."

"Mind out of the gutter, MacMahon. This is some highfalutin magic stuff I'm doing here. Take it seriously."

He gave a heavy sigh, but at last he closed his eyes and let the teasing expression fall away. I was sad to see it go, both because I could never get enough of playful Mac and because it meant it was time to begin.

"Do you remember anything from the last time?"

He cracked one eye open. "You mean when I was dead?"

That sounded like a no. "I'm going to send my magic into you, thread it through your body and look for what got left behind. If all goes well, the magic I left inside you will recognize its source and return willingly. Its natural state is to be together. It should want to be whole."

"And if it doesn't go well?"

"I could make it worse. I could end up leaving even more inside you, though I doubt that will happen. Last time, I think it stayed behind to continue healing you. I mean, you were dead. That's going to require more than the magical equivalent of two aspirin and a good night's sleep."

He studied me. "We have to take the risk, don't we?"

We both knew the answer. "I only plan to access the water side, but it may not be enough. The fire might come out. If something goes wrong, don't hesitate to dump me over the side of the boat."

I placed my fingers over his lips when he began to protest. "The water can't hurt me. I can't drown. You know this. But the water *will* help dampen the fire's power and keep that side of my magic from gaining a hold. I mean it. Promise me you won't let the fire claim me. If it comes to it, you can't hesitate."

It took him a long moment. It went completely against his nature to chuck a woman over the side of a boat and watch her sink.

"I promise I'll throw you over the boat if the fire shows up," he grumbled.

"Now can you say it like you mean it?"

He groaned, but at last he gave a single nod. "I promise I won't let the fire take you," he repeated, and this time the words were measured and honest, if still reluctant.

I had to trust he meant it.

"You'll feel it, as my magic moves through your body. You can talk to me if you want, but try not to make any large movements."

In answer, he closed his eyes again and let his body relax. His legs turned out, feet dropping to the sides, and his hands unclenched.

I called to the magic in my core, finding the water eager and strong. It had fed well these last few days, and it was sated on the canals and the sea. It flowed from me, its movement effortless and sure.

I let it rest on top of Mac's skin, covering his chest. I made no effort to send it through his skin, not yet. This should be a slow assimilation, not an invasion.

"It's warm," he said. "I didn't expect that."

I stretched it out, covering his shoulders and arms, moving up to his collarbone. "It could be a bit uncomfortable. Sure you don't want to be knocked out first?" He opened one eye, but that was all he needed to convey his scorn for that idea. "Fucking man," I muttered. "You probably don't take painkillers either, do you?"

His small smile told me I'd guessed correctly.

I let the magic drift into his body, passing the first layer of skin. Mac gasped once, but that was his only reaction. Once he relaxed, I allowed it to sink further, becoming part of him.

Inch by inch, I explored his body, this time from the inside. I kept my eyes closed, wanting as few distractions as possible.

I moved with great caution. It was terrifying, how much power Mac had given me. It would be so easy to take control, to speed or slow the flow of blood, to destroy cells vital to survival.

Every doctor knew this truth, how close healing was to destruction. They were opposite sides of the same coin, and with each slow exploration, I made the choice, again and again, to heal rather than harm.

Mac's breathing grew deep and steady. "You still with me?" I whispered. I couldn't believe he'd fallen asleep.

"I'm here." The words came out on a breath. "I can feel

you everywhere." I heard no fear. If anything, it sounded more like awe.

"Me too." It wasn't just the magic, though by now it had spread throughout his torso and into his legs. The length of his body was pressed against mine, and his shoulder was warm where my cheek rested against his skin. I felt the lines between us blurring, our two distinct forms melding together. Flesh and blood. Body and spirit.

It felt like I'd finally found the place I belonged. I never wanted to move. I never wanted to feel separate from him again.

I inhaled sharply, squashing that thought. I had to want my magic to return to me, want it with no reservations. I needed to believe in my very core that Mac and I must exist as two separate beings.

No doubts. No uncertainty. It was the only way I'd free him.

The magic moved again, winding its way past arteries and bones and organs. There was a tiny tug, a glimmer of recognition. I forced myself to keep the movement steady as I inched toward Mac's magic source.

It was in the center of his body, as mine was. I let my magic gather there, sliding away from his arms and legs until it pooled in his core. He shook once, an involuntary shudder caused by holding more magic than his body was built to handle. I rested my hand on his chest, above his heart, and waited for him to still before I continued.

I had no difficulty finding the water magic I'd given him, as familiar to me as my own voice. It leapt in greeting, recognizing its source, and the water swirled around each other, rejoicing.

There was another magic, one I'd come to know too well.

I'd used the water magic to find what I needed. I recalled

it, offering it gratitude, though it hadn't completed its job. It hadn't yet reclaimed its missing pieces from Mac.

That could wait. My first priority was the more dangerous fire, and I tapped into it as soon as the water quieted.

The fire was slower, more willful. It refused to make it easy for me. Hesitantly, I touched the magic that resided in my core, asking it to find and reclaim the forgotten bits of fire.

Without any anger to fuel it, it responded sluggishly, but it woke at last, crackling and hissing with pleasure as it was granted release.

I practiced every meditation technique I'd ever learned and a few I made up, demanding my body remain calm. This time, I would control the fire, not the other way around.

I kept my breathing regular, my attention on Mac. I was aware of nothing but the magic, his and mine, and the way it danced together. I'd been right. It wanted to be whole.

I fought against the exhilaration that came with the knowledge I could do this. I couldn't lose focus, not yet.

Even so, my lips curved in a smile as the magic bonded to itself. The lost threads were downright giddy, happy to return now that its healing work was done.

I couldn't rush, not yet. I whispered to the fire, calling it back. If I could just remove the most unstable magic from Mac, there should be no more surprises.

The fire laughed.

I gritted my teeth and tried again, giving the fire an order rather than a suggestion. It grumbled, but this time it returned to me.

It seemed to have fought me just for the joy of the fight, as it didn't really want to be in Mac's body. I could feel its pleasure as it returned to me and settled back in my core.

It hit me, then, a simple fact I should have recognized

months ago. To me, the fire was an intruder. I resented it, even despised it for what it would someday do to me.

To the fire, I was its home. It belonged to me. In its way, it loved me as much as the water magic did.

Mac felt me pause at the long-delayed realization. "Aidan?"

"Shh. We're almost finished." I sent the water back, seeking the lost pieces of magic it neglected to retrieve the first time. I gave them time to bond again, then I reached for that last invisible cord and called the water to me.

It didn't budge.

I tried again, a little harder, and then harder still, more than I was comfortable with. This wasn't an operation that could succeed with brute force.

Nothing. I still controlled my own water magic, but the bits that had been inside Mac for the last several weeks weren't moving.

If anything, it felt like they were digging in their heels.

I opened my eyes, fighting for control. This time, it had nothing to do with my fire side. It was the sort of good old-fashioned panic one feels when they don't know what to do.

"Does it hurt?"

"I can take it." He spoke in a whisper, and the words held a tension they'd lacked before.

I almost stopped right then. I could say I tried. No one would blame me, and I wouldn't cause Mac more pain.

Except he'd be trapped with a woman who couldn't control her own magic, let alone his, for the rest of his life.

If the direct approach wasn't working, I needed a different strategy. Rather than tugging again on the magic locked in Mac's core, I looked for the block. It didn't take long to find. The water magic wasn't alone.

Surrounding it was an unfamiliar power, one that felt

wild and pure and demanding.

His shifter magic.

I pulled again, this time paying attention to how the other power responded. As I tugged on my magic, Mac's tightened, creating a trap the water couldn't escape.

Chaotic and difficult to understand, my mother had said. She hadn't understated the matter. I felt the bear's eager hunger, and I had no idea how to convince it to release the water remnants from Mac's body.

This was taking too long. It was too much time for my magic to be inside Mac, too much time for something to go wrong. Already, I was feeling my energy falter, just a bit. It would take only one distraction, one slip, and I could kill him.

I spared no time to consider my choice. There was one remaining option, and I wouldn't take the time to debate its merits. Self-doubt and fear would only create unnecessary delays.

I remembered Trent Pond, stuck in the mental hospital in Eureka, able to manipulate water and ice together. I thought of Brian, grinning as he lifted soil with one hand and drew ice from the air with the other. Accessing both magics at the same time required more concentration than one person could manage. Based on the little I'd seen, the only way to do it was to fracture into two selves, to abandon the sense of oneself as a whole, complete being. I'd done it once before, when I'd healed Mac, and it had changed me. I was still discovering how much.

Now, I had to do it again.

"Remember your promise." I spoke the words against his skin, so quietly I didn't think he'd hear them. I forgot about shifter ears, though. He tensed, preparing to fight.

It was too late. The fire rose, grinning, and shot through my body, claiming every inch, every cell. It insisted it was as much a part of me as the water ever was.

And at last I knew, with absolute, heartbreaking certainty, that it was right.

I eased the fire back into his body, sending it along the same course the water had charted.

I pressed even closer to Mac. I let his warmth, his smell, the essence of who he was comfort and ground me as I guided the two magics through his body.

I felt strange and certain at the same time, my body both unfamiliar and how it was always meant to be. But there was no fear, only the same clarity I remembered from the last time I accessed both sides.

The fire reached his core and shielded the water, creating a barrier between my magic and Mac's.

"Now," I said, and I pulled.

He winced, the only sign of discomfort, as the threads struggled toward me, disengaging from their temporary host. It was going to work. Mac was going to be free.

Then his shifter magic decided to join the party.

I grunted at the unexpected intrusion, and Mac's eyes flew open. He stared at me, as surprised as I was.

His magic circled the water and fire, stalking it, preventing it from leaving. It almost seemed to growl, a silent insistence that I stay put.

"It's not me." The panic rose again, fear threatening to ruin everything. I couldn't lose my focus, not so close to the end. "Mac, you're holding me in place."

"I know." He gasped. "I'm trying." His ears grew round and small, the bear making its presence known.

"What can I do?" I tugged on the water again. Nothing happened.

He laughed with no humor. "Be less appealing to the bear."

I felt it then. It wasn't rational Mac holding me in place.

It wasn't the man. It was the beast, and it was staking its claim on the magic.

No, not the magic. It was staking a claim on me. The beast desired the connection between us. It craved the dependence our logical brains rejected—and the beast had no intention of giving up.

It didn't try to hold onto all my power. That would be too much for Mac's body to permanently handle. The animal just didn't want to give up the bits it had possessed since it returned from the dead, that tiny amount of magic that meant Mac and I would be connected forever.

I didn't fully understand the relationship between a shifter's human and animal sides, but I knew they didn't exist as separate beings. They were part of the whole, aware of each other at all times, regardless of which body was in charge at the moment.

Perhaps, if I gave the man enough reason to let go, the bear would relinquish its hold.

"The bear doesn't want me." A low growl emerged from Mac's throat in pronounced disagreement. "I'm just a skinny blabbermouth with a weakness for bread products. It can find hundreds just like me."

The growl rose in volume. I was pretty sure it was the bear equivalent of "That's my girlfriend you're talking about."

New strategy, then. "I'm not going anywhere. Magic or no magic, I belong with you, Mac. With all of you." The growl subsided, somewhat placated, but the beast didn't release its hold.

I felt its possessive need, the primal desire that had nothing to do with the human wish for independence or a healthy adult relationship. It was the part that was frustrated by our insistence on taking things slow, on dating, on getting to know each other when every irrational part of us had known from the beginning we belonged to each other.

I'd given Mac part of my purest essence, a silent prom-ise to stay with him always, and his bear showed no interest in releasing it.

I saw one final option. When all else fails, tell the truth.

"Mac, I need you to listen, and believe what I'm about to tell you. I need the bear to hear it, as well. I know I said I'd try to beat this whole dual magic thing. I said I'd hold onto my sanity as long as I could. We thought we had years." My throat tightened, and I blinked several times, trying to keep the tears from building. It didn't work. My face was still pressed against Mac's side, and he had to feel the escaped tears sliding down his skin.

"We're not going to have years. It's happening now, faster than I know how to fight it. The madness is taking over. It's using the fire as its tool, and my fire is kind of psy-chotic. It wants the world to burn, and when it has control, even my water half wants to watch. I'm not okay, and I'm not going to be okay again. If you don't release my magic, you'll suffer with me. You'll be tied forever to a woman with little resemblance to the person I am now. You have to let me go. You have to," I insisted.

Both the man and the bear were still.

"No." The word was rough, coated in gravel, and I didn't know who spoke it.

"We don't have a choice. It's bad enough that I have to face this for myself. Don't make me drag you down with me."

A shuddering breath escaped Mac, and I felt it then. The barest change, a tiny shift as his bear magic moved. "Take it."

I didn't hesitate. I could feel the bear's resistance, and only the strength of Mac's will allowed him to overpower the creature for a few moments. I wrenched on the magic, though I knew it would cause him pain. A little pain now was better than a lifetime of regret.

He grunted as the magic flew through him, head and shoulders rising from the mattress as his abdominal muscles clenched. His features contorted and twisted, brow and cheekbones reshaping themselves into the bear's face, and his mouth opened in a silent roar.

When I finished, Mac collapsed on the mattress. Sweat beaded on his forehead, but it was his human face once again.

The magic settled back in my core, but the relief was short-lived. The bear had only relinquished the fire magic in its entirety. Small drops of my water side remained inside Mac.

Unless we found a way to tranquilize Mac's inner bear, I doubted I'd be getting them back anytime soon.

"It didn't work." My muscles sagged in defeat. Now that I no longer needed to maintain uninterrupted focus, exhaustion claimed my body. My slow tears became a torrent of sobs. I tried to tell him I was sorry, but I couldn't form the words.

"It wasn't you, Aidan. You did your part. I guess I don't know what I want as well as I thought I did." He stared at me, pain and frustration combined with a tenderness that damn near destroyed me.

It was a look of pure honesty, and I returned it, though tears blurred my vision. As the magic settled into place, I let him see the struggle as I forced the fire to quiet, the cost to my soul each time I was forced to deny half my heritage. I let him see my anger, that I had no defense against a traitorous body that was so determined to send me into darkness. I showed him my sorrow, that the man who should be mine could never truly be.

He wrapped his arms around me, pulling me even closer.

Though there were many things I needed to do, and places I needed to be, I made no effort to leave, and when sleep came for me, I surrendered willingly to the only peace I could find.

CHAPTER 24

Whether it was exhaustion or just the comfort of sleeping in Mac's arms, I slept better than I had since arriving on the island. When I woke, I had a moment of pure peace, the certainty that everything was going to be okay.

The curtains were open, the earlier dreary day replaced by the lavender of twilight, that liminal space that was neither day nor night, bright nor dark. It was the time of day that whispered of quiet change, of secrets and possibilities.

The clouds looked even blacker than they had earlier that day, promising a wet night. I'd always loved summertime rain, and I decided it was a sign of a good night ahead.

I snuggled further into the blankets. They still smelled of Mac, though they no longer held his warmth. Reluctantly, I sat up, letting reality pierce my false sense of calm. It might feel like a perfect evening, but we were a long ways from that being true.

The quiet clatter of dishes and pans reached my ears, but before I could join him in the kitchen, the bedroom door opened. Mac entered, carrying a tray loaded with mugs and buttered toast. He put this on my lap, then sat next to me, careful not to spill the drinks.

"You made me tea." I sounded a bit stupid, but no one had ever brought me breakfast in bed. The fact that it was nearing nine o'clock at night didn't detract from the experience.

I took a sip. It was strong enough to put hair on your chest and milky enough to hide that fact, just the way I liked it. The man did pay attention.

"I thought you might need the boost."

I nibbled on a toast corner, unsure how to start the conversation. "Thanks. I'm okay, though." I was worried and scared, but okay seemed an acceptable shorthand. "You?"

"Okay." I wasn't convinced. He slid his eyes toward me, letting me know he hadn't believed me, either. "I sent the others a text, so they know we're both still alive. I wasn't sure what else to tell them."

"I guess we can tell them it halfway worked. I got the fire out, at least."

He was quiet, and I thought he was looking inward, examining his own magic.

"It does feel a bit calmer in there, which can't be a bad thing. Should I worry about you? Are you unbalanced now?"

I did a quick mental check. The water came easily, happy as could be to find itself in the middle of an ocean. The fire side remained quiet, almost patient. I wasn't sure I trusted that. "No more than before. How's the bear doing?"

"Pissed off." He gave a short laugh with little amusement. "He's not pleased he had to fight to keep you."

I took another sip of my tea, blowing on it until steam rose into my face. "Tell the furry bastard we're going to try again. Your health shouldn't depend on how close I stand to you."

"I'm not sure he's listening to logic. Maybe it'll be better now, without the fire." He picked up one of the napkins on the tray and began twisting it into knots. "I need to shift soon, Aidan. The furry bastard wants some payback after last night."

"The island probably isn't the best place."

"Probably not."

"Can you make it another day or two?"

He grimaced, but he also nodded. "What's the plan for tonight?"

I considered giving him sexy bedroom eyes, but in truth I felt stretched and brittle, as if a strong breeze could break me. I could still manage a few amorous thoughts—it was hard not to, sitting on a bed with Mac—but I didn't know that I had the energy to act on them.

"I'm waiting to hear from a few people who can help me with a theory I'm working on. Once they get in touch, I think I can finally confirm who killed Edith and Robin. If all goes well, tonight will find me pointing my finger at someone while saying '*J'accuse!*' in a dramatic fashion."

He smiled. It wasn't indulgent, either. He didn't humor me, as so many did when I opened my mouth. If anything, he looked proud. "I knew you'd figure it out."

"Don't jinx me," I threatened. "It's not over yet. But if all goes well, we should be on our way back to Tahoe tonight. If you're ready to go by midnight, I bet we can find a seat on the plane for you."

"I think I can manage that." He busied himself removing the tray and placing it on the floor next to the bed. Butterflies fluttered in my stomach once the bed was clear. Maybe I could manage some amorous intentions, after all.

"Tell me how bad it is."

The butterflies sat down, disappointed.

"You mean…"

He gave one more tug on the napkin, and it split in two. He looked at the pieces of fabric in his hands as if he had no memory of how they got there. Gently, he set them on the bed. "Is there no chance you can find a balance as the fire grows stronger?"

"I'm trying, but I wouldn't be optimistic," I said. "I don't feel like me, Mac. I feel stronger, more focused. Maybe more what a full-blooded elemental feels like, I'd guess. But I'm harsher, and crueler, and I'm pretty sure my fire side couldn't tell a joke to save her life." He watched me closely, and I knew he wasn't just listening to my words. He was absorbing them, believing them, and yet still trying to find a way out of this mess.

I needed him to understand how unlikely that was.

"I've talked to Sera about her fire, and mine's not the same. I think up till now my fire side has been absorbing all the crazy the dual magic's kicking loose, just because I never learned to control it, but eventually it will affect the water, too. I think. This is all guesswork, and most of it is based on what we know about Trent and Brian. They weren't exactly the most stable subjects."

He took my hand, intertwining my slim fingers with his massive ones. "You're right. There's a lot we don't know, and so long as there's any hope, I'm here." The words were quiet but filled with absolute certainty. "I'm not giving up on you."

My throat didn't just close. It locked up, unable to produce a single sound. I wanted to throw myself against him and bury my face in his chest. Another part held back, the part that insisted he was only being stubborn, and if he remained at my side, it was a recipe for more and greater pain.

Both parts shut up when he released my hand and grabbed my hips. With one easy move, he pulled me on top of him, putting my face even with his. With a low growl, he nipped my jawline. I felt his strength, barely contained. He was fighting for his own control.

"In the meantime," he murmured, lips sliding down my neck, "you may have noticed that we're actually alone."

The thought had occurred to me. I reached up one hand, threading it through his hair, and I tugged until his lips met mine.

Miriam's phone beeped.

Mac released a long, heartfelt groan. "Why? Why?" he muttered, glaring at the small device.

"I can't ignore it," I said, though I couldn't remember exactly why.

"I know, I know. Clues to the murderer, etc." Oh, yeah. That was why. I stretched as far as I could to reach the phone, not wanting to lose my place on his lap.

While I fumbled, Mac stared upwards, perhaps hoping a cure for unending frustration was written on the ceiling.

Two messages came through, one after the other. I read them once, twice, then a third time, letting the words slowly sink in. It was the last thing I expected to learn, and with it I finally had the missing puzzle pieces.

Unfortunately, they created two different pictures.

"I have to go," I said.

"I know." We shared one long look of regret, then I stood, ready to face a bunch of elementals and at least one murderer.

"This is the last time, though." I stopped pulling my shoes on to stare at him, uncertain what he meant. "This is the last time we're going to stop. I don't care what happens next time. I don't care if Simon is doing cartwheels next to the bed, or the agents decide they need you to save the world. I don't care. So go, tell everyone what you know, then meet me on that damn plane. Because I'm telling you right now, Aidan Brook, unless the world ceases to exist, tonight you will be in my bed."

———

Somehow, I managed to leave the boat after Mac's words, though I spent most of the trip back to the island convinced I'd lost my mind. I mean, no one had died in days. Surely the killer could wait a few more hours while Mac and I settled some unfinished business.

Then I remembered the look on his face when he spoke, and the heat in his eyes as he helped me off the houseboat, his fingers tight around my waist. A few more hours would only begin to cover all the things we needed to do to each other.

Instead, I focused on the main obstacle standing between me and a night I planned to remember till my very last shred of sanity ran for the hills. It was time for the last step of my plan.

As soon as I landed, I texted Sera, Grams, and my mother with instructions. Whatever happened next, I was going to make damn sure there were a lot of witnesses.

Then, I started toward the northeast side of the island and Grams' house. I followed the canals through the trees, drawing to a halt as an otter head poked out of the water. A black housecat trotted alongside.

"What have you been up to today?" I asked. They both shifted back to human form, though Miriam remained in the canal, her defined shoulders rising above the water line. They exchanged a conspiratorial grin. "So, spying then?"

Simon nodded. "The council spent most of the day trying to figure out how to deny our existence again after my little display."

"Glad to see they're focused on the important stuff. Did they come up with anything that didn't involve shipping every last one of you to Australia?"

"Not yet, but they were still at it when I left."

Simon looked far too pleased with himself. "The trees outside my grandmother's house are comfortable, then?"

The corners of his lips lifted in a small, close-mouthed smile.

I clapped him on the shoulder. Simon didn't mind hugs, but he had to be the one to instigate them. "You know, whatever you've learned from Carmen, she'll never be a better ninja than you."

"No, she won't," he agreed.

"Hey, can one of you stay with Mac? Maybe there won't be any side effects from retrieving the fire, but I don't want to leave him on his own just yet."

Without words, they held out one hand each, folded into a fist. They pumped them up and down three times, and Simon's paper wrapped around Miriam's rock.

Her face scrunched in protest, and it was a sign of how much I'd grown used to her that I almost felt no desire to ooh and aww. Almost. "Babysitting duty for me. Damn you, Brook." But her eyes weren't serious, and she didn't complain again before reverting to otter form and swimming toward the houseboat.

Simon looked uncertain. "That did not go as planned. I thought we were fighting over who would spend the evening napping on the sofa."

I started toward Grams' house. "Trust me," I told him. "If this goes the way I think it will, you're not going to want to sleep through it."

FULL NIGHT FELL as we walked across the island, but tonight the countless stars were hiding between thick clouds. As Grams' house came into view, the windows warmly lit, a few fat drops fell on my arms. I smiled, welcoming the rain's power. Simon hissed and ran ahead, scrambling up a large tree until he reached a nook on the second floor, one protected from the rain.

I wanted him nearby, as a witness and as support, but it was better he not come inside just yet. The next hour was going to be tense enough without asking the elementals to ignore a bone-deep prejudice they'd held pretty much since the birth of our race.

By the time I arrived, the group was already gathered in the library. Chairs had been brought in from other rooms in the house, and everyone perched on whatever was available.

Nearly everyone whose presence I'd requested was there. Lydia Pond, Deborah Rivers, and Michael Bay, the remaining members of the council who, technically, still held my fate in their hands. Grams, my mother, and Sera. Lana and David claimed the one love seat, sitting close enough for their thighs to brush. I hadn't invited my aunts, but Georgina, Marie, and Tina still perched on the room's largest sofa.

When I entered, they all spoke at once, demanding to know why they were there, what I'd learned, why I thought I had the right to give orders to my elders and betters.

I didn't answer any of them, going straight to my mother instead. "You got it?" She pulled a laptop from her oversized handbag.

I set it on the desk, next to the other computer, and turned it on. As I worked, the room quieted, their curiosity about my actions overpowering their indignation.

Sera worked on Grams' computer at the same time, connecting it to the internet and downloading the software we needed.

At last, we stepped back, having invited two more people to the meeting. Despite the serious purpose behind the gathering, my heart lightened to see Vivian's lovely face on the laptop screen. "You really cut this one close, you know."

"Well, next time have a shorter list of names to research,"

she grumbled. "Particularly when half of them are old ones practiced at living off the grid. It took a while."

I gave a small nod, hoping she didn't see my relief. She hadn't been ignoring us. She'd just been thorough. "Thanks for doing this. You sure you don't mind?"

She waved off my thanks. "I'm safe in Tahoe. The odds of you lot managing to blow me up are slim."

"You underestimate our powers, Viv," said Sera, popping up over my shoulder. "The other one's ready to go."

I turned to see Carmichael and Johnson filling Gram's computer screen. The council bristled at the inclusion of the human agents, but this was my meeting, and they were invited, damn it. Only I got to be angry at Carmichael. Everyone else had to deal.

"Can we begin, please?" Deborah asked, sounding deeply bored.

"Almost. Just waiting on one more."

We didn't need to wait long. The front door opened, and Josiah Blais entered the library. Self-possessed as always, he nodded at each person and took a seat, choosing a bar-stool for himself. Somehow, he managed to look elegant even while sitting on a chair that required his legs to dangle.

It was time, and despite my eagerness to get this over with and return to my life, I also felt dread building. One of these people was the murderer, and soon their identity would be known by all. I just couldn't see that ending well.

I studied them all, friends and family and strangers, and took comfort in the knowledge that I had plenty of backup.

Before beginning, I reached for my magic, sending some of it out to the ocean and attaching it to the water molecules. I fed on its peace, letting it fill me with a calm certainty. Whatever happened in the next hour, whatever was revealed, I had to remember I was a water. I was Aidan

Brook, descendent of the old ones, born from the earth's first magic. It was what I carried in my veins, now and always, and I could not forget that. Not now.

I moved to the center of the room and waited until every eye was on me. No one spoke.

"Thank you all for attending the island's first annual, one time only, murderer unmasking. It was a pretty exclusive invite, so I'm glad to see you could all make it. Quite simply, everyone in this room has either been a suspect for the killings or holds information that will help uncover the true killer. Or they're related to me and I couldn't keep them away," I added.

Everyone who wasn't a blood relation erupted at my words, filling the room with indignation and loud proclamations of innocence. I let them speak for a few seconds, then held up my hand.

"We're here to learn who's been killing waters. I have no idea why any of you would be opposed to that." I looked at each person with the sort of sincerity that might fool someone who's never seen an actual expression before. Everyone in the room recognized it as the threat it was. If they were vehemently against finding the killer, it only made them look guilty.

The room quieted again. Grams poured tea and coffee, as if she was hosting an afternoon salon rather than a murder investigation.

I looked at each person, trying to read them all. They appeared worried or annoyed, serious or amused, but none had a sign on their foreheads that said "Guilty" in blinking neon letters. I was just going to have to do this the old-fashioned way, then.

I smiled. "Shall we begin?"

CHAPTER 25

I spun in a small circle, trying to look perfectly at ease while a roomful of people stared at me with expressions ranging from curious to downright hostile. "There's this game I used to play with my aunts," I said. "The object of the game was to determine who committed the murder, where, and with what weapon. Players did so by sharing information and through process of elimination. Well, we know the where for Edith Lake, at least, and we think we know the weapon."

"It was fire, wasn't it?" Lana interrupted. "I'm pretty sure that's what we saw." She glanced to David for confirmation.

"Yes, but that's like saying someone was killed with a gun. It could have been a Smith & Wesson or a Glock. The trick is finding out the type of weapon and who used it." I thought I sounded pretty convincing. Mainly, I was pleased I remembered two kinds of guns off the top of my head. "The point is we don't know the who or the details of the how, which is why we're all here today. Process of elimination through shared information."

Everyone considered my words. Most of them even began to relax as they accepted my reasoning.

"Lana and David, I'm sure you understand why we need to consider you. You appeared on the island a day before bodies started dropping."

David looked serious. Lana, as usual, looked mildly surprised.

Michael stood up and immediately sat back down. "I don't understand why we're wasting our time with waters, or even that stone. We know who did it, don't we? It was a fire, and there are two in this room. One of them already confessed. Can't we wrap this up before someone decides to blow me up next?"

Josiah only offered him a mild stare, but fire sparked from his fingers. My father wasn't a man who lost control. He just wanted to mess with Michael. The councilman blanched, so I'd say it worked.

"Humor me," I said. "Lana, did you kill anyone since arriving?"

"Kill? Oh, goodness no. Why would I do that? That would be a terribly mean thing to do. My karma would never recover." She reached one shaking hand to her throat, wrapping her fingers around the crystal necklace she wore.

In truth, I had no evidence that would either exonerate or condemn Lana, but I'd also have an easier time believing a basket of puppies committed the murders than believing Lana was responsible. The bemused faces about the room suggested they felt similarly.

"And David, what about you?"

He gave a single shake of his head. Otherwise, his face was as immobile as the granite from which his powers were born.

Assuming, of course, he was a stone. There was still room for doubt.

I stared at him, my skepticism evident, until the room began to murmur questions.

"It would not be difficult for a fire to appear to be a stone, if he was motivated enough," I reminded him. The quiet murmurs rose, one voice after another adding to the growing cacophony. "Vivian, would you please share what you've learned about David Flint?"

Heads swiveled to the quiet earth on the computer screen. "David was raised with his family in Hawaii."

The voices became a roar, complete with pointed fingers. Sera and Josiah studied David with renewed interest, trying to place him. Vivian waited until the noise subsided before she continued.

"He lived there until he was in the fifth grade, when his mother died. At that time, he and his father moved to the mainland. They settled in North Dakota, but once David was old enough to pass as a human adult, he began moving. Frequently."

While Vivian recited these facts, I watched David. His teeth clenched, tighter and tighter, until a small muscle in his jaw began to pulse.

"Anything notable about where he moved?"

David began to rise, but Lana reached for him, pulling him back. He sat, looking defeated.

"He went back to Hawaii, living not far from the Blais compound, in fact. Then Southern California for a time, then Texas. Most recently, he lived in Lake Tahoe."

"Where he met me," Lana interrupted. "That's not a secret."

Josiah peered at David. "It's also where I was. I've spent time in each of those places when I was building new hotels. You aren't stalking me, are you, young man?"

David glared, but refused to answer. He might just make this easy for me, after all.

"There are two issues on the table," I said. "First, if we're assuming Edith and Robin's deaths weren't random, then someone had a reason for killing those particular women. Second, someone chose to frame the fires for their deaths."

Once again, I waited for the protests to die down. "I

know they're innocent, but don't just take my word. When Edith died, everyone was happy to point the finger at Sera, and then Josiah, but they've all forgotten one key detail. Neither of them are a fraction as stupid as they'd need to be to commit these murders. If they were going to kill anyone, they wouldn't light them on fire or blow them up, not when they were the only fires on an island full of waters. There's something else going on here."

I paused, hoping someone else would reach the same conclusion I had. My arguments would sound much more convincing if I wasn't the only person who thought they sounded obvious.

Georgina jumped into the silence. "But why? None of us really know Sera, though I'm sure you're lovely, dear. Why would any of us choose her to frame?"

"I think that was only the first part of a complicated plan."

The room fell into silence, and I waited, attempting a dramatic pause. I caught Josiah's eye. He looked downright intrigued. I was certain he'd already made the same leap I had.

Marie stared between Sera and Josiah. "Oh! I get it. You think someone either wanted Sera convicted, or they wanted a reason to bring Josiah to the island. Because he wouldn't let his daughter be convicted without trying to save her, would he?"

Again, the room broke into quiet murmurs, but they sounded less indignant than before. People were beginning to think about these murders rather than just blame the nearest target.

I exhaled, daring to believe this might actually work. I reached into my purse and withdrew a rock the size of my fist.

"David, your history indicates an interest in Josiah Blais.

Maybe even an obsession. We need confirmation you are what you say you are." I set the rock on an end table and stepped back.

I didn't want David to be guilty. He seemed like a nice guy, and anyone who could tolerate Lana for more than five minutes was far too patient to be a fire.

And yet, it made sense.

David glanced around the room and saw little support from the other elementals. Instead of arguing, he leaned forward and stared at the rock. A moment later, it crumbled into a hundred pieces.

The room sighed, both with frustration that a perfectly good suspect was innocent and with pleasure at the dramatic way he exonerated himself. I eliminated one of my possible scenarios, drawing a mental X through that picture.

David's words were quiet, with only the thinnest hint of reproach. "There are rock formations in Hawaii, you know." He put the rock back together, one piece after another merging until one would never know it had been broken, then he placed it in his jacket pocket.

Sera wasn't done with him, though. "You're not telling us everything. Don't pretend it was a coincidence, you living everywhere he did."

Though his hands clenched and released and his eyes held fear, David answered the question, chin jutting out in defiance. "I followed him because I hated him, and I wanted to kill him."

Then again, maybe he could be a suspect for a bit longer.

"I didn't know how. We all know what he is. One of the oldest of all the old ones, powerful and untouchable. I am a quarter stone. I couldn't kill him without extensive planning, and so I followed him, from one city to another, trying to find a weakness."

"Until you found one," I said. "His daughter."

David's brows furrowed. "No. I never found one. I still have no idea how to kill him. I didn't know he'd be here. I've been trying to get off the island since he arrived. I couldn't bear to see him." He looked around the room, eyes pleading for understanding, though he refused to meet Josiah's gaze. "I wish I could let it go, but stones, well, we can be set in our ways, and I've wanted to kill him since I was ten years old. That will never change."

I heard truth in his words, but I wasn't ready to trust it, not yet.

Josiah watched him, much as one watches a pet capable of performing quality tricks. "What did I ever do to you?"

David's eyes darkened, and one hand reached for the stone in his pocket, calling on his element for strength. "You killed my mother."

Jaws dropped. Mine landed somewhere around my navel. Even Josiah looked taken aback. "I believe you're confused. I don't even know who you are."

David met Josiah's dark stare. "I'm the boy in the car."

For the first time, Josiah looked bothered by David's words. "That was years ago."

"To you, perhaps."

They might as well have been alone, so intently were they focused on each other. When Josiah pulled his attention back to the room, he did so with a forced smile. "This is between the boy and myself. It has nothing to do with the murders."

"But could he be…?" I began, unsure how to finish the sentence in a room full of people. I feared saying the words "dual magic" aloud, lest someone draw the wrong—or right—connection.

"No," said Josiah. The single word was terse, leaving no room for argument.

Sera's head whipped between them, trying to read the unspoken meanings, but whatever truth the two were hiding, their faces offered no hint.

After a staring contest that seemed to last several days, David at last turned back to me. "I understand your suspicions. I am a stranger, and I freely admit to wishing harm on that man. However, that is between the two of us. The waters' deaths aren't on my conscience."

It was hard to believe a man who admitted wanting my father dead was innocent, but his words were weighted with truth. While I'd been fooled time and time again by people who claimed innocence, the gravitas David carried made it difficult to doubt his words.

Plus, there was another suspect I still wanted to hear from.

Setting aside the question of David's guilt, I again addressed the room. "Days ago, there were five council members, not counting my grandmother. Now, there are three."

"I killed Rachel." Everyone stared at Josiah, busy cleaning his nails with a letter opener. "It seems like a point worth clarifying. She threatened me, we fought, she died. I then said I killed the others to save Sera." His voice gave nothing away. He seemed to believe his own words, having absorbed the necessary lie until it became the truth. I almost wished I could believe that truth, too.

"And what?" Michael sputtered. "Are we supposed to simply forget what you did?"

"Of course not. I will have a trial, when you have enough members. It's worth noting, of course, that if you rush through my evidence as you did for Ms. Brook, the fire council would be quite displeased."

No one in the room missed the threat. A particularly astute banana wouldn't have missed the threat.

I glared at Josiah and Michael. Josiah held up his hands in mock surrender, but the twinkle in his eyes told me I was about as threatening as an angry toddler.

I did my best to keep the room focused. "So, we don't need to worry about finding Rachel Strait's killer. We do need to find Edith's and Robin's, however, and Josiah claims he didn't kill them. As he's confessed to the one death, can we assume he'd feel no compunction about admitting to the others?"

"If I killed them, absolutely." So helpful, my father.

"Which leaves us with the council."

Deborah stirred, her eyes slowly focusing back in the room. "There's still the other fire. I think it was her." Proclamation delivered, she disappeared once more into thoughts collected over thousands of years of life.

"It wasn't Sera." The council looked unconvinced by my certainty. "Fine, doubt me. How about this? If, in ten minutes, you still think it was her, I'll willingly hand her over to you."

Sera's eyebrows ran for her hairline, but she said nothing. She was surprised, but she trusted me.

I could only hope I was right.

"Grams?" She stood and left the room.

"One at a time, then. Deborah is the oldest member of the council. She spends most of her time in Key West, only emerging for council meetings. She has nothing to gain by framing Josiah or Sera for the murders and, so far as I can tell, no motive for murdering Edith Lake." Rivers blinked twice, her sole reaction. "Lydia, also, has no record of conflict with other council members."

"Michael, on the other hand, has a long history of despising Edith, particularly after she convinced him to invest in a real estate deal that's currently resting on the ocean floor off the coast of Dubai." The man protested, but no one was listening. All eyes were on me, which was as it should be. I was about to have my big *Murder, She Wrote* moment, and I'd hate to waste it on the disinterested.

"However, hating Edith isn't enough. As David has shown, wanting someone dead is a far cry from performing the act. Also, we must look at the full picture. Robin is dead. Someone tried to blow up Josiah, Sera, or me. Considering that the last time there was any crime on this island was when I shoplifted a candy bar in town, I don't think I'm going out on a limb to say these are all connected. Michael might have despised Edith, but he had no reason to commit the other crimes."

I studied every face carefully, looking for growing discomfort or even fear. Unfortunately, everyone looked nervous, the natural reaction when one is waiting to hear the identity of the worst killer the island's ever seen.

I stretched out my water magic and felt a tapestry of power, every water in the room contacting the water fountain, the canals, the ocean. It was our security blanket, and it was our defense. We were ready.

Grams returned, handing me several objects she'd gathered.

"Oh, good. You found them. Did you test them?"

She nodded, then rested one hand against my cheek, her eyes gentle. The touch held all the words she dared not say in front of others. Be strong. Remember who I was.

I was sure as hell going to try.

"Try this on for size, tell me how it sounds. Edith was preparing to announce an unusual punishment." I opened the small case, which held five unbroken vials of anti-magic serum, and displayed it to the room. "She was planning on blocking my magic with this drug for two months, as punishment for befriending shifters."

The room gasped in outrage. Some of the room, that is.

Several people already knew, and they only watched me.

"Josiah shattered twenty vials already. At the time, I thought he'd found all of them, but then Lydia told us he only destroyed most of them. Grams found the remaining ones." I nodded at my grandmother, grateful for her snooping abilities. "Out of curiosity, where was this one hidden?"

"The air vents."

I allowed myself a brief victory smile. I'd had the place right. I'd just been in the wrong room.

"Not everyone agreed with this punishment, and in an effort to stop it from happening, Edith was removed from the equation. One could be forgiven for thinking Sera was responsible. She's my best friend, after all. She wouldn't want to see me jabbed full of a drug that would destroy my magic, even temporarily. We're creatures of magic. Without it, we aren't whole."

The tapestry of magic grew richer, the room calling on it with gratitude for all it gave them.

"But she's not the only one who had a motive." I crossed the room until I stood before Lydia Pond. "You wanted it, too. You wanted it for Trent."

Lydia stared at me, eyes round, but she didn't deny it.

"My brother? Why would you do that?" Lana asked, even more confused than usual.

I swallowed. This part was going to be one hell of a balancing act. I turned from Lydia and Lana, addressing the rest of the room. "Trent is in a mental hospital in Eureka because he can't control his magic."

Behind me, Lana whimpered. "I thought he was just very sad," she said to no one in particular.

I prayed to any deity who felt like listening that Lana wouldn't choose that moment to remember I also had trouble controlling my magic.

Lydia still hadn't spoken, but she no longer looked lost.

She looked angry. Worse, she looked calculating. I needed to wrap this up before I lost control of the situation.

"A desperate woman, one who loved her nephew, who would take any opportunity to see him return to sanity, that's who wanted the drug." I held up the case. "This was found in Lydia's room. It's similar to the one Edith had at my trial. Maybe you remember seeing it on the table. Edith intended to inject me as soon as the sentence was read, before anyone could lodge a protest. When she exploded, someone pocketed the case. There was a backup set of drugs in the house, which Rachel guarded. Those are the ones Josiah destroyed. This case, you'll notice, still has twenty filled syringes Lydia planned to use on Trent."

Deborah was unconvinced. "This is all flimsy. It's a weak motive, and based on coincidence and supposition. There's no way Lydia could have done what you say."

Lydia cast a grateful look her way.

"That's what I thought, too, until I asked some old friends to help me with a bit of research. Take it away, humans."

The FBI agents looked less than impressed with my introduction, but they didn't miss their cue. Carmichael began. "Aidan inquired if there were ways to create an explosion that could be triggered with water."

As they spoke, I picked up the second item Grams had brought downstairs and displayed it like a game show hostess. When she caught sight of what I held in my hands, panic crossed Lydia's face.

Johnson took over. "There are, in fact, several ways one can create such an explosion."

I moved toward the fireplace. "You might want to move," I told my aunts. They stood, moving as far away as possible without missing a single moment of my demonstration. "Also, if you can all let go of your water, that will increase our chances of surviving the next few minutes."

I opened the airtight metal container that claimed to hold baby powder and used my fingertips to spread a small amount of the substance onto a kitchen towel Grams had helpfully provided. Once I'd coated several square inches of the towel, I opened a second, smaller container. Its label said it was a face serum, but the jar didn't hold a liquid. I sprinkled its contents on top of the the first one. Finally, I picked up the box Grams had brought from the kitchen and added several white granules to the mixture.

I backed away the second I was done. The rain was picking up outside, fierce drops lashing the windows, and if Carmichael's notes were accurate, this mixture was far from stable in the presence of water.

The agents looked nervous, which was the appropriate expression when watching me handle explosives. Carmichael hurried to finish their explanation. "A solution of ammonium nitrate, zinc, and table salt could have been sewn into pockets and hems, hidden in a locket, all sorts of places on a person. Like, for example, the oversized collar on the cardigan Edith was wearing the day she died. Get enough of the mixture, and it causes one hell of an explosion. Terrorists have used several ammonium nitrate mixtures in the past, and the chemicals have caused no shortage of industrial accidents."

Sera's eyes widened, and I gave her an imperceptible nod. She'd found a clue, after all. We just hadn't known it at the time.

"Then," I finished, "all it takes is a bit of water. It can come from the air, so if it had been a rainy day, the mixture would have worked instantly. If Edith's upper body had absorbed more of the ocean water, she would have exploded earlier. Perhaps she was supposed to. It wasn't until the last minute, when Lydia realized Edith was still in one piece and about to announce the sentence that would earmark the drugs for me rather than her nephew, that she called on her magic and added water to the chemical mixture."

The entire room held its breath. I still had some of my magic connected to the outside fountain, and I dragged it through the house. It was only a few drops, but I directed them onto the towel and stood back.

One loud boom later, and small pieces of a white kitchen towel fluttered to the ground. My mother grabbed the metal container from me and vanished for several minutes to put it in a safe location.

I plucked the largest bit of cloth from the fireplace and turned in a circle, letting everyone see the damage. I was on a roll now. "I don't think I need to say that the baby powder was really ammonium nitrate, and it was found in Lydia's room. It was only a small amount. She'd used most of it when she tried to blow up Josiah and, of course, when she killed Edith. There was too much to keep in Grams' house, and it was far too dangerous, so she stored it in Robin's shed until she needed it."

Everyone spoke at once, accusations and denials, a swell of noise that was felt more than heard. It took a full minute, but one voice rose above the others.

"That is not proof." Lydia's chin lifted, and her eyes blazed. "Those items could have been planted. People have been in and out of this house since we arrived, including you and Josiah. It isn't proof," she repeated.

She might claim innocence, but I noticed Michael was inching away from her, his eyes scanning the room for an exit.

"It also doesn't explain why she would want to kill Josiah." Lana's eyes were even rounder than usual, giving her a decidedly owl-like quality, though with less wisdom.

"It really was a neat little plan. Kill Edith and get the drug that might help Trent's sanity. Of course, that's a terrible reason to murder someone, especially when a good pickpocket could have retrieved the vials with fewer exploding body parts. But then she heard Sera Blais was accompanying me. The daughter of a man with a history of doing anything to protect his offspring. A man Lydia wanted dead. If Sera was accused of murder, Josiah would appear soon after. Lydia counted on this. She arranged for the explosives to be delivered, the ones used to turn the cottage into a beachfront scrapyard. Robin must have grown suspicious about the delivery and was coming to tell me. Lydia didn't have the time to plant explosives on Robin, which explains why her death was different. Based on my examination of the body, I'd say she was struck twice at the base of her skull, and then Lydia burned her, probably with some good old-fashioned gasoline and a match. Do you all see it? Edith, Robin, and the house explosion can be laid at that woman's feet."

When I finished, I expected at least a few dramatic gasps. There was only silence. "It was Lydia, on the beach, with ammonium nitrate," I added, worried my explanation hadn't been clear enough.

Everyone stared at Lydia. Many eyes held accusation, but some awaited her denial. She said nothing.

"Why would she want Josiah dead? Did he kill one of her family members, too?" David sounded almost sympathetic.

Sera blinked, distracted. David's story was one we needed to hear, perhaps after we dealt with the other psychotic murderer in the library.

"Not yet." Lydia's voice was barely a whisper. "But he would have."

The room waited. No one seemed to breathe, but Lydia

said nothing more. There was only one way I'd convince the room of her guilt. I had to share the piece of information I'd dearly hoped to avoid.

I couldn't act to save my life. However, if denial was an Olympic sport, I'd be a gold medal contender, so I called on that skill. I took the knowledge of who I was, of my own dual magic heritage, and I buried it so deep archaeologists would struggle to find it. I let myself believe, absolutely, that I was a water and a water only, before I raised the one topic I never wished to discuss.

The words I was about to speak would give Lydia a motive and exonerate Josiah.

And they would doom a man who deserved better. I took one last breath, and I made my choice.

"Trent Pond is a dual magic," I told the room. "He is both ice and water. Josiah has been researching dual magics, attempting to uncover their locations."

For me. He'd done it all for me, trying to find any way a dual magic could remain sane, but Lydia could never know that. No one could.

"I found a couple of them, actually," Josiah said. "We can discuss my findings later. Once I'm declared innocent of all crimes, that is."

Michael and Deborah and even my aunts all turned pale upon hearing that the unmentionable still existed, that the forgotten elementals capable of razing entire cities still lived among us. I suspected they'd happily take Josiah up on his offer if it meant he'd lead them to the closest thing elementals had to a boogeyman.

I had to believe he was bluffing. If he gave that information, the others would die. The council would not hesitate to issue an automatic death sentence.

The same sentence I'd just forced upon Trent.

It was too late to change course now. "Lydia learned

of his investigations and feared for her nephew's life. She tried to stop him. She is responsible for it all."

Lydia didn't say a word. Instead, she stood and walked toward the library door. Her steps weren't hurried, but they were intent.

The doorway erupted in flames.

"You can't leave that way," said Sera. Her face held as much rage as I'd ever seen. It didn't matter how complicated her own relationship with Josiah was. He was her father, and Lydia had tried to kill him.

He was my father, too. A man whose unrelenting desire to protect me had caused him to kill at least two women. Lydia was attempting to do the same thing, to protect her own family.

The irony was so rich I could choke on it.

She returned to her seat, and Sera extinguished the flames.

"How could you, Lydia?" Michael Bay stared at her with equal parts horror and sadness. "How could you kill all those people?"

Lydia avoided Michael's gaze and didn't answer him. She didn't look like a murderer, or even like a desperate woman with an elaborate plan to cure her nephew. She just looked small and scared. "What happens now?"

Michael and Deborah glanced about the room, hoping anyone else had the answer. It was their job to manage misbehaving elementals, but Lydia hadn't just acted a bit naughty. This was far beyond their comfort level.

It was Grams who answered Lydia's question. She was the only council member prepared to give voice to the words that needed saying. "You know what happens. There is only one sentence available to an elemental who commits premeditated murder."

Lydia did not argue. "Death, then?"

"It is our only option. You have proven yourself both dangerous and cruel. You have placed your needs above the needs of all elementals, and in so doing committed unforgivable crimes. You have tonight to prepare yourself. The sentence will be carried out at dawn."

I'd expected a raging elemental, trapped and unpredictable. Instead, Lydia accepted her sentence without protest. "That is fair. Am I allowed one last request?"

"Of course." Grams gave a gracious nod.

"Please, inject one of those vials into Trent before you kill him. Don't punish him for my crimes. I know it's not the best solution, but we have to try. If there's any hope of a cure, you must try. Maybe no magic at all is still better than the wrong kind of magic."

Grams only hesitated for a moment, and her stiff neck told me she was working hard not to glance in my direction. "We will do as you ask."

Lydia's shoulders slumped. She'd given Trent a chance. It was all she'd ever wanted.

I'd almost feel bad for her, if the memory of Robin's burnt body wasn't still fresh in my mind.

The doorbell rang, the sound overloud in the quiet room. We were still processing the news. I wondered to what extent Lydia's actions were based on cruelty and how much on a genuine belief that she needed to do this. I was beginning to think anyone could snap, given reason enough.

Grams opened the front door, and though I couldn't see who it was from my current position, the familiar deep voice reached me, and for that moment all my worries and fears vanished. "We were told to meet them at the plane fifteen minutes ago. Is everything okay?"

Everything was fine. For that moment, everything really was.

"We're just wrapping up," I called. "Be right there." The tension in the room rose noticeably with the arrival of the oversized bear shifter, and I didn't want to linger. "Do you need me for anything else?"

Though I asked the room, I looked at Josiah. I felt an unexpected stab of guilt. Even with extenuating circumstances, I was leaving him to face a murder trial for a death I forced him to commit.

He looked at me, and at that moment I saw Sera in his eyes. For the first time, they held softness, perhaps even understanding. "You know I'll be fine, Ms. Brook. I always am. You did a wonderful job today. You should be proud."

I didn't cry. I just thought about it for a moment or two.

"We've got this, dear," said my mother. "You need to be home now. If the council is determined to see you in person to deliver the sentence, they can always travel to you." She stared at Michael and Deborah, daring them to contradict her.

It felt strange to accuse and run, but my job was complete. There was nothing else for me to do.

I stood, knowing this could be the last time I ever saw my grandmother's house. Already, it felt foreign, a place I might wish to visit but would never call home. It was bittersweet to leave, but the emphasis remained on the sweet.

"How can you just go?" Lana asked. Her eyes darted around the room, and I was reminded of a china doll, beautiful to look at but so easy to destroy. One good hit, and it would smash into thousands of pieces. David clutched her hand, but for once she didn't seem to notice his presence. "Everything's just wrong. It's all wrong. You say my aunt is a crazed killer and blew up the cottage and my brother is something that isn't even supposed to exist but you want to take away his magic and it's just all wrong. Stop it. The world doesn't make sense. Stop it." She pleaded with me, begging to be returned to a time when everything wasn't awful.

I wished I could. I longed for that myself, for a world that made sense. I held out one tentative hand, not even sure if I was trying to touch her or hug her or just shake her hand.

It didn't matter. Lana wasn't even looking at me. As her tears broke forth, she called to the water just outside, pulling it to her for comfort. Thin waves ran through the room, heading straight for her. One of the waves passed over my outstretched hand—a hand I'd used to spread the chemical mixture on the towel.

There wasn't much, just a few grains on each finger. My hand didn't explode.

It just caught fire, flames dancing along the skin.

I didn't think. I let the fire magic loose, grabbed hold of the flames and pulled them through my skin, absorbing them into my body. In a matter of seconds, the fire was extinguished.

I don't know what I expected to see when I looked around the room. Concern or surprise, perhaps. Instead, no one met my eyes. They were too busy staring at my hand.

My perfectly smooth, unburnt hand.

CHAPTER 26

Once, while walking through a park in Tahoe, I passed a group of children playing a game. They called it freeze tag, and I watched for several minutes, fascinated by the way they would cease motion the moment someone yelled "Freeze!" and then burst into action once the game resumed.

That was how the room reacted. No one moved for what felt like a small eternity, during which I had time to appreciate that, after days of fearing Lana's words would unmask me, she'd managed to do the unthinkable with a single stream of poorly directed magic. I turned my head, catching my mother's eyes, Josiah's, my grandmother's, hoping one of them would offer a lead I could follow, but there was nothing. They were as frozen as the others, unable to think of a way to explain the impossible.

And then, just as quickly, the room burst into action.

Deborah grabbed a large cushion, holding it before her as a shield.

My aunts started shrieking, one question after another falling from their lips, filling the room with uncertainty and fear.

Mac, sensing something had gone terribly wrong, barged through the front door and joined me in the library, Simon and Miriam right behind him. The elementals were so fixed on me, no one cared that the hated shifters were in their midst.

Lana stared, baffled, and David looked at me as if I'd grown a second head—one I'd borrowed from Medusa, perhaps.

Lydia hissed, an inhuman sound. "You. All this time, you."

"It's not what you think," I sputtered, sure that if I could just delay long enough, I'd find a believable explanation.

"No?"

I felt it then, water controlled by Lydia brushing my other hand. Flames ignited where the chemicals still clung to my fingertips. "No one put it out," she ordered, voice thick with rage. The passive elemental prepared to accept her fate was nowhere in sight. Perhaps it had never been anything but an act to buy herself time.

I felt Sera grab hold of the flames and pull them toward her. She wasn't in the habit of taking orders from anyone, let alone recently unmasked murderers.

I looked at her, grateful, but my expression froze somewhere around horror, instead.

If I could feel her magic, it was because my own had risen to the surface.

I knew it was there, angry and gleeful in equal measure. It had waited years for this, maybe decades. Even before I knew it was a part of me, this was what it wanted. Freedom.

The secret was out. My fire side was done hiding.

"She doesn't burn." Lydia raised her voice, ensuring no one missed her words. I supposed, if there was one way to take the focus off her murderous deeds, it was to point out the other person in the room in need of a death sentence.

My fire crackled, full of energy and desire.

"Aidan." It was a single word, spoken in a low voice, but my magic responded. It knew that voice intimately. It had climbed inside his skin.

But it wasn't just the magic that answered. He'd called to the woman, and his voice found her, hidden somewhere beneath the panic and the pure blind fear and the fire's slow-building rage.

"This isn't good, Mac." I met his eyes, that dark melting brown I knew so well, no matter where my magic tried to take me. "We need to go."

"You cannot leave." Deborah blinked at us, and the haze over her eyes lifted, revealing a sharp intelligence only a fool would miss. "What you did, we all saw. You are a dual. You have fire."

Grams recovered first. "Don't be ridiculous. You know they're practically impossible. It requires two full elementals, both fertile. The odds are staggeringly slim. I'm still struggling to believe this Trent Pond is one. You think to unmask two in an hour when we haven't seen one in a century? I'm sure there's another explanation." Grams turned expectant eyes to my mother. Grams had only had a day to work up a cover story. My mother had been concocting lies for me since the day I was born.

Of course, she hadn't expected me to demonstrate my ill-fated abilities before the council. That was a little more difficult to cover up.

My mother stood, and though her spine was stiff and her face set, her hands shook. "I think I would know if my own daughter was a dual magic. If you recall, the reason they were banned was their rampant insanity. Aidan is perfectly sane. If you can cast your mind back a full five minutes, she was the one who solved these horrible murders while the rest of us twiddled our thumbs. That is hardly the sign of an unordered mind."

I kept my face still, thinking the sanest, most rational thoughts I could manage. Quadratic equations. Flow charts. Actuarial tables. The whole time, the fire churned through my core, gathering strength.

Deborah gave no sign she heard my mother. She consulted the notes she'd been given on my case. "Aidan is sixty-five. I seem to recall you took a long vacation six decades ago or so. To Hawaii. I believe I still have a postcard somewhere." The room hung on her every word. The damn woman had picked one hell of a time to appear lucid again. "Josiah Blais lives in Hawaii, does he not?"

Loaded looks flew between my mother and my father, between my sister and myself, trying to decide how much we could deny.

Considering the alternative, I was happy to deny it all. "This is ludicrous. The only reason I learned dual magics exist is because I met Trent." It was the absolute truth, and I would stick to the truth as much as I could. "I didn't burn because I'm surrounded by water and I used it to heal my hand when it caught fire." That part might have been a bit less true.

"Hmmm. And why, exactly, were you visiting Trent in the first place?"

Because I'd heard he was a half-water in a mental hospital and I was worried I might be going insane, too. Because Lana told me about him when I visited her, hoping for answers before I knew the truth could kill me. Because it was the only way I could figure out what I was.

I couldn't say any of it, and Deborah saw my hesitation. "Light her on fire," she instructed the room. No one moved. "Very well. I will do it. Someone bring me gasoline."

Josiah stepped between us. "This isn't a witch hunt, Rivers, where we throw the accused into water and watch them drown to prove their innocence. If you light her on fire, she will burn."

Deborah scoffed. "As she said, she is surrounded by her element. It will take her mere moments to heal herself.

Though Ms. Brook, I do suggest you wait at least a few seconds before doing so. A bit of singed flesh will prove your innocence much faster than this incessant prattling."

There was no way out. It was over, and part of me was relieved. The secret had only grown heavier the last several months as I became more and more of a danger to people I loved. I already felt like I'd been living under a death sentence since learning what I was. Making it official felt like the logical next step.

But there was Mac and Sera. Simon and Miriam. Vivian and the agents, watching the drama unfold with matching expressions of alarm. I wasn't ready to leave them, or my mother and Grams. Even Josiah might, on occasion, demonstrate a redeeming quality. My exposure as a dual magic would affect him and my mother as well. A century of incarceration for any parent who harbored a dual magic child.

The way Deborah looked at him now, she had little doubt who my father was.

There was only one thing for it. I had to run. I had to run before my status was confirmed, before my parents were condemned and all our fates sealed.

I had no second plan. This wasn't something I could talk my way out of. I needed to start running and never stop.

I sought Mac's eyes and found them, as ever, on me, full of a comfort no one else could offer.

He reached out his hand, my anchor in the storm. And somehow, in the middle of the worst moment of my life, I knew. I loved this man, with everything I was. It might be my magic that had staked a claim on his body, but he'd possessed me far longer than that. He would go with me, I knew. He would give up his life to run with me, as long as I needed him, and though it was weak and selfish, I'd never been so glad of anything in my life.

"Let's go." I took his hand, prepared to leave. Prepared to find whatever life awaited the condemned and the crazy.

I overlooked one small detail. I might have been willing to disappear forever, or at least until we came up with a workable plan. My protective parents had a different plan.

"No."

They weren't the only ones who spoke. Deborah and Lydia, Lana and David, they all wanted me to stay for their own reasons.

Josiah looked at each person in the room, turning his merciless black eyes on them one at a time. They all tried to hold his gaze, but only Deborah had the years and power to back it up.

At last, when he was certain everyone waited to hear his next words, he stepped next to me and curled his hand around my arm, the one that wasn't gripping Mac's hand. The touch was light, but there was no missing the strength behind it.

I'd known Josiah was my father for months now. He'd spent most of that time trying, and failing, to convince me he loved me as a daughter. In all that time, he'd never touched me.

Sera stared at his fingers, wrapped around my elbow, and her eyes turned even blacker than her father's. That was my only warning for what was about to happen.

"Aidan Brook is my daughter," he announced to the room.

I expected cacophony, screams and noise and an onslaught of question. Instead, everyone was too stunned to speak.

He continued, unconcerned with the room's reaction. He spoke with confidence an award-winning actor wouldn't be able to reproduce. He spoke as one who has walked upon the earth for thousands of years and wielded power most can only dream of. He spoke as a man used to getting his way, and one who expected to get his way this time, as well.

"She is my daughter, and she is a dual magic, and I will not allow her fate to be decided by an archaic law passed in the middle ages. As Fiona pointed out, she is not insane."

The fire unspooling through my body as Josiah sealed my fate was less certain. It was busy thinking this room would look better with flames kissing the wallpaper and carpets, with the door blocked by a thick wall of fire that would prevent anyone from following me. My enemies, all who knew what I was, they could die in that room.

I felt it detach, as it had before. I felt it stretch and grin, ready to deal death more eagerly than it ever had before. I was a spectator to its thirst for destruction.

I stared across the room, and the smile forming on my lips stilled. My mother would not survive that. My aunts and grandmother would not.

And so I pulled it back with a vicious tug. I couldn't even tell which part of me fought anymore, whether it was the water struggling to reassert itself or my fire hesitating in the face of my loved ones. It didn't matter. I took it back, controlled it, and beat insanity for one more day.

Josiah continued to speak, and the room still hung on his every word. No one had seen my lapse. No one except Mac, whose grip on my hand tightened enough that I might have a bruise the next day. It was a silent reminder that, whatever happened in this room, he wasn't letting me go.

"We created this law when there were hundreds of dual magics and we possessed few resources to track them. That is hardly the case in our modern world. Trent Pond's parents practically bought the institution, and it has done an excellent job of preventing him from harming others. We can learn about this condition, rather than eliminate it from fear."

Lydia's expression vacillated between suspicion and an uneasy hope. "That's why you were researching the dual magics. You weren't trying to kill them. You were looking for a cure."

"I was looking for a solution. You cannot cure someone of their magic. And yet, if the humans can treat schizophrenia and other mental diseases, shouldn't we be able to do the same to our own? I recognize that we do not like change, but neither do we like being surpassed by humans. We have not needed to face the problems of a dual magic in centuries. Now, we have no choice, and I am telling you we must do so with civility, rather than barbarism."

My family were still stunned, and I couldn't begin to fathom how many bottles of wine the aunts would demolish that night.

Lana and Lydia listened to every word. I guessed their thoughts were with a dual magic far to the south, living in a small windowless room in Eureka.

Deborah looked at no one but Josiah. "Change for its own sake is meaningless, and your argument fails to address the reasons we initially chose barbarism, as you put it. I remember the havoc wreaked by the duals. One thousand years ago, I watched a village burn because a child was denied a toy. I watched an entire island drown under the weight of one man's unrequited love."

"I too remember such events, Deborah. That does not negate the need for—"

Deborah continued as though he hadn't spoken. "I also remember you killed one of our own, Josiah Blais. Whatever the circumstances, Rachel's blood is on your hands. You are not a man whose opinion I will consider. The girl will have a trial, and if she is found guilty, she will die. That is our law, and it will not be broken. Not this day."

Josiah nodded, as if coming to a decision. "You are outnumbered by those who wish otherwise."

"Is that a threat? There will already be a severe back-lash against this island. Two of our number have died on its shores. If Michael and I fail to return, the Brook clan will be known as the family that slaughtered an entire council to protect their girl. Vengeance will be swift, and it will be absolute. Threaten me if it pleases you, but if you act on it, this island will be destroyed. You know what must happen. Lydia has accepted her fate and will die tomorrow. Aidan's trial will be postponed until a quorum can be assembled. Anything else would be disastrous to the residents of this island."

By the time Deborah finished, my aunts were standing, and for the first time since I arrived, there wasn't a single hint of intoxication in their eyes. My mother and Grams held hands, and I suspected it had less to do with comfort than with merging their magic together. Lana looked back and forth, appearing unsure of pretty much everything. The rest of us, we watched Josiah, waiting to see his reaction.

"You forget, Deborah. History is written by the winner. There will be no one left to tell your version of the story." He blinked, and her clothes were on fire.

The room took a moment to inhale, to accept what we were seeing, to choose a course of action.

Then battle was joined.

The fire only lasted a second before Deborah was drenched with water. It was impossible to know if she'd been the one to call it. I didn't think she had many friends in the room, but Lana rose and stood beside her, and David followed. Somewhere, in the back of my mind, I understood they were only following the law. They likely believed they were making the right choice.

The rest of my mind thought it was a betrayal.

Josiah didn't have a chance to strike again before Deborah retaliated, sending a thick stream of water soaring into his nostrils and mouth. He coughed, but she was relentless, filling his lungs with water until he was unable to steal a single breath. It didn't matter how fast he burned the water off. She had a limitless supply, and her focus never wavered.

Someone else jumped in, fighting to draw the water from his lungs and allow Josiah time for a breath. Someone powerful enough to neutralize the strongest water in the room. My mother and Grams, hands still locked and all their attention on Deborah, fought to save my father. As each stream of water rushed toward Josiah, they pulled another from his lungs, giving him precious seconds of oxygen.

I'd only fought one other elemental in earnest, and I'd killed him. I'd hoped to never do so again, but at least this time there was a key difference. This time, I wasn't alone.

Josiah now stood in front of me, my very own elemental shield. Mac remained on one side, and Sera moved to the other. They wore matching determined expressions. They would fight for me to the bitter end, if need be.

I took quick stock. On our side, we had the most powerful fire elemental I'd ever met and my sister, who could more than hold her own. Grams could easily take Michael. My mother and aunts were full waters, and though they were younger than Deborah, there were more of them.

On their side, they had a loopy half-water, her grudge-bearing stone boyfriend, one full-blooded council member, and possibly the strongest water in existence. By all accounts, they could not win.

No one had bothered to give them the memo.

Deborah showed no hint of fatigue as she continued to pour water into Josiah's lungs. It kept my mother and

Grams busy on defense, leaving no one available to help when Deborah split the stream in two and sent the other half toward Sera.

The water forced its way through the seam of her lips, the pressure too great to withstand. Water flooded her mouth and slid down her windpipe.

When she looked at me, she wasn't scared. She was pissed off, the pure anger of a fire. It didn't call to me. It shouted my name while stamping its foot and waving an enormous red flag.

I was so close to the edge. If I let the fire loose, I might never come back.

If I didn't let the fire loose, I couldn't battle Deborah.

I don't recall making the choice. I only knew the fire rushed through me, filling every cell in my body, ecstatic to be free. It demanded to be fed, and there was a target before me, one who would kill my sister and father if no one stopped her.

She was one of the oldest and most powerful waters in existence.

Me, I was a fucking dual magic, capable of harnessing two elements and bending them to my will. Also, I might be nuts.

The worst thing about battling a crazy person? You never knew what they would do next.

I didn't try to light Deborah on fire. Her clothes still bore black marks from Josiah's effort, but she'd doused the fire too quickly for it to do any real damage.

Instead, I enclosed her in a circle of flames, and drew them high, blocking her line of vision. She had no choice but to release Sera and Josiah, bringing the water back to herself in an effort to douse the flames.

I couldn't let her do it. She was trapped, and she needed to remain that way.

I sent a silent prayer into the void, that what I was about to do wouldn't seal my fate. While the fire burnt, I reached for my water magic. It hesitated, its uncertainty almost palpable.

Once, I'd been unable to use both elements simultaneously. Anger would trigger my fire and block access to the water.

Then I'd needed to use both, to save Mac, and I'd discovered the secret. All I needed to do was isolate the elements from each other and risk furthering the schism to my psyche.

Hey, crazy still beat dead.

I imagined the fire was limited to the right side of my body, and when it resisted, I slammed it into my arm, my leg, my torso, freeing up the left side for the water magic to roam free. As it did, something inside me disconnected. My compassion, or my empathy. Whatever part of me chose not to kill others, that part was silenced as I discovered what it truly meant to be a dual magic.

All this took a second, perhaps less. The water surged forward, grasping the waves Deborah was drawing toward the fire. I yanked and felt resistance from her magic, her full blood still stronger than my half.

The water wasn't enough on its own, so I added the fire magic. It boosted its power, pushing it harder and faster than it could move on its own. It was almost easy to steal Deborah's stream of water and send it toward my mother and Grams. I trusted they would keep it from her.

The two elements danced together in my body, more power than I'd have believed my skin and bones and blood could hold, and yet I did not crack. I grew to fit the power, my body expanding and stretching to make room for it all. I was shocked to discover my clothes still fit, my shoes remained on my feet. Based on how I felt, I ought to be nine feet tall.

This was why. This was why no one ever sought a cure for dual magics. It was why we were a threat to be eliminated.

We were pure power. We were stronger than the oldest of the old ones. Compared to Deborah, I should have been a mere speck, easily flicked and forgotten.

Instead, I was going to destroy her.

I made the flames spin around her, a deadly promise of the power I wielded, and I smiled.

Of course, the old ones also might have wanted us dead because dual magics really seemed to enjoy killing people.

Just one more, I whispered. I would find a way to control myself, but first I needed just one more death.

There was pressure on my left hand, squeezing so hard I could no longer move my fingers.

"Aidan, come back. God damn it, Aidan. Answer me."

I twisted my neck and was surprised I needed to look up, into brown eyes that told stories and promises I still hoped to hear someday.

"Your eyes." The words were low, a horrified whisper. He'd never seen me like this, I remembered. "They're so dark. Almost slate. Aidan, this isn't right. I can feel it, too. The water, it's not stable."

"It's who I am. It's who I've always been." It just took me this long to realize it.

I was ready to end this. I tightened the circle of flames around Deborah.

I yelped, a sharp pain on my right arm demanding my attention. "What the hell?" I turned to see Sera, face set in harsh lines, pinching my arm over and over again, her fingers practically meeting through the walls of skin and muscle.

"Knock this shit off, H2O." I sensed her own magic then,

reaching for the flames I controlled and trying to push me out of the way.

She wouldn't succeed, not unless I chose to let go. I wasn't ready to do that.

"Let the fires handle this." I knew that voice. I knew the certainty and confidence I'd borrowed every day of our friendship. She was right.

I didn't want her to be. "No." I whispered the word, but the force of my refusal was so loud I might as well have shouted it. I held fast to the fire, ready to finish what I'd begun.

I didn't get the chance before I found myself on the library floor, struggling under the weight of a well-muscled otter shifter.

"Gotcha, Brook," said a grinning Miriam. "It didn't look like you were responding to logic, so I went with something a little different. Did I ever mention I won a national flag football title?"

The tackle might as well have been a reset button, shocking my magic loose. My hold on both the flames and the water lessened, the magic flowing back into my core.

I almost felt like myself again. I pushed weakly at Miriam's shoulder, but she didn't budge. "I thought you didn't tackle in flag football."

"I like to experiment with the rules. If I let you up, do you promise not to fucking kill anyone?"

I looked around the room. True to her word, Sera had taken control of the fire, and I suspected Josiah was adding his power to hers. They'd widened the flames, keeping Rivers trapped. She would be warm, but alive.

Water hovered above her, being yanked to and fro by my family and Deborah. Lana still fought on the side that didn't seem interested in burning people to death, and I was no longer sure I could blame her for that.

"You don't let a girl have any fun," I muttered to Miriam, but this time when I pushed on her shoulder, she stood and offered me a hand up.

The room stilled enough to watch me, their eyes telling me they thought my claim of being a stable dual magic had been rather overstated.

"How does this end?" I asked the room.

"She dies," said Josiah, as calmly as he would tell me what he ate for lunch. "She has to."

"We can't just keep killing everyone who knows what I am."

He turned to me with one eyebrow lifted, and in that moment he looked so like Sera I almost loved him, this man who lived by his own moral code, who'd given me my sister, who would literally find a way to move mountains if that's what it took to save his daughters. He wasn't a good man, but at least he was on my side.

"Do you have another option?" Josiah asked.

I didn't. Some people could be trusted with my secret. Deborah was not one of them.

And yet, I couldn't speak the words. A moment ago, I'd been ready to kill her myself, but I couldn't condemn her, not when I was in control of my own mind.

Josiah didn't wait for my permission. As I watched, the flames intensified, the heat felt throughout the room.

"This is barbaric." David stood, glaring at each of us.

He was right. The room was about to watch a woman burn alive.

And once she was dead, Josiah would move on to Michael, and Lana, and David. No threat to my life would leave the room unscathed.

"Stop." It was my voice, though I didn't recall making the decision to speak. "No more."

The flames dipped, and Josiah frowned at me. "Have

you thought of another way?" It sounded like he was humoring me.

"Pull the flames back." When he didn't, I looked at Sera. She nodded and fought Josiah for control of the fire. Her attention was fixed on the flames, but her features were marked with sadness. She knew what I was about to say.

It was what needed saying.

"No more death. No more protecting me by destroying others."

Josiah began to protest, but I talked over him. This wasn't up for debate.

"You know this is the right call." I spoke to my mother, Grams, and Sera. I met my aunts' sad eyes, and even dared a glance at the others, those I'd just fought against. "Josiah can't keep killing in my name. It would destroy me. And if that wasn't reason enough, it's only a matter of time before I start doing the killing myself."

My mother shook her head, but words failed her.

"It's the truth, and while I still have the capacity to regret my actions, I have to do the right thing. I don't want to be a killer. Please, honor my choice. Take me to Eureka, put me in a room across from Trent, and let me have my trial. We can make the case for treatment instead of execution. But no more hiding, and no more killing. I can't take any more."

My throat closed on the words as I finished, and a strong arm wrapped around my shoulders. I leaned into Mac, borrowing his strength.

No one was happy with my decision, but no one fought it.

Sighing heavily, Josiah walked up to Deborah, now standing in a ring of burnt carpet. My eyes widened when he held out his hand. "No hard feelings, old girl?"

They turned downright bug-like when she took his hand

in hers. "You were protecting your own, Josiah. Though I don't agree with your choices, I understand them. And, as everyone is still alive, no elemental laws were broken tonight. I see no reason to take this further."

And they worried that I was the crazy one. Millennia of life might give one a different perspective on life and death, but this was still unexpected. I was starting to think, if my time in Eureka got me far away from these batshit old ones, it would be time well spent.

"What the hell is wrong with you people?" asked Miriam, echoing my thoughts.

All our eyes were on two of the most powerful creatures in the world as they forgave each other for attempted murder.

No one was watching David.

We had one warning, a small cry from a tinny speaker. I stepped toward the computer, to ask Vivian to repeat herself, and almost missed seeing what she'd already spotted.

The letter opener in David's right hand, just as it plunged between Josiah's ribs and deep into his heart.

Screams and gasps and magic filled the room, everyone trying to stop him as the letter opener was withdrawn and inserted again and again, piercing the heart twice more.

David was soaked, covered in the water with which the others had tried to slow him, but he was smiling, a grim, satisfied smile as Josiah fell to the floor.

Some things, even magic couldn't cure.

His eyes were open, wide and black and so like Sera's, except now they were empty. A man who'd practically glowed with the energy that fueled his every movement was still, and forever would be.

Beside me, Sera didn't sob. She wasn't there yet. She drew short, jagged breaths, her shocked body struggling to remember how to survive. I felt her grief, waves of horror and disbelief that this man we'd believed was practically immortal was gone.

It took seconds for my sister's life to irrevocably change, for a pain that would never truly heal to take root in her soul.

Despite what Josiah was, she loved him, and her father was dead. Our father was dead, and one man was responsible.

That was when I finally lost my mind.

CHAPTER 27

The fire shot through me, taking over my entire body. Arms, legs, hands and feet filled with heavy strands of magic. It slid into my throat and climbed the back of my neck, creeping like a spider across my skull. It filled every cell, every pore with unrepentant rage.

I'd given in before. I'd accepted the fire's embrace, its absolute knowledge that what I did was right. Those times, there'd been a quiet voice I chose to ignore. The voice insisted that I couldn't give in. It told me to fight the fire's ravenous ways.

Now, the voice was silent. It was just me and the fire. This time, I wanted to be consumed.

"If you want to live, you should leave now." My voice sounded foreign, flat and hard. "This house is going to burn."

I sent a burst of flames toward the curtains. In a room full of waters, it was extinguished immediately.

I hissed, the sound more animal than human. "Do not interfere."

My aunts stood. I saw fear on their faces, but still they faced me. "Aidan, you can't win." Georgina searched my face, believing her niece still hid just below the surface.

Tina nodded. "Think of the books. You like books. They'd all burn."

Marie chimed in. "Or be ruined by water. This isn't like

you."

I stared at them until their brave faces crumbled, until they no longer trusted themselves, let alone me.

They were wrong. This was exactly like me. This monster had been inside me all along, waiting for an excuse to escape its bindings.

I cast flames throughout the room. The carpet, the desk, the shelves of books. Books were replaceable. Josiah was not.

One after another, each fire was doused. I set more, and more, and all were extinguished by the waters in the room. Marie grabbed Tina's hand, and Tina grabbed Georgina, pooling their magic together. Three fulls working in tandem were unimaginably strong. Behind me, my mother and Grams also worked together.

Everyone in the room was fighting me.

Everyone except Sera.

I clutched her hand, my fingernails digging into her skin until they drew blood. She was no more gentle. Our magic combined, crackling and sizzling and unbearably angry. Something needed to be destroyed.

Someone needed to die.

The room was full of people. I knew this. My mother and my grandmother and my aunts watched my every move. Lana stared between us with wide eyes, making strange squeaking noises. Michael and Deborah glared, and any hope I might have clung to that I would receive a fair trial vanished.

If I released the fire, my life was over. They wouldn't allow me to live long enough to see morning.

Together, Sera and I set the room ablaze. If it was made of wood or fabric or paper, we torched it, and every time the flames were put out by the waters. We were outnumbered.

I looked at Sera, my fire sister. We didn't need to speak.

I tugged the hand Sera wasn't holding, trying to free it from someone else's grip. There was no give. Growling, I sent fire toward the stubborn flesh and was rewarded with a low curse.

"I'm still not letting go."

I paused. The voice was familiar. The hand was, too. I was forgetting something, something worth remembering. I scrambled after it for a moment, but it scampered away, unwilling to be caught. Not yet.

Instead, I sent heat toward David, igniting his clothes even as I tapped into my water side. It came eagerly, craving the man's execution as much as the fire did.

Even as I knew the perfect clarity that only came when my magic worked together, darkness slipped over my mind. The shadow threatened to consume me, and part of me welcomed it.

I fought the elementals who were determined to put out the flames. They sent water to him, and I hauled it away, one wave after another. They'd overpower me eventually, but first David would burn.

He screamed, and I smiled to hear it. I laughed as he collapsed to the ground, using the damp carpets to smother the flames.

The fool thought he might get to live.

I stopped fighting the waters, instead taking the fire and sending it through his skin. He coughed, trying to expel the intruder.

"Why did you do it?" I built the heat, raising his temperature.

Sweat broke across his brow and his cheeks grew flushed. More heat, and more, until he was writhing in pain, struggling to find words.

"I told you. He killed my mother." He gasped the words, and the pained face he turned to me was clear of deception.

That should mean something. Josiah hadn't been a good man, and he'd probably earned his death. In all likelihood, he'd deserved it several centuries ago.

He was also my father, the only one I had, and in his way he'd loved me.

Though David's words were steeped in memories of a child's unspeakable pain, they left me cold. I was someone's child, too.

It was a bitter irony that the hotter my fire burned, the more I felt like ice, hard and immovable. I could destroy this entire room, and I would not care.

Instead, I took the fire and wrapped it around David's heart, around his lungs and windpipe and spine, and I let it burn. Hotter and hotter, until he was screaming and begging for mercy. I felt the tentative touch of a water, hoping to heal him, and I expelled that magic without hesitation. I would not allow the damage to be repaired.

Someone sobbed, and when her hand slid from mine, I knew it was Sera. She'd had enough.

I didn't think I could ever have enough. The fire, so long contained, would never be silent again. It would never fit back into its little box, never allow me the comfort of pretending I was just another water.

I'd accessed it too many times. My body was not the same one Sera found on that porch in Oregon months ago. This one was marked by my own magic, scorched and scarred from the inside out.

Lana knelt at David's side, her cries wild as only the screams of grief can be. I think she looked at me once, possibly even spoke to me.

I think many people spoke to me. Somewhere, underneath the rage and the certainty and the perfect knowledge that I was never coming back, there were familiar voices.

I ignored them all, and I watched David burn.

It only took seconds for the magic to incinerate the organs he needed to live. Seconds for a man to cease to exist.

Seconds for me to become a murderer.

I'd killed before, with Sera. It had been an accident, and I spent ten years punishing myself. I'd killed once after that in self-defense. Just a day earlier, I'd caused Rachel's death.

This was different. This time, I'd chosen to kill. I'd *wanted* to watch him die.

The voices continued to hammer at me, demanding I release the fire. I knew what would happen if I let it. I would return to myself. Forever altered, but in some way the Aidan I'd known my whole life.

If I let go of the fire, I would feel again. Grief and guilt and rage and more pain than one soul could bear.

I could never let go of the fire again.

Someone else needed to burn, and the fire turned to Lydia. Whatever her motivation, whatever her original plan, she was the reason we were all here. It didn't matter that she never could have foreseen this outcome. She'd wanted Josiah dead, and now he was.

"Any last words?" A collective gasp filled the room, and I replied with a cruel smile. "She's already condemned. Let's end this now."

Lydia said nothing. She fixed calm eyes on me and waited. With a shrug, I withdrew my magic from David and sent it towards her.

At once, I met a block. Sera's magic surrounded Lydia in a protective barrier.

I called on the water, letting it boost the fire's power, and sliced through her magic.

"Goddamn it, Aidan, stop." Sera almost never raised her voice, but she was screaming now. She stood in front of me, her face tilted toward me until she was only an inch or two away. "It won't bring him back. You have to stop. Aidan, please. I can't lose both of you." Her voice hitched.

But no one could stop me. No one in this room was strong enough. I felt my aunts' magic push at me and I waved it off with no more effort than I would a bug. Grams and Deborah and my mother stretched their hands toward each other, trying to combine the full-blooded magic of three old ones, but they wouldn't be on time. Already, my magic threaded through Lydia, easing through her veins and arteries. I might make her death quick, just to see how that differed from David's slow torture.

Around me, everyone screamed. They called my name and pulled on my arms, fighting for my attention. It was all just noise, and it meant nothing.

The power was so intense I felt myself growing again, rising from the ground until my feet no longer had to touch the floor.

I blinked, confused. I wasn't touching the floor. My feet were, in fact, about two feet above the ground, and my view of Lydia had been replaced by a close-up shot of a green t-shirt.

"No. Put me down," I cried. More power than anyone on the island, and I was reduced to a petulant whine as Mac hauled me from the room, unceremoniously tossed over his shoulder.

I couldn't see ahead of us, but one voice drew us forward, toward the study rather than the front door. "This way. Through here, quickly," said Simon, standing back and allowing everyone into the passageway, then closing the door behind us before the council had even exited the library.

I had a vague impression of a bookcase turned at an odd angle, a dark hallway, whispers and footfalls around me as

Sera and Miriam followed Simon's lead, and then we burst into the kitchen pantry.

No one paused. The kitchen door was wrenched open and we tumbled out into the night, fleeing down the rocky path, the shortcut giving us a vital head start on those who would chase us.

I beat my fists against Mac's back, pummeling the kidneys. His stride never broke as he carried me away from Grams' house, running along the eastern shore. He was carrying me away from the people I could hurt.

I disliked that plan. "Take me back," I cried. No one answered me.

Rain poured down, soaking both of us within seconds of stepping outside.

"Stop them!" Deborah's voice cut through the night. We were downwind, and every word reached us clearly.

I raised my head to find Sera, Simon, and Miriam right behind us, and nearly a hundred feet further back, everyone who'd been in the library was now spilling from Grams' front door. They didn't yet have our speed, and their steps were unstable, as if they were still deciding whether they should risk their own lives in pursuit or just watch me go.

Deborah felt no such uncertainty. "She is a dual magic. She is too dangerous to live." She clasped Lydia's cheeks between her hands and stared into her eyes. "If you can stop her, no one will ever hear what you did on this island."

At those words, Lydia found her feet and began the chase.

Mac didn't turn, but he picked up speed, legs pounding against the ground with each step.

The fire slammed back into my body as he built the distance between me and Lydia, carrying us beyond the limits of my power. As long as he ran, I couldn't hurt anyone else.

Lydia continued to chase us, seeming determined to put

herself back in harm's way, but with every step Mac pulled away from her.

The sound changed. No longer did his feet crunch against rocky paths. A solid thud greeted each step as he landed on the wooden pier.

"Stairs?" He yelled behind him.

"No time." Simon didn't pause. One second he was running on two legs, the next he was on four and leaping for the seaplane's door. He shifted back mid-air, his human hand catching on the handle and drawing it downwards, opening the door in a single movement.

Sera stepped onto one of the floats and pulled herself up with Simon's help. A second later, Mac lifted me toward them. They yanked me inside the plane, but as soon as they released my arms I turned, determined to leap out and run for Lydia. This wasn't over. It wouldn't be over until one of us was dead.

"Oh, hell no." Sera hauled me backwards, dropping me into a chair. I struggled to free myself, and she forced me to still, sitting on my legs to keep me in place. "Do not think I won't knock you unconscious if I have to, Ade. How much longer?"

Miriam required an assist from Mac to make it inside, but she hustled to the cockpit the minute she was clear of the door. "Just need the keys."

Simon cursed and flew out the door in feline form. He sailed over Mac, who was effortlessly pulling himself into the plane.

"I've got her." Mac took the seat behind mine and wrapped his arms around me, pinning me in place.

Sera paced to the door, peering into the night. Clouds covered the moon and stars, and thick sheets of rain made it impossible to see more than ten feet ahead. Simon blended into the night so thoroughly we didn't see him until he came barreling out of the darkness, jaw wrapped around a pair of jeans. He was instantly back in human form, pulling a set of keys from the front pocket and chucking them to Miriam. "Go. We don't have much time."

He'd barely finished the sentence before the propeller whirred to life.

"How close is she?" Sera asked.

Simon didn't have a chance to answer before fingers wrapped around Sera's ankle. She kicked, hard, but the hand didn't loosen its grip.

Lydia's head appeared in the doorway. I grinned.

"We have a stowaway," I murmured, the fire roaring to life.

"Miriam," Mac called, urgency filling every syllable.

"Get us the hell out of here," Sera said, still struggling to free herself from Lydia's determined grip.

We were fighting to escape. Lydia was fighting for her life. Few things evened the playing field like desperation.

"Doing what I can," Miriam gritted. "The Air Force didn't train me on fucking seaplanes."

We pulled away from the pier, heading toward open water, and still Lydia refused to release her hold. "She's going to pull Sera out." I spoke to no one in particular. "She can't do that."

Once again, I stretched the fire out, reaching for Lydia. Sera's magic was already on the woman's hand, and I added my power to hers, burning Lydia until she screamed and released Sera's ankle.

The plane rose from the water, fighting its way through the choppy waves and the pounding storm. "Hold on to something," Miriam yelled.

Mac tightened his grip on me. Simon stood behind Miriam's shoulder, peering nervously through the windshield as we climbed fifty, then one hundred feet into the air.

"Let me go," I whispered.

He said nothing.

"Please. I can't see the island from here. This may be the last chance I ever get."

I sensed his uncertainty, and his arms relaxed, just a tiny bit.

It was the best I was going to get. I sent the fire to his forearms, just enough to sting, and flung myself forward as he yelped. Two steps and I was at the door, peering down at Lydia, still clinging to the plane.

Sera shoved me backwards. "That's enough fire. Find your water and get this damned storm under control."

I laughed in her face and staggered back to the door. When Sera tried to push me a second time, I clung to the doorframe and refused to move.

"Damn it, Ade. Stop this and come back to us. You always come back." She was screaming, or pleading. Maybe both.

Lydia had both arms inside the plane now, uncertain eyes locked on me. She knew, whatever Deborah promised, there was no happy ending for her. We don't get to escape the things we've done.

"I can't do that, Sera." I sent my fire toward Lydia in a rush, and when Sera tried to block me, I boosted it with the water. It poured into the woman, claiming her entire body.

The tiny plane shook, jolting as it passed through the pounding storm. Lydia's fingers lost their grip.

Two hundred feet above the ocean, she fell.

I whispered to the magic, told it to burn her before she fell out of my reach and into the welcoming arms of her element. I told it to end this.

The magic was silent. The world grew dim.

Unburnt, Lydia landed safely in the water, and I could only whimper at my failure.

My arms were heavy, and my legs threatened to crumple

beneath me. A tiny pain on my neck vanished. I turned my head, fighting to understand.

Mac stood at my side, an empty syringe in his hand. "Forgive me," he whispered, "but I keep my promises." I blinked at him, then fell against his side, unable to support myself.

Right before everything went dark, I thought I saw several large bodies in a distinct black and white pattern swim toward the woman who'd set us all on this path.

Then I closed my eyes and saw nothing else.

CHAPTER 28

When I woke, I was fairly certain the dwarves from *Snow White* had found their way inside my head and were mining for gold in my skull. Every cell in my body ached. Every organ screamed in agony, until I was pretty sure I could identify my gall bladder by its pain signature alone.

It was excruciating, worse than anything I'd ever known. I felt like a giant had consumed several bottles of cheap liqueur while eating some bad fish, then performed a spell to transfer the sickness to my body.

I wasn't ready to wake. Fatigue called to me, and I nearly gave in, slipping back into a perfect sleep, where there was no pain, no insanity—and no murders on my conscience.

I shied away from that thought, unwilling to examine it. It would insist on my attention soon enough.

"Water," I whispered.

"Water? You can feel your water magic again?"

I cracked one eye open. It was crusty, the lashes sticking together. I didn't just feel gross. I looked it, too.

Sera stood at the end of the bed, twisting her hands together.

"No, water. In a glass. To drink." I didn't go looking for my water magic. I wasn't ready to know what I'd find.

A rough hand brought a glass to my lips, and another reached underneath my shoulders, propping me up so I wouldn't choke.

Wakefulness came slowly, a reluctant separation of the dark dream world and harsh reality. Mac was behind me, I knew. The bed was warm and soft. Music filled the room, a song I loved and one that caused Sera to make gagging sounds whenever I played it.

"The Civil Wars?" The words were slurred, but Sera understood.

"Yeah, well. I figured it couldn't hurt to remind you that you're the sort of person who prefers banjos to electric guitars."

I listened to several bars, hoping I was still that person.

"You drugged me." It was a statement of fact, rather than an accusation, and neither Mac nor Sera denied it.

"If he hadn't, I was a second away from knocking you upside the head until you had a bad case of unconsciousness."

I took another sip. My stomach rumbled in protest, and I pushed the glass away.

"You keep threatening to do that, but we both know you're too little." I eased my way into a sitting position, still finding my bearings. I was in a bed, and Mac's arm was around me, and that was an excellent place to start. He propped a single pillow behind my back for support.

Sera snorted. "Yes, but unlike you, I actually have muscles." Then, with no warning, she started crying. Sera, the woman who never shed a tear, stood at the foot of my bed and sobbed. "Damn it, Ade. It's you, right? You're still in there?"

I didn't know how to answer. I was still Aidan, yes, but not the same woman who'd walked into Grams' library. The magic might be quiet for the moment, but a shadow lived inside me now. Already, I felt it, a darkness that watched my every move and would prey on any weakness. It was both a stranger and an integral part of me.

I might control it, at times, but it also controlled me. It brushed against my mind, a caress. A promise. It wasn't going anywhere.

But for this moment, I was Aidan. I was filled with fear and regret and a small mountain of horror at what I'd done, but I was still me. "I'm here. But keep those syringes close, okay?"

Sera's tears were already drying up. She released one shuddering breath, then put her game face on. If it weren't for the red eyes and tear tracks that still marked her face, no one would ever know she'd cried.

"I don't want to, if we can help it. We have no idea what effect that drug will have longterm. It could make everything worse." Even so, she glanced to her right, and when I followed her eye line, I saw the small black case one of them had pocketed. They'd been prepared for whatever I was when I awoke.

"Well, I'll do my best not to kill someone else, but if I get close to that point again, you have to do it. If I even look a bit unstable, you do it. No questions. I just wish…" I didn't finish the thought. I wished one of them had thought to jab me before I killed David, but I wouldn't blame them for my crimes. It had been me, and me alone, and I would live with it for the rest of my life, another body for the growing graveyard in my soul.

No one had much to say. Mac hadn't spoken a word since I woke, but when I cautiously turned my head to face him, repositioning the hammering dwarves in my head, I found him looking at me with eyes as warm as I'd ever seen. I fought against my own breakdown at that moment. Really, only one of us should be crying at a time.

"How can you not hate me?" I looked at Mac, but the words were for both of them.

Sera moved to the other side of the bed and sat gently on the side. "Let's get a few things straight. First, David killed our father, and I can't forgive that. I won't mourn his death, and I won't allow you to torment yourself for years to come over what you did, not when you need to focus your energy on saving yourself. I don't even care if he had his reasons, if he could justify killing Josiah. David was not one of my people. Despite everything, my father was, and you definitely are. You always will be, you know."

Fuck it. I was going to cry, and there was no help for it. I gave in, talking through the tears. "Do we have any idea what that was about? The whole 'boy in the car' thing?"

"No, but Vivian's already digging deeper into David's history. If there's an answer to find, you know she'll uncover it. And if you're wondering, she's been monitoring the island. Nothing's happened so far between the council and your family other than a lot of yelling, but she'll let us know if that changes."

That was good. My entire life felt like an open-ended question these days, and I didn't want to add any new mysteries to the existing pile.

There was another question I needed to ask, though I dreaded their response. "After what I did, aren't you scared of me?"

Sera shook her head so fast, her curls bobbed from side to side. "No way. I'm not scared, and I never will be. No matter how batshit you got, you never tried to hurt me, or your mother, or Mac. You may lose your best judgment when the fire and the crazy takes over, but Aidan is still in there somewhere. I am absolutely certain of this."

Mac's chin rested on my head, and I felt his nod of agreement. "You could have burnt me so I'd put you down and you could go back to Lydia. When you did fight me, you only singed me a tiny bit, no worse than a sunburn. You noticed when Lydia was trying to pull Sera from the plane, and you fought to stop it. You were as far gone as you've ever been, and you still protected us."

I wanted to believe him. He painted a pretty version of my actions, but I couldn't trust his words. He hadn't been inside my head. He hadn't known how, when the madness came, I cared about nothing but the kill.

I jerked my head toward Mac, wincing at the pain. "Wait. How were you okay when my magic went kaput?"

He shrugged. "I have no idea. All I know is, when your power was squashed, so was the part that's inside me. I just felt like a bear again. Maybe I still fed off your magic, maybe not. I haven't had the chance to find out."

Sera shook her head in mock disgust. "It's been sickening, really. He hasn't been more than ten feet from you since we stole the plane." Her cynical tone might have been more believable if she wasn't wrapping a fresh blanket around me as she spoke.

"How long was I out? What are we going to do about the trial?"

"Trial?" Sera sounded way too innocent.

"Yeah. There were a few too many witnesses to bury this one. Oh, god. My family didn't kill them all, did they?"

I felt a warm breath of air on my head as Mac snorted. "You haven't really looked around, have you?"

It hurt to crane my neck even an inch, but I managed. There was a narrow door behind Sera, lined in aluminum. A table with a mystery novel. A bathroom so tiny I'd once wondered how Mac possibly fit inside.

"We're in the Airstream. The trailer. Why are we in the trailer, Sera?"

"Since you never told anyone where we'd parked it and the Bronco, no one knew to follow us here. Miriam flew us to Bremerton, and we left the plane floating there.

I'm assuming it's been found by now and the island was informed, but that doesn't even matter. By the time they knew where to begin looking for us, we were at the Oregon state line. Since we returned the plane, I don't think they can get us for grand theft seaplane. Though we're already fugitives for aiding and abetting a dual magic. They can't really hit us with much worse." She didn't sound too concerned either way.

"Oregon? We're in…" I had to stop, needing to organize the whirlwind of thoughts. The two of them were far too calm, considering our lives had pretty much fallen apart the minute I revealed what I was to the council. "So, what's the plan, then? Head for Mexico, knocking over convenience stores all the way down?" It was a bad joke, but I had to try. It was joke or fall apart, and I was tired of doing the latter. "Oh, god. Is Miriam a fugitive, too?"

"Among others." The voice came from the door. Joy and regret collided when I saw the speaker. I wished I could say regret won, that I was a big enough person not to be happy one of my friends was risking her life for me, but I didn't feel like that person right now.

Her dreads were pulled back neatly, and for the first time since she left the cabin, she was once again in proud nerd wear, this time in a t-shirt that read "Back in my day, we had nine planets."

"Vivian." My voice came out in a squeak, too happy to also manage dignity. Simon crept in behind her and sat on the built-in table. Miriam followed.

"Glad to see you're not dead, Brook."

Shadow be damned, I thought I might be glad I wasn't dead, too.

"Room for two more?"

I blinked several times, fairly certain I wasn't actually seeing two FBI agents in the bedroom of the Airstream.

"I'm hallucinating, aren't I? None of this is real. Any minute now, a bunch of hobbits are going to appear and start jumping on my bed."

Carmichael's brows drew together. "What is she talking about? Did the drugs do this?"

Sera rolled her eyes. "*Lord of the Rings*, Carmichael. I understand it must be uncomfortable to sit in a movie theatre, what with that stick up your butt, but you really should try it sometime."

I couldn't be certain, but I thought Carmichael smiled.

"Anyone else tucked away up front?"

Mac wrapped his arm a little tighter around me. "This is it. We're stopped for the night. We'll pick up again in the morning."

"Where the hell is everyone sleeping?"

Johnson moved to a window and pushed the patterned curtains to the side. A camper van sat outside. "Carmichael and I are in that one. We've been stopping in campsites so far, so Vivian sleeps on the ground. Sera's been on the Airstream couch. Miriam's taking the Bronco's back seat. No one knows where Simon sleeps."

"Wherever I want," Simon answered. Damn cat.

I looked at this tiny circle of humans, shifters, and elementals risking their lives for me, and I didn't even know why. We could run for years, and it wouldn't matter. I couldn't outrun the darkness inside me.

It took everything I had in me, but I said what needed saying. "We can't do this. I can't ask this of you. I won't ruin your lives. Just drop me off at the next gas station, and I'll call the council."

Sera gave me that look she'd perfected, the one that strongly suggested I was an enormous idiot. "And you think Deborah will just forgive us for helping a fugitive escape and making her look like a damn fool? It doesn't matter. You didn't ask us to be here. We chose it. End of discussion."

It really wasn't. "And them?" I nodded at the agents.

Carmichael smiled. "We're not fugitives. The elementals don't care about humans. Besides, we're still the FBI liaisons for the supernatural. We're just doing our job. If our job helps you stay off the grid while you figure out what happens next, well, I'd say you're owed that." He spoke the final sentence to Mac, not me, and some of the tension eased from Mac's arms.

Miriam stepped forward. I noticed she already had a drink in her hand and wondered how long I'd have to wait before they'd let me have one, too. "What are they going to do to me? Elemental laws don't apply to shifters, and I'd like to know how they'd name us fucking fugitives when they're not prepared to admit we even exist. I'm here because it's a road trip, and I don't ever turn down the chance for one of those. Don't fight me on this, Brook."

I doubted anyone fought Miriam on anything, ever. I sure as hell wasn't going to be the first.

"Thank you." It wasn't enough. No words were going to be enough, but right then it was all I had.

They began to file out. I let the agents and Miriam go. "Stop," I said, before the others could follow.

They paused expectantly.

"Why?" Again, the word was insufficient, but I knew they'd understand.

"You mean, why am I not at Carmen's, learning more about what it means to be a cat?" At my nod, he gave me the same look Sera had a moment ago, coupled with a cat's disdain. "You are my friend. You need me. I made my choice." He slid off the table, walking to the bed just long enough to pat my calf, still covered by the blanket. "I know my own priorities, Aidan."

If they didn't knock this off, I was going to start crying again.

"What about Olivia?" I asked Vivian.

"It's complicated."

I shook my head. "I don't want a Facebook status. You can't give up your life for this. You have someone who loves you."

She smiled, small but kind. "I love her, too, but sometimes it's not enough." She hesitated, weighing how much to tell. We waited, giving her the silence to find her words. "I saw David grab the letter opener. I tried to warn you, but no one heard. Not until it was too late. If I'd been there, your father might still be alive."

Sera protested. "You can't blame yourself for that, Viv."

"I don't, not really. But it doesn't change facts. When I'm with you, I matter. I make a difference. It's scary, and sometimes people get hurt, but I also get to help people. I was so worried about something hurting me that I never thought about the pain I could help prevent. When I'm with Olivia, we watch TV and eat brunch on weekends. It's not a bad life, but it's not enough. I want to matter."

"You sure about this?" Nothing in her words suggested uncertainty, but I wanted to hear her say it.

"I've made my choice, too. I'm good with it." She walked to the side of the bed and bent over to kiss my cheek. "We're going to fix you, and this time I'm going to help."

I gave up the fight. Those damn tears weren't going anywhere.

Vivian and Simon left, once again leaving me with Sera and Mac. They both looked considerably the worse for wear, with wrinkled clothes and messy hair. It occurred to me that Mac wasn't the only one who'd been at my side for days.

"That's the plan? We're going to fix me? When thousands of years of elementals couldn't find a cure?" I didn't want to sound too pessimistic, but I was pretty sure, if that's what they thought, they were going mad alongside me.

"Thousands of years of elementals didn't have Josiah's research. He wasn't lying to the council. He did figure out where the one in the southwest lives. It took him so long because the person moved a couple of years ago, to eastern Texas. There was a map in his notes, with a big old X drawn over a small town about a hundred miles from the Gulf of Mexico. Josiah was too cautious to spell it out, of course, but it feels like a safe bet. We know he wouldn't have stopped looking until he found a way to help you." Our eyes met in silent, shared grief for the man, then we let it go. There would be time for many things later, including time to mourn.

"And if this dual magic's insane and tries to hurt us?"

"Such a Debbie Downer. If she, or he, does, we'll have Carmichael shoot them next."

It wasn't much of a plan. It wasn't really a plan at all. But it was more than I'd had a few days ago. I was still free, and while the shadow in my mind never stopped whispering, never stopped poking and prying and trying to find a way out, I still knew who I was. For these people who were risking everything for me, I'd make sure I never forgot.

"Can you...?" I asked. Sera gave me a blank look, which I suspected was deliberate. "Oh, get out already."

Her face cracked into a smile, but she didn't argue.

At last, it was just me and Mac, still wrapped up together.

"Oh, god."

"Yes?"

"How many days has it been? Where are we? Most importantly, how badly do I stink? I haven't showered since the island."

He held up his fingers, ticking off the answers. "Three days. We're outside Bakersfield, in southern California. It's taking a while, because we're trying to stay off the main roads, but we're heading steadily south. And you don't smell, because you've been bathed and changed." He didn't miss my suspicious look. "By Sera. What kind of pervert do you think I am?"

I grinned. I couldn't help it. "The best kind, I'm hoping."

"I like my women conscious when I see them naked for the first time, thank you very much." Still, I earned an answering smile.

"This wasn't what you meant when you said I'd be in your bed that night, was it?"

"No, but I'm adaptable. And, apparently, really patient." He pressed a kiss to my temple, which still throbbed. I reached delicately for my magic, almost afraid of what I'd find. The water was still there, front and center, though there was a veil between it and me, some residual effect of the drug. Still, I was able to access it enough to heal myself, using the water glass at my side. The headache receded, just a little.

"I'll let you sleep." Mac stood, filling the entire room. I wanted to appreciate the sight, but already my eyes were drooping.

He was almost to the door before I stopped him. "Wait. The others all told me why they're here. Why are you? Is this still about the magical tie?"

"You don't really think that, do you?" I didn't. I just wanted to give him an out, if he wanted to take it. "You know why I'm here. It's why I'll always be here."

I did know. I had for a long time, and right then the words didn't matter. I'd hear them someday, and I'd say them in return. When our lives didn't hang in the balance, and they could be spoken simply, a quiet affirmation of what we both already knew. This wasn't a matter of the words being feeble or weak. They just weren't necessary. Mac was mine, as much as I was his, and we would be as long as we were both able, however long that was. And so I only said, "Me too," and watched the smile warm his face, and that was enough.

The door closed behind him, and I was alone, with only my weak magic and memories and a guilt that would never go away. That was as it should be. We don't get to escape the things we've done.

But I was loved, by so many people, and I thought that might balance out the rest. At the very least, it would give me a fighting chance.

I closed my eyes and waited for sleep to pull me under. As I slid toward temporary oblivion, I felt the shadow stretch, long inky limbs spreading over my mind, claiming my dreams. I weakly pushed against it, but I was too tired, and it was too strong. That night, I would belong to darkness.

Tomorrow, it would be different. I had reasons to fight, both outside that door and inside my own soul. Tomorrow, I would start fighting again.

I would always start again.

Acknowledgments

I am, as always, grateful to all who helped get the words onto the page and this book into readers' hands.

Kaari Busick went above and beyond this time, and I thank her for every extra hour she spent whipping my words into shape.

Carrie Stewart swooped in at the last minute and gave the book a final polish. She has also been an invaluable sounding board when I needed second opinions on cover art, back cover copy, and all those pesky details that come with publishing independently.

Thanks to Jessica, Rachel, and Shelly, my awesome beta team who continue to outdo themselves. They insisted I clarify every murky motivation and confusing plot point, and the book is immeasurably improved because of their feedback. Additional thanks to Rhiannon and Dani, who generously offered their time to review the book during various stages of its life.

Lynsey Taylor has worked her tail off in support of the Elements series, creating one gorgeous graphic after another and helping with the marketing in so many ways. Fist bump as well to Janice, her partner in crime, for all her help promoting the books.

I am thankful to whichever government body chose not to interrogate me after I spent hours researching how to create an explosion in which water is the trigger.

Finally, thanks to my mother, as always. Just because.

About the Author

Mia Marshall spent time as a high school teacher, script supervisor, story editor, legal secretary, and day care worker before deciding she would rather spend her days writing about things that don't exist in this version of reality. She has lived all along the US west coast and throughout the UK, during which time she collected an unnecessary number of degrees in literature, education, and film.

These days, she lives somewhere in the Sierra Nevadas, where she is surrounded by her feline overlords.